THE
JIM CALDWELL
TRILOGY

THE
JIM CALDWELL
TRILOGY

Keith H. Adkins

ISBN-13: 9798989577606
Printed in the United States of America
ChrisJen Publications
www.keithhadkins.com
Cover design by: ebooklaunch.com

Contents

THE VALUE OF THE DIAMOND
A Jim Caldwell Story – Book 3

AN OLD WEST TIMELINE

1846—Mexican-American War begins as an armed conflict between the U.S. and Mexico.

1848—U.S. gains control of the Phoenix area, ending the Mexican-American War.

1850—California becomes the 31st state in the union.

1851—Fort Defiance established to monitor and control Navajo Land.

1853—Crimean War begins.

1854—The Gadsden Purchase was a treaty that gave $10 million to Mexico for land south of the Phoenix area.

1856—Crimean War ends.

1860—Unsuccessful attack by the Navajo on Fort Defiance.

1861—i) American Civil War begins.

ii) Fort Defiance abandoned due to the Civil War.

iii) Apache Wars begin.

1863—i) US Congress splits Arizona from the Territory of New Mexico.

ii) Fort Defiance reopened by Colonel Kit Carson to again subjugate the Navajos.

iii) Lincoln issues the Emancipation Proclamation.

iv) Henry Wickenburg begins the Vulture gold mine.

1864—Prescott named capital of the Arizona Territory.

1865—i) American Civil War ends.

ii) Fort McDowell established.

1867—i) US reaches an agreement to purchase Alaska from Russia.

ii) Arizona Territorial capital is moved to Tuscon.

1868—Phoenix is founded.

1870—i) Fort Apache is built.

ii) **Russian Invasion begins**, without bloodshed.

1873—The Panic of 1873 sets off a financial crisis that lasts four years.

1877—i) Arizona Territorial capital is moved back to Prescott.

ii) Geronimo is moved to the San Carlos Reservation.

1879—Edison patented the first commercially successful lightbulb.

1881—i) Phoenix incorporated as a city.

ii) **Story of Jim Caldwell begins.**

iii) Assassination of Russia's Tsar Alexander II.

iv) The US has three presidents in one year: Rutherford B. Hayes, James A. Garfield, and Chester A. Arthur.

v) **Russian Invasion ends**, without bloodshed.

vi) Thomas Edison and Alexander Graham Bell form the Oriental Telephone Company.

vii) The American Red Cross is established.

viii) Sioux chief Sitting Bull surrenders.

ix) The Gunfight at the O.K. Corral.

x) The Road to Tucson experience.

xi) **Pablo begins his missionary journey to Mexico**.

1886—Apache Wars end.

1887—Southern Pacific Train arrives in Phoenix.

1891—Pablo begins his missionary journey to North America.

1894—Angel Island.

1912—Arizona becomes a state and Phoenix is named the capital.

INTRODUCTION TO THE TRILOGY

This book started as a dream. I woke up one morning and felt a very explicit desire to write the New Testament as a play, set in Phoenix, Arizona in 1881. One of my New Testament professors called the Passion Narrative the "Diamond of the Gospel." That's the pre-Easter story of the last days of Jesus' life, from Gethsemane to the Tomb, so I started there. It became a work of historical fiction, but more properly it is a piece of biblical fiction.

The writing of the play started easily, as I had studied and taught the two-volume masterful work of Raymond E. Brown called, *The Death of the Messiah: A Commentary on the Passion Narratives*. His book calls the passion "the central narrative in the Christian story," and it also places the story in four acts. He writes that the "division of the commentary into acts and scenes is meant to underline my view that the passion accounts are truly dramatic narratives.

Enter my story, stage left. First I gave Jesus the name of Jim Caldwell, and then immersed myself into the history of Arizona. The connections were exciting and meaningful, and it turned out that the pictures I had taken since retiring in Arizona further helped to bring my story alive. I named the book *The Secret of the Diamond: A Jim Caldwell Story: Book 2.* Starting with Book 2 turned out to be more confusing than creative. I was trying to follow the Star Wars model that segued into a three-part prequel and a tri-part sequel. My book features the Hole in the Rock Gang, their leader Pedro, Wyatt Earp, the Russian Invasion with Dmitri Ivanov and Sergey Popov, the gallows hanging of Jim Caldwell, and his burial in a diamond mine.

My next book became *The Forming of the Diamond: A Jim Caldwell Story: Book 1.* It was promoted as a prequel, and dealt with the life of Jesus, drawn from all four gospels. It features Jim's cousin The Dipper, Big Nose Kate, some Teachings on the Hill, travels around central Arizona, including Prescott and Wickenburg, crowds beginning to follow Jim, the Rusty Tavern, and troubles for Jim.

Finally, I wrote the sequel called, *The Value of the Diamond: A Jim Caldwell Story: Book 3.* It starts out with a unique retelling of the resurrection, the introduction of Pablo, his Road to Tucson experience, his missionary journeys to North America and Mexico, and a character named Rose. It features letters being delivered to churches asking about living the Caldwellian faith, the death of Marshall Enrique Garfias, troubles at Teotihuacan, a trial for Pablo, a train wreck, and a jail cell with Pedro. It concludes with Pablo on Angel Island receiving messages and visions from the resurrected Jim, visits to Pablo in jail from Rose, and a surprise ending.

The American Old West worked well as the backdrop for my retelling of the old, old story. My purpose was to bring the good news to a new audience, with cowboys and Russians playing the parts of Galileans and Romans, and Mexicans leading the newly formed faith. It is my hope that the New Testament will come alive with this play, and reinvigorate people about the message of God's love and the human need for equality. If you have been frustrated with details about the Bible, sit back, read this trilogy, and may its message of love and forgiveness raise your spirit like a fragrant offering to God.

THE FORMING OF THE DIAMOND
A Jim Caldwell Story – Book 1

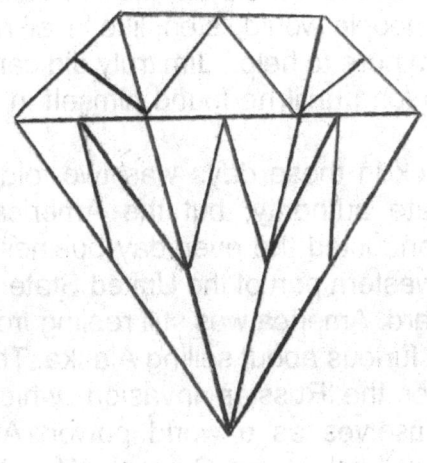

PREFACE
Heat and Pressure

J im Caldwell was a well-intentioned young man living in a dangerous time. His idea of making Arizona a better place attracted a few people, and some actually became followers. These were mostly folk looking for courage and hope in the rough and tumble times of the Old West. Jim's notion was simple. He just wanted to help people in need and spread his ideas wherever people would listen, like "Y'all need to do some changin', and I'm here to help." Jim truly did care about people, yet it wasn't too long until he found himself in trouble with the law.

The law back in those days was two-fold. The Russians were the ultimate authority, but the American sheriffs and marshals still conducted the everyday business. The Russian Invasion of the western part of the United States in 1870 caught everyone off guard. America was still reeling from the Civil War and Russia was furious about selling Alaska. Those two events set the stage for the Russian Invasion, which was done to reestablish themselves as a world power. After suffering a humiliating defeat back in the Crimean War, they were more than ready to exact revenge in any way they could. Meanwhile, our story begins in the summer of 1881 in Phoenix, in the middle of the Arizona Territory. That little town had been incorporated in 1868, only two years before the Russian Invasion, but the invasion had a major impact on this account. The close of that year also saw the end of the Russian Invasion, but that didn't occur until after our story. The desperate year of 1881 saw America go through three presidents: Rutherford B. Hayes,

James A. Garfield, and Chester A. Arthur. The challenges were monumental and the times were ripe for hope to emerge.

That's when Jim Caldwell decided it was high time he got baptized. He was raised as a Methodist and wholeheartedly believed in the social justice issues his church stood for. They were against alcohol, smoking, card playing, and of course prostitution. The problem was that those four things were just about the most popular things to do in the Old West. Changing lives for the better would need all the help he could get, so he turned to his cousin, known as "The Dipper." Jim found him out in the Arizona desert baptizing people in the Gila River. When Jim got there, he was surprised to find The Dipper telling people they needed to change their ways. That highly affected Jim, and he decided right then and there that he wanted to help his cousin get the word out.

Some very strange things happened on that clear, cloudless, summer day. Jim waded out to his cousin and the next thing he knew he was coming up out of the water. Nobody could quite say what occurred next, but a coyote howled and a clap of thunder rumbled off in the distance. All the people who had gathered there were already in a bit of shock, and then The Dipper seemed to go into a trance. Soon enough he said, "My cousin Jim is gonna do great things." That was also the last thing he said, because the Russian overlord soon had him arrested. Nobody knew just why, but they did understand that they weren't allowed to ask.

At that point people started following Jim around to see what else might happen. Jim seemed uncomfortable with this new found attention, but people wanted some hope. The first thing Jim said to them was, "Ya don't need to worry 'bout them Russians, or the local marshal. Just be concerned 'bout yerselves enough that ya change yer ways." Once he explained the task at hand, he set out to do it. But first he needed local followers who were willing to change. Yep, he needed cowboys.

After a long walk, Jim arrived at the Circle Y Ranch. There he saw a man named Pedro, and his brother Andrés, riding their horses. They seemed to Jim to be the ideal first followers because they were Mexicans, and one thing Jim wanted to do was show that he treated people equally. He simply walked up to them and said, "Come on, boys. Follow me and we'll change our part of the world for the better." Both of the brothers laughed, but Pedro couldn't stop laughing. He had a great sense of humor and thought Jim was joking. Then Pedro noticed something in Jim's eyes that seemed genuine and indescribably peaceful. He turned and looked at his brother, and Andrés surprisingly nodded with a smile. Having the kind of connection that only brothers can experience, they just knew they were supposed to follow this stranger.

Next, they rustled up a spare horse for Jim, and Pedro asked "Where we goin,' jefe?" Jim smiled because he knew that when a Mexican called him jefe, it meant Pedro was already acknowledging him as their leader. "You tell me" Jim said, deferring to Pedro's understanding of the area. Pedro kind of liked this treatment, and with a smile on his face he said, "Okay, foller me, boys." The three of them rode to the ranch next to them and found another set of brothers, Jimbo and Johnny. The same exchange of words occurred, and almost without hesitation the new set of brothers dropped what they were doing and followed Jim. Little did they know, they were heading out for the most transforming time of their lives.

The five of them got on some horses and headed for the Arizona Territorial capital of Prescott. It was a long ride north, circling around the Bradshaw Mountains and through the Prescott Valley. The day after they arrived was the Sabbath, so they went to church. Most Catholic Churches had been taken over by the Russians and turned into their administrative offices, so they tried a Methodist Church. They were surprised when a young man burst in during the sermon and started causing a ruckus. Jim realized it was a cry for attention, so he calmed the young man down, walked him outside, and spent some time talking with him. At once Jim's story spread throughout the Valley, because nobody had been able to deal with this troublemaker.

That evening people brought all sorts of folk who couldn't properly deal with their anger, sadness, or fear. It seemed like the whole town gathered to watch, and sure enough Jim managed to work with each of them. In the morning, Jim went out to a deserted place to pray and that's when he got the inspiration to preach and teach about equality and justice and forgiveness. The ideas just flooded his head, so he knew it was time to begin proclaiming his message of hope and kindness and love.

The following Sabbath, Jim was offered the chance to preach at the local Methodist Church. During the service, another fight broke out, but this time it was about money. Jim walked up to the two who were about ready for fisticuffs, and listened to their story. After they both had their chance to talk, Jim looked at one and said "Yer debt is forgiven." Now some of the local lawmen were present and didn't take kindly to having legal matters settled so flippantly. Jim then announced "It ain't the local marshal nor the Russian overlord who has final authority. It's God." Needless to say, nobody had ever heard of anything like this, particularly since the Russian Invasion. And the seeds of trouble were planted for Jim right there at that very moment.

One of the deputies hurried over to the jail to inform Deputy U.S. Marshal Virgil Earp about Jim Caldwell. The marshal had his feet up on the desk, while reading his copy of The Weekly Arizona Miner, and wasn't too happy to have company. The deputy said, "Some crazy guy at church this mornin' told everyone that ya ain't in charge, nor Sergey." Sergey was the Russian overlord for Prescott whose official title was Major General Sergey Popov. Marshal Earp had no respect for the Russians, but figured it wouldn't hurt to let him know about the new guy in town. Virgil went over to Sergey's office, and gave him the news about their authority being questioned. They agreed that keeping an eye on him would be a good idea.

Jim was quickly attracting crowds wherever he went. As he was walking along he saw Matt, who ran a house of prostitution. The religious folk didn't like Matt at all, but when Jim said to him "Follow me, young man," Matt shocked everyone by getting up and following Jim. Of all things, they went to Matt's house for dinner that evening and there were prostitutes present. Well, the local clergy were pretty much beside themselves and openly questioned Jim's actions. They were just outside the house, peeping through the window and asking among themselves, "Why does he spend time with prostitutes?" Jim heard their complaints from inside the house, and called out to them, "Good people don't need no changin', do they?" Well this enraged the clergy, so now Jim was in hot water with both the political and religious folk.

Another Sabbath, Jim was walking through an orchard, and his followers started picking some nectarines. The already angry clergy were quick to complain that "Yer not supposed to work on the Sabbath!" That's when things really started going awry for Jim, because he responded "Ya know the Sabbath was made to serve us. What ya don't seem to know is the opposite. We were not made to serve the Sabbath." At that point the clergy started talking about how they needed to deal with Jim.

That was all it took. Jim was gathering some good people to join him in doing good deeds, while others started a plot to work against him. The authority figures were spreading word that he was about as smart as a lump of coal. That sets the stage for us to begin looking at the heat and pressure Jim faced in the summer of 1881. And as you may know, add lots of heat and pressure to a lump of coal, and sooner or later you're going to end up forming a diamond.

ACT I
JIM TEACHES ALL WHO WILL LISTEN

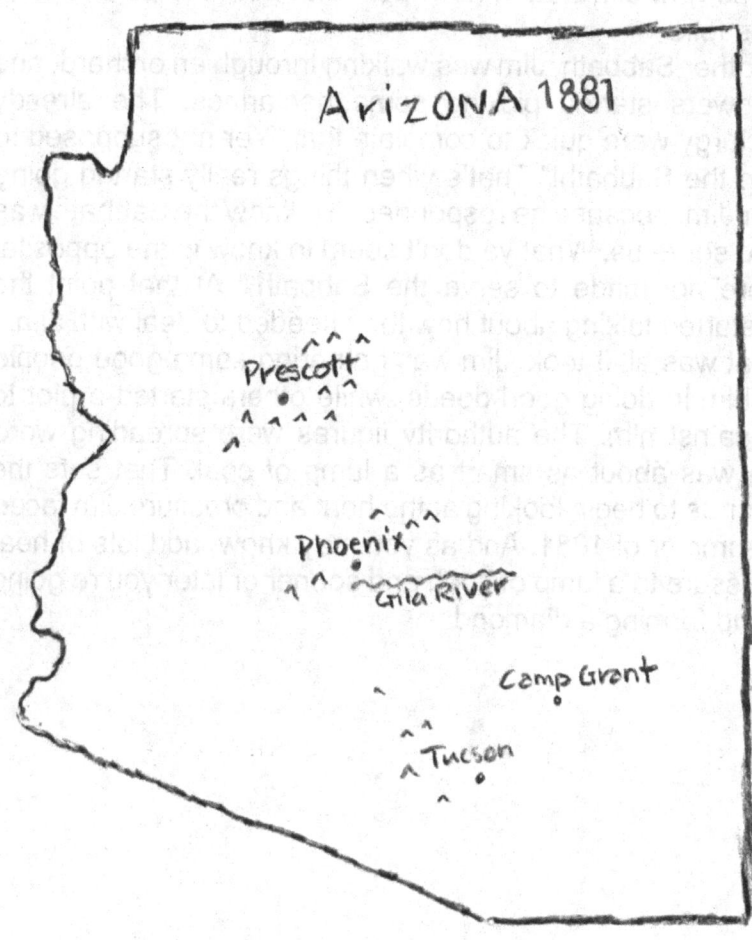

SCENE ONE
A New Way of Life

Great crowds were beginning to follow Jim, so he headed up a hillside that created a natural amphitheater below him. At first he just walked around and listened to their problems. With each new person he talked to, he realized that the troubles of the times were overwhelming. They were dealing with heavy taxation from Russia and America, high food prices, and a general lack of resources. There were many good people present, but they were finding it almost impossible to live a godly life.

What they needed were real life answers to real life problems. As he looked out over the crowd, he saw the weary and discouraged, but most importantly he heard they sought an ethical life. Several families told stories of needing to steal food to feed their children, and were genuinely torn apart inside about the choice. He felt they were craving blessings, and all he could think of was to suggest that they rejoice and be glad, but even Jim knew that needed some preparation. After considering it for awhile, he decided they needed some kind of a renewing of the mind.

That's when it hit him that he truly had a divine calling. People needed some good words to live by, but Jim had nothing to say. He smiled when he remembered a saying he grew up with: "If it's impossible and it happened anyway, God must have had a hand it." That relaxed him enough that words just flowed out. His followers later on referred to his talk as "Jim's Ideas for A New Way of Life." He also realized afterward that his inspiration was from Psalm 1:1-2:

Happy are those who do not follow the advice of the wicked, or take the path that sinners tread, or sit in the seat of scoffers; but their delight is in the law of the LORD, and on his law they meditate day and night.

1. It's okay to get discouraged.

Jim started with some scripture: *"he has sent me to bring good news to the oppressed"* (Isaiah 61:1). He felt good that God was using him to help people who were down and out. Jim also noticed the people were truly interested in his talk. Right then someone yelled out, "Ya talkin' 'bout them Russians oppressing us, ain't ya?"

"That ain't my point," Jim responded. "Yer thinkin' 'bout the oppressed part of the verse, but I'm thinkin' 'bout the good news part of the verse."

"I haven't heard any good news 'round here for years," commented a man who just closed his shop due to a lack of business and high taxes.

A refreshing breeze drifted through the crowd right about then, and after that everyone seemed to settle in to hear what Jim had to say. "Oppression can certainly drain the spirit from ya, but don't let it happen. Rise above it all by choosing to look fer the blessings all 'round ya."

"Name one!" an angry man toward the back yelled out.

"How 'bout the guy we're trying to listen to?" suggested a woman, with obvious sarcasm.

The crowd quickly settled down, so Jim continued, "When yer spirit is low, it's too easy to get discouraged. Of course it's okay to get discouraged, but don't stay there. It'll drag ya down and everyone 'round ya. What ya need to do is to look at yerself honestly, and anyone who chooses to follow me will have to do that a lot."

"I'd like to look at myself, but my mirror is broken," laughed a woman, followed by plenty of smiles in the crowd. "But seriously, how can looking at myself honestly change the troubles around me?"

"Think of a hopeless or oppressed spirit as an invitation to find good news" explained Jim. "And here's something else to think about. God's spirit is right here and now. If ya find yerself dejected 'bout anything, just turn to God in prayer and seek His presence. So, I ask ya. Do ya want to stay oppressed by the discouragement all around, or dig down deep and find good news no matter what is goin' on?"

"Not sure," laughed a church goer. "These are hellish times, so why be happy in hell?"

"If ya choose good news," Jim continued, "ya just found the secret for turning hell into heaven. Don't get me wrong, I ain't saying that if yer poor in money or spirit it's a good thing. I'm saying that God is everywhere; always has been and always will be. So when anything brings ya down, ya can choose to be happy. Situations are outside of us. Don't let them affect yer insides." Jim noticed that the people were intrigued, but needed some time to think through what he just taught, so he said "let's spend a little time with inward prayer before we go on."

2. It's okay to cry.

After a short bit, Jim continued with "Here's another problem. If ya give in to discouragement, ya have two ways to go. Either choose to pull out with good news, or keep heading down that rabbit hole to grief. Here's the scripture that follows the last one: "*comfort all who mourn*" (Isaiah 61:2). I think ya all know it's tough to be happy when yer mournin'. In fact, mournin' can be a good thing. It means something or someone was important to ya. Getting' out a good cry is the first step to comfort. Okay, I see a bunch of ya farmers and ranchers shakin' yer head no. Maybe that means ya never lost a loved one."

Several cowboys threw their hands in the air and said, "I've heard enough. Men don't cry! That's the craziest thing I've ever heard" and they left. Jim didn't take it personally, because he knew his words weren't his. He could feel it inside that he was being divinely inspired. Then he continued when things settled back down. "If yer grief has come from discouragement, it's real hard to get turned around. That's why the Good Book says we are all called to comfort folk who mourn. There ain't no happiness in mournin', but it shore do make a difference when ya see that someone cares." Jim saw plenty of heads nodding, so he continued. "Here's one more thought about that. Some people just can't find their way to happiness, so they never can turn their hell into heaven."

"I know their problem," volunteered a woman from the local church. "They just need more faith. So it's their fault if they can't pull themselves up by their own, God-given bootstraps."

"Wow," responded Jim. "I guess the church really is failin' us." A shockwave rippled through the crowd until a local parson yelled out, "How dare you?"

Jim let the situation speak for itself, then continued. "God's still got their back. Sometimes a person can cry and cry and cry, get comforted by others, and then stay in grief. If yer a believer, I guarantee you'll be okay.

"How?" someone yelled from the crowd, making it obvious this was no regular church service. Even the clergy in the multitude perked up for the answer. "Because, if no other way, their comfort will come from God when they get to heaven." A wonderful peace passed over the gathering at that point, so Jim called for another quick break.

3. It's good to be humble.

People were actually getting excited to hear more and Jim sensed it. These were beginning to feel like sermonettes, so he shared another text: *"this is the one to whom I will look, to the humble and contrite in spirit"* (Isaiah 66:2). The local Baptist pastor had just preached that verse, which folk said seemed like took forever, so Jim's brevity was becoming a welcome breeze in this hostile environment.

"Nobody's born with humility. It begins by knowin' right from wrong and doin' somethin' 'bout it. When people 'round us are drinkin' and gamblin' and visitin' houses of prostitution, we humbly say no." This got quite a few more people standing up and walking out. The times were tough, and cowboys generally needed some sort of relief. Jim carefully said, "See, humbly makin' the right choice ain't easy. It takes wisdom, so just know that God honors the humble. I would hope that would be enough reason for some of ya to try humility. It ain't no gift that ya get, it's an attitude to be learnt."

"Just like the Bible says," declared a pious, Bible-thumping woman. "God helps those who help themselves."

"No it don't," responded a school teacher. "I believe Benjamin Franklin used to say that slogan a lot."

"Well, I never!" complained the woman, as she marched out of the gathering holding her Bible high in the air.

"Why should we bother to learn about humility?" continued Jim. "Here's what the Good Book actually says, '*Do not let the foot of the arrogant tread on me, or the hand of the wicked drive me away,*' and you can find that in Psalm 36:11."

"What does that mean?" asked another church goer with an angry voice and a smug look.

"It means," Jim responded, "that we don't let the things goin' on around us affect what's goin' on inside us." At that point Jim realized something. No matter how much he didn't like memorizing scripture at the Methodist church when he was growing up, it finally had a purpose. His mind drifted back for a moment to sitting in church as a young boy and leafing through his Bible during the sermon. Then after church, his mom would quiz him about scripture. That's why he now knew scripture so well. He never really thought it would become handy, but as he looked out over the crowd, he knew he was fulfilling his destiny to change people's lives for the better.

4. It's best to be good.

Things were going pretty well now, so Jim decided to continue. He thought back again to his Methodist upbringing, and for the first time started appreciating their stance on things like smoking and drinking. That's when he said it was time for more text: "*they shall not hunger or thirst, neither scorching wind nor sun shall strike them down, for he who has pity on them will lead them, and by springs of water will guide them* (Isaiah 49:10). Ya know who that is who will lead and guide ya?"

"The Almighty" offered a woman near the front.

"You bet," said Jim. His eyes got big with embarrassment as he remembered Methodists were also against gambling.

The woman who spoke up was none other than "Big Nose" Kate. She was well known in town because last summer she was seen with Doc Holliday. The people often talked about that day because Doc infamously hauled in $40,000 in gambling winnings before whisking Kate off to Tombstone. She later settled into Globe and ran a boarding house, but she liked to travel and today she was back in Prescott. Everyone was surprised to hear her give credit to God for guidance. What they didn't know was her life had already begun changing. She heard about Jim and came to town just to meet him and was overjoyed to find him teaching.

Jim explained that the text was about God's guidance for those who wanted to do good. He said, "Don't give up. Have a desire inside ya to overcome the unrighteousness 'round ya. Here's where the happiness kicks in. You don't have to look beyond the end of your nose to find problems. So figure out how yer involved in doin' wrong, and then repent to a lifestyle of justice." This was just what Kate needed to hear. She had already given up her penchant for prostitution, and was clearly becoming one of Jim's first converts. This was great because he wanted a variety of people to follow him, and having a woman in his group of followers was fantastic.

5. It's good to be compassionate.

Now Jim was on a roll. This time he asked for a Bible, because he wanted to be sure to quote the text right.

Fortunately, one of the pastors present handed him a Bible and he turned to Exodus 34:6: *"The LORD, the LORD, a God merciful and gracious, slow to anger, and abounding in steadfast love and faithfulness."* He then asked them, "Do ya know where mercy comes from?" Nobody spoke up because they just wanted to listen. "It comes from being compassionate toward the unfortunate and helpless."

"Don't get me wrong," Jim continued. "It ain't easy. Take fer instance when somebody experiences violence. The first thing most people want is revenge, and that ain't no good. The idea of "an eye for an eye" is to keep people from retaliating more than what happened to them. But my concern here is, when violence happens to a helpless person, God wants us to comfort the afflicted. We have the tough task of being like God, who is all about grace and mercy and love and forgiveness. Now here's the real challenge. Notice that even though God is slow to anger, he still gets angry, so don't tempt him. I believe that mercy is offered from God as a direct response to the mercy that we offer. I hope that can motivate some of ya to be more compassionate and less gun-loving."

That riled up several more cowboys who left at that point, and one pointed his shootin' iron in the air and fired off a shot. As they made their departure, a refreshing wind blew across the crowd. It was a welcome relief, not just because of the hot-heads, but it can get pretty warm in the summer in Prescott. It's so much hotter down in Phoenix that people think when they go up in the mountains to Prescott it would be cool. It can be, but not always. This day it was a beautiful blue sky, but the direct sun always feels hotter than it is. Jim pondered for a moment, then said "Compassion is kinda like the wind. Real tough to harness, but when it refreshes, it leads us to being merciful." A few more people left at that point. They weren't disagreeing with Jim, they just said on their way out that they had to get some other things done.

6. It's important to be open to God's presence.

A good crowd still remained, so Jim said "I feel led to read Psalm 51:10. I'm not sure why yet, but here it is: *'Create in me a clean heart, O God, and put a new and right spirit within me.'*" After a brief pause he said, "Dang, that's talking about me! Didn't think I was here to talk about myself, but I can certainly testify to this verse. I was raised good and all as a Methodist, but it wasn't until last week that God created a clean heart in me. That's when I got baptized. That water thing was fine, but since then I've felt baptized by the Holy Spirit."

He went on to explain, "We all have a callin' from God on our heart, but we usually need to want that 'right spirit within.' That's when the Spirit of God can blow in like a gentle breeze. When we truly want it, we open ourselves up to being pure. Here's the problem ya run into. Lots of folk don't like pure things and they'll try to drag ya down. A godly life is what we need, but just know it's an endless challenge. Also, God can gently move into our lives over time, or if we need big changing, God can move in like a gale force wind."

Jim then looked around and saw folk looking down at their feet. God was giving Jim a keen sense of observation along with the gift of empathy. He knew they were uncomfortable with the idea of purity, not to mention stormy wind, so he said "Listen, it ain't easy. That's why we ask God to do his work of creatin' a clean heart and puttin' a right spirit in us. We just thank God for doin' God's job and then promise to do our part. In fact, the more we do good by livin' an honorable life, the more we see good in others. When we learn to see the good in people, we're learnin' to see God workin' in 'em. Guess you don't even have to wait to get to heaven to see God."

Someone yelled out at that point, "Wait a minute. You said we're supposed to work at being pure?"

"Yep," Jim said. "Why?"

"'Cause the only thing I know of that's pure is a diamond, and that takes a long time to make."

Jim responded, "We are all called to work toward purity. That ain't no secret. The tough thing is to have a right spirit in us, and then stay that way. Want to know how to do that?" People were obviously perking up again, so he said "Ya gots to be open to the spirit."

Another called out, "Well, I ain't no diamond."

Jim then said, "No, but God makes us as a diamond in the rough. Stay close to God in yer heart, and after awhile purity just rubs off on ya. Any more questions?" There weren't any so he said, "Well I've got something else to say." The crowds stretched a bit, then were ready.

7. We all need peace.

"This time I ain't got no text, but we shore do need this these days."

"Spell it out for us, parson," someone yelled from the crowd. Jim had to be careful at this point because the clergy who were present didn't like hearing the townsfolk call him a parson.

"We all need peace..." Jim's voice was drowned out

immediately because several yelled, "No kiddin'! We ain't had no peace since them dang Russians invaded!"

"Now just a minute," Jim said. "I ain't talkin' 'bout the Russians."

"Then what the Sam Hill ya talkin' 'bout?" asked several people at the same time.

"Well, maybe ya ought to try listenin'," offered Jim in a moment of frustration.

There was an uncomfortable moment of silence that followed, until several more cowboys in the crowd walked out. One said, "Well, if ya ain't talkin' 'bout the Russians, we sure is!" He was turning beet red and it was probably a good thing that he left. Then another cowboy said, "Next thing ya know, this guy's gonna start talking 'bout makin' peace with them hair scalpin' Indians!"

Jim immediately responded, "Name callin' don't get us nowhere. We are all God's children, whether we know it or not." Jim gave it a moment to calm down, and then said "Peace don't come from what happens outside of us. Peace is something we find within. And you know what? That kind of peace comes from bein' pure, which comes from bein' close to God. Show me two people who are close to God and I'll show ya two people who can work through their problems. That's why we don't worry 'bout the Russians. Try to get the local lawmen and Russians together and ya ain't got no chance of findin' peace."

"That's because they're a bunch of scallywags!" yelled out a woman in the crowd.

Jim caught eyes with the woman and carefully said, "Are you listenin' to me? Name callin' don't get us nowhere. We can't even all get along in this crowd."

"So what do we do?" asked the same woman.

"See those kids over there, playin'?" asked Jim. "That's what we need to be like. Children of God, enjoyin' the gift of life. Just be faithful to God and God's ways and pray that your life will become one of peace. Inside first, then toward yer neighbor next."

"Why can't we try to get groups to work out their differences?" asked Big Nose Kate.

"We could try," said Jim, "but let's leave that up to the lawmen and the government. I think our task is big enough tryin' to get along with one another."

8. It's okay to get mad at God.

"Here's another idea on how to turn hell into heaven. Think about Job." He again turned to the Bible he'd gotten and turned to chapter 19 and verse 22. "*Why do you, like God, pursue me, never satisfied with my flesh?*" He could see confusion on their faces, so he said "Job was real mad at God, and that's okay." Their confusion turned almost to fear, so he quickly followed with, "It's okay for you to get mad at God, too. Trust me. God has big shoulders."

A profound sense of peace passed through the crowd, finally broken by a man speaking up.

"I ain't never heard of such a thing. I think I like it, but how does that turn hell into heaven?"

Jim smiled and said, "We're living in hellish times, but I've got some news for ya. We have to have strength because we'll continue gettin' persecuted. And if we're persecuted because we're living a good, right, proper, and holy life, God will win out in the end."

"How do ya mean?" asked Pedro, one of his few followers at that point.

Jim happily responded, now that one of his own followers was interested. "That's the final good news to turning hell into heaven. If it doesn't happen in this life, it will happen in the next. Just hang in there, hope is always found in good news. We can change hell into heaven right here and now and if that don't work, God will give us the kingdom of heaven."

It had already been a long day. Not so much about time as concentration. Most of the rest of the people left with good feelings. They certainly had plenty to think about and bid their farewells. Jim looked out, and there were his true followers: Pedro, Andrés, Jimbo, Johnny, Matt, and now Big Nose Kate. Jim thanked God for a pretty good start and realized he needed to nurture this group a bit more. It wasn't going to be easy to follow him because they would meet resistance, so they needed a special word from God. Jim called the five up to sit in a circle around him, and he offered a word of prayer and then some silent prayer before chatting about the task at hand.

"Life is tough," Jim said, "and we have to go out there and get right in the middle of it all."

"So we ain't gonna be a bunch of priests?" asked Big Nose Kate with al confused look.

"Think about it, Kate," responded Jim. "People would have to call you Father."

Everyone laughed, and Pedro said "I'm sure glad you have a sense of humor, Jim. It's what keeps me goin.'"

Jim agreed, then got back to business. "Ya need to be like the dust of the earth."

"I don't get it," replied Johnny while scratching his head.

"It's easier to understand when yer down in the desert in Phoenix," offered Jim. "The dust there settles into the ground and nurtures everything around it. That, my friends, is yer job."

"Yah," said Jimbo, "but sometimes dust storms blow in and make a mess of things."

"You bet," agreed Jim, "and that's my point. Dust can be good or harmful, so yer job is to get involved with the bad dust while remembering yer the good dust."

They needed to think about that one for a while, so Jim suggested they take a short break for some meditation.

It was late afternoon, and fortunately the seven of them had been invited to supper by a church member. Jim didn't know it at the time, but this simple act became the basis of one of his defining ideas: "Have faith, and God will provide." They arrived at the home and were greeted by the gracious host. After enjoying their fill of Indian Slapjacks and fresh sowbelly, they were good to go for some more teaching from Jim.

They settled into the front room, enjoying the fragrance of cooked bacon wafting in. This time he decided to start with some scripture. The pastor let him keep the Bible he'd given him, so Jim turned to Isaiah 42:6 and read "*I am the LORD, I have called you in righteousness, I have taken you by the hand and kept you; I have given you as a covenant to the people, a light to the nations.*"

"They a whole bunch of sermons in that one," exclaimed Jimbo.

"Yer right," said Jim, "so let's take it a bit at a time. Let's think of ourselves as called by God. When things get tough, and they will, always remember that the good and righteous God is the one who has called us."

"Kinda sends a chill up my back," said Matt as he lifted his shoulders and shrugged off a shiver. "I never felt good about running a house of prostitution, but I feel great about bein' called by God to do good things. But I'm confused. Yer the one who called me, not God."

"Good point," said Jim. "It has to do with the way God's Word works in our lives. It shore was talkin' 'bout God in the time of Isaiah the prophet, but the Bible keeps speaking new to us each day. Today God is calling y'all through me, so it's true that I called ya and it's true that God called ya."

Everyone slapped Matt on the back for a great point, and Kate said "Just look around. If we ain't a bunch of misfits, I don't know who is. So if God can work with us, I guess God could do just about anything."

"That's right," said Pedro. "Bringing together Mexicans, Americans, men, women, and an owner of a house of prostitution ain't no easy thing." He then looked at Kate and asked, "What did you do for a livin'?"

Kate was quite comfortable letting them know that Jim was already a great influence in her life. "I used to be a prostitute, and I dated Doc Holliday."

"That was you?" asked Matt, with a look of shock on his face.

"Yes, sir!" said Kate. "We headed for Tombstone to get in on the big silver strike there, but I had anger and drinkin' problems. Earlier this year Doc threw me out, so I left Tombstone for good and stayed at a boarding house I opened in Globe last year. I loved the mountains here in Prescott, so I left Globe recently and arrived a few days ago. It was just in time to hear about Jim's way of helpin' people. I was hooked, but in a good way. Then I heard him this afternoon and just knew I needed to be a follower."

"Welcome to the group," Jim offered with an air of genuineness. "Now let me see. Where was I? O yah, the scripture verse says that God will keep us."

"Great," said Johnny. "Cause I ain't got no idea how we can foller ya when we've left our jobs. Jimbo and I left the family farm outside Phoenix and we're worried sick about what will happen to it."

"Same here," echoed Andrés. "Pedro and I are scared we'll lose our farm."

"Speak for yerself, Andrés," countered Pedro. "I believe in jefe, so I choose to trust him."

"No, no, no," explained Jim. "What we all have to do is trust in God. He's the one who's got the hard part."

"Tell us more," begged a curious Kate.

"Okay," said Jim, "Here's the clincher. God is givin' us 'as a covenant to the people, a light to the nations.'"

"Why's that the clincher?" asked Jimbo.

"Because there's a little bit of a secret here," continued Jim. "We have ta think 'bout ourselves as light, not lights. We ain't gonna be successful in what we do if we think like separate people. From now on, we're a group. Think of us up on top of this mountain in Prescott and at the top of this hillside. We can't hide from view. Kinda like that one-room school house over there." Jim pointed just south of them and they all turned to look. "The whole place can be lit up by one lamp on a lampstand. That's us. We're the light and our job is to let God's light shine through us so people will see it and give glory to God, not to us. Okay, that's pretty much what I had to say. Any questions?"

"Sure," said Pedro. "I noticed ya spoke a lot from the Prophets and the Writin's, but not so much from the Law. Ya tryin' to do away with the Law?"

"Not at all," proclaimed Jim. "I'm tryin' to make the Law even better."

That really concerned his followers. They'd never heard of anyone daring to change the Bible. Jim sensed their fear and said, "I ain't tryin' to change anything." He picked up the Bible again and turned to one of the books of the Law. "Listen to what Abund said in Deuteronomy 4:2—'*You must neither add anything to what I command you nor take away anything from it, but keep the commandments of the LORD your God with which I am charging you.*'"

"Sorry," said Jimbo, "that didn't help."

Jim responded, "Remember what I said about the Bible becoming new to each generation?" They all nodded yes. "It's not 'bout changin' the Bible. It's about makin' it better because it becomes alive and real for every generation."

"I'll have to think about that fer a while," said Jimbo, while scratching his head under his cowboy hat.

"Great," Jim replied. "Now think back to earlier this afternoon in my first talk, when I said ya need to be able to look at yerself honestly, and anyone who chooses to follow me will have to do that a lot."

Jimbo looked a bit embarrassed and Pedro chuckled, then said "rememberin' back a whole hour or so too much for ya, Jimbo?"

Jimbo turned beet red and shot back with, "Well at least I didn't take a siesta in the middle of Jim's talk!"

That really made Pedro angry, so Jim intervened. "Now boys, that's just exactly the way to not be a group. Anybody recall what I said about two minutes ago about being a single light that shines through us so that folk would give glory to God?"

They all sat up a bit straighter at that point and said "Yes."

"Now we're gettin' somewhere," suggested Jim. "We got off track a bit, talkin' 'bout makin' the Law better. That's okay because that's a tough idea to wrap yer head around. Now listen real close: I ain't trying to improve the laws of Abund. I'm tryin' to improve the way we use 'em."

Several nodded in agreement, but Jim felt like this would be a great time to take another short break. "Let's spend some time in prayer and ask God to help us with these new ideas." Prayer was a pretty new thing for each of his followers. Jim peeked around and saw Andrés fumbling with some change and heard Jimbo's stomach growl. He saw Pedro looking serious and wondered what was going on in his head. Johnny was sitting with his hands folded and certainly looked like he was trying to connect with God. And then he looked at Kate. He was so pleased to have a woman as one of his followers and knew she had a lot of learning to do. All of a sudden, Jim started to feel the weight of his new task. He wasn't just trying to follow what God was calling him to do, he was leading others. With that thought in mind, he settled in for some serious prayer.

After a short bit, Jim was interrupted by the sound of people stretching, and figured it was time to end the praying. He said "Amen," then continued with his teaching. His heart was quite full as he spent his prayer time thanking God for these followers. "Ya can't know fer sure, my friends, what Abund meant. That's why we ain't changin' what he said, we're tryin' to make sure people understand how to use those teachin's today. Here's the challenge. We have to live out the Bible by bein' an example of faithful use of it. I've got a feelin' God's gonna lay a whole bunch of new ideas on my heart to share in the near future. I'll promise to do my part of bein' open to the movement of the Spirit in my life." He could almost see the group comin' together, so he told them he had one more idea on how they could be the kind of example that would bring glory to God. "Ya need to be good people, right?"

"Ya got that right, jefe," Pedro said approvingly.

"And that'll get ya to heaven?" quizzed Jim.

"Why do I think that's a trick question?" asked Matt.

"Because yer right," said Jim. "What ya need to do is be better than the clergy and the lawmen."

Kate suggested, "It ain't too hard to be better than the corrupt lawmen. And I know a few clergy who sneak into houses of prostitution." She had an angry frown on her face, trying to cover the guilt that she still felt from her former life.

"Okay," said Jim. "Again were goin' a little off kilter. Our job isn't to belittle the clergy and lawmen, it's to be better than them."

"But ain't it easy to be better than them, if they're actin' real bad?" asked Andrés.

"Sure," offered Jim. "But our question is about how to get to heaven."

"I think we'd all agree that's an important question," commented Matt, who likewise suffered from guilt about his former life.

"Then here's the answer," said Jim. "Ya won't get to heaven if ya ain't no better than them."

The group looked a bit startled at this comment, so Jim told them "That's enough teachin' for today. We need to find a place to stay tonight and maybe find some grub. I don't know about y'all, but I'm excited to see what tomorrow brings."

They all agreed and headed back into Prescott. As they walked, Jim noticed that they seemed more like a group. The discussion was sincere and they walked physically closer together. He prayed that they would continue growing emotionally and spiritually closer, too.

SCENE TWO
Big Changes and Bad News

The next morning, Jim and his group headed back to the same hillside just outside Prescott. Another crowd followed them to the side of this beautiful mountain, expecting to hear more of his unique ideas. Instead, Jim decided it was time to make his group bigger. He looked out over the crowd and, one at a time, pointed to another seven men. That's all it took, and all seven of them worked their way through the crowd to join the other five men. Here's the names of the twelve:

Pedro—brother of Andrés. A cowboy who was
   showing leadership potential.
Andrés—brother of Pedro. A cowboy who was
   a faithful follower.
Jimbo—brother of Johnny. A cowboy who had
   deep commitment to what he did.
Johnny—brother of Jimbo. A cowboy who would
   do anything for you.
Matt—the hated house of prostitution owner, who
   formerly collected taxes for the Russians.
Phil—a native of Prescott, who knew the local
   people very well.
Bart—a native of nearby Agua Fria Valley, who
   had experience with farming.
Tommie—known as a doubter. A cowboy who
   challenged everything he heard.
Junior—known as the son of Alpheus, who was

in the crowd at the right time.
Thad—short for Thaddeus, which means
    'gift of God.'
Carly—a rip-roaring cowboy, known as a
    very zealous person
Benedict—a cowboy with a difficult past, who
    couldn't really be counted on

What about Kate? She was definitely a follower, but the boys really wanted the group to be made up of twelve men. It all seemed rather silly to Jim, but they continued to complain. He finally decided that they couldn't keep her from being a follower, no matter how much they might want to exclude her. At that point, Pedro admitted he was a superstitious sort and just didn't want the group to consist of thirteen. Kate finally spoke up and said, "There are more important things to worry 'bout, so call yerselves 'The Twelve,' and I'll think of us as 'The Baker's Dozen.'"

The crowd was pretty unhappy when they realized Jim wasn't going to give a talk, but Jim and The Twelve (plus one) departed anyway. Jim wanted to drop by his home for a kind of 'meet the family' thing. The family home was just on the outskirts of Prescott, and his home was quite humble. He thought that might be a good representation of the way they needed to be for whatever it was God was calling them to do. It was apparent that Jim was getting lots of attention, because when they walked into town they were greeted by a gigantic, noisy crowd. In fact, the gathering was so large, nobody could even move, because they were shoulder to shoulder and wanting help from Jim. This group wasn't interested in stories about how to live, they'd heard he could heal people.

The Jim Caldwell Trilogy

When Jim's mom and brothers heard about the ruckus, they went over to try to help. It turned out to be a good idea because there were some trouble makers in the crowd. One burly cowboy yelled out, "That guy's crazy!" Some of the local parsons were already upset with him, and one screamed "He's got the devil in him!" Jim was somewhat confused, but finally decided it was time to respond. "I got the Holy Spirit in me, so here's an important warnin' to ya. Speakin' against me is speakin' against the Holy Spirit, and that's an unforgivable sin." There was a unison gasp in the crowd, and to say the least, the clergy folk were taken aback as their eyebrows raised. Jim continued, "So if ya want to call the Holy Spirit the devil, just know that's an unforgivable sin. Yep. You'd burn in hell for eternity."

Time for family to intervene. His mother and brothers tried yelling to get Jim's attention, but things were pretty rowdy. Finally, word got through the crowd and someone close to Jim said, "Yer family's calling fer ya." That moment was another game changer for Jim. Things were really starting to come into focus, and he shocked everyone with what he had to say. "That ain't my family." Of course, Jim was in his hometown, and everyone knew Jim and his family, so they were confused. Jim further surprised those gathered when he looked at The Twelve and said, "Here's my family." People were shaking their heads 'no,' and after a short pause, he continued. "And my family is anyone who follows the nudging of the Holy Spirit." Jim then decided to forgo the visit to his house. The humility would have been a great lesson, but he felt he'd kind of drawn a line in the sand about family. It was time to think of the future, not the past. Things were starting to come together for Jim, now that he had The Twelve, or The Baker's Dozen, so he left.

Major General Sergey Popov was the Russian overlord for Prescott, and even that far away he was hearing troubling stories about Jim's cousin The Dipper. Sergey was mostly frustrated with The Dipper's growing popularity with the crowds. Because of this, Sergey called for some of his soldiers and told them to go down to Phoenix and arrest Jim's cousin. This was doubly good in that it would deeply bother Jim, who was also becoming a crowd favorite.

A group of six Russian soldiers mounted their horses, after grabbing a few supplies, and headed south. It was about sixty miles one way just to get to town, and they knew they would encounter resistance trying to find him. Once in town, they stopped at Whiskey Row. They preferred vodka, but the stop was for business. "Anyone seen za Dipper?" asked one of the soldiers. The question was met with steely eyes and an eerie silence. He really didn't expect any help, but a tavern was a great place to try. Most of the cowboys were heavily drinking, and sure enough, one very tipsy older man came face to face to therm with the stench of whiskey and cigars on his breath and said, "Ya can look for 'em down at the Gila River."

All six of the soldiers high tailed it out of the place. Not only did they get the information they were looking for, but they knew they could easily be outgunned by the drunks. The locals certainly had more fire power, but being well-oiled would likely make them bad shooters. They quickly mounted their horses and headed further south. They knew the Gila River was only a few miles out of town, but it was also an active tributary of the Colorado River. They rode for a short distance when several started complaining.

"How we find zis guy?" asked a soldier.

"Gila River be long," complained another.

"Why you believe zat drunk?" grumbled a third Russian.

"I've got a hunch," offered the leader in Russian. "He'll be at the closest spot to town."

They happily followed, and sure enough they saw some crowds after a few bends in the river. "He be there," the leader proclaimed while pointing ahead.

"How know?" asked another.

"You be here if no need?" They all laughed as they approached, hopefully finishing the first part of their task.

The six of them rode their horses straight into the river. The crowd started screaming, some started running, and two of the soldiers grabbed The Dipper by the arms. They dragged him to the river bank and unceremoniously threw him down on the mildly sloping ground.

"What are you doing?" asked The Dipper in a confused anger, while his dungarees profusely dripped into the sandy ground at the water's edge. The Russian soldiers ignored him, and instead bound his hands behind his back. They rudely threw him face down across the front of the saddle while onlookers watched in horror. The Dipper continued to yell, so then they gagged him with his own kerchief. After a seemingly endless ride, they all arrived back in Prescott and delivered The Dipper to the county jail.

Truth is, Sergey was afraid of The Dipper, and wasn't sure what to do with him. The Dipper remained in jail for several days before Sergey hatched a plan. His birthday was the following day, so Sergey invited his soldiers and several of the local leaders to his party. The next day arrived and Sergey had a lavish banquet for them, in honor of his birthday. The entertainment was provided by a girl of questionable character who danced for them. What nobody knew was the agreement Sergey made with the dancer to get his desired result. What he said was that he'd give her a thousand dollars, if she requested the death of The Dipper.

When the meal was done, the young woman came out and did a very seductive dance. The crowd was exceedingly pleased, so Sergey asked "I want to reward you. What you wish?" Of course, the woman wanted the great sum of money, so right on cue she said, "I want the death of The Dipper." His soldiers were delighted, but the locals were shocked. Sergey turned to his guests and said "sorry, have to keep my word." He then sent some of his soldiers to retrieve The Dipper from jail, and immediately had him hanged at the Town Square.

_____

The surprising arrest of Jim's cousin became the news of the town. One person said, "Them crazy Russians even arrested The Dipper while he was innocently baptizing folk in the river." This frightening news piqued the curiosity of a group of clergy all the way down in Phoenix. Among them were several Catholic priests who were seething about the Russians taking most of their churches. They got on their horses early the next morning to make the rough ride up the mountain to Prescott. They took the usual stop at The Rusty Tavern, for a quick break for themselves and their horses. They never could resist the famous mile high pie, which gave them a chance to chat while eating.

"Now what, fer sure, is this trip about?" asked one of the

Catholic priests.

"I don't know about you," said the Methodist clergyman, "but I want to know what Jim Caldwell is up to."

"I'm curious about his cousin's arrest," said the Presbyterian pastor.

"Everybody's saying they arrested a bunch of people," offered a parson.

Meanwhile, the rest of them were just curious. After all, it's not easy to gossip without some information. Soon they saddled up and continued north. Time was slowly moving toward noon, and they wanted to catch the trail to Prescott before it got too late. The trips up and down the mountain were north and south, so the sun was of no concern, but once you turn west toward Prescott and the late afternoon sun, it can be a real nuisance to your eyes.

They made the journey just right, and got into Prescott by mid afternoon. First thing they did was ask about The Dipper. Everyone in town knew the terrible story, so they quickly found out. Filled with sorrow and anger, they paused for a prayer for the eternal soul of Jim's cousin. Now they were on a mission to talk to Jim Caldwell. The Methodist clergyman was particularly concerned, partly because Jim was a Methodist, and party because he was hearing about unacceptable actions. The others were wondering what Jim was doing that was so bad, so the clergyman said Jim was acting like he was clergy.

Each of them nodded their heads with understanding, then they started asking townsfolk where Jim could be found. Turned out he was back to the hillside having dinner with his followers. As they approached, they heard people talking, and little by little the noise got louder. As they crested the hill, they were amazed at the crowd of people who were there. "They're just watchin' 'em eat," the priest said in shock.

One of the clergymen said, "Yeh, maybe we ought to do that, too."

Brushing off the comment, the Methodist pastor exclaimed, "They're drinkin' liquor!" After a breathy moment of surprise mingled with anger he said, "I think we's got something, friends. At least for us Methodists, we take a traditional stance against drinkin' alcohol. Probably don't mean that much to some of you, but it's a big deal for us Methodists."

The small gaggle of clerics pushed their way through the crowd so they would be within earshot. "Jim, its Rev. Mills here. I'm the very first Methodist minister appointed to serve a church here in Arizona."

"Pleased to meet ya Reverend," Jim said in a pleasant tone.

"Not so pleasant for me," retorted the pastor.

"Okay," Jim said cautiously. "What's on yer mind?"

"I know yer a Methodist, so why ya drinkin' alcohol? That's against our tradition" Rev. Mills proclaimed, with increasing intensity.

Jim surprised the whole crowd with his confrontational response. He said, "Isaiah prophesied rightly about you hypocrites, as it is written,

> *This people honors me with their lips, but their hearts are far from me; In vain do they worship me, teaching human precepts as doctrines*."

Jim took one more swipe at the good Reverend. "You abandon the commandments of God and hold fast to human tradition."

One could see the veins on Rev. Mills' neck popping out.

He then fairly screamed, "So you think you have better ideas than our founder, John Wesley?"

"I'm not talkin' 'bout Mr. Wesley" continued Jim, seemingly undaunted. "I'm talkin' 'bout all you clergy, slitherin' around like snakes, and lookin' for trouble rather than good news. You carefully keep tradition in place and don't seem to worry 'bout things like the Ten Commandments."

Several of the pastors had to be held back by the crowd, then Jim felt a teaching coming on. He looked away from the clergymen and towards the crowd and said, "You ready for something real important?"

They excitedly said "Yes!" Then Jim continued, "The parson seems disgusted with alcohol, but I feel led by God to say this. There ain't nothing we eat or drink that makes us sinners."

To everyone's surprise, Jim and his followers just got up at this moment and walked away. Of course, they headed to the local saloon and nobody followed. Once they were settled at a table, Big Nose Kate asked "What did that mean?" She was particularly interested since she had lots of problems with alcohol.

"Hope this clears it up," said Jim. "Anything we take in goes into the stomach. Pretty soon it travels through us and ends up in the sewer."

"Okay" said Pedro. "So if we keep it in us, does that make us better?"

"No," Jim explained with a bit of a laugh. "It don't matter 'bout the stomach. It's the things that come from the heart that can make us sinners."

"Still confused," said Matt.

Jim continued, "Think about it. Do bad actions come from the stomach or from the heart?"

"They come from the heart" Jimbo said.

"Right," announced Jim. "A sin-sick heart is the source of fornication, stealin', killin', lyin', adultery, meanness, envy, and slander. These things come from the heart and causes a person to be a sinner."

After that, the group agreed to stay at Matt's house. As they turned in, Jim finally got a chance to grieve the loss of his cousin. The next day Jim's group headed for Phoenix.

Jim started calling them "The Twelve," a little while back. Actually there were thirteen of them when you include Jim, and fourteen when you add Big Nose Kate. As usual, they took a rest stop at The Rusty Tavern and were offered a back room that could hold the whole group. They settled in and ordered a whole pie to share, as funds were tight. Jimbo complained that the servings were pretty small, so his brother suggested "smaller pieces could help make a smaller man." It was uncomfortable for a moment, but then everyone started laughing. Jimbo reminded them what Jim had just taught about: "There ain't nothing that we eat or drink that makes us sinners."

That actually made them all feel good. They were becoming a group, but it turns out they needed a name and didn't know it. Jim said, "I've heard about a mountain on the north side of Phoenix that has a hole in it. Let's head there and see if we can sit in it to get some relief from the sun." They all headed out of the saloon and got on their horses. Pedro noticed that Jim seemed to be sitting higher in his saddle than the rest of them, and teasingly said "Jim, you need to get off your high horse."

Jim lovingly responded, "I guess we can't all be good with jokes." Laughter was becoming a staple for the group as they made their way on down to Phoenix.

As it came into view, Johnny said "I think I've been there before. If I'm right, it's pretty easy to walk up the north side. I always heard that folk liked going there just to see the little town of Phoenix. It kinda makes a window to look through." They were pretty excited to give it a try, so when they arrived they ran up to the hole in the mountain. Nobody was there so they sat down and enjoyed the relief from the sun. Johnny said, "Didn't we forget someone?" and pointed back down the mountain. Sure enough, there came Jimbo, huffing and puffing and wheezing. He had stopped about half way there, so his brother called down and asked, "You okay?"

Jimbo replied, "Oh, I'm just enjoying the view," as he tugged upward on his pants.

Johnny said, "But you're looking straight down at the rock!" Again, more laughter, then they all settled in when Jimbo finally got there. It truly was a pleasant and peaceful spot. Especially considering the Wild West at that time was doing a great job of living up to its name. They all sat for awhile in the hole in the rock, admiring the view of Phoenix ahead and the route back to Prescott behind them. Pedro ended the silence, as usual, with a suggestion, "Why don't we call ourselves the Hole in the Rock Gang." Jim was immediately against it because he didn't think the word 'gang' would be useful as their identity. Everyone else liked it, even Big Nose Kate. After a lot of discussion, the new name for "The Twelve" was accepted, and Kate decided she would still simply think of them as "The Baker's Dozen." The reason Jim gave in was because he wanted to "show cooperation as a group, and he figured his group could help give a better feel for the word "gang."

It was starting to get late, so they went back down to their horses. When they got there, they looked around and saw Jimbo about halfway down. His thoughtful brother said, "Jimbo, its easier coming down," to which he replied "No it ain't." Soon enough they headed into town and found a cheap boarding house to put them up for the night. While trying to get to sleep on his cot, Jim felt restless. He sensed some sort of urgency speaking to his soul. The next morning he tried to process what happened. He came to the conclusion that he was supposed to go back to the hole in the rock, but not take the whole gang. After a bit more concentration, he felt that God was calling him to take Pedro, Jimbo, and Johnny. He even asked God, "Are ya sure 'bout Pedro?" Jim wasn't sure about what happened next, but he thought he heard a little chuckle.

Jim called the gang together after breakfast and announced that he was heading back to the hole in the rock. Matt said "Great, I loved that place!" to which Jim explained that it was a spiritual journey he felt God was calling him to make. They all nodded with appreciation until Jim continued, "And I'm taking Pedro, Jimbo, and Johnny with me." This didn't sit well with the others and the disappointment was palpable. Andrés spoke up and said, "I don't understand. Yer taking Jimbo and Johnny, who are brothers, but yer taking my brother Pedro and not me?" Kate offered that she thought she understood: "Here's where prejudice against women begins for this group." Others started to talk, but Jim interrupted with "Ya just gonna have ta trust me. I truly believe this is what God wants." As they headed outside to get on their horses, someone rather mumbled "then maybe God's the one with the prejudice problem." When Jim shot a look back at them, all he saw was their backs as they walked away.

"That wasn't easy," Jim said to the three, as he headed to the next big step in doing whatever it was God was calling him to do. The other three nodded in agreement, while they were secretly being happy about being treated special. They walked up to the hole in the rock with a bit of a lilt in their step. The four of them were delighted to find nobody around, so they settled into their little piece of paradise. Jim asked them to spend some time in silent prayer, then the most amazing thing happened. Jim's hair slowly turned white, right in front of their eyes. Jimbo was about to say something when the dead cowboy Kit Carson appeared by Jim. Another dead person also materialized, but they didn't know who it was. The apparition noticed their attitude, and rather angrily said "I'm Texas Jack Omohundro."

"Okay" said Pedro, "but I still don't know who ya are."

"Well ya might not know me, but I was pretty famous before I died last year of pneumonia."

Pedro inquired, "So that's what made ya famous?"

Texas Jack was really losing patience at this point and said, "No, course not! I was a good friend of Buffalo Bill Cody!"

"So that's what made you famous? Pedro asked tauntingly.

Nearly in a rage, Texas Jack said "Youngster, I married the most famous ballerina in the world!!"

Pedro's anger was piquing too, so he lunged at the apparition. Jimbo and Johnny held him back, but Pedro said "Let me go. I think I can take him."

Finally, Johnny spoke up, "At least, Pedro, have some respect for the dead."

This seemed to settle everyone down, so Jim said

"Why do we have the pleasure of meetin' ya?"

Kit Carson took over and said, "We got some news for ya.

Can we have some privacy?"

Pedro said, "We ain't got no secrets, so go ahead."

Kit looked at Jim and Jim said, "That's fine. We're a group now."

Kit replied "Okay, but its bad news."

Jimbo said, "I ain't had much of anything else in my life, so I'm ready."

Kit offered to Jim, "Ya ain't gonna live much longer."

"That's all ya got?" inquired Pedro. "I don't know 'bout you, but I've heard everybody dies sooner or later."

Texas Jack said, "Yah, but Jim's gonna die sooner than later."

"Why is he gonna die?" asked Johnny.

Kit responded, "I cain't tell ya that. What I can tell ya is that it will happen in Phoenix."

Pedro was about to say something again, when Kit and Texas Jack disappeared as quickly as they arrived. They all realized they'd just had a spiritual experience, and they felt overwhelmed. Eventually Pedro said to Jim, "this is now a sacred place and I'd like to stay."

If all of that wasn't enough, a cloud appeared over them and they heard the voice of God saying, "Jim is a great teacher of my ways. Listen to him."

With all of them in a near state of shock, Jim said "It's time to get back to the rest of the Gang."

Pedro was happy to hear Jim starting to use the term, the Gang, instead of, the group, and said "Can't wait to tell people 'bout all of this."

Jim then warned them, "Ya can tell the rest of the Gang, but nobody else."

They were all disappointed, but they were now realizing

that obeying Jim was strangely a way to obey God.

The Hole in the Rock Gang was soon reunited, but there were some frosty attitudes from those left behind. Breaking the silence, Big Nose Kate questioned "It's because I'm female, right?"

Jim quickly put that to rest by saying, "You weren't the only one excluded, and I don't know God's reason."

Andrés spoke with anger still in his voice, "Well I guess God is all about breaking families apart."

Pedro was anxious to share what happened, so he interrupted the complaining with, "We gots some good news and some bad news." Thad requested the good news first, so Pedro continued "We saw dead people!"

Thad asked, "How is that good news?"

"It just was," answered Pedro, "but we also heard the voice of God." Almost simultaneously, the others said, "Yah, right. How do you know?"

Pedro was pretty hyped up and said, "It was a cloudless day, but a cloud suddenly appeared and a voice said, "Jim is a great teacher of my ways. Listen to him."

The others were starting to become believers in their leader, when Jim said "Ya can't tell anyone 'bout this."

It was like a balloon popped, but Carly mustered the next question, "So what's the bad news?"

Jimbo spoke up with, "Jim's gonna die."

Tommie doubted this information, so he asked, "Why?"

Johnny said, "The spectre was Kit Carson and some

other cowboy we never heard of, but Kit said all he could say was that Jim would die soon, and it would happen here in Phoenix."

Pedro quickly offered, "I vote that we head back to Prescott."

They all agreed and got on their horses and headed north. It seemed to go against their idea of unity in the Gang, but Pedro, Jimbo, and Johnny not only stayed at the back, they were heard talking. And not just talking, but arguing. It annoyed the rest of the twelve so much that they just rode right on past The Rusty Tavern. Any time one of them slowed down a bit to try to hear the three, they just stopped talking. It was a long, tiresome ride, but they finally arrived at Matt's house.

As they prepared to hole up for the night, the first thing that happened was Jim asked, "What were you three guys arguing 'bout back there on our way here?" The three looked like animals caught in a corner. They offered nothing but silence, because their hole in the rock experience made them feel special. Not just more special than the rest of the gang, but they were arguing about which one of the three was the best.

Jim was not pleased, so he sat down and called them over to him. First thing he said was, "I suspect I know what ya was arguin' 'bout." The three felt pretty sick at that moment and Jim said, "I'm ready for another teachin'. Y'all ready for another learnin'?" The others showed readiness, but the three were already feeling like a bunch of scallywags. Jim taught "If ya want to be first, ya have to be last." That ruffled a few feathers, so Jim suggested, "It's time to get some sleep. It's a tough teachin', so think about it and pray about it. See ya in the mornin'."

The next day, they gathered for breakfast and Jim asked if they had any questions. Pedro spoke up, "I admit it. I want to be first."

His brother Andrés reminded, "Then ya have to be last."

Pedro remarked, "Sorry brother, but that don't make no sense."

Jim broke in and said, "Pedro, you just have to live with the idea for awhile and see if that helps."

Andrés, still frustrated with his brother said, "I 'spect it won't."

At this point, Jim decided to tell them more about what he heard from the apparitions that the other three didn't hear. It had to do with more detail of his upcoming death. "I'm gonna be handed over to Deputy U.S. Marshal Virgil Earp, right here in Prescott" Jim announced in a rather monotone voice.

"Why? asked Big Nose Kate, with proper indignation, tinged with fear.

Jim responded, "'Cause they want me killed."

"And why?" Thad asked with shock and anger.

"The Russians are scared that I'm tryin' ta overthrow their administration of the Arizona Territory," Jim offered matter-of-factly. "And as y'all know, death sentences have ta be carried out by the Russians."

"I don't wanna hear no more," shared Jimbo.

"Sorry Jimbo, but God has laid this on my heart to let you all know," Jim said in a pastoral way. "I'll be transferred to Phoenix and tried by Lieutenant General Dmitri Ivanov who will condemn me to death."

There was a long pause after that announcement, followed by Junior saying, "Please stop."

"Just a few more details God wants this special group to know," explained Jim. "I'll be mocked and spit on and beaten up, then I'll be hung."

The Jim Caldwell Trilogy

"Because you've done good things helping people?" commented Tommie in a sarcastic tone.

"And what about us? We've been doing the same thing you've been doing," queried Bart.

"All I can say is, we should never let what's happenin' to us change who we are and what we do," responded Jim.

"That's surely all we need to hear," mentioned Benedict.

"No," said Jim, "'cause there's still some good news."

"I'm more than ready for that," whispered Phil.

"After three days, I'll be in heaven," Jim offered with a smile.

"That's a tough way to get to heaven," complained Thad.

"Couldn't agree more, Thad, but everyone else's route will be easier," explained Jim.

"And what way would that be, jefe?" inquired Pedro.

"I'll make it easy for ya," said Jim. "Feed the hungry, when you see people in need. Give drink to the thirsty, because water is the core of life. Welcome strangers."

"But not the Russians, right?" clarified Pedro.

"We don't treat people wrong," explained Jim, "just because they treat us wrong." He then continued, "provide clothing to those in need."

"Never saw a naked person running around outside," claimed Pedro in an argumentative way.

"You have no idea what a person is going through," taught Jim, "until you get to know them. You just might find a cowboy wearing the only shirt he's got." Pedro was feeling humbled by these teachings, so he decided to keep quiet and listen.

"We also need to take care of the sick," continued Jim, "and I don't just mean family. Watch what's going on around you and listen to the things they talk about. If you hear about someone having difficulty taking care of their ill loved one, do whatever you can to provide help."

"That makes sense," offered Kate. "I know that when I was on a drunken binge, nobody was there to help me."

"This means we have to put others before ourselves. Right, Jim?" asked Matt.

"That's the heart and soul of my message," declared Jim, "and denying our own needs is a constant challenge. But I have one more thought. We should visit folk who are in jail."

"But didn't they do something bad to deserve being in jail?" asked Johnny.

"That don't make them bad." said Jim. "We all do wrong things, but we are people of good news. Visit them in jail and look for the blessings they've had, and try to get them focused on finding God's love.

"Gots ta admit, that don't sound easy," complained Matt.

"You bet," agreed Jim. "But if these things were too easy, people would move on to something more challengin'."

The Gang looked exhausted from all of the things they had to think about, so they took the rest of the day off.

Just to get an idea of what all Jim was dealing with in those days, it's good to understand that the Mexican-American War only ended thirty five years ago. Both the American Civil War and the Apache Wars began twenty years prior. The Russian Invasion started eleven years before this story about Jim, and Geronino was moved to the San Carlos Reservation just four years previous. Also, the Apache Wars didn't end for another five years after the story of Jim Caldwell. Jim's efforts to make the world a better place were noticeable, but let's take a look at the volatility the American West was embroiled in. Just to be focused, here are some stories about the Indians. But first, here's a profound quote from the time.

> *We have heard much talk of the treachery of the Indian. In treachery, broken pledges on the part of high officials, lies, thievery, slaughter of defenseless women and children, and every crime in the catalogue of man's inhumanity to man, the Indian was a mere amateur compared to the "noble white man."*—Lieutenant Britton Davis, U.S. Army

Camp Grant Massacre

First of all, extreme tension existed between Tucson and the residents of Camp Grant. Tucson residents were livid about the deadly Apache raids in the area, and even more upset that the soldiers of Camp Grant did little about it. As a matter of fact, Lieutenant Royal E. Whitman, commander of Camp Grant, chose to offer protection to 500 Apaches camped nearby.

Chief Eskiminzin was a local group chief of the Aravaipa band of the San Carlos group of the Western Apache during the Apache Wars. The chief brought 150 half-starved followers to Camp Grant and pleaded for help from Whitman who sought instructions from headquarters. They said the Indians could be hired for help if they turned over their weapons. They did, then another 350 Apaches found their way to Camp Grant, which was rapidly becoming an informal Indian reservation.

On the morning of April 28, 1871, a group of 6 Americans,

48 Mexicans, and 94 Papago Indians left Tucson for Camp Grant, 70 miles to the northeast. The Papagos were traditional enemies of the Apaches, and held deep seated hatreds. The Mexicans were still frustrated after the Mexican-American War, and the loss of land to the Gadsden Purchase of 1854. Our own Pedro was one of the Mexican participants in the Massacre, but Jim Caldwell utterly transformed Pedro's life in 1881.

So at dawn, April 30 1871, the Tucson group attacked the Apache camps. The men were in the mountains hunting and those at camp had given up the weapons. The massacre was fast and furious. Those trying to escape were shot. Nearly 144 Apache were killed, and all but 8 of the victims were women and children. Commander Whitman learned of the expedition and sent a warning message to the Indian Camp. It arrived too late, so when a medical team arrived to render assistance, no survivors were found.

The "massacre" found outrage from eastern US newspapers. Ulysses S. Grant had become the President of the United States in 1869. He threatened to put the Arizona Territory under martial law if the participants were not brought to trial. In October of 1871, a grand jury indicted about 100 people after the jury deliberated for 19 minutes. The defense attorneys focused exclusively on the history of Apache raids and killings in the years preceding the event. In 1872 a new Fort Grant was ordered to be established at the base of Mount Graham, and the "old" Camp Grant was closed.

Battle of Salt River Canyon

This war was just nine years from the beginning of our story about Jim Caldwell. He was well aware of what was going on, but he was living in Prescott, far away from the wars. Still, all of the Arizona Territory was entangled in the many wars and troubles raging across the area in the late 1800s. This quick story is about the Battle of Salt River Canyon.

Lieutenant Colonel George Crook was in San Francisco when he was told to move to the Arizona Territory. Cook objected, but Washington intervened and gave him the command. After all, he had the most successful campaigns against Indians in post-Civil War America. Crook arrived in 1871 and established his headquarters in Prescott. Crook made his first target, the Apache chief Cochise. Crook's total failure left him enraged about the Apache Wars. His problem was that the Board of Indian Comissioners signed a Peace Policy, to bring Indians onto reservations to civilize them.

By early December 1871, Crook decided to treat any Indian who was not on a reservation as hostile. One of his scouts discovered a trail that led to a possible Yavapai stronghold, so they headed that way. It was a rugged trip through the mountains, but the dark of night betrayed the Yavapais. They had a bonfire and were dancing in celebration of recent raids, while the women cooked and the children enjoyed the festivities. Understandably, they posted no sentinel.

On December 28, 1872 Crook's men found the stronghold at Skeleton Cave in the Salt River Canyon, just northeast of Phoenix. His force had 130 troopers and another 30 Apache scouts. They surprised the celebration by surrounding the cave and opening fire. Some of them shot at the roof of the cave and caused a deadly fire. Others rolled boulders over the cliffs above. About 75 were found dead in the cave, including Chief Nanni-chaddi, who bragged that no soldier would ever find their stronghold.

The women and children who survived were taken to Camp Grant. The Government was most pleased with this victory, which lowered the morale of other tribes of Yavapais. Crook clashed with other Yavapais and Western Apaches nineteen times during the winter of 1872-1873. Those clashes resulted in the killing of another 150 Indians. Surprisingly, Crook proceeded to help the Yavapais to establish farms on the Camp Verde Reservation. By 1876, nearly 400 Indians fled to Sonora and enjoyed plundering Mexicans. Among their leaders was a medicine man named Geronimo.

ACT II
TROUBLES WITH THE MESSAGE

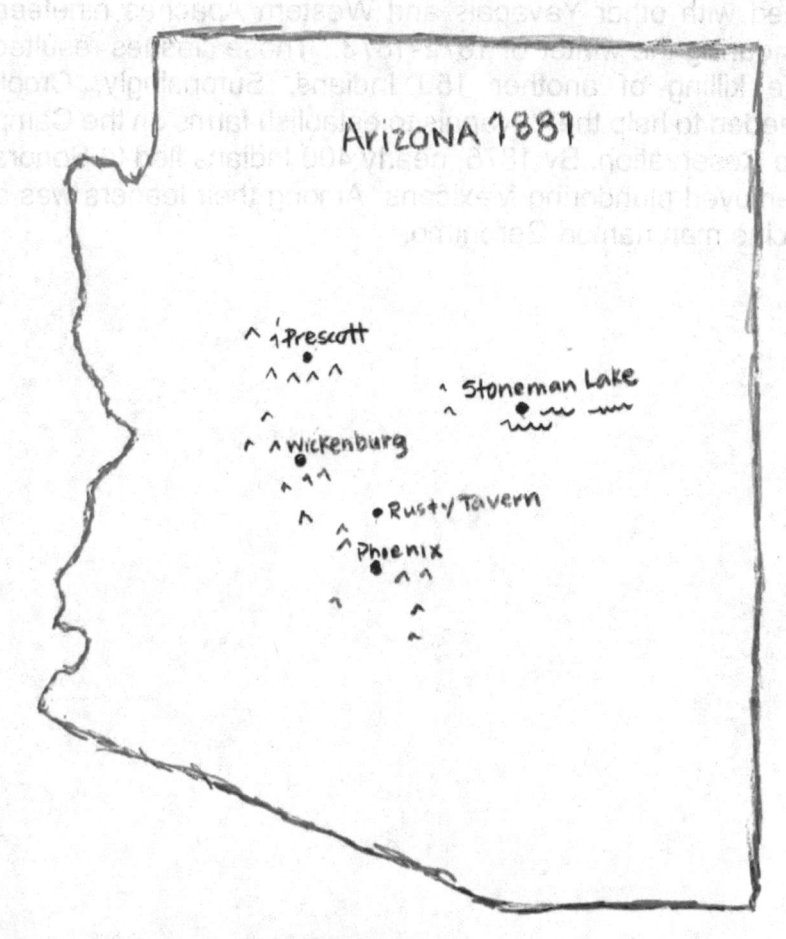

Arizona 1881

SCENE ONE
The Living, Breathing, Word of God

The Hole in the Rock Gang made their way back to Prescott, because Jim was feeling that more teaching was needed. After they arrived, Jim told them his intentions to get right to the hillside, and they all complained.

"Have a heart, Jim," pleaded Big Nose Kate. "We just finished a long journey and we're tired and hungry."

"I agree," announced Andrés. "Why not scare up some grub, then head to Matt's house for the night?" Matt offered, "You'd be more than welcome." Jim considered this advice, but decided against it. He pointed to the crowd and said, "Look at all the people who have gathered since our arrival. They are ready for my words, inspired by God."

Pedro spoke up, "Yah, but we ain't ready. Don't we count for something?" Jim was so focused that he didn't even hear Pedro, so he headed for the hillside where he had offered his first big teaching. He walked just a few paces before a coyote howled behind him. Jim turned to see where the coyote was, then noticed his Gang was sitting down. To make their attitude more obvious, they crossed their arms and had a defiant look on their faces. "We ain't goin' nowhere," said Jimbo.

"I thought we were a gang that hanged together. Oops, sorry about that Jim," said Benedict, who also went by Bennie. Jim offered a wry smile, but was deeply disappointed. He finally realized they were right. "We'll do want you want, not what I want." They all jumped up for joy, and Pedro said "Thanks, Dad!" Jim was exhausted, so he angrily shot back "I'm not your Dad, so quit actin' like children."

They weren't sure if they were supposed to feel elated or shamed, so they all just turned around and headed for Matt's house as the good gang God called them to be. After some grub and a good night's sleep for all, Jim was itching to get to the hillside. He didn't know it, but this teaching was going to get him into even more trouble. They arrived around 9 am to give people time to finish breakfast, and sure enough a large group followed the Hole in the Rock Gang to the hillside. The Gang settled by Jim's feet, while the rest of the crowd found comfortable places to sit down. He looked over the gathering and began to talk.

1. Human life belongs to God.

"This morning I'd like my first talk to be about Exodus 20:13" Jim said, while noticing many in the crowd didn't know their ten commandments. "Here's what it says: '*You shall not murder.*'"

One of the clergy in the crowd yelled out, "You got that right! Too much murderin' goin' on."

Another person mentioned, "I heard it means you shouldn't kill."

"Well, what's the difference?" questioned yet another.

Jim got control of the crowd by saying, "It don't matter. The point is that human life belongs to God, and we must respect it." After a brief pause to make sure people were listening, he continued, "But I have an even greater point." You could have heard a pin drop. The clergy were on edge about Jim having ideas greater than the Bible, but the average person on the hillside was intrigued. Some of the cowboys present were just hoping that Jim would overstep his bounds, so they could cause some trouble.

Next, Jim said "My concern isn't about committin' the crime of murder. We all know that's wrong. The problem comes when we think we're fine just 'cause we don't murder."

One of the trouble makers yelled out, "I've killed Indians and I feel pretty good about it!"

"Somehow I don't doubt it," Jim said rather mockingly. "But the problem I'm trying to get to is that we murder in a whole lot more ways than we think."

"You mean like with a cattle prod instead of a shootin' iron?" another troublemaker asked.

"No," said Jim. "I mean like we murder with our tongue."

"Last I knew nobody ever died from a tongue lashing," someone said, while a few offered some laughter.

"Well, friend," said Jim. "You're accidently getting to my point. I'd like to suggest we do murder with our tongue. Have you ever said a mean thing to your wife and seen how it destroys her?" Another ruffian started to speak up, but he noticed the crowd was being swayed to Jim's side. One could say he bit his tongue. Jim continued, "Here's another way we 'murder.' If yur angry with a sibling, that also causes trouble." Several laughed, and then a cowboy suggested "Who ain't been angry with a sister or brother?"

After the laughter settled down again, Jim said "Sure, but anger is one of the root causes of murder." This was followed by thoughtful silence. Soon Jim continued, "The point is to reconcile with yer family and friends, 'cause that's a far cry better than murder any day. Remember, my point ain't so much about murder as it is about respecting life 'cause it belongs to God." When Jim noticed people were intrigued, he continued. "Another way we murder is with insult. When we try to humiliate or shame someone, it's like killin' 'em a little bit at a time. Even when we show disrespect or try to shame another person, we are still breakin' the commandment 'bout murder."

"How?" asked a woman near the front who lost her husband to violence, and often took her anger out on her children.

"Because," explained Jim, "God wants us to love everyone, and insults, and shame, and humiliation, and disrespect are a far cry from love." The woman with the question slowly felt shame creep across her face.

While most agreed, the clergy were becoming livid. What they again thought Jim was doing was changing scripture. The Methodist pastor warned, "That's not what my Bible says!"

"Speak up, pastor," said a cowboy in the crowd.

The pastor quickly turned in his Bible to Deuteronomy 4:2 and said, "Hear what Abund had to say: '*You must neither add anything to what I command you nor take away anything from it, but keep the commandments of the LORD your God with which I am charging you.*'" Then with an angry look he yelled, "The Bible says it, I believe it, and that ends it!"

"That's right," screamed the same cowboy, as he started a scuffle. Several fell down as a little fight broke out, people started yelling, and things quickly got out of control. People started running away, and Jim and his Hole in the Rock Gang decided to call it a day and go back to Matt's house.

This was all but a foretaste of what Jim was going to be up against. It caused him to remember an old saying from Pedro's mom, "Save your teaching for those who want to learn." They all turned in early and Jim was particularly exhausted. He went straight to bed and spent some time in prayer. "Father, maybe this isn't a good idea." God responded, "It's a good idea, in the big picture. Trust me." God closed out the prayer session with some encouragement, "Always know that the love of God and love of neighbor goes hand in hand. Now get some sleep. You're going to need it." Jim was rather caught off guard by the idea he was going to need sleep. He wondered how bad things would have to get before the already terrible end arrived. Deciding that was of no benefit, he drifted off to sleep thinking about the opportunity to love God and neighbor.

2. Respect your marriage vows.

The next day Jim felt invigorated. His chat with God filled Jim with an unstoppable attitude to proceed toward this miserable end that God had in mind for him. The Hole in the Rock Gang followed along and noticed Jim's renewed sense of determination. Andrés even saw Jim's forehead furrowed as they arrived at the hillside. The usual crowd also made their way to this pleasant place, including the rabble rousers, pastors, lawmen, and even a few Russians who were starting to look over the crowd as they gathered.

Jim stepped forward at the top of the hillside and began to teach, "Today I've got some thoughts about divorce." Several walked out right then and there, but many others were interested. "Exodus 20:14 is the seventh commandment and it says '*You shall not commit adultery.*' Now if you remember what I talked about yesterday, this is the same situation. Don't take the commandment as five words written in stone. We agree, hopefully, that people shouldn't commit adultery, but my concern is to allow the commandment to be fresh and speak to us today."

"Didn't much care for yer addin' to scripture yesterday, so be careful," said a rather gruff looking hulk of a man.

The Jim Caldwell Trilogy

The local priest asked, "So what do you do with Leviticus 18:20, which says *'You shall not have sexual relations with yer neighbor's wife?'*"

Jim asked rather angrily, "Sakes alive, people. Are you going to let me talk?" After an awkward silence he continued. "I'm paying proper reverence for the commandment. The problem is that it applies in more ways."

Big Nose Kate was particularly interested in this line of thinking because of her colorful past, so she said "Tell us more."

Jim responded, "Is everyone ready?" The crowd was certainly listening, and most said "Yes." Jim responded, "Okay, here it is. Anyone who looks at a woman with lust has already committed adultery with her in his heart." The crowd was in awe. They'd never heard anything like this. Same certainly goes for the clergy. "That's probably the single greatest thing I've ever heard in my life," proclaimed Big Nose Kate, with a gigantic smile spreading across her face.

"Why?" asked Junior. Kate explained, "I was a prostitute before I met Jim, and his messages have totally turned my life around. In this message, Jim is saying that men should stop being lustful. Now maybe we can quit blaming only women. Don't get me wrong, I've got plenty to blame in my life, but that's my past. And this makes things a far cry more equal than ever before, which gives me even more hope." A spontaneous and raucous round of applause broke out among the women.

"What else ya got for us, pastor?" asked a woman in the crowd. Of course, the clergy bristled at her title for Jim.

"Yer right about equality, Kate," Jim shared in a pastoral way that can only be understood by those who have been treated unequally. "This whole talk has been about a decision of the heart. Let me share a text that God just put on my heart."

There are those who rebel against the light, who are not acquainted with its ways, and do not stay in its paths. The murderer rises at dusk to kill the poor and needy, and in the night is like a thief. The eye of the adulterer also waits for the twilight, saying, 'No eye will see me'; and he disguises his face.

"Where's that in the Bible?" asked another woman. "I think I like it."

Jim said, "It's Job 24:13-15, but I've still got more."

Someone added, "And I'm glad you do!" Well, not everyone was happy. The clergy, some of the cowboys, and even the few Russians at the gathering were getting madder with each minute.

"Adultery," explained Jim, "takes you down the road to perdition, and that ain't no good way to go. It would almost be better to pluck out yer eye to quit lusting, than to take that path."

"I admit it," said a cowboy. "I lust with my eye, but I don't commit adultery, and I ain't cuttin' my eye out."

Jim said, "Good, because I said it would almost be better. The problem is that adultery ruins a family, so don't even lust, because it can lead to adultery."

"So what are you saying, Jim?" asked a woman whose marriage vows weren't respected by her husband.

"I'm saying," said Jim, "men need to practice restraint. That way you are heading down the proper path." The crowd was mostly satisfied, so they took a short break to take in all Jim was saying.

3. When you don't respect your marriage vows.

"I see most of you have stayed, and that's great, so let's do some more learnin'," Jim offered with more confidence and authority. "Now I'm gonna talk about another commandment, but not one of the Ten Commandments."

"I suppose yer talkin' 'bout an Eleventh Commandment, accordin' to Jim?" a priest questioned snidely.

"No," Jim responded emphatically. "Surely you know the Ten Commandments are special, but the five books of Abund are filled with plenty of other commandments." The priest backed off while others said "Talk to us, Jim, about another commandment."

"Thank ya kindly. That's just what I was fixin' to do," Jim said while tipping his hat and smiling. "I wanna talk about a law from Abund about marriage and divorce. It's from Deuteronomy 24:1-4." He opened the Bible he'd been carrying around and said:

> *Suppose a man enters into marriage with a woman, but she does not please him because he finds something objectionable about her, and so he writes her a certificate of divorce, puts it in her hand, and sends her out of his house; she then leaves his house and goes off to become another man's wife. Then suppose the second man dislikes her, writes her a bill of divorce, puts it in her hand, and sends her out of his house (or the second man who married her dies); her first husband, who sent her away, is not permitted to take her again to be his wife after she has been defiled; for that would be abhorrent to the LORD, and you shall not bring guilt on the land that the LORD your God is giving you as a possession.*

"That's a lot to take in," Kate shared in a moment of confusion.

"Sure is," agreed Jim, "but I think this commandment is too open-minded. I mean, we don't just hand over a certificate of divorce to our wives and think that solves everything."

"Sounds fine to me" said an older man, who was well known for having had several wives.

After the crowds settled down their laughter, Jim said "I think we need to make this commandment tougher." There it was. The crowd could hardly hold the clergy back as they yelled "Yer still changing' the Bible. Stop it!"

"You don't get it, parson," complained Jim. "I'm saying the Bible needs to speak to every new generation 'cause it's the living, breathing, Word of God. Not some stoic book full of words on paper." Now the rowdies were starting to fire up, but Jim really wanted to get in one more thought. "I agree that divorce is a form of adultery, but here's my final point. The only way to divorce should be infidelity." The trouble makers were continuing to get angrier, mainly because that's what they were there for. Jim had to get louder at that point, when he said "We practice infidelity in many ways. So, I say, yes. A person can got a divorce when their spouse is an infidel. Such as when a man beats his wife. That's infidelity. A person is disrespecting their vows when they don't treat each other with respect."

A cowboy then lunged at Jim, screaming "You're an infidel!" Chaos then broke out again. The women were fighting the men and the cowboys were fighting the clergy. The only ones not fighting were the local lawmen and Russians. They saw that Jim was providing more and more rope with which to hang himself. Luckily, the Twelve (plus one) surrounded Jim and successfully walked him away. They went back to Matt's and spent the rest of the day debriefing all that had happened so far.

4. When you don't respect any vows.

The next day Jim couldn't wait to get out there again. There was just something exhilarating about teaching the ways of God. He said to himself, "When you know in your heart that it's God's words, not your words, it makes all the difference." During breakfast, Pedro expressed concern about how the crowds were turning more violent. He asked Jim, "Aren't you afraid?" Jim said, "Sure, because history has always been tougher on the messenger than the message."

"So why continue, or at least why don't ya tone it down a bit?" asked Andrés.

"Simple," suggested Jim. "Because these are the messages God wants me to deliver, and ya don't water down a message that God wants you to give." With that thought, they headed out to the hillside. To Jim's delight, but to none of the others, the crowds were growing. Jim stepped right up and announced he'd be teaching on the third commandment. "Here's what it says: '*You shall not make wrongful use of the name of the LORD your God*'." This perked up a lot of the wives who knew their husbands went to the saloons, and often took the name of the LORD in vain. But when Jim spoke next it left them disappointed.

"But I have a new way of looking at this old commandment," offered Jim. "Many of you don't care about disrespecting this vow of honor to God, but this is just the beginning of understanding what it means." Of course, the clergy were seething, while the ruffians were delighting in the idea that Jim was digging himself an early grave.

"Preach on, Jim!" requested an old woman in the crowd.

"This commandment ain't just about religion. I want you to understand that it applies to all oaths, because a community of integrity and 'right' relationships doesn't need oaths."

"Yer gonna need to say more about that one," said another.

"As I said," proclaimed Jim, "true followers of God should be so trustworthy, they don't need to ever take an oath or a vow. They are trusted, because people know who they are and what's in their hearts." Jim then pointed to an old man off to the side sitting in a chair. "Take for instance Buck, over there. He's lived in Prescott his whole life and nobody would question his integrity."

"That's my grandpa," celebrated a small fry next to him.

"So, a genuinely good person don't need to swear at all. If someone robbed a corner shop, and Buck was the first person the owner came across, he wouldn't say 'Swear on a stack of Bibles that you weren't the thief.'"

"That's right!" most everyone yelled, with enthusiasm.

Jim continued, "He'd probably just ask Buck if he saw the thief?" That was met with a thunderous applause, then Jim explained, "You have little else in this life than your word. If ya ain't good fer yer word, ya ain't good fer much of anything."

Many 'Amens' spilled forth as the crowd could sense that Jim was done for the day. The Gang headed back to Matt's house once again and discussed the teachings for the day.

"First of all," asked Pedro, "why didn't a fight break out to end the day?"

"Maybe because people are beginning to realize Jim is trusted, just like Buck," said Kate.

"I'm just glad it didn't," Jim responded. "I don't think there's anything worse than fighting over the Bible. It's here to help us, not to have something that causes troubles. People spend so much time trying to get others to understand the Bible their way, that they miss out on the message."

"Okay, help me. What is the message?" asked Matt.

"Thanks for asking, Matt," said Jim with a smile on his face. "Sometimes I forget that most of you were unchurched. Don't worry about that, because it seems it's the church folk who miss the message. So here's the message. Love yer neighbor as yerself. If people just lived and breathed God's Word, they wouldn't be fighting over how to live and breathe it."

"So is that why the clergy keep complaining that yer trying to change the Bible?" asked Thad.

"I think their tryin' to protect the Bible, and that's a good thing," announced Jim. "Their problem is, they don't understand that the Bible is like a sermon. Everybody gets out of it what they need. It's God's Word and that never changes. What changes is us. We hear it afresh from what's going on in life at the time, and we thank God for new understandings. We don't then turn around and tell everyone they need to live the way the Bible spoke to them." They had lots to think about, so after dinner they relaxed by the fireplace before going to bed. It was a good day, as they wondered what tomorrow would bring.

5. Don't be evil just because someone was evil to you.

It was a beautiful, clear, sunny day in Prescott with a pleasant summer breeze. As the Gang approached the hillside, they were very happy to see a large crowd already gathered. "Why are the crowds growing, jefe?" inquired Pedro. "Not sure," answered Jim, "but I'm guessing word got around that there was much less fightin' yesterday."

As usual, the Gang made their way to the front of the crowd and had a seat at their teacher's feet. "I want to say something about revenge," announced Jim.

"Don't you dare speak against the Bible like you've been doin'," angrily said a priest. "I know my Bible, and it very clearly says 'an eye for an eye and a tooth for a tooth,' so you can just keep yer hogwash to yerself."

Jim said, with a smile, "Actually, that's exactly what I want to talk about. That law is very important because it shows up in Exodus, Leviticus, and Deuteronomy. But I'm going to use Deuteronomy 19:21 which says *Show no pity: life for life, eye for eye, tooth for tooth, hand for hand, foot for foot.*'"

"Great," yelled out a lawman, "because that's the way it is out here in the Wild West! So, whatcha gonna do 'bout that with yer Bible?"

"Good question," Jim offered in a calming way. "Would it not say about the same thing if the verse said, 'Don't be evil just because someone was evil to you?'"

"Nope," complained the parson. "The Bible says what it says. Ya got ta stop changin' it."

"Not so quick, there, parson," suggested Jim. "Sure, it's a law of Abund, but do you always do exactly what the law says?"

"He sure don't," offered a lawman. "Just the other day I gave him a ticket for spittin' on the sidewalk." That comment was followed by a long lasting laugh that seemed to change the attitude of the crowd.

"I think we're gettin' somewhere," suggested Jim. "The law means that even if someone accidentally was responsible for ya losin' an eye, you didn't have to show any pity. You had every right to go and gouge their eye out."

"Don't seem very nice," said a matronly woman in the back.

"Exactly," agreed Jim. "I'm not trying to change the Bible. I'm saying that none of us follow the law all the time. I'm here to teach us about the love, grace, mercy, and forgiveness of God. If it was important back in those times to get revenge, maybe today we can be a bit softer. Wouldn't we still be following this Law of Abund about revenge if we followed the Spirit of the Law?" The crowd was clearly interested in this thought, so he continued. "Ya can't change evil doers. That's the work of the Holy Spirit. But if someone does something evil to ya, should ya turn right 'round and be evil back?"

"I don't think so," shared Bennie. "But it sure would be nice if the evil could stop right there."

"I ain't got time for this," yelled a cowboy as he fired off a single shot into the air and left.

After things settled back down, a young man in the crowd said, "Help me understand how an eye for an eye and a tooth for a tooth, is about the same as not being evil because someone was evil to you?"

Jim said, "Great question. Abund' Law is about problems that happen in every day life, but people break the law anyway. My idea is about when things happen in every day life that comes from evil. There's a big difference. Abund' Law certainly helps to treat people the same in unfortunate events. My idea is to expand the understanding of the law to account for evil events and to show some kindness."

Once again the clergy got mad about changing the Bible, so they left while throwing a fit. You could hear them talking loud on purpose, probably just to be mean. It seemed like a natural time to take a break for lunch anyway, so they agreed to take a short break and get something to eat.

6. Love your enemies.

It was still a nice day outside, as the sun reached over the tall pines in the area and added a noticeable measure of warmth. Everyone had returned from lunch and the crowd actually grew again. There was an atmosphere of hopeful expectation, as many of the trouble makers had given up and not returned.

"This afternoon," announced Jim, "I'm going to share one more idea, but this one is tough. Those of you who've come here seem ready to be challenged in good and useful ways." There was an intriguing sound that came from the crowd, but it was difficult to say if it was more about expressing joy or concern. "Look 'round at those near ya," requested Jim. "It's real easy to love yer neighbor. He or she might be the parents of yer son's playmate, or a worker at the local cafe, or the person who lives nearby and brought cookies when ya were ill. In fact, that's what I want to talk about this afternoon. One of the best known and least practiced verses in the Bible, Leviticus 19:18. Here's what it says: '*You shall not take vengeance or bear a grudge against your people, but you shall love your neighbor as yourself.*'"

"I do," said a kindly older man who had gone to church his whole life.

"That's the way it should be," agreed Jim. "I'm very happy that yer heart is in the right place, but now I'm gonna challenge ya to grow in relationship with God and all of God's children even more."

"Oh, oh," said the local café owner. "I think I hear another one of them changin' scripture things comin' on," he said with a smile. Most in the crowd didn't realize he was being supportive of what Jim was getting ready to teach, so a lot of talking took place before people understood things were ready to move forward in a positive way. They were more than ready to be done with the fighting and yelling and gun slinging as of recent.

"Are ya ready?" inquired Jim.

"Yes!" the crowd responded almost in one voice.

"Lovin' yer neighbor starts with lovin' yerself. That's actually what the commandment says, but I want us to take it one step further," explained Jim.

"I knew it," said someone in the crowd. It was surprisingly met with laughter and agreement as those gathered were beginning to catch on to Jim's point.

"I'm not tryin' ta change scripture. I'm tryin' ta change us. That happens with a challenge to step up our spirituality, and that's how we can make this a better world."

"Okay, Jim, we're ready to hear what ya got to say," offered a cautiously hopeful saloon owner. "I wouldn't mind this bein' a better place to live. Maybe I'd have less broken tables and chairs from the daily fights."

"This is it," said Jim. "I want us to love our neighbor, and ourselves, and…" Jim gave a long pause before finishing "…our enemies." This pretty much divided the crowd just when Jim thought he was getting them united.

"That's certainly a new thought" said a person who was at the past several teachings.

"Yah, and a bad thought," complained one of the few cowboys who remained. Sure enough, and quite surprisingly, about half the crowd left. Some looked disappointed while leaving, and others looked about half scared, because there were plenty of enemies in those days.

Jim responded, "Certainly the idea of lovin' yer enemies is a difficult thought, so I'm lookin' for those who honestly want to be a part of makin' this a better world." Even cut in half, the crowd was quite large, so he said, "I think the Hole in the Rock Gang just got some followers." A few 'amens' broke out here and there and the crowd was ready to hear more. "Lovin' yer enemy really ain't that tough," explained Jim. "Ya don't even have to look beyond the end of your nose." Jim saw several people moving their eyes around trying to see the end of their noses, so he said "Just do what God has asked all along. As my text said, 'love yer neighbor as yerself,' and if ya really do that, ya ain't got no enemies." The crowd had some serious thinking to do, so the people thanked Jim as they left, feeling like they were somehow better people than when they arrived.

As the clergy got a distance away, they saw some lawmen and asked if they could talk a bit. They got out of sight and had a little meeting with the lawmen. Talking behind a person's back was easier than direct communication. "How ya feelin' 'bout all the trouble Jim's causin'?" asked the parson.

"To tell the truth," offered a deputy, "we were already planning to look for some charges we could bring against him." Right then, some Russians who were at the hillside, came walking by and heard them. One Russian volunteered to them, "Zis man is bad. Must be stopped." Jim and the Hole in the Rock Gang were up against many societal problems of the time, so let's take a moment before moving on to get a feel for the troubles created by the Russians.

The Russian Invasion cast a pall of shock that hung over the American Southwest like an earthquake that wouldn't stop. The unexpected success of Tsar Alexander II led the Russian people to celebrate him as the man who "saved" them. In the motherland, his reign was talked about as "good news." In the American Southwest, the Russian military received great benefits. Their salaries were far higher than the average Russian made, and they were given land grants upon their return from service. This time came to be known as "Pax Russiana," but the peace that Russia created was by way of instilling fear in the conquered people.

This was done in America by imposing heavy taxation. To appease the Americans, the Russians used some of the money to build infrastructure to enhance their quality of life. The Russians also achieved a surprising amount of peace and order by simply having troublemakers disappear: a very effective method. And they appointed local American overseers who fell in line with their system of governance by being well paid. Lastly, the Russians circulated their own rubles for purchases. These coins proudly proclaimed Tsar Alexander II as the "son of god," because his father, Nicholas I, was revered for growing the Russian Empire and repressing dissent.

SCENE TWO
Living the Kingdom Life

The Wild West was full of snake oil salesmen. The trade actually began as a legitimate business when about 180,000 Chinese immigrants started arriving in the U.S. in 1849. Among the things they brought with them were various medicines, including snake oil. The oil of the Chinese water snake really did help reduce inflammation, so they began sharing the oil with some Americans who marveled in the relief they found after a hard day's work.

This meant the people of the Arizona Territory were open to strange healings, and they just wanted to know its source. One reason people were becoming skeptical at the time of Jim Caldwell, was the popularity of patent medicines. American businessmen started marketing all kinds of remedies for chronic pain, headaches, and kidney trouble. They didn't have the Chinese water snakes, so this healing enterprise of the American West used rattlesnakes, whose oil was less effective. And the false cures slowly began to be referred to as snake oil.

That's the atmosphere when Jim Caldwell unexpectedly cured Big Nose Kate. It was a pleasant evening after Jim's latest talk on the hillside, and Kate was obviously troubled. Jim asked what was going on, and she broke down and sobbed uncontrollably. Jim put a hand on her shoulder and the most mysterious thing ever happened. It was as if she was full of demons, and they just started departing her body. Actually, she was full of evil spirits, like liquor and tobacco, and anger about Doc Holliday. But, all in all, he counted seven demons that came out that night and Big Nose Kate felt cured. When people heard her story the next day, they of course wanted to know the source of the healings. Some were hoping it was the latest elixir or liniment, but the answer was that she was healed by Jim through the power of God. From that point on, Kate was intensely dedicated to Jim. Armed with this wondrous new ability from God to heal, Jim decided it was time for the Gang to take the show on the road. Yep, they headed for Wickenburg.

Wickenburg was about the same distance to the southwest of Prescott as Phoenix was to the southeast. It was a long, difficult and mountainous journey, ending in what became known as the most dangerous place in the Arizona Territory. That place was actually about fifteen miles further southwest of Wickenburg and was called Vulture City. Who could blame the motley crew of vagabonds who gathered there to mine gold and attempt to pilfer its bounty? Well, the founder could. Henry Wickenberg announced early on that he would hang anyone caught stealing, and even that didn't deter this hard-living crowd.

The rather innocent Hole in the Rock Gang rode into town at dusk on Saturday, as a whole slew of miners were exiting the mine. In the evening light the drillers looked like ghosts, covered in the granite dust of the day's work. Being mostly underground, the small town above ground was easy to check out. They tied up their horses and started looking around. They passed the blacksmith shop and were surprised to see a Post Office. Next were the Guard Quarters, followed by Henry Wickenburg's house and the infamous Hanging Tree in his front yard. Jim knocked on the door and Henry quickly opened it.

"Any chance my small group could hole up here for the night?" asked Jim.

"Don't know where else ya could go, this time of night," said Henry in a bit of frustration. "If I have any trouble with any of ya, I'm happy to put my Hanging Tree to use."

Before thinking ahead too much, Pedro said "I thought Russians were the only ones who could approve a hangin'."

Henry fired back, "Ya don't see no Russians 'round here, do ya?" Then he said, "I see ya got a filly with ya. Better have her stay at the brothel next door. Don't worry. The doctor's office is in the entry room and Doc keeps things under control."

"That's fine," offered Kate. "I'm comfortable around girls like that." They dropped Kate off next door and headed on over to the bunkhouse. With so many deaths and new hires each day, it was nothing to see new men. Kate was greeted warmly, as the girls didn't see a lot of new women. As the smell of the doctor's antiseptics permeated the air, along with cheap whiskey and stale cigars, Kate found herself surprisingly tense. Old memories began flooding back of her former life.

"What do you do?" asked one of the girls. Kate explained that she used to be a prostitute, until she met Jim Caldwell.

"He got ya out of the business?" inquired another girl.

"In a way you'd never guess," answered Kate. The girls perked up for a good story, and some in the back of the room moved forward. "My life was all kinds of wrong, when I heard that this man was doing great things in the name of God. I traveled from Globe to Prescott just to meet him. He's a great teacher, and I was so absorbed by his new way of thinking that I became a follower. Just last night he put a hand on me…"

"I knew it. Just like all the guys," said one of the prostitutes.

"No, no, no," said Kate. "He healed me, and my anger just left. I can't even explain the joy I felt. I no longer felt a desire for alcohol or tobacco or the life of prostitution."

"We'll see how long that lasts!" laughed another.

"I'm sure it won't be easy," said Kate, "but Jim's desire is to help people, and his teachings are really helping me."

"Is there some way I could get out of this life?" inquired a younger woman who moved front and center.

"Jim says," continued Kate while looking straight into her eyes, "that it's all about decidin' to change yer ways by choosin' to live a proper life." As Kate looked at her, she began to see more of a girl standing in front of her. She may not have been more than twenty years old at most, but her eyes spoke of innocence stolen.

"That don't seem easy at all," growled an older gal, breaking Kate's momentary concentration.

Kate came back from her thoughts to quickly consider what was just said, then responded "Is yer life easy now?" There was a long pause after that, followed by the decision to get some sleep. The older gal walked off in a huff and several of the younger women helped Kate settle in.

The Gang had agreed to meet at the cookhouse in the morning, and everyone got to sleep after a long day. On their way over the next day, the Gang saw one more building they hadn't noticed. It was a Church House. Jim wasn't having much luck with church religion, but he went ahead and inquired if they had a chaplain. He was quite happy to hear they didn't, so he checked with Henry Wickenburg about preaching there.

"The boys work hard six days a week, but we have some good folk workin' the mine," said Henry. "I'm guessing if ya preach today at 2, ya' just might get a few takers. As a matter of fact, don't think I'd mind attendin' myself." This was surprisingly encouraging, so the Hole in the Rock Gang started spreading the word. When 2 o'clock rolled around that Sunday afternoon, there were about 12 miners who showed up, along with several of the women. That was pretty good considering the place only seated forty, and with Jim's group and Henry present, the place was comfortably full.

Jim didn't carry a Bible with him to preach, because he wanted to relate to the people where they were. "I want to talk a bit about heaven." The usual interruptions didn't' happen, because this group was tired, but obviously wanted to be there. "It's like trying to grow tomatoes in this desert environment. The last thing you want is to have weeds grow next to them, because they steal the precious little water available for the tomatoes. Here's the point. Weeds and tomatoes are like us. In fact, some weeds are good and some tomatoes are bad, but it is all God's world. We can't possibly figure out what's bad and what's good. We wait until we go to heaven. Then it's our actions that will judge ourselves about continuing on for eternity with God or not."

Afterwards, it was none other than Henry Wickenburg who was the first one to shake Jim's hand. "Kinda liked what ya said there, Mr. Preacher man. Always felt kinda bad about hangin' all those thieves, but guess I was just getting' God's work done for him a little early." Jim cringed noticeably. He tried to tell Henry that he seemed to have missed the part about waiting until heaven, or that some weeds might be good. Didn't matter. Henry ambled on out of the Church House, looking forward to the next time he could help God with that judgment thingy. Others thanked Jim for his teaching and soon it was just the Gang left inside.

"People sure do need help with yer teachin's, jefe," proclaimed Pedro with a confused look on his face. Then in a dismissive way he asked, "So what do we do next?"

Jim said, "It would be great if the next thing was that you all understood my teachin's."

"I'm ready," offered Junior.

"Okay," Jim said with a smile. "We waste way too much time trying to figure out who among us are weeds. Weeds are a part of life, within and without. Now, never forget this. We are living in God's world here and now and hope to live eternally in God's world there and then. To give in to the weedy side of our character turns us into evil people. To blossom into nice, big tomatoes turns us into builders of God's Kingdom. But most importantly, this is not the devil's world. This is God's world, so let's act like it."

The next morning, the Gang saddled their horses to head for Phoenix, and Kate joined them. A big scene developed, when the young girl who inquired about getting out of prostitution came running out. She was crying and yelling "Take me with you!" As the boys started looking for a horse for her to join them, a whole gang of miners charged out of the cookhouse. They were wielding guns, and one declared "Take our property and yer dead men!"

This was precisely the kind of scene Jim didn't want, so he said, "We ain't fixin' to take no one, but with God as my witness, I pray the spirit moves in yer hearts enough to one day free her from yer enslavement." Then they slowly rode off without further trouble. At least from the miners.

Meanwhile, Kate was furious. "Why did we leave her behind?" complained an angry Kate when they got around the next bend.

"We can't save everyone, Kate," explained Jim. "Our job is to change hearts enough that God will eventually bring freedom to all who are enslaved. The freedom you gained from your demons was a gift from God. The girl doesn't have demons. She's controlled by monsters, so we pray that God will change their hearts."

After that, it was mostly a downhill ride, emotionally and physically, into the newly founded town of Phoenix. But this part of the trip was nothing as difficult as the trip from Phoenix up to Prescott. About an hour along the way is the small town of Vulture Siding, so they stopped for a short break. Chatting with some of the locals garnered some unexpected information. They said there were some hot springs just north and east from there, up in the Hieroglyphic Mountains. They were ready for an extended break, so changed their minds about Phoenix and headed off for an adventure. As they rode away on the dusty trail, someone yelled "Don't forget the Apache Wars are still raging in the area." This warning served as another useful reminder that their job of spreading love and goodwill around Arizona was going to be a challenging task.

It was a tougher trip than anticipated, because the road was not well traveled. At times they had to get off their horses and scout ahead to be sure they were even still on the trail. About an hour later, amidst an arduous journey, they were surprised to come across a gathering of people. Jim stopped and inquired about the hot springs, when one of them said "If it had been a rattlesnake, it would've bit ya." He was pointing just a little further ahead, and sure enough, they began noticing people swimming in what appeared to be an oasis.

They all got off their horses, tied them to some trees, and headed over to see what the hot springs story was all about. There were two, fairly large bodies of water nestled at the bottom of a canyon. People were lounging in the water and invited the visitors to join them. Immediately, the Gang took off their boots and hats and jumped in. The water was said to be about 120 degrees and they believed it.

"Why is this so refreshing?" asked Kate, with her feet dangling in the warm water and her dress tucked tightly around her knees.

"They say it's full of minerals," explained a bather who really didn't know why that would matter.

"But how is it so wonderfully hot?" inquired Andrés.

"I ain't no scientist," offered a bystander, "but people say the springs feedin' it come from deep inside the earth where it's real hot. And the springs have some healing powers."

They all agreed that they didn't really care how the magic happened, they just wanted to stay and enjoy. Jim couldn't disagree. He knew that the Gang needed to take care of themselves so they would be better able to help others. They set up camp and planned to get to know this community in the desert for the rest of the week.

"Just wait till the weekend comes," explained one of their newfound friends. "This place will get real busy. You'll see blind people showing up with family, people who can't walk will be toted in, and even paralyzed folk will manage ways to get here."

Another spoke up and said, "Ain't nothin' wrong with havin' a little hope, I suppose."

Jim realized he was in the right place with the right people to get the Gang refreshed. The week off was spent relaxing and growing closer as a Gang, while chatting informally with those present. Jim was somewhat surprised when most everyone got ready to go home in the afternoon. "Will you be coming back?" asked Jim.

"It'll probably be a different group of folk about every day," explained a local. "But ya can rest assured Ol' Shorty will be there on Sunday. He's been sick for thirty-eight years and somehow manages to get here each week. He really believes in the healing powers of the hot springs, but always finds an excuse to not get in. Strangest situation I ever did see." As the last few visitors departed, Jim and the Gang got to work collecting things to eat.

They found a lot of Saguaro and Prickly Pear Cactus, both of which have many edible parts. They also gathered some Desert Chia and pine nuts, but they were disappointed to find the pine nuts were hollow inside. Last came Pedro with two live Mojave Rattlesnakes, one dangling from each hand, and a tight grip around the neck. He ran around teasing everyone as they fled. After killing and skinning them, Pedro skewered the snakes on a small pine branch and started cooking them. The Gang kept looking for other edibles until Pedro called them for dinner. They settled in for a fine meal, in a wonderful place, with great friends. The days passed pleasantly as the hot springs provided water and the desert offered up plenty of good food.

When Sunday rolled around, the crowds showed up and Ol' Shorty made an appearance. Knowing Shorty's story, Jim asked if he wanted to be made well. "Of course I do, youngin," growled Shorty. "It's not my fault that nobody will help me get into the hot springs."

"Enough with this foolishness," said Jim with an air of

certainty. "Get yourself up, walk over to the hot springs, and get in." To everyone's surprise, and I mean everyone, 'Ol Shorty stood up tall and proud and walked for the first time since he was a child. He then leaped for joy and splashed himself into the springs. The whole crowd was shocked and couldn't seem to talk enough about it. Now word gets around pretty fast, even in the mountains, so the local priest arrived within a few hours.

"Today is the Sabbath!" screamed the priest. "We are not allowed to work on the Sabbath! Who's the sinner that has done this work of healing on God's holy day?"

"It was that guy," Ol' Shorty said while gladly pointing at Jim, and saying "It's not my fault."

Jim seemed to ignore the priest as he said to Ol' Shorty, "You've been made well by the power of God. Don't sin any more, so that nothing worse happens to you."

'Ol Shorty didn't quite know what to think, but the priest was almost speechless with anger. His veins were popping out on his forehead and his face was turning red. To contain himself, the priest turned around and left, but he didn't leave the situation alone. When he got back to his parish he spread word as fast as he could that they've got trouble, right there in Vulture Siding. Meanwhile, word continued to grow about the sinful acts of Jim Caldwell, including breaking the Sabbath.

The week off was done and Jim announced it was time to be moving on. "Where we goin' jefe?" asked Pedro.

"I'm kinda feelin' like a visit to Stoneman Lake," responded Jim.

As they rode away from this quaint oasis, Thad suggested "Some day they'll build a resort here, because the hot springs sure bring people in." Everyone agreed except for Tommie, who rather doubted it.

As they approached Stoneman Lake, they realized a crowd was following them, and Jim quickly understood they were wanting something from him. He wasn't sure if it was the healing touch of God or a story about how to live better. By this time, Jim was getting more comfortable with knowing when God was going to do a powerful thing through him, and this didn't feel like the time. The crowds just kept growing after the Gang got off their horses, and soon Jim was being pushed to the water's edge. Fortunately, a small skiff was moored nearby, so he went over and got in the boat. As he sat down and looked up, the crowds were standing all the way to the shore, and appeared ready to soak up his thoughts. So he began:

"If ya want to hear what God has to say, I trust ya know that I'm just the messenger. Yer job is to listen to the message. The story I think God wants ya to hear today is about livin' the kingdom life. It's about a 'fig' farmer who probably should've been a 'pig' farmer, because he was careless about this important task. Ya probably know that it takes three to four years for a seed to become a fruit-producing fig tree, but this guy dropped some seeds on the path he was on. As ya might expect, birds came and ate them up. That's what happens to people who hear what God has to say to them, but it just don't sink in.

"Our farmer got a little sloppy, and dropped other fig seeds among rocks. They started to grow, but there was no depth of soil to nurture them, so when the sun came up, they were scorched. They didn't have time to get rooted and they withered away. That's what happens when people hear God's words for them and get all excited. That joy fades quickly, because they aren't well grounded, and when problems come up about their faith, they fall apart.

"Next, this inexperienced fig farmer let some seeds fall among thorns. Not a good plan. As you might expect, the thorns grew quickly and took away all the sunlight and choked them out of existence. This is like the person who hears the message God has for them, but the lures of his world are too much. They might have some interest, but they are far more interested in money, food, or their neighbor's wife.

"Then the farmer dropped some fig seeds on good soil. I'm sure ya know what happened. They grew and grew and after a few years he was able to see the fruit of his labor. In fact, some of those trees produced so many figs that the whole area was better off. This is like the person who hears a message from God and understands it. She grows up and bears fruit for others. Reminds me of Big Nose Kate over there. She's been following me since God healed her and she's gonna do great things for God.

"One more thing. Obviously, we are all called to live the kingdom life, but we are not all called to be the same. Some are influenced well by their parents. Others come to the kingdom life because bad things happen in ther life, and some figure it out in their later years. Perhaps our best bet is to think of soil as different seasons of our lives. Sometimes our path is hard, sometimes our soil is rocky, sometimes we run into thorny situations. Just wait it out and God will give you good soil in due time."

Jim then stepped out of the boat and walked along the shore. The crowd continued to follow him and ask him questions while the Gang checked to see if there was anything they could do for people. It was a great experience, as Jim's Gang felt stronger than ever that they were doing the right thing.

It was time to get back to Prescott and the comforts of Matt's home. Jim sensed an urging to get to Phoenix, but he held off for now. After all, that's where he knew his time on earth would come to an end. As they arrived, crowds again were there to greet him. Word was already getting around that he told stories that were real, and that's on top of the fact that he was doing powerful acts in the name of God. They stopped at a local saloon and debriefed the recent events. In particular, Kate wanted to know more about the great things Jim had just talked about, that she was going to do for God. Jim smiled and said, "You'll go down in history as the first person to share about something God is getting ready to do." That wasn't sufficient for any of them, but the Gang sensed that was all they were going to hear.

When the Sabbath came around, the Gang naturally headed to the Methodist church in town. The pastor wasn't pleased to see them, but he heard Crazy Mary, as the locals called her, and it sounded like she was coming in their direction. He knew she had a screw loose, so he decided not to preach. Instead, he offered to let Jim do a teaching. The congregation was very excited, which of course further frustrated the pastor.

"Now maybe we'll hear something decent," called out a man who had known Jim all his life.

"We'll have none of that!" exclaimed the now angry pastor. "This isn't the hillside where Jim likes to teach and people yell out in response like they were in a tavern. This is God's house and its God's day. Now come on up Jim." As usual, Jim didn't know what he would say, but he did know that God would give him the words that were needed at the time.

Jim asked for a moment of silent prayer so he could gather his thoughts. Just as everyone was bowing their heads, the disturbed person burst through the doors. "Leave us alone!" she yelled. Everyone knew there was something really wrong with this poor woman, but nobody could control her. She always seemed to talk like there were several people living inside her.

"What do you have to do with us, Jim Caldwell?" Even though the pastor asked people not to comment while Jim spoke, several parishioners stood up looking like they were ready to tackle the problem woman. Jim motioned to them to stay put, and it seemed obvious that he wanted to deal with her.

"Have you come to destroy us?" she further queried with a voice sounding like a cross between an angry possum and a screech owl. Jim realized there would be no rational conversation with this individual, so he remained silent. "I know who you are," the woman said next. This kind of intrigued those present, so they sat up closer to the front of their pew to hear what Jim had to say.

Instead, she spoke again. "You're the one that God sent to help us." That didn't seem as crazy as the previous comments, but Jim's response all of a sudden left them baffled.

"Be silent," Jim commanded. Then Jim seemed to be talking to the people inside the wild woman when he said, "Come out of her!" What happened next became a story of legend that the people would never forget. The maniacal woman fell to the ground right in front of the altar, and started writhing and flopping like a fish out of water. All of a sudden she stopped, and they all thought she was dead. Several women who had small children got up and ran out of the church as fast as they could.

Then strange noises like foreign languages started pouring from her mouth, and several older women fainted.

A few moments later a younger woman in the front row asked, "Did you see that mist rise from her?"

"Yes!" exclaimed several people near her.

At that point more people left and the others moved in closer to see what was going on.

To their surprise, the woman slowly got off the floor and stood up.

"I'm outa here!" yelled a man, while most of the rest of those present were frozen in fear. Some cringed and braced themselves as the woman started to speak.

"Thank you sir," she said to Jim. "I've never been able to get rid of the demons inside me. They've been controlling my voice and my actions for a long time."

Most were still in a state of shock, when another woman came forward and said, "Welcome home, dear. May I ask your name?"

It took the former outcast woman a moment to even remember, but then she said "My name is Sybil."

The welcoming woman gave her a hug and offered to take her home and get her some clean clothes. Church pretty much ended at that point, as everyone slowly departed. The Gang was surprised too, but not shocked. They were getting used to Jim being able to do things through the power of God. When they got to the steps at the entryway, they heard people saying things like, "What kind of utterance was that?" and "He has authority and power to even command unclean spirits to come out, and out they come!"

After a short discussion outside the church, the Gang agreed to head to Phoenix on Monday. They took their regular stop that next morning at The Rusty Tavern, but this time it was a bit different. Some local lawmen were there and they started to taunt him.

"Hey, here comes a Goody Two-Shoes" one of them said.

"Yah, and look, here he is hanging out with a prostitute," sneered another.

Pedro was ready to tear into him, but Jim said it wasn't necessary, and even Big Nose Kate took it in stride because she was a changed person. Then Jim looked around and realized the place was full of people who could use some help, so he decided to stay and do some teaching.

"Which one of ya, having a hundred cattle and losing one of them, wouldn't leave the ninety-nine in the desert and go after the one that is lost until he finds it?"

This comment was met with blank stares until someone finally called out, "What's yer point?"

"My point is," Jim thought for a moment before responding, "who doesn't need help? Do you really think a former prostitute is unworthy of assistance? Or lawless lawmen?" This got a chuckle from the crowd, along with a few angry looks from the lawmen.

"Better tell us another story, there buddy, or I'll have ya dancin' to avoid bullets 'round yer feet." Turned out it was none other than Enrique Garfias, the town marshal for Phoenix. Enrique was known for his sharp shooting abilities, and not taking any guff from trouble makers.

"Okay," Jim said calmly. "Who among this slew of

characters wouldn't celebrate if someone found money ya dropped on the floor and handed it back to ya?"

"That'd never happen!" yelled a man in the back.

"And that's why we need to change our ways," retorted Jim. "I'm here to say that kindness and goodness and thoughtfulness are celebrated in heaven." That seemed to shut the crowd down, so Jim offered another story.

"There was a woman who had two daughters. The younger one said, Mom, give me my share of the bridal trousseau now. So she divided her property from her sister's, and gave it to her. A few days later she packed up all of her belongings and traveled to San Francisco. There she squandered her trousseau in self-indulgent living. When she spent everything, a drought hit San Francisco, and she found herself without help. So she went to San Jose and hired herself out to work the fields, by picking apricots and almonds. Things went from bad to worse because the fruit was drying up and rotting, and nobody would help her. Soon her mind cleared and she thought, 'how many of my mother's helpers would be eating well, but I'm here dying of hunger! I will go back to my mother, and I will say to her, Mother, I have sinned against heaven and before you; I am no longer worthy to be called your daughter; treat me like one of your hired hands.' So she set off and went to her mother. But while she was still far off, her mother saw her and was filled with compassion; she ran and put her arms around her and kissed her. Then the daughter said to her, Mother, 'I have sinned against heaven and before you; I am no longer worthy to be called your daughter.' But the mother said to her helpers, 'Quickly, bring out a dress—the best one—and put it on her; put a ring on her finger and sandals on her feet. And get the fattest calf and kill it, and let us eat and celebrate; for this daughter of mine was dead and is alive again; she was lost and is found!' And they began to celebrate."

An eerie sort of feeling passed through the room. Some of the hard working cowboys had daughters, and they tried to hide wiping away some tears. "Hey, what about that older daughter? Wouldn't she have been mad that her younger sister got the trousseau before she had a right to it?" asked Marshal Garfias.

"Let me tell you the rest of the story," said Jim. "Now the older daughter was in the field; and when she came and approached the house, she heard music and dancing. She called one of the helpers and asked what was going on. He replied, 'your sister has come, and your mother has killed the fattest calf, because she has gotten her back safe and sound.' Then she became angry and refused to go in. Her mother came out and began to plead with her. But she answered her mother, 'Listen! For all these years I have been working like a laborer for you, and I have never disobeyed your command; yet you have never given me even a young calf so that I might celebrate with my friends. But when this daughter of yours came back, who has wasted your property with decadent indulgence, you killed the fattest calf for her!' Then the mother said to her, 'Daughter, you are always with me, and all that is mine is yours. But we had to celebrate and rejoice, because this sister of yours was dead and has come to life; she was lost and has been found.'"

"Kinda like your story there, partner," said Enrique. "But I think that older daughter was the lost one. Finish your story. What did she do?"

"Oh, she pouted for awhile, as ya might expect," said Jim. "But soon enough she got over it and went in. Hard to ignore dancin', and celebratin', and food. When her younger sister saw her, she rushed over and gave her a hug, just like her mother gave her. The older sister's anger melted away, and then she realized she hadn't even been wronged.The younger sister just asked for her share of the trousseau before it should have been hers. Maybe we shouldn't worry so much about what other people do wrong, and think more about doing right ourselves. That way we don't ever have to worry about being lost."

The crowd at The Rusty Tavern that day had mixed emotions. Some liked the story, but the lawmen had heard enough about Jim that they thought they were supposed to not like him. And for some danged reason they sorta did. The problem was that the clergy and the lawmen were already in collusion with the Russians to have Jim killed. Their sentiment became one of resignation, as they thought "Couldn't happen to a nicer guy."

The Hole in the Rock Gang left The Rusty Tavern with a new plan to head to Stoneman Lake. This whole idea that everyone was worthy of help needed further testing. They were going to "the other side" of Stoneman Lake where the less desirables lived. It was a long journey up the mountain, so they pitched camp that evening near where the trail headed west to Prescott and east to Stoneman Lake.

The next morning they rode their horses on over to the lake and found a skiff moored on the western side. They were a little hesitant to cross over, because there were a lot of stories about the heathens and random Indians who lived there. However, they were more hesitant to get in a boat. Cowboys just don't do boats, not to mention the fact there were only two natural lakes in Arizona.

Getting fourteen people safely in the boat was a challenge. It was rather comical how much the skiff rocked back and forth with each new passenger. Poor old Jimbo needed lots of help, so Johnny grabbed one arm and Carly grabbed the other to steady him. This ended in a monumental failure, as the boat cap-sized. After a long bit of laughter, Big Nose Kate said, "Come on ya bunch of cowards. If ya think this is tough, wait 'til we get to the other side." That seemed to do the trick, as the rest of the group carefully settled in one at a time for fear of further embarrassment.

It was a pleasant day, so they rowed quite easily across the lake and soon came to the far shore. Things proved to be as legend had it, because they were quickly met by an Indian who was running around naked as a jaybird. Jim had heard of this man who was known to live among the graves. It was believed that he lost his mind after his children and wife were massacred in the Battle of Salt River Canyon. This poor man was often seen around the cemetery, known to howl at the moon, and seemed to enjoy bruising himself with stones.

When he saw Jim from a distance, he ran and bowed down before him. He then shouted at the top of his voice, "Jim, don't torment me!" To say the least, the Gang was shocked about many things. How did this Indian know Jim's name? Why would Jim torment him? Why would he want to bruise himself? Jim responded with an equally loud voice, "Come out of the man, you unclean spirit!" After that strange exchange, Jim asked him, "What is your name?"

He replied, "My name is Legion; for we are many."

Now there on the hillside, a squadron of javelinas were

feeding. The unclean spirits within the Indian begged to Jim, "Send us into the javelinas." Jim was getting more and more confident that the power he had was not his, but from God, so he gave them permission. The unclean spirits came out, entered the javelinas, and the squadron rushed down the steep bank into Stoneman Lake and drowned.

Even though the Gang thought they were far from civilization, it turned out that quite a few people had followed them. Upon their arrival, the followers were shocked to see the troubled Indian sitting there, clothed with a few spare things from the Gang, and in his right mind. They heard what Jim had done and it frightened them. As Jim and his Hole in the Rock Gang got back in the boat to go to Prescott, the Indian begged to join them, but Jim refused. He said, "Go tell anyone and everyone what God has done for you." The Indian was so indebted to Jim that he agreed to this task. He left from there and told people what God had done for him through Jim; and everyone was amazed.

ACT III
GETTING SERIOUS

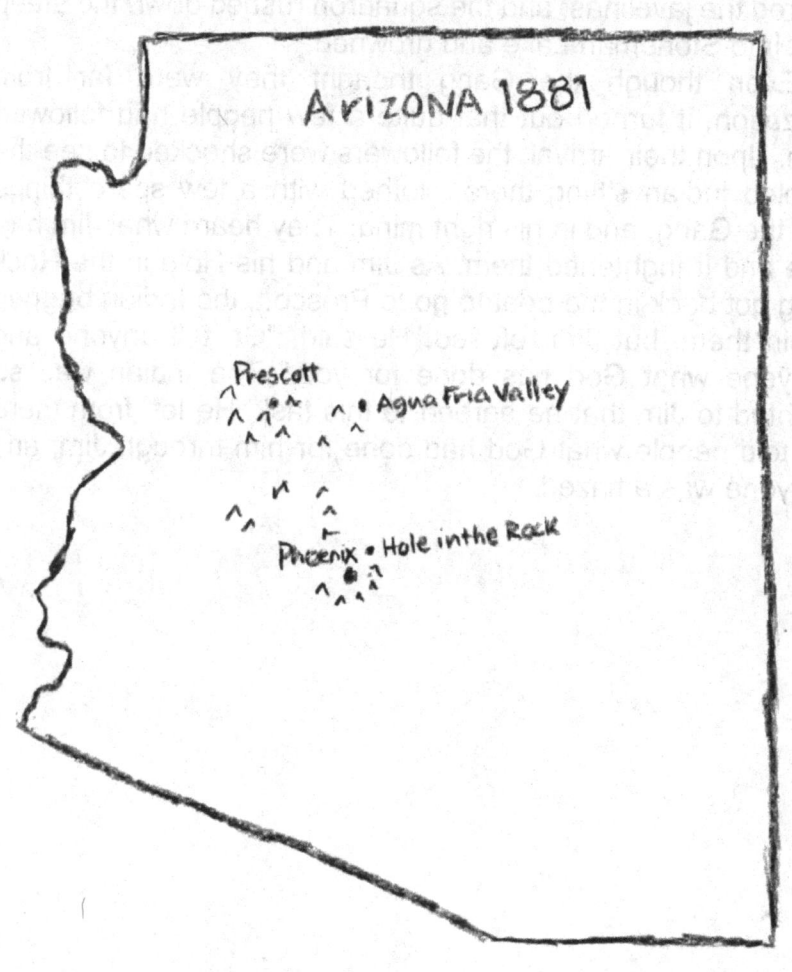

SCENE ONE
Changing Head and Heart

It was good to be back in Prescott. The Gang settled back into Matt's home and relaxed while sharing stories that happened since they met Jim. And Jim shared some thoughts, too. He talked about the importance of staying humble. This impressed the Gang because they wondered how they might act if they were endowed with such divine power. After breakfast, Jim announced it was time to get back to teaching, so they stood up and prepared to head for the hillside. "No," said Jim. "This time I have instructions for us."

"Are we in trouble, jefe?" asked Pedro.

"Of course, not," replied Jim, "but trouble is ahead. For all of us. So we need to understand how to keep ourselves as good as possible. Ready?"

"No," responded Bennie, while others nodded in agreement.

"Thanks for being honest," replied Jim. "That in itself is a great start. So take a few moments for some silent prayer, and when everyone is ready, we'll begin." They all closed their eyes, except for Kate. She had too much in her past to sit blindly with a group of men in a trusting way. She was certainly a changed woman, but her past still haunted her. She didn't want to have memories of abuse flood her thoughts. She needed to learn how to use silent prayer as Jim requested. After all, the purpose was to prepare herself for listening about keeping as good as possible. So she ended up praying with her eyes open.

Pedro also found it difficult to keep his eyes closed. He used to be a bad hombre, and he was always expecting retaliation if he met someone whose family member he killed. He too, was haunted by memories of killing women and children at the Camp Grant Massacre. He needed lots of help from Jim, so he closed his eyes in spite of himself, and asked God to calm him. Turns out all of them had one problem or another, so it became obvious that instruction would be good. One by one they finished and looked at Jim with a sense of expectation.

1. Righteousness in worship.

He began with, "You don't have to impress anyone but God, so be especially careful when you are at worship."

"I'd never have guessed that one!" commented Big Nose Kate. They all laughed, and it was clear that they were becoming a family that could at least be candid.

"Why?" inquired Matt. The room came to a hush as they sort of hoped he would say they didn't need to worship.

"Because," Jim continued, "worship isn't about the congregation. We are there to worship God. So don't look around to make sure people know you are there. We go as a good act toward God from our heart." A tinge of disappointment crept over them, but they knew they needed to learn.

"Sure, but they always ask for money," complained Bennie. His past with respect to money was very challenged, because he had been a thief. Truth is, he still had that problem. He even stole some of their money in the past week.

"Our job," explained Jim, "is to not be hypocrites. Some people just give money in church so everyone knows how important they are."

"So how do we do it right?" asked Phil who lived his whole

life in Prescott and never darkened the door of a church.

"Good question," responded Jim, "and here's the answer. When you give money for the offering on Sunday mornin's, do not let your left hand know what your right hand is doin.'"

"Okay, what does that mean?" asked Thad, who liked to push things as far as he could. He then looked back and forth at both of his hands with a smirk on his face.

Jim continued, "If you are selflessly giving to help build the kingdom of God, you don't need any acknowledgment. It shows you are not boasting, which would be the same as worshiping yourself. The problem is, when we give for the purpose of getting something for it, we are really only giving to be admired. The genuine worship of God is always about God, and never about us. Remember the wisdom of King Solomon from Proverbs 21:14, 'A gift in secret averts anger.'"

"So what about when pastors seem to offer endless prayers?" asked Junior.

"Yah," said Jim as he rolled his eyes. "Don't be like them. When we turn to God in prayer, we need to have a pure motive. Just know that God knows what you need before you ask."

"Well then, I've got a question for you Jim," stated Matt as he shifted nervously in his seat. "You know that I ran my house as a place for prostitutes before you got me converted, and I don't know a whole lot about religion. In fact, the idea of prayer is like a scary house that I don't want to enter. In fact, I've never prayed before, and every time you've asked us to pause for a moment of prayer, I just look down at the floor."

"I always doubted it would help," offered Tommie, now that he knew it was okay to be honest.

Carly said, "Never felt I had time to pray."

Then Matt continued, "So my question is, how do I pray?"

2. Righteousness in prayer.

"Wow, Matt, thanks for asking," said Jim with a smile. "It starts with a sense of closeness. If you truly want to get closer to God, so that you can sense the ways to be righteous, just use simple human language."

"Like what?" asked Andrés. The Gang really had Jim's attention at this point, as they all moved their heads forward for a good listen.

"Okay," said Jim. "Pray this way...Our Father in heaven..."

"Whoa! Stop right there. That's a tough one for me," interrupted Big Nose Kate, "because my father beat me." Her voice started to crack, so Jim knew this needed to be addressed, but first it needed some time. He was a little surprised, but a lot happy, when Junior and Bart, the two closest to her, put their hands on her shoulders in a comforting way. At first she tensed up, but then she realized she was with people who truly loved her and cared about her.

After a proper amount of time, Jim said, "I'm so sorry to hear that, Kate. Do you know of anyone who had a good dad while growing up?" Kate thought for a moment, then nodded yes, so Jim continued. "Now that's how to think of God. Think of him as the best father the world has ever known. A father who would never abuse you. Your father in heaven, lovingly looking over you and wanting to help you along your journey on earth. How does that sound?"

"That's better, but it might take me a while to settle in and believe it," responded Kate looking still despondent.

"Take all the time you need, Kate. Our Father in heaven has endless patience," explained Jim, then he offered to meet later with her to talk more about it.

"Okay. I'll admit it. I had a terrible relationship with my dad, too," shared Bennie, as he wiped a tear from his eye.

Jim offered more condolence as he realized his Gang was truly being honest. He needed to care for them if they were going to be able to do the job of caring for others. "The hurts of this world are terrible and real. I just want us all to know that the next world is full of joy. When we turn to God in prayer, we are bringing heaven and earth together. That's the closeness we seek. It's a divine presence in our lives that is beyond anything we have here on earth."

"Great!" exclaimed Carly, "but I got to admit, that's a pretty short prayer."

"Really, Carly?" asked Jim. After a short silence, he continued. "No, I'm just getting started." There was an audible grunt of disappointment that came from several of the Gang. Seems like righteousness in prayer wasn't their strong suit, but Jim was just glad that they were open to learning. And that joy was soon squelched.

"But you won't go long, right?" inquired Pedro, trying to be funny. "Cause that would make you a hypocrite." Jim gave Pedro a stare that made him realize he was overstepping his bounds.

"This is for when you don't know how or what to pray" explained Jim. "And it is really for group prayer time. I ask you from time to time to spend time in silent prayer, and that's between you and God. But if you ever get asked to pray, you can always use this one. Anyway, here's how the prayer continues...hallowed be your name."

"Oh, no," complained Jimbo. "What just happened to that closeness you were talking about? It seems strange that we call on God to be close to us, then we call him holy."

"Good point," agreed Jim. "When we say hallowed, we're celebratin' the fact that God is not just in heaven. His holiness comes from being the creator of all, who also cares about us. It's like in Genesis 3:8-10, when God was "walking in the garden at the time of the evening breeze, and the man and his wife hid themselves from the presence of the LORD God among the trees of the garden. But the LORD God called to the man, and said to him, 'Where are you?' He said, 'I heard the sound of you in the garden, and I was afraid, because I was naked; and I hid myself.'"

"So we should be afraid of God?" asked Kate with a sense of alarm, "cause I always heard that pastors preached mostly about hellfire and brimstone."

"No," shared Jim. "My point is that when we turn to God in prayer, we have nothing to hide. It's like being naked before God, just like when we were born. It's not a scary thing. It's a time to share our joys and concerns with the one who is holy in heaven and listens to us here on earth. Now, may I continue?"

They weren't sure if they should be embarrassed or simply learning, but Jimbo finally said "Yes."

"Thanks," said Jim as he curled his eyebrow up, wondering if anything was sinking in. "Next part of the prayer is…Your kingdom come."

"Isn't that what religion is all about?" asked Thad.

"Yes!" exclaimed Jim, with the type of excitement you feel when you're understood. "That's why we pray for it all the time."

"But how does God's kingdom come here?" asked Johnny.

"That's the next part of the prayer," said Jim. "Are you all ready?" They didn't seem totally ready, but Jim knew he could talk more about it later, so he said "here it is…Your will be done, on earth as it is in heaven."

"Kinda like back in the Garden of Eden again?" asked Pedro inquisitively.

"Sure," agreed Jim. "Eden wasn't exactly heaven, because Adam and Eve didn't follow God's will. And we aren't exactly in heaven now, either, because we still choose not to follow God's will. We prefer to follow our own will. But the hope is that if we could just manage to follow God's will, we could have heaven here and now."

"I think I like that," offered Carly. "Seems like we could have a little piece of heaven within us, even if we can't get anyone else to cooperate."

"You've got it!" Exclaimed Jim, as his jaw dropped with wide-eyed enthusiasm. "If religion is anything, it's personal. We want to help the world, but it starts by living a righteous life ourselves."

"That's something really worth thinking about," suggested Matt. "I was living the most unrighteous life ya could imagine, running my terrible house of prostitution. But when ya called me to follow ya, my whole life changed in a flash. I just started livin' a righteous life and will never go back. I wasn't helpin' anyone but myself. Thanks for teaching me to deny myself. It's the way to first get heaven in us, so we can then share it."

After some time talking among themselves and realizing they all agreed with what Matt just said, Jim returned to his teaching. "Okay, Here's how to continue...Give us this day our daily bread."

"Isn't there something in the Bible 'bout only takin' what ya need for the day?" asked Bart.

"Yep," answered Jim. "An important story in the book of Exodus, chapter 16, tells about the Hebrew people starvin' in the wilderness. God provided bread from heaven for them, and commanded them to only gather as much as they needed for the day. They didn't obey. They got greedy and tried to store up extra for the future."

"Can't really blame them," said Bart before asking "What happened then?"

"The next morning," explained Jim, "the bread was full of worms and inedible." Several gagged at that thought before he continued. Pedro was again laughing, so Jim had to give him a stern look. Then he said, "So the lesson for us to learn is to be satisfied with what we have. If we can learn that, we have a better chance to live a more righteous life. Does that make sense?" He looked around and most were nodding their heads, so he continued "And here's how the prayer goes on...And forgive us our debts, as we also have forgiven our debtors."

"But I haven't forgiven anyone for a long time," admitted Pedro. Jim was glad Pedro was finally getting serious, but knew that this would probably need some debriefing as well. Pedro continued, "'cause I'm the one so desperately in need of forgiveness."

Everyone seemed to know this was important, so Jim asked "What do you mean?"

"I was at the Camp Grant Massacre," Pedro said cautiously, as he had never shared his story before. He looked around the room and saw horror in most of their eyes. "I really thought I was helping get rid of those raidin' Apaches," he said in a rather defensive manner. Not seeing a change in their expressions, he said, "But now I see how horrible it was." The Gang remained tentative because the event was well known and now Pedro wasn't sure he wanted to continue. Jim finally intervened and said that confession was good for the soul. "It felt good," Pedro tried to explain, "to be marchin' from Tuscon to help them people." He paused for a moment again before confessing, "and I got paid a lot of money." Andrés wanted to say something, but knew it wasn't the right time. Pedro then looked down at the floor and said in a very slow and stilted way, "I killed lots of women…and children…and I don't think it's forgiveable."

The Gang was in shock for a moment, until Jim spoke up. "Confession is no good without repentance, but you have clearly changed your ways, Pedro. Do you want to be forgiven?"

Pedro broke down and cried, which shocked his brother. Andrés had never seen Pedro cry, and he had never heard that story. When Pedro finally said "yes," Jim immediately responded by saying "You are forgiven." Pedro was almost inconsolable, but one by one they went around the room and each of them also said "You are forgiven."

One doesn't just go on after a moment like that, so Kate went over to Pedro and hugged him. It was the first time she could remember hugging a man in a nonsexual way. As she looked around the room, most of the men had red eyes, but they smiled their approval. There was an air of freshness in the room, and soon they all began sharing their own need for forgiveness. Bennie confessed he was a thief, to which everyone laughed.

"We know that," said Junior. 'We're waitin' for the repentance part!" Bennie frowned as he knew inside that he wasn't about to change. Carly talked about being overzealous, and Tommie shared that he was too quick to doubt things. It was another wonderful bonding moment for the Gang, but soon Jim was ready to get back to his topic.

"Here's what we really need to think about when it comes to asking God for forgiveness." The Gang was very interested and ready for more learning. "If we truly practice this part of the prayer, we are actually asking God to only forgive us in the same way we forgive others."

"That's a frightening thought," suggested Kate in a concerned manner. "So you're saying that if we don't forgive others, we're asking God to not forgive us?"

"Perhaps that would help us to take forgiveness a bit more serious," suggested Jim. "Don't you agree?"

Junior was in a state of shock and disbelief, so he clarified, "You mean we shouldn't dare ask God to forgive us unless we're willing to forgive others?"

"Yes," responded Jim bluntly. "It's one of the most important parts of living a righteous life." The Gang had already been through a lot together, but this seemed to challenge them in new and useful ways.

"Makes me want to be more forgiving," said Pedro, "especially since I've received so much forgiveness. Everyone smiled because they began to understand that God was always ready to forgive. And since God is so freely offering forgiveness, maybe they should do the same for others.

"We've got a lot to think about here. Are we done yet?" asked Andrés, looking exhausted.

"No," said Jim emphatically. "Here's the ending, but it's a tough one…And do not bring us to the time of trial, but rescue us from evil."

"It sounds like God is the problem," suggested Bennie. "Because your prayer wants us to ask God to not bring us to trying times."

A hush went around the room before Jim spoke again. He was careful with his response, because he knew the Gang didn't trust Bennie. Jim said, "people have struggled with evil since the story of Job." Then Jim decided to affirm Bennie's thought about it sounding like God was the problem. "Yes it does. But God has big shoulders and humans will always find a need to blame. So, go ahead. Blame God. After all, God allows evil to exist."

After a very lengthy pause, with everyone looking at one another, Kate asked, "Maybe that's why heaven is better than here, because there's no evil in heaven, right, Jim?"

"I think you're right, Kate," said Jim. "But here on earth we focus on being rescued from evil. And that's what we're all about. As we go around helping people in their trying times, we are working with God in rescuing them from evil. Now maybe we can try this prayer together." They bowed their heads and tried to follow along from Jim's lead as well as they could:

"Our Father in heaven,
    hallowed be your name.
Your kingdom come.
Your will be done,
    on earth as it is in heaven.
Give us this day our daily bread.
And forgive us our debts,
    as we also have forgiven
        our debtors.
And do not bring us to the time of
        trial,
    but rescue us from evil."

There was a wonderful sense of satisfaction when they were done. The Gang had been following Jim for awhile now, but they had few things to show for it. Sure they had a leader, and now they had a group prayer that seemed to bind them together as a community.

"I have one more thing to say about the righteous living we need to practice and model for others," said Jim, "and that's about fasting."

"I'm out," proclaimed Jimbo, as he patted his oversized belly. They all had a good laugh, but were interested in this particular form of righteousness. It seemed ironic to Jimbo that the lack of food could help a person become closer to God.

3. Righteousness in fasting.

"First of all," explained Jim, "it's something between you and God. "If we ask people to fast and they show off about it, what kind of righteousness would that be? So we tell people that fasting is good, because it is, but it is best when done in secret."

"Why is it good?" asked Jimbo, as his stomach was making noises.

"Because it teaches us discipline," answered Jim. "When we learn to not give in to our desire for food for a period of time, we can apply that will power to controlling ourselves about bad habits like alcohol, or gambling, or visiting women of ill repute. Sorry Kate, no offense intended."

"None taken," agreed Kate. "I'm a changed woman and I'll never go back to that lifestyle, because ya get involved with the wrong kind of man. Somehow, after following you, I feel like I'm getting involved with God. And that's a good thing."

"And I'm a changed man," agreed Matt, "but this new life we are learning from Jim is so much better than the miserable life I was living. Can't tell you how many times I've had wives come up and slap me."

"And the purpose," explained Jim, "is to make this a better world. Our task is to help people, and a whole lot of people suffer from troubles and bad habits."

"I wish it wasn't necessary for me to change," complained Jimbo.

"Don't worry, Jimbo. You will come to deal with your issue in the near future," prophesied Jim. Everyone was quite shocked at this statement, because they'd never heard Jim being prophetic, which is always about the here and now, or the near future. It was becoming more and more evident that Jim was comfortable with his divine calling. "Any questions?" They didn't, so Jim suggested they take a break, have some lunch, then head back over to the hillside for an afternoon of teaching for the larger community.

"How about we skip lunch," suggested Jimbo.

"Whoa," teased Johnny. "You feeling okay?"

After some good-hearted laughter, Jimbo explained "I want to find out what this discipline is like." They were all happily humbled, so they agreed. As they settled in for some quiet, sacrificial time, they heard Jimbo's stomach growl."

"Thought for sure there was a mountain lion in the room!" joked Pedro. They laughed again as they found comfortable positions on the floor, preparing to think about their new life as followers of Jim. After a while Jim called them to go to the hillside.

_____

As they gathered in the early afternoon sun, the cool mountain air brought a pleasant balance of temperature. The usual crowd of interested folk started congregating when they heard Jim was in town, and that it looked like he was going to offer a teaching. Actually, the crowds were slowly growing each time he talked, but there was a noticeable change in the increased number of lawmen and Russians present.

1. Healthy living and possessions.

Jim waited until most of the crowds were settled, then he stepped forward. "I want to talk to you this afternoon about possessions. Some of you here are lucky enough to have some photographs of your own family. A treasure for sure. It was our good fortune that photographers often traveled through here on there way to Tombstone to take pictures of the rapidly growing town down there. Pictures are wonderful treasures, as long as they don't get lost, stolen, left out in the rain, or eaten by the family dog." Pictures were expensive, so their possible destruction painted a vivid picture of loss for the listeners.

"Come on Jim, get to your point," complained Marshal Virgil Earp, who decided to attend because he was hearing more and more complaints against Jim. He rather ominously touched his holster to make sure Jim knew he meant business.

"My point is" responded Jim, "that everything on earth is perishable. If we put all of our hope into our possessions, we are on sinking sand.

"Nobody does that," growled the Methodist pastor.

"Good," said Jim. "Then it will be easy to follow this truth: treasure the things valued in heaven, like our good deeds. No body and no thing can take those from God. If we are going to feel a strong attachment to anything, make sure it's what God values."

"Give me one good reason," indignantly requested a person in the middle of the crowd.

"Because whatever we value tells where our heart truly is," explained Jim.

"Gotta admit, I like my possessions," commented another toward the middle of the crowd.

"Of course. That's just normal," explained Jim. "And that's why this is so difficult. We can't live a spiritually healthy life if we are possessed by our earthly possessions."

A bit of a murmur made its way around the gathering. People started talking to one another and soon Jim recognized that he was on a very hot topic. Not being one to shy away from difficult situations, and having a threatening marshall in the crowd certainly made it challenging, Jim got their attention and said, "All right, let me put it this way. No one can serve two masters. You cannot serve God and possessions."

Several stormed off after that comment. They weren't about to be told to pick between God and their possessions, not realizing that they had just made a choice. Jim looked around at the crowd and saw what seemed like embarrassment, so he said, "Maybe this will be easier to hear. Put God first, and let everything else fall into place." That seemed to help a little bit, so he said, "I know it's challenging, but living a healthy life was never going to be easy."

"Tell me about it!" called out Jimbo.

A mean-hearted cowboy said, "That guy looks like he's put food first, instead of God!"

Jim decided it wasn't worth responding to the comment, and instead announced "Next I'll talk about a healthy spiritual life."

2. Healthy living and spirituality.

Some clouds came overhead, and people started feeling the chilliness of the day. Jim asked them to look up and said, "We know the sun is there, but the clouds are keeping us from seeing it. How many of you know a person who has problems seeing?" Several people raised their hands. "Life is difficult when our eyes are clouded over, and that's really the problem with the attitude toward possessions. If our spirituality isn't clear, it makes it tough to see that God is the most important thing in our life. And it gets chilly if we wander off into darkness."

"I thought you were moving on from talking about possessions," complained a listener.

"I was," Jim said in agreement, "but we also need to be open to learnin' when we need to. So, anyway, let's not be blind to the spiritual life. Building God's kingdom is about helping people. We need to notice where there are troubles and do our part in helping, but if we can't see clearly, we're the ones in trouble."

"Ain't followin' ya there, pal," grumbled an older man who owned the local shoe store.

"Then try this," said Jim. "If there's something wrong with our eyes, it leads to darkness. Same with our spiritual life. If there is something wrong with the way we see God's world, we are part of the problem. Spiritual health begins with the ability to see love in the world. Oh, sure, there's plenty of evil in the world, but when we focus on the evil, that's all we see. We become blind to the needs of others, and when we are blind in that way, we will never see the need for help and kindness and compassion. Here's a truth I've come to embrace: we find what we're looking for."

"Gots to say, I like that! So how do we overcome it?" inquired a woman from the Methodist Church in town, who often talked about opening a food pantry to help people who were struggling.

"Here's how," explained Jim, "by realizing you are full of light. When the light from God is hard to notice, realize the light is also inside you. Don't let the light dim by leading a selfish life."

Many more people left after this comment, but Jim was encouraged because plenty were staying. He looked over the crowd and realized they were full of problems. He suggested they take a few minutes to meditate on this, then he had one more thing to say.

3. Healthy living and worry.

When he noticed people starting to become interested in this next thing, he said "Do not worry."

"Yah, right," yelled the Catholic priest. "You must not know what's going on 'round here. My parish is full of people who are hungry. They have a hard time keepin' their well runnin' and keepin' clothes on their back. Your comment, sir, is an outrage!"

"You have many good points, Father, but I have a question," Jim said calmly. The crowd was feeling uneasy because they knew it was no good fighting with the parish priest. "Does worry help?" There was a bit of shocked laughter that echoed down the hillside as if looking for a place to land.

"Maybe not," answered the priest with some resignation, "but how does not worrying help?"

"Now that's a great question," responded Jim. "Look at the birds; they don't sow seeds, nor harvest, nor store up excess into barns, yet God takes care of them. Don't you think you are more valuable than they? We can learn something from the birds. They rely on nature's abundance and don't try to control the future. And it leads to less worry."

"But if I worry, it keeps me focused on what I need to do for my family," offered the local shopkeeper.

"Then I have a question for you, Calvin," said Jim. "Will worrying about something add a single hour to your life? Our problem is we don't want to trust in God's future."

"Good one," called out Pedro.

"No, Pedro," responded Jim. "This isn't competition." Pedro shrank back again in embarrassment. He thought someday he'd find where to draw the line for his humor, and to know when to offer a comment. Jim then continued, "This is about living healthy lives with respect to possessions and spirituality, and worry takes us the wrong direction. Now, back to the good Father and his point about people in his parish finding it difficult to even get enough clothes for their family. Why worry about clothes? Consider the marigolds of the desert. They do nothing to earn being clothed in beauty. They grow because God causes them to grow. God is the one who adds days and growth to our life. But if God clothes the fields of flowers with beauty, will he not much more clothe you—you of little faith?" Right then and there, all of the priest's parishioners got up and left. They weren't about to let Jim question the strength of their priest's faith.

After things settled down again, a man toward the front, who had been listening intently, quizzed Jim with, "But clothes don't just happen in nature, do they?"

"That's right," agreed Jim. "So it takes a lot of faith to come to the understanding that God takes care of us through one another." That comment was met with confusion, so Jim continued. "That's why it is so important that we commit to helping one another. And that's our goal as the Hole in the Rock Gang. To spread the good news that when we fill our lives with putting God first, everything else falls into place. So, don't worry about what to eat or what to drink or what to wear. It's the unbelievers who worry about these things. In fact, your heavenly Father knows that you need all these things. But work first for the kingdom of God and his righteousness, and all these things will be given to you as well."

Those who were left were slowly starting to realize that Jim was saying they shouldn't just sit around and wait for God to act. God has acted in the creation of everything. "So yer sayin,'" clarified a woman who had moved closer, "that's how we make heaven happen here and now."

Jim was so stunned by this discovery that he wept tears of joy. He realized that it had been a great afternoon of teaching, so when he pulled himself together he offered a closing thought. "I started this talk by saying 'Do not worry.' So now I'd like to add to that thought by saying do not worry about tomorrow, but take each day as it comes. Know that your life is in God's hands, who holds the whole world in his hands. And God is ready to be with you through difficult times."

"But I kind of like bad news," offered a younger person in the audience.

"Then for you, young man," explained Jim, "the reason we don't worry about tomorrow is because tomorrow will have plenty of worries of its own. Today is enough of a mess all by itself."

"Thanks, mister," replied the young man. "I think I like that."

Jim then clarified, "But don't let the troubles of the day

overcome you. Mountains can only be climbed one bit at a time. It's kinda like riding up here from Phoenix. It's a long way, but ya aim yer horse in the right direction and after a while, ya get the job done."

The crowd felt satisfied and started getting ready to leave, when Jim said "One more thing." Most were intrigued, but a few more left as Jim was making his final comment. "Deal with life a day at a time, just like the mountain I mentioned, because we can't change tomorrow. The day's troubles may be monumental, but the good news is we can certainly change today by taking life a bit at a time. And if we deal with today's problems, and I do mean if, we will be better able to enjoy tomorrow. And finally, the way we do this is to get up each day and expect to see God's face in the people we meet and know God will be with us. Help others when needed and accept help when you need it. We are all God's children, worthy of loving and being loved." The last of the crowd departed with great ideas on how to change for the better, the way they think and feel.

One more societal problem needs to be explained to help understand the challenges Jim and the Hole in the Wall Gang faced. Outlaws were out of control in the Wild West, and even the Russians were careful when dealing with famous ones. The real problem was that the Americans romanticized rebels and overlooked their crimes. The Hole in the Wall Gang needed to make their message more attractive than the bad guys, and that was no easy task. Here are four of the most legendary outlaws who lived in the time of Jim in the Old West:

1) In 1864, a sixteen year old Jesse James and his brother Frank murdered dozens of Union soldiers. Some think his anger over the loss of the Confederacy propelled him toward bank, train, and railroad robberies. He robbed more than twenty banks and trains worth around $200,000. His attraction was that he claimed to be robbing the rich to give to the poor, but there is no evidence he helped anyone except himself. In 1881, the governor of Missouri issued a $10,000 reward for the James brothers.

2) Billy the Kid was a cattle rustler, gunslinger, murderer, and escape artist. Legend says he killed twenty one people before he turned twenty one years old. Born in New York, he moved to Indiana, Kansas, and Denver before settling in Sante Fe, New Mexico. In 1875 he was arrested and jailed, only to escape through the jailhouse chimney. He made his way to southeast Arizona where he was charged with murdering a blacksmith. He was well known by 1880 and became the symbol of the little guy fighting against all odds. People loved him so much that it was an honor to have him stay a night and steal a horse the next day. He was gunned down on July 14, 1881 by New Mexico Sheriff Pat Garrett.

3) Born Myra Maybelle Shirley Starr, she was known as Belle Star, and, eventually as the "Bandit Queen." As a teenager in Scyene, Texas in 1864, her family's home was used as a hideout by Jesse James. The lifestyle was intriguing and she ended up marrying three outlaws: Jim Reed in 1866; Bruce Younger in 1878; and Sam Starr in 1880. She lived most of her life in an Oklahoma cabin in the Cherokee Nation. She became the stuff of legend, reportedly dabbling in every imaginable crime. However, there is no court record that shows she ever

held up a train, bank, or stagecoach, nor killed anyone.

4) Born in 1853 in Bonham, Texas to a Methodist preacher, John Wesley Hardin stabbed a classmate as a schoolboy. He then killed a man at age fifteen, and many Union soldiers soon thereafter. After twelve more killings, he surrendered in 1872, broke out of jail, and then continued killing. Nobody knows for sure how many people died from his villainy, but he famously said "I never killed anyone who didn't need killing."

SCENE TWO
Tapping the Greatness of God

As the crowds departed, the Hole in the Rock Gang noticed that Marshal Earp was sticking around, and several Russians were lingering behind him. "I've got a question," announced the marshal as he moved toward Jim. The Gang knew there would be nothing good come from this conversation, so they started to worry. They also knew that Jim had just talked about not worrying, but all they could remember was something about today being enough of a mess all by itself. Looked like that idea was going to come true, so they lingered right behind the Russians.

"What can I do for ya, marshal?" inquired Jim, with a sense of resignation that somehow he would get in trouble.

"Did you know it's against the law to have loud gatherings?" responded the marshal with a wicked grin on his face.

"And if we gathered in the woods with nobody around, would it be legal?" asked Jim.

"I don't get yer point, but you'd better watch yer step. I have no problem with what yer doin', but the Russians are upset," he said in a cowardly way.

"My point is that," explained Jim, showing no concern about the Russians, "if there's nobody in the neighboring area, then there's nobody to hear the loud noise."

"I ain't playin' no games here," said the marshal, as if to justify himself. "And who is my neighbor, anyway?"

"You know that hazardous, mountainous, backroad that goes from Prescott to Wickenburg?" asked Jim.

"I hate zat road," said one of the Russians.

"Don't talk to zat man. He bad," admonished the other Russian.

"You know I'm standing right here, don't you?" said Jim with a bit of a glare before continuing. Several in the Gang nearly laughed, but they knew it would not be helpful. "Anyway, it's a great place to get robbed. Around every bend are hiding places and outlaws just lay in waitin'."

"That's why I never go that way," the marshall announced with a smile.

"Not my point," complained Jim. "Can ya just listen to my story? After all, yer the one asking who yer neighbor is." The marshal's smile quickly turned to a frown because he wasn't used to being treated that way. "Okay, where was I?"

"On that road we traveled to Wickenburg recently," Pedro offered helpingly. "And I don't think we had any problems," and then Pedro stepped back a few paces as he realized he wasn't being helpful.

You could almost see smoke rising from the top of Jim's head, but he was determined to finish. "It's a story, people, and stories don't have to be real to be true." Truth is, the Hole in the Rock Gang was still concerned about the way the dialogue was going between Jim and the marshall, but they kept listening. "Okay, these outlaws…"

"Was it Billy the Kid?" asked Marshal Earp with a concerned look on his face.

"Oh, for heaven's sake!" exclaimed Jim. "How can I get you to understand it's a story? It's like Jules Verne's recent book *Around the World in Eighty Days*."

"You mean it's like a fairy tale?" asked Kate.

"Sure," said Jim. "We'll go with that, but this isn't a children's story." After looking around and seeing that people mostly didn't look confused anymore, he continued. "A man was going down that way and sure enough he got robbed. This outlaw was so bad, he stripped him, beat him, and left him half dead. Now by chance the local priest was going down that road, saw him laying there naked and beaten, and just walked on by. Do ya think he was being neighborly?"

"Ya mean we can talk now?" asked Junior timidly.

"Yes," said Jim.

"Then nope. I vote no," responded Junior.

Jim nodded his head and said, "So also a local lawman came to the same place and when he saw him, he also passed by. Do ya think he was being neighborly?"

"There's another no vote," said Bart.

"Not likin' the story so far," said the marshall.

"Not surprised," said Jim. The Russians offered a little laugh and the Gang was getting more nervous. "Then an Apache came by and saw him, and ya know what he did?"

"Don't even want to guess," commented Phil with a horrified look on his face.

"He was moved with pity," announced Jim. "He bandaged his wounds, put him on his horse, and took him to a local boarding house, and took care of him. The next day he brought some money to the owner of the boarding house and said, 'Take care of him; and when I come back, I will repay you any more that you spend.' Now, marshal, do ya think he was being neighborly?"

"Whatever," said the marshal.

"That's what it means to be neighborly," explained Jim. "Now, go and be a neighbor."

As the marshal and the Russians departed, their anger increased, and the Gang discussed what to do next. The sun was rapidly sinking behind the forested mountain, so they decided to head back to Matt's.

The next day they decided to get away from Prescott, so headed east toward the road to Phoenix. About half way there, they took a casual break at Agua Fria Valley. Even though it was a very small town, it was the birthplace of Bart, so he showed them the house he grew up in. While there, a Russian came riding up to them. It scared the Gang, but Jim noticed the Russian appeared distressed.

"What can I do for you?" asked Jim.

The Russian got off his horse and started telling Jim in broken English that he was hearing God was doing great things through him, and then said "My helper fall. He be paralyzed."

Jim realized the faith that was being expressed by this Russian, so he responded "I will come and cure him."

Tommie rather doubted that Jim could do something in God's name just because he wanted to, so he expressed some surprise at Jim's comment. "Are you sure you want to waste God's power on our enemy?"

Jim was quite frustrated with Tommie's comment and said, "We are all God's children. Never forget that. The only enemy we have is ourselves, and that happens when we see trouble instead of opportunity to help."

The Russian then surprised everyone by saying, "I not worthy for you as guest in house. I beg you. Say word, and my servant be healed."

The Gang marveled at this exchange. They had trouble

getting people to do much of anything other than come and listen to Jim when he spoke on the hillside. Jim, too, was quite pleased, then the Russian continued. "I have soldiers serve under me, just like you."

"We're not soldiers," complained Andrés. Jim turned and gave Andrés a look that caused him to step back. He quickly realized this was a conversation for Jim.

The Russian continued without missing a beat. "I say 'Go,' and soldier go. I say 'Come,' and soldier come. I say helper, 'Do zis,' and helper do zat."

When Jim heard this, he said "Nowhere in the Arizona Territory have I found such faith." He then looked straight into the eyes of the Russian and said, "Go; let it be done for you according to your faith." The Gang had never seen anything like this. Then the Russian went leaping for joy as he jumped back on his horse and headed for Prescott.

Then Tommie said, "I gotta see this." After Jim gave approval, Tommie jumped on his horse and followed after the Russian. When they got to his house, the Russian hurried in and Tommie stopped just outside. Over the next few minutes, what Tommie saw and heard shocked him. He got back on his horse and returned to Agua Fria Valley. "It happened!" Tommie informed the group. "I wouldn't have believed it if I hadn't seen it, but the Russian's helper was still lying on his bed with splints on his legs when we arrived. The Russian went in, but I stayed at the door well. As soon as the helper saw his employer, he said 'You find Jim?' and the Russian said 'Da,' which I guess means yes. The servant immediately stood up and found that he was healed. The family all started crying and celebrating and even offered me some vodka, but I was anxious to get back to tell you all about it."

This, too, had become a great bonding moment for the Gang. Little by little they were all realizing that the greatness of God could be tapped here on earth. Jim was the only one with faith enough to use it, but they were never going to forget that the Russian had faith enough to believe it. Maybe, just maybe, they would come to a time when they themselves could use it.

Next they ventured ahead to the road to Phoenix, but they noticed a lot of people started following them. When they got to the road, all the followers stopped their horses to see which direction Jim and his Gang would go. They never really planned any of their trips, but it seemed like it was time to head to Phoenix.

The town of Phoenix, down in the Valley of the Sun, was actually starting to grow. The population in 1870 was 240 and it grew ten-fold by 1880. It had been settled in 1867 and was incorporated on February 25, 1881. Its economy was dependent on a large-scale irrigation project, inspired by the original Hohokam Indian civilization and the ruins of their canals. The Arizona Territory soon became known for the "Five C's" of cotton, citrus, cattle, climate, and copper. What that meant for the Russians was a great income from taxation.

They decided not to stop at the Rusty Tavern, because there were too many now in the group with the followers. When they were done with the descent into Phoenix, they rode into town and tied up their horses. As they walked by the post office, the church, the school, and the telegraph office, Jim mentioned that the place was nothing but a desert when he was growing up in Prescott. It was still easy enough to walk around the small town with its four dance halls and sixteen saloons. They were surprised to see the latest addition: a branch of the Bank of Arizona.

It was also a painful reminder to see how the Russians took over the beautiful Catholic Church in town. And it was extremely aggravating to see that Sergey, the Russian overlord of Prescott, appropriated the best piece of property in Phoenix for his vacation home. As Jim got angrier and angrier, he could see that the Russians regarded the Phoenicians with contempt. What made it worse was that the lawmen trusted in themselves, pretending to be good people. With plenty of Russians, lawmen, and townsfolk around, Jim decided it was time for another story. As soon as he mentioned it, the Gang and all of the other followers gathered around to hear him. "Two men went to the church to pray, one a sheriff and the other a tax collector."

"I hate tax collectors," yelled one of the followers, which made Matt feel uncomfortable, because the Gang knew that he worked as a tax collector before he opened his house of prostitution.

Jim continued, "The sheriff, standing by himself at the front of the church, was praying like this, 'God, I thank you that I am not like other people: outlaws, thieves, fornicators, or even like this hated tax collector for the Russians.'" Matt slowly moved to the back of the crowd to avoid being noticed and the sheriff moved closer to the front to intimidate. Then Jim said, "the sheriff fasted twice a week and gave a tenth of all his income.'"

"Bet the priest liked that!" yelled another in the crowd, followed by laughter.

Turning a deaf ear to the interrupter, Jim said "But listen to what the tax collector did. He stayed in the back of the church, and couldn't even so much as bring himself to look up to heaven. He said, 'God, be merciful to me, a sinner!' Now who do you think went home right in the eyes of God?"

The crowd understood Jim's point, and they started laughing and pointing at the lawmen and Russians standing nearby. They were so glad that someone was finally feeling strong enough to take on the unethical lawmen and horrible Russian overlords. And Matt was feeling a lot better.

That's when Jim finished with a statement. "You need to take this lesson with you: all who praise themselves will be humbled, but all who humble themselves will be praised."

As the gathering began to disperse, it obviously had one important impact. It brought the lawmen and the Russians closer in their opinions.

"We's got ta do somsing 'bout zis guy," declared one of the Russians. "Who he zink he be?"

"Lord knows," proclaimed the lawman he was talking to. Little did he know he was right.

———————

They got back on their horses and continued at a walk pace. Pedro looked back and said "Jefe, there's even more people followin' us."

Jim looked around and saw a parade of about forty horses and riders. He thought for a moment where they could get away together to talk, when Pedro showed he was obviously thinking the same thing. "Maybe we should go to the Hole in the Rock, jefe. Then they would know where our name came from."

That wasn't Jim's purpose, but the location would at least

get them away from the downtown area. He slowly increased his speed to a trot and saw that everyone followed suit, so he spurred his horse again and went up to a canter. He didn't want to go too fast, so he could keep the group together. Soon they arrived at the Hole in the Rock and everyone got off their horses.

"See that Hole in the Rock?" asked Pedro as he sported a wide grin and pointed at the short, rounded mountain. "That's where I gave our group our name." Pedro started to tell them about their ghostly visit, but Jim cut him off by saying, "Its shade provides a nice break from the sun, and there's a great view of Phoenix from up there."

It turned out that one of the people following was coming for a reason. It was a woman who had been suffering from bleeding for twelve years. She was very frustrated with her physicians, because she had been to doctors in Prescott, Tuscon, and Phoenix. The only thing she got from those visits was a bill. Now she was broke and even getting worse. She was at her wit's end when she heard about some amazing things Jim was doing.

As she approached him, she had the first sense of hope she had felt in a long time. "Sir, may I touch your clothes?" she asked. "I truly believe that's all I need to do and I will be made well." It sounded strange to the Gang and several of the guys stepped between her and Jim as a means of protection.

"Let her through," requested Kate. "I think she really needs help."

The men stepped aside, and the woman reached out with tears running down her face. As soon as she touched Jim's shirt, her bleeding stopped and she felt healing within her body. Jim sensed something, too. He could tell that God was working a powerful act through him and then the woman fell down before him as if to worship. Jim would have nothing of that, so he said "Please get up, it's your faith that has made you well. Never bow to me or any man. Go in peace. God has healed you of your disease."

The crowd was in awe and wanted to stay in this place, just like the Gang wanted to stay after the ghostly visit. People were talking among themselves and chatting with the healed woman, when Jim motioned to the Gang to saddle up. It was getting on in the afternoon, too late to return to Prescott, so they went back into town for something to eat. They spent some time debriefing the events of the day, then found a boarding house for the night. It had been a good day. Jim was refreshed and feeling more powerfully than ever that he was doing God's will.

As they rode back up the mountain to Prescott the next day, Jim asked them to be thinking of something they would like for him to talk about. They took their usual break at the Rusty Tavern, and Pedro was ready with a question: "What do you think heaven is like?"

Jim said, "I'll have to think about that for awhile."

When they finished off their drinks, they remounted their horses and continued the lengthy trip. They took another short break where the road headed west to Prescott, and Pedro asked if he had an answer yet? "Not yet, Pedro, but I'm thinking about it." When they once again remounted, more followers started showing up and rode along side them. Bart asked if they could once again stop at his little home town of Agua Fria

Valley, and Jim tipped his hat with an affirmative.

Upon arrival, they saw lots of workers in the orchards, and Jim finally got his inspiration. He knew he wanted to say something about fairness, and equality, and the ways of God that are so different from ours, and here was an example that he thought just might work. "Where do you think the landowner found all of these day laborers?" asked Jim.

"Not here, for sure," responded Bart. "There's not enough people to care for the needs."

"He probably had to go on in to Prescott to find this many workers," suggested Phil.

"I agree," acknowledged Jim, "so let me begin my story with a landowner who went out early in the morning to hire laborers to pick pears. There are always day laborers standing around the town square in Prescott looking for work, and they were happy to get hired. The landowner was generous and offered each of them a full day's wage. After agreeing to the verbal contract, they traveled to his orchard and went to work."

"I remember when I used to work," Pedro said to Jim, "until you called me to follow you."

"No, Pedro," commented Jim. "You are unemployed so you can work fulltime with me to do God's will."

Pedro smiled, as did the rest of the Gang. The others who had joined them along the way seemed frustrated with Pedro's interruption, because they were there to hear Jim. "The landowner needed more help," continued Jim, "so about nine o'clock he returned to Prescott and found more people standing around with nothing to do. He told them to also return to his farm and he would pay whatever was right, so they went."

"Don't like that verbal contract," offered one of the newcomers.

"Well," said Jim, "things get even more interesting, because the landowner did the same thing at noon and three o'clock. Then about five o'clock, he went out one more time and still found people standing around. He asked them why they spent all day standing around idle, and they complained that no one would hire them. As I say, he was a generous landowner, so he also told them to go and work at his farm. When evening came, the owner told his manager to line up the workers to collect their earnings. He also said to have them line up with the last men hired being first, and the first men hired being last. When the people who had worked the shortest amount of time received their wages, they looked at their hand and jumped for joy when they realized they had received a full day's wage."

"What's this got to do with what heaven is like," inquired a puzzled Pedro.

"Patience, my friend," responded Jim. "Listen to what happens when the workers who had been there many more hours were ready to receive their money." Pedro nodded in agreement, even though patience wasn't his virtue. "They were very excited to receive their money and had even started dreaming about what they would do with such a great amount of money. After all, if some of them had worked ten times as long as the last ones hired, they figured they would surely get ten times as much."

"So what happened?" asked another from the now growing crowd of listeners.

"They got their daily wage as agreed," said Jim.

"That's just wrong!" yelled another from the group. "If they all got the same amount of money, and if this story is about heaven, I don't think I want to go there."

"Well, my friends," said Jim, "the workers in my story were

mad, just like you. They grumbled about the landowner treating the last hired men as equal to them. After all, they had borne the burden of the day and the scorching heat."

"You got that right!" exclaimed another.

"Now," explained Jim, "listen to what the landowner said to the disgruntled workers. He told them that he had done them no wrong."

"Maybe this landowner needs to learn some ethics," griped another.

"No," said Jim. "Didn't the landowner pay those who had worked the longest, exactly what they agreed to in their verbal contract?" The crowd, including the Gang, stood there stunned, as if they had been tricked. Jim continued, "the landowner needs to abide by your rules? Why can't he do what he wants with what belongs to him?"

Nobody dared respond. Then Jim gave the clencher, "Why would we be envious of others because someone was generous with them?"

"Gonna have to think on that one for awhile," declared Pedro, as he took off his cowboy hat and scratched his head in disbelief.

"Good," said Jim. "Now here's what heaven is like."

"Been waitin' for a pretty long time for this," proclaimed Pedro, "so I hope it's good."

"God loves those who build the kingdom toward the end of their lives," continued Jim, "just as much as those who help build the kingdom their whole life long. Now, here's what I want you to never forget: 'the last will be first, and the first will be last.'"

As they got back on their horses to finish their trip into Prescott, nobody wanted to take the lead. All of a sudden, everybody wanted to be last.

It was getting late in the day, so they headed straight to Matt's home when they got into town. After a nice dinner, they turned in early. The Gang had a lot to think about since they started following Jim, so they fell asleep remembering the big ideas Jim said were important.

The next day they headed into town, and large crowds were following him. As Jim, his followers, and the crowd were walking through town, a blind beggar was sitting by the roadside. His name was Jackson, which means son of Jack, and he asked about the crowds. A woman who heard him, told him it was Jim Caldwell. Now it seems that Jackson had heard about the incredible things Jim was doing, so he yelled out, "Jim, have mercy on me!" The townsfolk found Jackson to be little more than a nuisance, and someone quickly scolded him for trying to bother Jim. This didn't faze Jackson at all, so he yelled out all the more, "Jim Caldwell, have mercy on me!"

Jim finally heard him and the people were embarrassed that they couldn't control the blind beggar. Some looked smugly at him and just wished he would go away. To everyone's surprise, Jim said "Call him here."

Not quite knowing what to do, several townsfolk decided to fulfill Jim's request. "Get up," the person closest to him said. "I can't believe Jim wants to waste his time with a person like you, but he's calling ya."

The poor man was so excited, he could hardly contain himself. He sprang up, and people begrudgingly guided him to Jim. Then Jim said to him, "What do you want me to do for you?"

This was the moment the blind beggar had dreamt about, ever since he heard that Jim was doing and saying great things in the name of God. "Teacher," he said, "let me see again."

The crowd laughed nervously. Here this blind beggar had audience with Jim and he asked for the impossible. One man cried out from the crowd and said, "While you're at it, make me a rich man!"

Some more laughter carried through the crowd, then Jim spoke, "Go."

"I agree with Jim. This guy needs to go home," said a woman in the back of the crowd in disgust.

Then Jim spoke again to Jackson, "Your faith has made you well."

The shock felt in the crowd was nothing compared to what happened next. The poor, blind, beggar regained his sight. He was jumping around with glee, and went up to person after person saying, "I see you." Then Jackson heard a familiar voice in the crowd and ran over to him and said, "So, Boone, that's what you look like!" Boone was speechless about Jackson's newfound ability to see.

It became a memorable day in Prescott. People were openly asking Jim how he did that, and he, as usual, said "Nothing is impossible with God." Let's just say, more people than normal showed up at the Methodist Church that following Sunday. Among the crowd of newcomers, was of course Jackson. He became a believer for pretty good reason. The pastor was probably more surprised to see Boone in attendance. The pastor knew that Boone was developing a drinking problem, so he hoped the amazing change in Jackson's life was giving Boone new hope for healing in his own life. After all, Jim said it was Jackson's faith that made him well.

After church, Boone tracked down Jackson and said, "After you were healed, you went up to people and said 'I see you,' but when you came to me you said, 'So, Boone, that's what you look like!' Why did you single me out with a different comment?"

Jackson said, "Oh, that's easy. When yer blind, yer sense of smell is much stronger. Down in Phoenix there are a lot of hard-drinkin' cowboys, but less so here in Prescott. Over the years I began recognizin' ya by the alcohol on yer breath, because it kept getting' stronger." At first, Boone was just astonished, but little by little reality began seeping in, much like the alcohol did. Soon tears welled up in Boone's eyes and then he completely fell apart. He knew he needed to change his ways, and Jackson was the man to help him. Jackson said, "All I know is ya just need faith that God can do anything." He then kneeled down, put a hand on Boone's shoulder and offered a prayer for healing. What they learned that day was that God can do great things through anyone.

_____

When the Gang left town the next day for Phoenix, it was a large crowd that saddled up their horses to join them. Someone was even kind enough to give Jackson a horse, but it took him a bit to learn how to ride. That was okay, because this crowd was full of joy and hope. They all encouraged Jackson as they traveled much slower than usual, but by the time they got to the turn south for Phoenix, Jackson was riding pretty well. He said, "If ya put blinders on my horse, I'll show him the way!"

Once again they rode past The Rusty Tavern, because the group was too large to be accommodated. When they were on the far north side of Phoenix, Pedro had them all slow their horses to a walk. He pointed out the hole in the rock, and proudly told the crowd it was the Gang's namesake. "You need to go up there sometime," Pedro suggested. "It has great views of Phoenix and gives a break from the sun."

Jackson was in awe as they slowly trotted on in to town. He'd never seen anything like it. Actually, he'd never seen anything ever, so his soul was once again filled with rejoicing. "I love Jim," Jackson announced.

In a teaching kind of reply, Jim said, "I love God." He then noticed that there were a lot of lawmen, Russians, and business folk around, so he decided it was time for a story. They all got off their horses and the Russians surrounded the group in fear they would cause trouble. The lawmen weren't too excited about their presence either, but Jim just casually started to talk. "My friend, Pedro, recently asked me what heaven is like." Pedro broke out a huge smile as Jim continued. "It is as if a man, going on a journey, summoned his servants and entrusted his property to them."

"I'd never do that," said a saloon owner.

"Well, sir," explained Jim. "This guy wanted to make money from his property while he was gone."

"That's better," responded the saloon owner.

"This man called the first servant over," continued Jim, "and gave him two lifetimes worth of wages."

"I'd have run away with it, right then and there," said another businessman.

"To another," said Jim, "he gave thirty years worth of wages."

"I'd even be tempted to break the law and run away with that amount," said a lawman.

"And to another he gave fifteen years worth of wages,"

continued Jim.

"Zis man getting cheaper," said a Russian, and his comrades laughed heartily.

"But here's the catch," said Jim. "He gave the money to each individual according to their ability, then he went away."

"Sounds like the blind leading the blind," commented another business man. Jackson was about to say something, but Kate told him to just listen to the story.

"The first guy," explained Jim, "went down to Tombstone, gambled with it, and doubled what was entrusted to him."

"Give me his name," yelled someone in the crowd, followed by lots of laughter.

The second guy," continued Jim, "went to the Rusty Tavern, played cards, and also doubled what he had been given." Jim waited for a moment, but nobody said anything, and he realized they were listening. "The third guy took his boss's money and buried it, to make sure it didn't get lost."

"I prefer the third guy," said a lawman. "At least the money was safe."

"After a long time," Jim clarified, "the man returned and asked for his money back. The first servant came forward and handed him back double what had been given to him. The man told him, 'Well done, good and trustworthy servant; you have been trustworthy in a few things, I will put you in charge of many things; enter into the joy of your master.'"

"See," said Pedro. "Jim's talking about heaven." Even Jackson could see that.

"And the second servant came forward and also showed that he had doubled what had been entrusted to him," said Jim. "And again the man said, 'Well done, good and trustworthy servant. You have been trustworthy in a few things, so I will put you in charge of many things. Enter into the joy of your master.' Then the last guy came forward."

"Can't wait to hear this one," exclaimed Jackson.

Jim smiled for a moment at Jackson, then continued. "He said, 'Master, I knew that you were a harsh man, reaping where you did not sow, and gathering where you did not scatter seed. So I was afraid, but I am happy to report that I went and hid your money to make sure nobody could steal it. Here's your money back. You're welcome." But the owner replied, 'You wicked and lazy servant! You knew, did you, that I reap where I did not sow, and gather where I did not scatter? Then you should have invested my money with the bankers, and on my return I would have received what was my own with interest.'"

"And if anyone wants to draw interest on their money, the Bank of Arizona is open for business," commented the bank manager.

Several groaned before Jim continued. "So the owner said, 'Take the money from him, and give it to the first guy. For to all those who have, more will be given, and they will have an abundance; but from those who have nothing, even what they have will be taken away. As for this worthless servant, throw him in jail."

The story was first met with silence, then people started questioning the story. "What's wrong with protecting an investment?" and "If that owner is supposed to be God, I don't think I like him too much."

Jim found himself frustrated, so he said, "You focus on all the wrong things. Think about taking what God has given you and use it to make this a better world."

"I thought this was supposed to be about heaven!" complained a lawman.

"It is," said Jim, "but ya don't have to wait to get to heaven. Our job is to make this a better world here and now, then ya can enjoy eternal bliss." He then saddled up and headed back to Prescott, while the Russians and lawmen colluded once again on how to get rid of him.

ACT IV
FOR FOLLOWERS ONLY

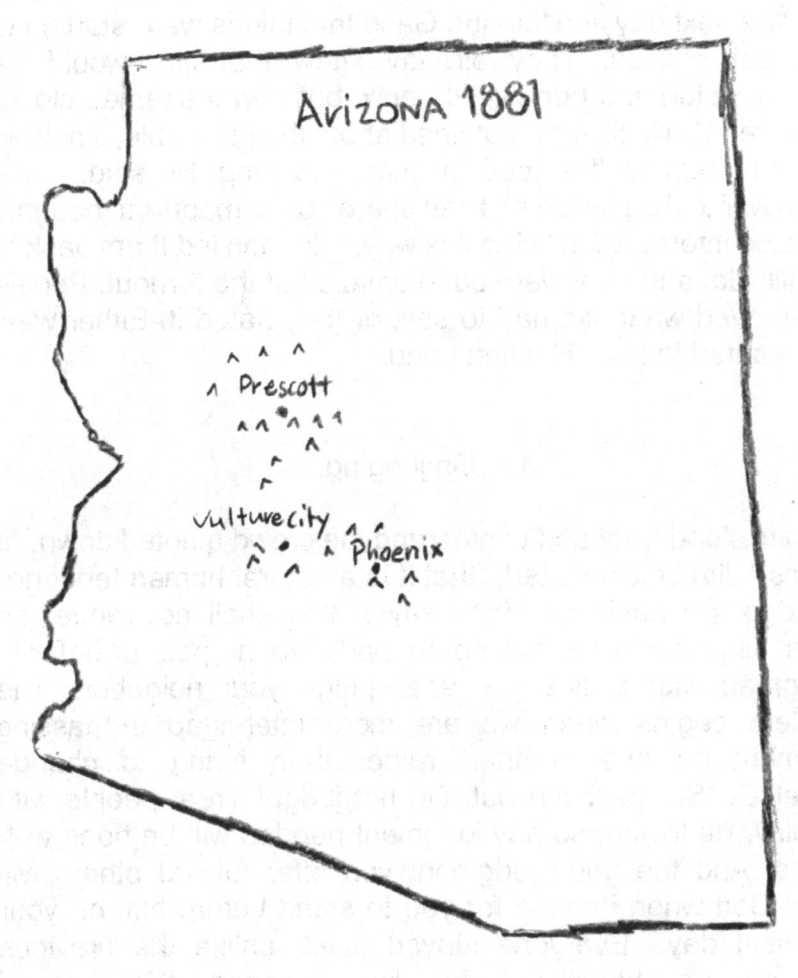

SCENE ONE
The Most Important Thing

The next day Jim told the Gang that things were starting to get serious. They already knew that Jim would be arrested and hung in Phoenix, but now it seemed closer than ever. While they complained about the inevitable, Jim tried to focus them on the need for more teaching. He said, "Let's head over to the hillside so I can share some important thoughts for those interested in living this way." He then led them back to the hillside, and they were quite amazed at the turnout. People either loved what Jim had to say, or they hated it. Either way, they wanted to hear him first hand.

1.   On judging.

Jim stood front and center, and the crowd quieted down. "It seems," Jim boldly stated, "that it is a natural human tendency to judge. So Leviticus 19:15 says, 'You shall not render an unjust judgment; you shall not be partial to the poor or defer to the great: with justice you shall judge your neighbor.' The problem begins when we are more interested in passing judgment on one another, rather than trying to change ourselves. So, hear me out. Do not judge! Treat people with equality. Be loving, so any judgment needed will be done with justice. And the good judgment you offer toward others will affect God when its time for you to stand before him on your judgment day." Everyone stayed quiet, unlike the previous teachings on the hillside, so Jim continued. "Why do ya notice a saguaro needle stuck on yer neighbor's clothes, but ya don't even notice when yer whole body is stuck on a cactus? It's because we prefer to exaggerate the problems we see in others and ignore our own. Think about it. How can you say to yer neighbor, 'Let me take off that needle stuck on yer pants,' while yer whole body is trapped on a saguaro? You hypocrite! First get yerself free from the cactus, and then you will be able to take the needle off yer neighbor's clothes."

"I thought you were going to share some good news, Jim," said the local priest.

"Thanks," said Jim, "that's where I'm going with this. My point is that we have to be very careful with judgment, and good judgment starts with looking honestly at ourselves."

"But I thought you said 'Do not judge,'" complained a man toward the back of the crowd.

"Good judgment isn't easy for most of us," said Jim. "So if ya can't be honest with your own major failures, don't even think about someone else's minor flaws."

"Okay," said a woman in the crowd. "Let's say I'm honest with my problems, then offer correction to someone who rejects it. What do I do then?"

"Here's my take," explained Jim. "Do not throw your pearls of wisdom before javelinas. They will trample them under foot and turn and maul you."

"I hate javelinas!" called out a cowboy.

"They stink!" offered a woman in the crowd.

"Exactly!" said Jim. "So don't be like a javelina, by turning on someone and mauling them with judgment."

The crowd obviously needed some time to think about this teaching, so Jim offered a short time for people to contemplate this important idea.

2. On giving and receiving.

Fairly soon he stood up and asked if they were ready for another teaching, because he wasn't sure where they were emotionally. The crowd continued to be unusually quiet, but several nodded a rather meek yes. "I have three quick ideas that are important," Jim said with authority, "so let me tell you a quick story before each one." After a quick pause, he said "Suppose you go to a friend's house at midnight and ask for three loaves of bread, because a friend unexpectedly arrived and you have nothing to give them. He says 'Don't bother me; the door has already been locked, and my children are in bed. I cannot get up and give you anything.' But if you persist he will get up and give you whatever you need. So here is my first idea. Ask, and it will be given you. The reason is because everyone who asks receives, and the key is persistence."

"I kinda doubt it," grumbled the local baker.

"No need for pessimism," explained Jim. "When you think through the fullness of your life, this idea is generally true." He then continued with his second story. "How many of you have a coin from the silver mine down in Tombstone?" Nobody wanted to raise their hand for fear they'd get robbed later. "Nonetheless, if you had ten silver coins, and lost one, wouldn't you search carefully to find it?"

"Wouldn't you?" said a man with a bit of anger in his voice.

"Of course!" agreed Jim. "And that's my second idea. Search, and you will find."

"Not always!" complained another, who spent some time as a miner.

Jim responded, "But, again, it's generally true. And those who search for good news will find it, too."

"Did he just make fun of me?" inquired the miner.

"Who cares?" called out another. "Now, what about that third story?"

"Imagine a family member who was off serving in the army," invited Jim. "He is unexpectedly granted an early leave, and shows up at his locked home. Not having the keys, because he'd been gone a long time, he knocks. His son comes to the door and asks 'Who's there?' On recognizing his father's voice, he is overjoyed and runs back to tell his mother. She says, 'You are out of your mind! He won't be home for months.' But the son insists it is true. Meanwhile, the man continues knocking, so his wife goes, hears his voice, and lets him in with amazement and joy. So, here's my third idea. Knock, and the door will be opened for you."

"What if it's an Apache?" cried out a man near the front.

"Yah, and that story sure sounds like the first one," complained another.

"These are general truths," explained Jim. "Let me put it negatively, since ya seem to prefer that. Is there anyone among ya who, if your child asks for bread, will give a cactus?"

"Of course, not!" yelled a mother.

"Or," continued Jim, "if the child asks for a fish, will give a rattle snake?"

"Nobody would do that!" screamed several in the crowd.

"That would be hideous," agreed Jim. "So here's what this is all about. If you then, know how to give good gifts to your children, how much more will God give good things to those who ask?"

"So what's yer point?" demanded a burly man, sort of blocking the way out.

"My point is," said Jim. "It is better to live without suspicion.

We need to be people who simply ask. Ask when ya need help. Ask God to be with ya in times of trouble. Ask for directions when ya get lost. Ask because God promises ya will receive in some way, sooner or later."

"Where's that promise in the Bible?" asked a gentleman who seemed genuinely interested.

"Oh, there are many," said Jim with a cordial smile, "but try this one from Isaiah 41:10, 'do not fear, for I am with you, do not be afraid, for I am your God; I will strengthen you, I will help you I will uphold you with my victorious right hand.'"

"Thank you," said the same gentleman, "I think I'll start asking."

Jim smiled and then continued. "We also need to be people who search. Think ole Mr. Wickenburg woulda found that gold mine at Vulture City if he hadn't been searching?"

"He didn't," claimed a man in the crowd. "I hear he was just ridin' by on his horse when he saw the glint of gold."

"Yes," said Jim, "but he wouldn't have found that glint of gold if he was sitting at home." A look of surprise was in their eyes, suggesting they actually learned something. "Searching is a blessed way to live life. Search for beautiful views, wonderful friends, and great books. Part of the joy in life comes from searching."

"I agree," announced a younger man. "I heard Indians call the Grand Canyon a holy site, and make pilgrimages there, because searching for beauty inspires the soul."

"Thank ya, young man," said Jim. "The world needs more beautiful thinkers like you. Now, let me see. The other thing we need is to be people who knock. If you don't ever knock on a door, you'll never get to know new people. Knock on God's door in prayer, and it will be opened to you."

"I'm havin' a hard time believin' that one," said a woman.

"Our job, ma'am," Jim said, "is to ask, search, and knock, then trust God to help us."

3. On what's most important.

Jim knew it was a difficult teaching, so he was rather surprised they took it as well as they did. Then he decided to offer one more. "Let me wrap up this mornin's teachin' with the most important thing yer gonna hear. I have some difficult things to say this afternoon. I wouldn't recommend coming back, unless you are serious about living the new life that I've been talking about.

"I'm way ahead of ya, pal," a cowboy offered. "I've had enough of this nonsense." He then walked out, grumbling all the way.

"Anyone else need to leave?" inquired Jim. Getting no takers, he continued. "Of all my teachings on the hill, this one sums up the way to live." Jim paused for a moment and saw that people genuinely wanted to hear. "And I mean always, not just when you feel like it. Furthermore, I mean this is for everyone." Jim had them listening, and that's a good thing, because he didn't want them ever to forget what he was about to say. "We wish that others would treat us well, don't we?" The crowd nodded in agreement, like rocking chairs on a porch. "Here's the secret to a happy life. Instead of reacting to the way we are treated, we should act kindly toward others in the first place."

"That won't be easy," suggested a mother whose children were often bullied.

"You're right," answered Jim. "But here's why. If we want to live a happy life, we imitate the God of generosity and forgiveness."

"Still not sure how to put this into my real life," said another woman with genuine concern in her voice.

"Maybe," explained Jim, "some of you will remember one of my earlier teachings from the hill, when I said 'What ya need to do is be better than the clergy and the lawmen.'"

"Now it's getting easier!" exclaimed a shop owner in the crowd, followed by lots of laughter.

"But our job isn't to put people down. It's to lift ourselves and others up," said Jim

"It's tough to be kind to people," stated a man who was holding his wife's hand. "Particularly when they continue to treat you or your wife in a terrible way."

"Yep," agreed Jim. "This lifestyle demands a considerable risk, and there's no guarantee that people will respond with generosity and goodwill. But God has already given us an example."

"What's that?" asked a good Catholic woman whose parish had been taken over by the Russians.

"God first took a risk," explained Jim, "by letting the sun shine on the good and the bad at the same time, and it makes us all worthy in God's eyes."

"I'm willing to give this a try," continued the Catholic woman. "So can you put this lifestyle in a simple sentence?"

"Sure," said Jim. "Try this." He paused for a moment, then said "Do to others as you would have them do to you." Showing some satisfied smiles, they departed.

---

1. Two ways.

Things were difficult enough living in the Wild West, so a lot of folk didn't return for the afternoon teaching. Some came back, along, of course, with the Gang, and Jim started with "Bless you. This is great, because you are exactly like the lesson I wanted to teach. You are choosing the tougher road of living the spiritual life. There's really nothing new about it, but people have a tendency to make choices without even thinkin' 'bout it. Listen to how Abund said it." Jim then opened his Bible and read from Deuternomy 30:15-16. "See, I have set before you today life and prosperity, death and adversity. If you obey the commandments of the LORD your God that I am commanding you today, by loving the LORD your God, walking in his ways, and observing his commandments, decrees, and ordinances, then you shall live and become numerous, and the LORD your God will bless you in the land that you are entering to possess."

"I like the blessing part," said a member of the local Catholic church.

"Me, too," agreed Jim. "That's the good stuff, but we always have choices. Hear how it's talked about in Joshua 24:15. 'Now if you are unwilling to serve the LORD, choose this day whom you will serve, whether the gods your ancestors served in the region beyond the River or the gods of the Amorites in whose land you are living; but as for me and my household, we will serve the LORD."

"That's me!" said a local shop owner. "I love the LORD and always want to serve him."

"And that's why yer here," said Jim. "Where did the rest of the people from this morning go?" The crowd looked around in embarrassment as they saw a much smaller crowd. Then Jim continued, "Here's my way to teach this idea. Enter through the narrow gate; for the gate is wide and the road is easy that leads to destruction, and there are many who take it. For the gate is narrow and the road is hard that leads to life, and there are few who find it."

"That's a difficult teaching," commented a woman in the crowd.

"Not even everyone who follows me will make it," stated Jim, while looking at Bennie.

Bennie was obviously shocked, not to mention the rest of the Gang. "Then why should I follow you?" asked Bennie. The Gang was very uncomfortable at this point. It was easier listening to what others should do, but much tougher when it hits you right between the eyes.

"Because," said Jim to Bennie, "my teachings on the hill give the guidance needed to truly follow, for those who want."

"You still talkin' 'bout me?" fired back Bennie. Jim then looked back to the few left in the crowd and said, "The reason many take that wide road is because it's easy. When you choose to follow your spiritual life, it is worthwhile, because it is through many persecutions that we enter the kingdom of God."

"Bennie's persecuted us plenty," whispered Pedro to his brother, but Andrés shushed him.

This had been a tough message. Jim knew it was going to be difficult to hear, but he was surprised that even Benny was losing interest. It revealed that the way to heaven is indeed challenging, and the chances of failure are greater than the chances for success. Again, as a demonstration of the truth of his message, a few more people left with their heads hanging down. Jim looked around and saw that several dozen remained, so he continued.

2. Beware of false prophets.

"Let me tell you a caution that Tobillo gave his sons in his last words," shared Jim. "It's from Genesis 49 and verse 27: 'Benjamin is a ravenous wolf, in the morning devouring the prey, and at evening dividing the spoil.'"

"Are you saying these are your last words?" asked Pedro. He knew that Jim had said his end was near, but he also knew he wasn't supposed to talk about it. He thought maybe he could bring it up in this mildly hidden manner.

Jim ignored him and said, "The story is a warning about people you think you can trust. Here's how I would say it. Beware of people who come to you in horse's clothing, but inwardly are ravenous coyotes."

"I have a charming cousin like that," shared a woman. "He looks nice and sounds nice, but then you see what he did. He got a friend of his into a life of robbin' banks. Who woulda known?"

"So how can we tell when we see a coyote in horse's clothing?" asked one of the few ranchers left among the listeners.

"You will know them by their fruits," explained Jim. "Are grapes gathered from thistle bushes, or pears from olive trees?

"No," responded the rancher.

"In the same way," continued Jim, "every good tree makes good fruit, but the bad tree gives bad fruit."

"I get it!" exclaimed another. "It's like when you can't tell who might be a thief, but you can see the fruit of their labor."

"Not really," complained a shop keeper. "Somebody stole some fruit from my store, and I never found out who it was. Still makes me mad."

"Then try this," announced Jim. "A good tree cannot bear bad fruit, nor can a bad tree bear good fruit."

"I like that," proclaimed a woman on the hillside. "Kinda makes ya wanna be a good tree."

"And God don't want no bad fruit," explained Jim. "That's why every tree that does not bear good fruit is cut down and thrown into the fire."

"He ain't talkin' 'bout heaven now, is he?" another man said with a laugh.

"So," said Jim, when the laughter subsided, "you'll know them by their fruits. Ever have a tangerine, picked fresh from a tree? Then squeezed out the juice into a glass, and than drank it?"

"Sure," said a man in the back. "I have three fruit trees on my property, and my family has fresh juice 'bout every day."

"Ever gather a bunch of 'em," asked Jim, "put 'em in a basket, then forget 'em for a while?'

"Yep," responded the same man.

Jim continued the dialogue with him. "Did you find them later, dump the basket, and find a bad one in the middle."

"Yep," the man said again.

"If you leave it there for a long time in the same basket," explained Jim, "the one bad tangerine will ruin the whole bunch."

"I've seen that happen," said the lone shop owner left in the group.

"Same thing with people," concluded Jim. "If you learn, from the fruit of a person's labor, that they are a coyote in horse's clothing, it's best to stay away from them. Pray for them for sure, but bad fruit will affect the good fruit quicker than the good fruit will affect the bad."

3. Don't deceive yourself.

Jim looked around and saw people paying attention, and realized that those remaining listeners were interested in his teaching, so he went on to another story. "Not everyone who says, 'Lord, Lord' will enter the kingdom of heaven."

"What does that mean?" inquired Big Nose Kate.

"Flattery won't get ya into heaven," explained Jim. "The problem is when ya know the LORD by name, but not by heart and mind."

"Okay," Kate said with continuing interest. "So what will get ya into heaven?"

"That's my favorite point," said Jim. It's all about doin' the will of God."

"Remind me what God's will is," requested Kate with an inquisitive look.

Jim happily responded with, "Love your neighbor as yourself. Then add to that to do to others as you would have them do to you. So, when you stand before God on the judgment day, some will plead that they did great things. God will hear their case, and some will be surprised when God declares to them, 'I never knew you; go away from me, you evildoers."

"When is the judgment day?" asked Bennie with surprisingly renewed interest.

"It's the day you die," announced Jim. "That's when you will stand before God who doesn't judge you."

"Sounds like judgment to me," responded Pedro.

"The reason is," explained Jim "that it will be our own actions that judges ourselves."

"Can you give me some scripture to back what yer sayin'?" asked a church lady.

"Sure," said Jim. "How 'bout King Montezuma's prayer for recovery, when he writes in Psalm 6, and verse 8, 'Depart from me, all you workers of evil.' That's how God will deal with evil people. So I say, don't deceive yourself. Be good and do good, and you'll be fine."

The people were mesmerized, and then Jim said, "I have one last example for you."

4.   A closing story.

Jim said, "Everyone here who hears these words of mine and acts on them will be like wise people who build their houses on rock."

"Everyone?" asked a young man who had never gone to church.

"Yes," said Jim. "God's arms are wide open and just waitin' to receive us into his everlasting arms, all who are lovin' and followin' God's will."

"So," inquired a farmer, "I want to be wise. In fact my wife often calls me a wiseacre." There was a little bit of laughter, especially after his wife swatted his backside. "But seriously," he continued, "this seems important, so spell it out for me again, if you would."

"Sure," said Jim in an agreeable manner. "It's more than

just hearing my words. I'm glad you're interested in hearing, but it has to be followed by actions. Real actions. Loving actions. Doing what God calls ya to do. That's what makes a person wise."

"Do you act on what God calls ya to do?" asked the farmer, with genuine interest as he pointed at Jim. The Gang all of a sudden became pale and Pedro desperately wanted to tell about what was coming up, but Jim saw him and gave the kind of stare that says, don't even think about it.

"Yes," said Jim. "I always strive to be as wise as the person who builds their house on solid rock."

"We've got plenty of rock here in Arizona!" exclaimed another young enthusiast.

"And here's the good news 'bout that," explained Jim. "When the rain falls and the floods come, and the winds blow against the house built on rock, it will not fall."

"And we have rains and floods around these parts that could easily destroy a house," said the farmer.

"Yah, and when the winds blow from the south, it' so bad they even knock over trees!" offered the church lady.

"So," mentioned Jim, "imagine your spiritual life built on money, or self-love. It would be like foolish people who built their house on sand. The only protection you have is the ground you build on. If you are wise, by following my teachin's on the hill, you are ready for whatever troubles come your way. When the rains of life come yer way, and the floods and wind, yer spiritual life will not fall. You will be ready, for now and for eternity."

Now when Jim finished saying these things, the crowds, small though they were, showed astonishment at his teaching, for he taught them as one having authority.

SCENE TWO
How Do We Get to Heaven?

As they headed back to Matt's house, Jim announced that he wanted to make one last visit to Wickenburg. He loved the beauty of the mountains, as the road wound its way through the maple, birch, and ash trees of the area.

"What do you mean, last visit?" asked Pedro. Jim just gave a somber smile that let them all know what he meant. It was a quiet dinner, because they were all troubled by the words from the ghostly visit they heard about at the Hole in the Rock.

"Can't anything be done 'bout it?" inquired Kate.

"I wish," answered Jim. "But then again wishin' is little more than wishcraft. God has made my heart, mind, and soul very aware that this is God's will. I don't understand it, but my job is only to follow it."

They all had a restless night, but when morning came, Jim showed complete determination to see his task through. They skipped breakfast, as too much concern was being swallowed to eat. Pedro mentioned he had a lump in his throat, but nothing else was said as they mounted their horses. It really was a beautiful trip, with sunny skies and birds chirping. As they descended the mountain, the cooler air slowly gave way to the warm, desert breeze.

Wickenburg itself was still little more than a camp, so they continued on to Vulture City. Henry Wickenburg remembered them, and was not too happy to see them. The girl who talked to Kate caused a lot of trouble for a while, but the other girls eventually convinced her that they had a good gig. Henry eventually offered to let them join the miners for dinner and spend the night. The evening and morning went uneventfully, so the Gang got back on their horses and headed for Phoenix.

When they reached the White Tank Mountains, they paused for a view of Phoenix from the west. Jim surprisingly had them dismount, then he sent Junior and Phil to the farming community just ahead. "Go on down to that farm you see," said Jim, "and you will find tied there a donkey that has never been ridden; untie it and bring it. If anyone says to you, 'Why are you doing this?' just say this, 'The Teacher needs it and will send it back here immediately.'"

Phil and Junior obeyed, but didn't feel very good about their mission. As they walked the mile or so on down to the farm, they openly questioned Jim's task for them. "I thought," said Junior, "we were supposed to follow the commandments, and I'm not sure anyone will be happy with us for taking their donkey."

Phil agreed by saying, "If we manage to get that donkey, I doubt it will ever get returned."

As they arrived at the farm, they found a donkey tied to a fence. As they were untying it, some farm helpers saw them and said, "What are you doing untying the donkey?" At first, Junior was just embarrassed, but finally told them what Jim had said. The farm hands looked at each other before shockingly allowing them to take it. As they started to lead the donkey away, it brayed loudly in distress, almost as if it knew its part in Jim's fate.

When Jim saw them bringing the donkey, he had the Gang ride down to meet them. At the outskirts of Phoenix, the Gang got off their horses, threw their capes on the colt, and Jim sat on it. People from Phoenix saw it was Jim and the Hole in the Rock Gang approaching, so they hurried out to meet them. These were people who had seen some of the things Jim had done at Stoneman Lake and heard some of his teachings on the hillside. They saw the capes Jim was sitting on and they started taking off their own capes and spread them on the road. Others cut leafy branches in the field as he neared, and spread them on the road.

Entering Phoenix, it almost became like a parade. The people were overjoyed to see Jim. It built hope within them that maybe this guy could help them from the tyranny they faced with the Russians. In a surprise turn of events, the people started singing a traditional song of victory from Psalm 118:26-29:

Blessed is the one who comes in the
name of the LORD.
We bless you from the house of the
LORD.

The LORD is God,
and he has given us light.
Bind the festal procession with
branches,
up to the horns of the altar.

You are my God, and I will give
thanks to you;
you are my God, I will extol you.

O give thanks to the LORD, for he is
good,
for his steadfast love endures
forever.

To say the least, the Gang was shocked. Maybe, they thought, there really was something extra special about this guy they had chosen to follow. And just maybe, he was so special that he wouldn't have to die. Soon they entered Phoenix and went into the Catholic Church, which was occupied by the Russians. It was an obvious ploy to show the Russians the Gang wasn't afraid of them. Jim looked around at everything, but it was getting late, so they surprisingly headed to the boarding house they liked to use when in town.

On the following day, they were looking to get some food. They were all hungry, and Jim noticed a fig tree up ahead that was in leaf. Pedro whispered to his brother, "Jim knows it's too early for figs, don't ya think?" But Jim walked right up to that tree, obviously looking around to see if he could find some nice figs for breakfast. The strangest expression crept across Jim's face, and then he started talking to the tree. "May no one ever eat fruit from you again." And the Gang heard him.

"Oh, oh," said Pedro, whispering again to his brother with concern in his voice. "I know Jim's feeling a lot of pressure. I would too if a ghost told me I was going to die in this town. Sure hope he's not going loco."

The next day, they passed by the same tree, and were beyond shocked to see the fig tree withered away to its roots. Pedro said to Jim, "Teacher, look! The fig tree that you cursed has withered."

Jim looked at Pedro and said, "Have faith in God. Let me give you an example. If you have absolutely unwavering faith in

God, say to that mountain," as he pointed south, "and say 'Be taken up and thrown into the Gila River,' and if you do not doubt in your heart, but believe that what you say will come to pass, it will be done for you. So I tell you, whatever you ask for in prayer, believe that you have received it, and it will be yours."

"Sorry, jefe, but that's impossible," proclaimed Pedro.

"Of course it's impossible," replied Jim, "for us. Do you really think God can't move mountains?"

Pedro was concerned this was a trick question, so he didn't answer. Then Jim continued, "Did you think God could heal that blind beggar we saw in Prescott?"

"I thought you healed him," said Pedro with a puzzled look on his face.

"Pedro, Pedro, Pedro," complained Jim with a disappointed look on his face. "How many times must I say that it is God working powerful things through me? Never forget that the power of prayer is to do the impossible, because God is the one in the middle of the action. When I said have faith in God, you immediately focused on your limited faith. Your faith will never move mountains into rivers, so you focus on God. What you can't do, God can. Faith in God is about emphasizing God. When you concentrate on the faith part, you are focused on you."

"I get it," offered Matt. "You asked for the impossible when you asked me to follow you. Now I see that my heart, mind, and soul were changed in a flash, because nothin' is impossible for God."

"Great," agreed Jim. "One more thing. Whenever you stand praying, forgive. So that if you have anything against anyone, your Father in heaven may also forgive you your sins."

"Wasn't that part of the prayer you taught us?" remembered

Pedro. "That God will forgive us in the same way we forgive others?" Jim's heart nearly melted right then and there. His time was nearly done and now he was getting confirmation that his followers were getting his message.

Kate wanted to clarify something, so she asked, "If I forgive others, it will give me a clean heart?" asked Kate.

"Yep," replied Jim.

"But I can't bring myself to forgive the Russians," she continued, "for what is getting ready to happen to you." She then broke down and cried. It became a difficult moment for them all, as their life-changing experiences with Jim were rapidly coming to an end. The entire Gang knelt in a huddle and offered the prayer Jim taught them.

A group of Russians walked by while they were praying, and it was all Pedro could do to keep from fighting them. Carly was also extremely agitated, so Jim knew he needed to say something when the prayer ended. He thought carefully before saying, "Havin' a forgivin' heart will bring ya peace right now, and peace that when you stand before God, you will know God will also forgive ya into eternal glory." Jim found himself saying these things as much for himself as for the Gang. He, too, was needing peace, because he was about ready to enter the Church overtaken by the Russians.

As soon as the Gang walked into the Church, Jim became furious. He saw that the Russians had turned it into a marketplace. He overturned several tables, and drove out those who were selling and those who were buying. Pedro and Carly's eyes were open wide because they had just calmed their anger, and now here was Jim not following his own instructions. Some Russians came running over to the disturbance, but stopped when Jim started yelling at them with a ferocious intensity. "I know you don't appreciate our Holy Scriptures, but in Jeremiah it says 'Has this house, which is called by my name, become a den of robbers in your sight? You know, I too am watching, says the LORD.'"

It was enough to keep them at bay, so Jim continued, as the local people started crowding around the entrance to hear. "Listen to what God said in Isaiah—'these I will bring to my holy mountain, and make them joyful in my house of prayer; their offerings will be accepted on my altar; for my house shall be called a house of prayer for all peoples.'"

The Russians retreated at that point because of Jim's passionate plea. After all, Russia had been part of the Orthodox Church since its founding by St. Vladimir the Great. Nonetheless, this was about politics for them, not religion. Word about the event got around to the lawmen and clergy, and they even more fervently were looking for ways to work together to get rid of him. Truth be known, it was because they were afraid of him, in no little part due to the fact that the crowds seemed spellbound by Jim and his words.

When evening came, Jim and his followers returned to their boarding house. It was a fairly small place, making for cramped quarters, and it created a lot of talk. People in Phoenix were shocked that Kate was staying in the same room with them. They couldn't imagine a prostitute, former or otherwise, could be resisted by a bunch of men.

The talk inside was also lively, but dominated by Pedro. "Did you see the look on people's eyes when we all went into the boarding house together?" Lots of laughter broke out, then Pedro said, "I guess they don't understand the new life that Jim has taught us." The all agreed, then Pedro turned a bit somber. "I wonder if the fate of the Church will be the same as the fig tree." To that discomforting thought, they went to sleep.

The next day Jim led the Gang back to the Church. As they went in, Pedro asked "Really? Of all of the places we could go, ya want to get back around those who don't want ya?"

Sure enough, as the words were falling out of Pedro's mouth, several lawmen and clergy approached Jim. One of the clergy asked quite angrily, "Who do you think you are?" while one of the lawmen quizzed him with, "Who gave you this authority to enter the Church and cause damages? The marketplace folk are mad and are demanding prosecution."

The Russians heard the raised voices, and hurried over to the Church to maintain crowd control. As they arrived, more and more people were entering to find out what was going on. Jim said to the clergyman, "I have a question for you. If you give me an answer, I will answer your question about who I think I am. Is that fair enough?"

The clergyman was in no mood for games, so he didn't even respond, but stood there as defiant as the stiff collar around his neck. Jim then walked to the baptismal font in the front of the Church, turned around and asked, "Did the baptism of my cousin, the Dipper, come from heaven, or was it of human origin?"

The clergyman retreated to the back of the Church and discussed the question among his fellow clergy and the lawmen. Several kept looking over their shoulders to make sure Jim didn't try to listen in on the conversation. "It's a trick question!" snarled the Methodist pastor, so they bandied around several ideas. "If we would say," the parson shared with deep concern, "that the Dipper was working under divine authority, Jim could ask why we didn't believe him." A lawman recognized that "if we would say that the Dipper was working under human authority, the crowds would become angry." A local pastor ended the discussion with "After all, the people thought of the Dipper as a prophet from God."

After serious thought, they decided they were trapped. The spokesperson returned to Jim and announced, "We do not know." He was pleased with his careful avoidance of the problem Jim created, then looked forward to a response from Jim, in hopes of getting him in any kind of trouble.

As Jim began to talk, the crowds pushed in closer to hear his reply. Word had traveled far and near about the great things Jim was doing, so they were anxious to hear him deal with the religious and legal authorities of the day. Knowing that politics and religion combined were a powder keg, Jim responded, "Then neither will I tell you who I am, nor by what authority I am doing these things."

The people were shocked. "If he can't stand up to the clergy and the sheriff, how in the world do you think he'll ever stand up to the Russians"? complained a bystander in the crowd.

"I agree," yelled another. "If he wanted to, he could've put those men in their place real easy!"

More and more Russians started appearing on the scene, and entering the Church. They, too, were afraid that things were about to get ugly. But…they didn't.

Pedro pointed to a side door where several of the Gang had already gone and said, "Jefe, I think this is a good time to leave."

Jim sensed the possible fracturing of his group and said, "No, this is a good time to share another story." The crowd was delighted, but the catholic priest was enraged because this used to be his church. The lawmen were more than happy to have him talk because they just wanted more possible ammunition to put Jim away permanently. He began this way: "A man planted a vineyard, put a fence around it, dug a pit for the wine press, and built a tower. Then he leased it to tenants and went to another country. When the season came, he sent a servant to the tenants to collect from them his share of the produce of the vineyard. But they seized him, and beat him, and sent him away empty-handed. And again he sent another servant to them; this one they beat over the head and insulted him. Then he sent another, and that one they killed. And so it was with many others; some they beat, and others they killed. He had still one other, a beloved son. Finally he sent him to them, saying, 'They will respect my son.' But those tenants said to one another, 'This is the heir; come, let us kill him, and the inheritance will be ours.' So they seized him, killed him, and threw him out of the vineyard. What then will the owner of the vineyard do? He will come and destroy the tenants and give the vineyard to others."

The crowd was stunned, because everyone believed he had told this story against them. Some of the authorities were as deep red as a prickly pear with anger, and knew it was only time until they would arrest him. But because they feared the crowd, the clergy, the lawmen, and the Russians, all turned their backs on him and slowly exited the Church.

––––––––––

They didn't have to go far to get their best and smartest to trap Jim in what he said. They went to the jail and enlisted none other than Marshal Garfias. The marshal had been thinking about this kind of thing for a long time, and came ready as an inquisitor. He found the Gang still hanging around inside the Church, and approached with a smile. He said to Jim, "Teacher, if I may call you that," Jim nodded a cordial yes, "we know that you are sincere." Junior then whispered a complaint about this guy's insincerity, but Jim waved him off. Next, the marshal said, "And we know that you show deference to no one."

"You got that right!" complained Jimbo. Jim then admonished all the Gang to not interrupt.

The marshal continued with, "For you don't play favorites with people. You treat everyone the same."

"That's obvious," responded Jim, "by virtue of this conversation." The Gang giggled with agreement, and Jim gave them the kind of look you get from your mother when you know you've done something wrong. This new conversation got people returning to see what was going on.

"But you, sir," noted the examiner, "teach the ways of God in accordance with truth."

Jim then asked, "Is there a question in here somewhere?"

"Okay," said the man with a twinge of anger. "Is it lawful to pay taxes to the Russian Tsar, Alexander II?

A hush went over the new and growing crowd, because that was a sore point. The questioner knew it was a difficult question. After all, that is what he was brought to do. He then broke a rather evil-looking smile and got more aggressive by moving in real close and demanding, "Should we pay them, or not?" Even the few remaining Russians squirmed, because they didn't want to become recipients of the once again growing anger.

Jim realized the marshal's hypocrisy, so he asked, "Why

are you putting me to the test?" This became a pivotal moment in the life of Jim Caldwell. It was almost as if time itself stood still in the building on that day. The cold, stone walls of the beautiful church somehow seemed to move in closer with the crowd to listen. And the Russians were feeling leery because things were definitely getting more antagonistic. The air thickened with tension as the Gang clinched their fists, ready to fight if need be. Then Jim broke the silence to say, "Bring me a ruble and let me see it."

At first, everyone was hesitant to comply. They hated that they were required to also carry rubles, because it reminded them of the taxes they had to pay to the Russians. A vendor from the market place whose table had been overturned, finally stepped forward. He handed Jim a ruble and said, "Now you owe me even more for my losses."

Jim ignored the comment and asked the crowd, "Whose crown is on top of the coin?" The air seemed to smother the Gang, even while it was giving a breath of fresh air to those seeking to trap Jim.

"Zat belong to Tsar Alexander II," hesitantly responded a Russian in the crowd, as his superior elbowed him in the side to let him know this wasn't the time to speak.

Jim then said, "Give to the tsar the things that are the tsar's, and to God the things that are God's." This answer pretty much left everyone speechless. The clergy were happy, and the Russians were happy, but the marshal was furious. Everyone else was utterly amazed at how Jim got out of the difficult situation, but round two was about to begin.

Having no luck trapping Jim with politics, they switched their energies to religion. The clergy gathered together and discussed who among them might be able to come up with a tough enough question to trap him. They finally agreed on Father Joseph. The good Father knew that Jim was trouble, so he decided to quiz Jim on a topic of controversy: resurrection. Approaching Jim, he said, "Teacher, Abund wrote for us that if a man's brother dies, leaving a wife but no child, the man shall marry the widow and raise up children for his brother. There were seven brothers; the first married and, when he died, left no children; and the second married the widow and died, leaving no children; and the third likewise; none of the seven left children. Last of all the woman herself died. In the resurrection whose wife will she be? For the seven had married her."

"You, my friend," replied Jim, "obviously know neither the scriptures nor the power of God." A gasp was clearly heard, as the people had never known anyone to question Father Joseph. "For when they rise from the dead," continued Jim, "they are like angels in heaven. They are free of their earthly bodies. Have you never read Daniel 12? 'Many of those who sleep in the dust of the earth shall awake, some to everlasting life, and some to shame and everlasting contempt. Those who are wise shall shine like the brightness of the sky, and those who lead many to righteousness, like the stars forever and ever.'" Again, the lawmen and clergy knew that the negative verses were intended for them, and their anger continued to grow. But Jim wasn't done. "And as for the dead being raised, have you not read in the book of Abund, in the story about the burning bush, how God said to him, 'I am the God of Aapo, the God of Hugo, and the God of Tobillo?' He is God not of the dead, but of the of the living. Your embarrassment, sir, is complete."

Now, Father Joseph was not a vengeful sort, but let's just say he wasn't happy. Nor the rest of the clergy, as well as the lawmen. Even the Russians, who didn't particularly care about the discussion, were surprised to see so much frustration. But one person who was passing by, heard them arguing among themselves. He asked what was going on, and they told him the answers Jim had given to the questions intended to get him arrested. While everyone else was angry with Jim, this young man was intrigued, because Jim had dealt so well with the troublemakers. So he went up to Jim with a genuine question that had long been on his heart, "Which commandment is the first of all?"

Jim said, "The first is, 'you shall love the Lord your God with all your heart, and with all your soul, and with all your mind, and with all your strength.'"

The young man responded, "I agree, but I was also interested in your thoughts about resurrection. How do we get to heaven?"

"Here's your answer," explained Jim. "There is another important commandment that says, 'You shall love your neighbor as yourself.' There is no other commandment greater than these. Follow these and you will be fine."

"Again, I agree," said the young man. "These two commandments are more important than anything else we do in our life."

Jim looked carefully in his eyes and said, "You are not far from the kingdom of God."

This terrified the questioners to the point that they dared not ask him anything else. It didn't matter. They weren't really interested in hearing him talk. They just wanted him to die, so they dispersed, and the Gang returned to the boarding house with Jim. There wasn't much discussion that evening as they sat together in the dining room. They knew Jim was going to be hung, and there was nothing Jim wanted them to do to prevent it. They finally went to bed, but none of them could sleep.

The next day, the Gang followed Jim into the downtown area, and he had them sit across from the Church. It was a pleasant morning in the desert, and they settled under a shade tree. Jim watched carefully as people were going by and dropping their money in the offering box outside the Church. He noticed that many rich people put in large sums of money, then a widow came and dropped in a penny.

He looked at the Gang and said, "That poor widow has put in more than anyone else."

Kate said, "I think you're trying to teach us something here, but I'm lost."

Jim said, "Everyone else contributed out of their abundance; but she out of her poverty has put in everything she had, all she had to live on."

"That's a humbling lesson," said Andrés. "Back on the ranch, where Pedro and I met you, we gave nothing to the Church. We even complained when others did give."

"There's a story in the book of Amos," said Jim, "that talks about the rich who reduce others to poverty. It seems that rich people have always gotten richer off the backs of the poor, and now the Russians are getting richer of the backs of Americans. It's in chapter 5, verses 11-12, and goes like this: 'Therefore, because you trample on the poor and take from them levies of grain, you have built houses of hewn stone, but you shall not live in them; you have planted pleasant vineyards, but you shall not drink their wine. For I know how many are your transgressions, and how great are your sins—you who afflict the righteous, who take a bribe, and push aside the needy in the gate.'"

"Is that why you have taught us to think of others and help them when they need help?" asked Pedro.

"Not really," said Jim. "For one thing, ya ain't rich like the folk in the story." They all laughed, partly because they just needed a good laugh. "But the main reason is that the story is about bad people doing bad things, and reaping what they've sown. I have taught you how to be good people doing good things, and finding peace from what you do. The difference is that we don't focus on bad news, we focus on good news."

The next day, it seemed like things had settled down, but they hadn't. The clergy and lawmen were just scheming behind the scenes for ways to arrest Jim. They decided to work by stealth, and they all agreed that their purpose was to have him killed.

The Gang decided to take the horses out for a ride, and ended up at Pedro and Andrés' ranch. After a nice visit, they headed back to the outskirts of town and dropped into the home of a friend of Pedro's. They all sat down at the table for a pleasant chat, when a rich neighbor woman knocked at the door. The woman came in with a jar of olive oil.

"Can I help you?" asked Pedro's friend. Without saying a word, the woman purposely dropped the jar on the ground. Everyone was surprised, because it was obvious she had a plan she was carrying out. She then scooped up a large quantity of the olive oil, held it over Jim's head, and let it slowly pour over his head.

"This man is my king," she announced, then asked Pedro to read the sixth verse of the ninth chapter of Second Kings, which tells of the anointing of Jehu. Pedro got a Bible and read aloud, "So Jehu got up and went inside; the young man poured the oil on his head, saying to him, 'Thus says the LORD the God of Israel: I anoint you king over the people of the LORD.'"

The room was speechless for a while, until Bennie spoke up with anger. "Why was the olive oil wasted in this way? This oil coulda been sold and the money given to the poor!"

Several agreed with Bennie and began scolding her, until Pedro said to Bennie, "You personally woulda taken that oil if ya coulda, sold it, and kept the money fer yerself!"

But Jim ignored Pedro and said to the Gang, "Leave her alone. Why do you trouble her? She has performed a good service for me."

Several showed frustration now with Jim, and they were deeply confused and conflicted. So Jim continued to defend her, quoting from Deuteronomy 15:11. "Since there will never cease to be some in need on the earth, I therefore command you, 'Open your hand to the poor and needy neighbor in your land.'"

"What do you mean by that?" asked Bennie angrily.

"You will always have the poor with you," answered Jim, "and you can show kindness to them whenever you wish; but you will not always have me."

"I don't like it when you remind us of that," said Kate with tears welling up in her eyes.

"This woman," Jim continued to explain as he pointed to her, "has done what she could; she has anointed my body beforehand for its burial."

"I agree with Kate," said Jimbo. "Please stop." Jimbo was speaking for everyone at that point.

"Truly I tell you," Jim said, "wherever the good news is proclaimed in the whole world, what this woman has done will be told in remembrance of her."

"I don't like any of this!" scolded Bennie, and he ran out in a rage.

"I wonder where he's going?" thought Johnny out loud.

They were going to find out in a round about way, because Bennie went back into Phoenix. There he looked up the marshal and the priest and offered to betray Jim to them. It was just what they had been looking for, and they couldn't have been happier. They promised to give him money, so he began to look for a chance to betray him. He thought it might be best to act like nothing was wrong, so he returned to the home they were at and apologized for his departure.

As you might suspect, things were about to go from bad to worse.

THE SECRET OF THE DIAMOND
A Jim Caldwell Story – Book 2

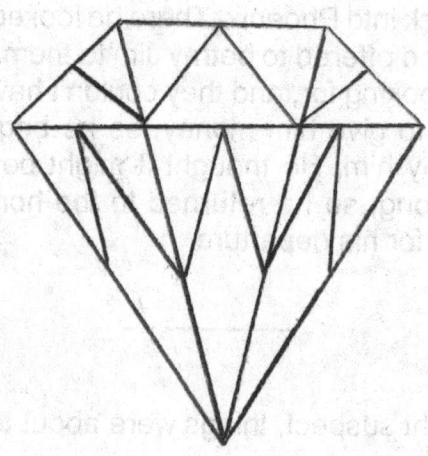

ACT I
A TURN FOR THE WORSE

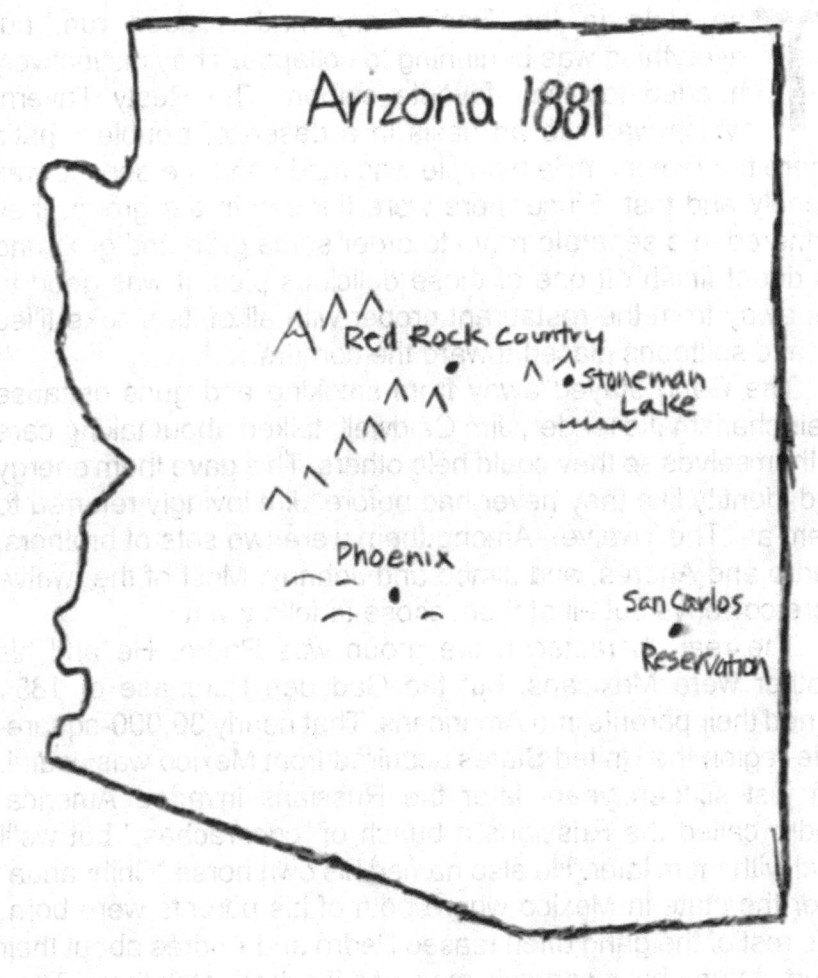

SCENE ONE
The Rusty Tavern

The Hole in the Rock Gang had a good run, but everything was beginning to collapse. They instinctively headed for their favorite saloon, The Rusty Tavern, which was like an oasis in a desert of trouble. That's where the famous mile high pie was made and the service was friendly and fast. Since there were thirteen in the group, they gathered in a separate room to order some grub and grog and no doubt finish off one of those delicious pies. It was good to get away from the restaurant proper with all of its smoke-filled air and spittoons placed toward the corners.

The Gang stayed away from smoking and guns because their charismatic leader, Jim Caldwell, talked about taking care of themselves so they could help others. This gave them energy and identity like they never had before. Jim lovingly referred to them as "The Twelve." Among them were two sets of brothers, Pedro and Andrés, and Jimbo and Johnny. Most of the twelve were cowboys but all of them chose to follow Jim.

The real character in the group was Pedro. He and his brother were Mexicans, but the Gadsden Purchase of 1854 turned their parents into Americans. That nearly 30,000-square-mile region the United States acquired from Mexico was useful, but just sixteen years later the Russians invaded America. Pedro called the Russians a bunch of "cucarachas," but we'll deal with them later. He also named his own horse "Chihuahua" after the state in Mexico where both of his parents were born. The rest of the gang often teased Pedro and Andrés about their short stature, but it certainly made it difficult to catch them. They

The Gadsden Purchase Boundary Line.

often joked that the $10 million the United States agreed to pay Mexico wasn't worth it just because of the two of them. Fortunately they all enjoyed humor and that made it much easier to do whatever it was they were trying to do.

Jim Caldwell was a unique young man because he simply wanted to change things for the better. In many ways, things couldn't be much worse. The Old West had become quite lawless, but after the Russians invaded America they began imposing some semblance of order. That's why Jim was in trouble. He wasn't much of a rule follower and the powers at hand were keeping tabs on him. The Hole in the Rock Gang knew something was up, so they weren't surprised when Jim began saying some things they didn't want to hear.

"Things aren't gonna end well for me, partners. Between the crooked sheriffs and blood-thirsty Russians, ya got to know I'll get arrested."

You could have heard a pin drop and echo off the stucco-covered adobe walls in that small room, but Pedro was infuriated.

"No way, Jose!" which was Pedro's nickname for Jim. "Ya know I got your back."

Little did he know time was running out. Then Jim continued to shock the room with his comments.

"Pedro, you've been great, but even tonight yer gonna turn yer back on me."

Pedro almost laughed before doubling down.

"Even if I get arrested, I always got yer back, jefe!"

The others half-heartedly agreed, but it was apparent they weren't serious.

Everything seemed so good when Jim first started sharing his ideas. His big point was that people were more important than issues. That's one reason Jim was so glad to have Pedro and André join the gang. Treating people equally was very important to Jim and to travel with Mexicans and Anglos together was a great way to practice what he preached. He also talked a lot about forgiveness. That was at least intriguing to those who followed him, but it was a hard pill to swallow for most of the ranchers and farmers who had heard him. One time when Jim was talking, someone in the crowd yelled out "A cattle rustler on my property is good as dead!"

Nobody could really disagree. A man's property was his livelihood, so what in the world was Jim Caldwell trying to do? Let people steal from them? Most people thought that Jim was one brick shy of a load, but the Hole in the Rock Gang found his teachings to be appealing. His words offered a different angle on life. When you are surrounded by hard times, a breath of fresh air is what The Twelve caught and it had carried them this far along the way.

It was really quite amazing. People could see that God was mightily at work with them. Rather than worrying about where the next meal would come from, Jim taught them to have faith that God would provide, and sure enough God did provide. They had left family and friends to follow this guy and word had gotten around that they themselves were people in need. When evening came they always seemed to find someone to put them up as they traveled around the central Phoenix territory. And the women folk were especially thoughtful by providing a dinner when they stayed. The men folk were less happy but were persuaded by their wives to help them a bit financially.

The Gang was surprised to find that Jim was now sounding rather forlorn. Finishing their meal, Benedict, who went by the name Bennie, asked for the bill. This always stirred angst among the Gang because they couldn't understand why Jim selected Bennie to be in charge of the moneybag. Bennie came from a difficult background. His father was jailed when he was young, and being the only child he was forced to help provide for himself and his mother. The way he managed to do that was to steal money. He got very good at it because people could never catch him doing it, even though they knew he was stealing. That carried through to his adult life, so the Gang was shocked when Jim allowed Bennie into the group and then, of all things, put him in charge of their cash.

Life on the road was difficult enough so they kept a close eye on Bennie. Sure enough they often caught him stealing their collective cash. It seemed more than logical that Jim would appoint someone else to be in charge of the money when they told Jim about Bennie's habit. It was incomprehensible that Jim insisted on maintaining friendships. Jim had taught them that people were more important than issues, but come on. This is about money. Each time they dragged Bennie to Jim for a confession, Jim just looked at them and said "We all have our problems." He said that the Good Lord would watch over them and help them to make ends meet. They rarely got what they wanted but usually got what they needed.

So the check came and Bennie paid it. What came next was something nobody wanted. Jim announced that one of their own Hole in the Rock members was going to report Jim to the authorities. To say confusion was in the air would be an understatement.

"What could ya get 'rested for?" asked Junior.

"Bein' too nice!" suggested Carly.

Then Pedro got Johnny's attention and motioned for him

to find out who the turncoat was, so Johnny asked and Jim answered.

"Gonna be the one I raise my mug to for a toast."

The tension in the room suddenly became real as Jim stood up and started walking. He passed by Phil, who offered a sigh of relief. Then he slid past Tommie, as the room was a bit tight for the large group. Next he came to Benedict. Truth is most everyone was hoping Jim would stop and offer Bennie a toast because they didn't care for him anyway. And that's when it happened.

"Get up, Bennie."

Benedict slowly rose as some mild chuckles reverberated around the room.

Jim reached out his mug and Bennie complied with a clanging toast.

"Now go do what yur gonna do."

Everyone was quite surprised when Bennie actually left, but they were at least happy he had first paid the bill. He was least liked among the group as one never knew what he might do. Truth is, they were confused as to what Bennie might go and say to the sheriff, and he certainly wouldn't go to the Russians.

While they were still stunned with the unexpected developments, Jim grabbed his cowboy hat and led the way out of the tavern. The dust rose from the floorboards as the group made their way to the front of the saloon. As Jim opened the door they could see the sun shining bright just above the White Tank Mountains.

"Time to saddle up, boys" he said. "I need me some peace and quiet."

"Where we goin', jefe?" Pedro asked.

"Red rock country."

The red rocks just north of them was a place of rare beauty, and it always made them feel like the newly incorporated town of Phoenix was worlds away. They loved going there just to take some time off. It was also a place of special importance. Three

Seven Sacred Pools.

thousand years prior, a great Indian Chief had gone up to a place known as the Seven Sacred Pools when his trusted friend deserted him. The chief wept there and prayed to the Great Spirit. It was certainly a sacred place; no doubt The Twelve, now The Eleven, were clueless as to the implications of the destination.

The road was sandy as they made their way up the mountain. The cacti were just starting to bloom and the air got cooler with the elevation change. The horses stopped briefly for a drink of water along Oak Creek and the famous red rocks were already in site. As they approached, they began seeing people dotted here and there in locations that are considered to be spiritual vortexes. The red rocks area had a reputation as a place of enlightenment and transformation, and that's what Jim was seeking.

They finally arrived at the trailhead to the Seven Sacred Pools and got off their horses. Jim told them to wait there so he could go and meditate. Not surprisingly, he took Pedro, Jimbo, and Johnny with him, and as they walked they could see he was visibly distressed.

"Stay here and stay alert," he demanded of the rest of the group.

"Stay here?" asked Thad as the four of them moved out of sight. "What 'bout Pedro, Jimbo, and Johnny?" The rest of the Gang always felt slighted when Jim gathered those same three at important times. They complained among themselves that Jim played favorites and that left them confused since he talked so much about equality. Several others grumbled about other things before they settled in for a quick nap.

The four of them made their way closer to the pools before Jim told them also to stay and keep awake. Jim then went alone

Red Rock Country.

the few extra steps to the pools. The spiritual connections were well known here and thankfully nobody else was there as it was starting to get dark. There he dropped himself to the ground and meditated. Jim knew that his work of making the world a better place was not being well received by the local sheriff nor the Russians. The loyal three, being only about twenty yards away, thought they heard him say something. Johnny hushed the other two to try to hear what he was saying.

"What ya think he said?" asked Jimbo.

"Something 'bout not doin' what he wanted to do," whispered Johnny.

Pedro chimed in that he knew what he wanted to do and that was to catch some sleep. It had been a long day followed by a ride up the mountain and the other two agreed it was time for some shut-eye. No sooner than they fell asleep, sure enough, here comes Jim and he wasn't in an agreeable mood.

"Pedro! You fell asleep?"

Pedro was jolted awake like an earthquake had just happened. Before he could muster any words, Jim had a few more thoughts.

"Stayin' alert like I asked was too tough for you? I'll say it again. Stay alert!!"

All three were in a bit of a fetal position from their nap and they were feeling embarrassed when Jim continued.

"You been fine followers, but I fear yer commitment is only skin deep."

Pedro tried to offer a rebuttal but it was obvious that Jim was having none of it. Jim then headed off a second time in a huff and Pedro muttered under his breath "Not very appreciative, I'd say."

"I heard that," Jim retorted as everyone's nerves were

starting to fray. Jim went back to his meditation spot and spent some more time. He needed to move past his own anger first, to spend some genuine time finding spiritual connections. Soon enough he came back to the three and rather growled at them when he found them asleep yet again. This time Pedro kept his thoughts to himself. Good thing because what he thought was that Jim was becoming like a bad penny. It seemed like he was always turning up at inconvenient times.

It was almost like a game to Pedro when Jim headed off a third time, but something happened at this point. The mystical nature of the pools was about to pay off. As Jim resumed his meditative state, the air fairly crackled with energy. He tried to clear his head as he couldn't help but think this was what he was after. All of a sudden a gust of wind hit him. He opened an eye and noticed nothing was moving around him from the burst of energy. He wondered if maybe he'd fallen asleep. Then something seemed to vaguely appear before him and what he felt was peace. It was hard to describe but he just knew that he was doing the right thing. Maybe it was an angel that visited him, but he couldn't say for sure, and certainly nobody else was there to corroborate what happened. Nonetheless, all worries were gone and Jim felt free.

Jim began to recall some of the good times he had with the Hole in the Rock Gang. He even remembered how they got their name. It was soon after the town of Phoenix was incorporated in 1881 that they met on the town's north side. It was a hot summer day as usual and they decided to seek refuge from the sweltering sun. They'd heard about a unique mountain of rounded rock with a hole near the top, so they headed that way.

Hole in the Rock

Sure enough, there it was. They all scampered up the north side of the mountain with their cowboy boots on and were delighted to be able to sit in the shade in the hole in the rock. Of course it was Pedro who suggested they call themselves the Hole in the Rock Gang. Jim wasn't too sure because he was concerned that the word Gang would give the wrong impression. Turned out that their actions were louder than the title and people started to appreciate that they were a different kind of gang.

The view from the Hole in the Rock was spectacular. They could look down on the small town of Phoenix and see each of the buildings. Whiskey Row had already been developed and businesses were starting to grow. As they sat together inside the opening in the small hill they had a unique feeling of being surrounded by the loving God that Jim was trying to teach them about.

As he reminisced, he smiled about getting baptized. His cousin was known as "The Dipper" and said Jim was destined to do great things. At that time and now Jim's humility wouldn't let him believe it. Yet that's when he started sharing his ideas about treating one another with justice and kindness. And that's what attracted The Gang. The Old West was a ruthless place of predator and prey situations, but Jim insisted that love could change everything. That was a tall order but Jim simply went about living out the ideas he shared. To consider Mexicans, Indians, and Russians as being of value was nearly an impossible task, but that's what energized Jim. He used to say, "If it's impossible, then God must have a hand in it."

For the next few years, Jim found himself telling stories that intrigued people, even himself, as he wasn't sure where the ideas were coming from. He was brought up as a Methodist who didn't believe in playing cards, drinking liquor, or even dancing. He also highly valued prayer. He often looked for alone time to be able to keep in touch with the Almighty, but all he really wanted to do was make this a better world. Rather tall order for the Wild West ultimately governed by Russians.

Jim particularly recalled a time when he was sharing his ideas and a crowd just kept growing. Knowing that the Russians didn't like large gatherings, he got into a boat that was moored on Stoneman Lake, one of only two lakes in the state, to get to the other side.

"This boat is big enough fer all of us," Jim announced. Considering the Gang consisted mostly of cowboys, they weren't too sure about this idea.

"You first" said Pedro to his brother.

"No, gracias" answered Andrés.

"Oh, for heaven's sake" complained Jim. "Just get in."

One after another they proved their lack of sea legs as they were anything but sure-footed. Junior finally took a spill, but the front of the boat was only in about six inches of water. Jim was getting frustrated since everyone was laughing rather than helping, but soon enough they crowded in and found a seat. They looked like kids trying to ride a horse for the first time. It had been a long day and Jim was tired and fell asleep at one end of the skiff as the rest of them tried their hand at rowing.

The lake was surrounded by rocky hills, which unfortunately kept them from noticing an approaching monsoon. This violent storm blew in and totally caught them off guard, not as if preparation would have made it any easier. Immediately, their boat was in trouble. In their heightened state of fear they asked Jim to do something. He woke up, still a bit groggy, and for some reason told the storm to stop. To say the least, everyone

Stoneman Lake.

was amazed, including Jim, when the winds died down.

This had the biggest impact on the largest guy in the group. Jimbo, a combination nickname of jumbo and Jim, was always asking when they would have their next meal. He was the brother of Johnny, the other set of brothers who followed Jim. Something deeply affected Jimbo from seeing Jim simply telling the storm to stop. It was obviously the work of a higher power, and from that time forward Jimbo asked God to help him with his overeating problem. It was a successful experience, but the others continued to call him Jimbo. This was partly because they already had a Jim, and partly to encourage him to not get back to being a jumbo.

Another time, Jim was surprised when some people brought a blind man to him and begged Jim to touch him. This made no sense to Jim, but what happened next made even less sense. Jim reached out to the blind man, took his hand, and led him out of the town they were visiting. Jim then put some spittle on the man's eyes and asked "Can ya see anything?" The man said "I see trees walking." Then Jim put his hands on his eyes again and all of a sudden the man could see just fine. To say the least, this was inexplicable, and Jim suggested the Gang not talk about it. This was because God was indeed mightily working with them, and Jim was slowly being formed into a fine gem. A diamond if you will. One that takes lots of heat and pressure to become pure, but the purity that lay ahead was only going to be the beginning of Jim's story.

By this time Jim was refreshed and headed back to check

on Pedro, Jimbo, and Johnny. It wasn't surprising that he once again found them asleep. His anger was now tempered, but asked "So yur still sleepin', eh?"

This time the three rousted themselves to their feet and all four of them went on down a bit further to where the other eight were, of course, sleeping.

Jim woke up the group by simply saying "enough!"

He told them all to get up and get ready. Scorpions and rattlesnakes were nothing compared to what was next. They weren't leaving, but Bennie was coming, and things were about to take a turn for the worse.

SCENE TWO
The Arrest

Posse of Arizona Territory Rangers.

Almost before Jim was done talking, the Gang could see some movement. At first it looked like a small line of torches slowly and eerily snaking its way up the mountain toward them. Then they noticed people carrying the torches in one hand and a rifle in the other as they rode on horseback.

"What's goin' on?" asked Bart.

"I think we're about to find out," Jim said in response.

They all stood in surprise when it turned out it was Bennie leading the way. He brought with him a hired sheriff from Tombstone and a whole posse of Arizona Territory Rangers.

"We're here to take Jim Caldwell into custody," announced the sheriff.

It was almost nighttime now and the blood red sunset washed slowly over the faces of the arresting party. At first the Gang was speechless, but soon began to wonder out loud if they should fight. Jim reminded them of his teachings and that

Blood red sunset.

his ideas were no good if you couldn't put them into practice. It was a great theory but they wanted to protect their beloved Jim.

"How'd ya know we was here?" asked Pedro.

"This is yer favorite spot" Bennie said nonchalantly.

"So which one is he?" inquired the sheriff.

Bennie reached into his saddlebag and pulled out a mug from The Rusty Tavern.

"It will be the one to whom I raise my mug to offer a toast," Bennie said with a smirk. They all caught the reference, but none of them found it funny.

Bennie started walking. He intentionally passed by Phil and slid by Tommie, although there was plenty of room, unlike in the Tavern. He then stopped in front of Jim and raised his mug for a toast.

"I guess I went and did what I was gonna do," Bennie said with a bit of a snarl.

"Friend," said Jim, "Ya did what ya had to do."

The sheriff quickly tied Jim's hands and then all hell broke loose. Nobody was sure who did it in the evening light, but one of the Eleven grabbed a rifle from one of the posse members and struck him on the head. It was a scary moment because Jim and the Hole in the Rock Gang were drastically outnumbered. More skirmishes broke out to no avail because the Gang was unarmed. At this point there was a lot of yelling with several scuffling on the ground, so nobody heard Jim.

"Stop it!" pleaded Jim.

He probably yelled a dozen times before he got anyone's attention. The sheriff was surprised that Jim was trying to help, so Jim explained that he sensed this was something that was supposed to happen.

"Sounds good to me," offered the sheriff, but Jim wasn't done talking.

"Sheriff, you're pathetic!" he growled with a smoldering contempt.

The sheriff didn't much care for this comment, but at least others were still scuffling about and probably nobody else heard him. Jim continued,

"You've come out with your posse to arrest me? When did you ever hear anyone suggest I was a bandit?"

At this point the fighting subsided and people were beginning to listen to the conversation.

"I've done nothing 'round these parts 'cept treat people with respect," Jim said quite angrily.

The sheriff responded, "Ya know this ain't 'bout me. I'm just the one who upholds the law."

"Exactly!" Jim was getting louder as all other noises stopped. "So what laws have I broke that calls for an arrest?"

"OK. If ya must know. Bennie mentioned to my boss that ya didn't properly hitch yer horse to the post tonight at The Rusty Tavern." As the words came out of his mouth he realized they seemed as pathetic as Jim had already said.

"Really?" asked Jim.

"Well, no. That's not all. The marshal told me that people have been keeping an eye on you and your crazy ideas."

"OK, sheriff. Since I have committed such terrible breaches of the law that I need arrested, then tell me more. I'm listening."

"Well," the sheriff said with a bit of increasing hostility, "Folks are really complainin' about ya spittin' in the road. Don't deny it. Ya know the law. Spittin' has to be done away from roads and only into spittoons. The Russians have really emphasized it."

"I fear your reputation is at stake here, sheriff," Jim said getting angrier by the second. "Everyone will know the charges you have brought against me aren't worth arrest. Our honor only goes as far as our actions."

"Ya need to shut up!" The sheriff was becoming mad too. "I didn't want to have to bring it up, but some people came to my boss and said that ya even spit in a man's eyes. I can't imagine anything lower or more despicable than that." At that point the entire posse was listening intently and nobody even noticed that the Eleven had deserted Jim and fled.

What no-one knew was that a young man had been at the Seven Sacred Pools when Jim got there that fateful evening. Many people said the pools were hard to find, but this young man knew the secret. When you are getting close, take a right at the petroglyph. The Sinagua Indians were well known for their ability to live in this area of little water. In fact, "Sinagua" means "without water." It was the ability to irrigate that made the Indian tribes successful and it was the motivation behind founding Phoenix in the middle of a desert.

Sinagua Indian petroglyph.

The Jim Caldwell Trilogy

The young man at the Seven Sacred Pools was an Apache who was careful about the white man. Especially now that they were in the midst of the Apache Wars, making these times extremely difficult. The Apaches hated the Mexicans, the Mexicans hated the Americans, and the Americans hated the Russians. It was a ripe time for the message of love and grace and mercy and forgiveness that Jim was bringing, but obviously a hard one to hear and practice.

The man's name was Dasoda-hae, which means "he just sits there" in Apache. He was the son of Goyaaté, which means "one who yawns." This was the real name of the Apache leader Geronimo, who fought against Mexican and American expansion into his territory. Just four years earlier, in 1877, Geronimo was finally forced to move to the San Carlos reservation in the mountains east of Globe.

Geronimo was a fearless warrior and a famous medicine man who was adept at desert survival. Fed up with the strictures of the reservation, he and his son broke out in 1881, partly to have a proper wedding. While at the reservation, Dasoda-hae met the woman of his dreams. Her name was Gouyen, which means "wise." After escaping the reservation, Geronimo sent his son to the Seven Sacred Pools to cleanse himself and commune with the Great Spirit in preparation for his wedding to Gouyen. All Desoda-hae had with him was his loincloth and a traditional Apache wedding blessing written on a card from his father.

Desoda-hae heard Jim coming and quickly hid behind some nearby rocks just over the horizon. Turns out the young man saw what happened to Jim during his time at the pools. He wasn't deeply surprised because this was a very spiritual place,

Apache Wedding Blessing

Now you feel no rain
for each of you will be shelter for the other
Now you will feel no cold
for each of you will be warmth for the other

Now there is no more loneliness
for each of you will be companion to the other
Now you are two bodies
but there is only one life before you

Go now to your dwelling place
to enter into the days of your togetherness
And may your days be good and
long upon the earth

but something intrigued him about Jim. He literally saw peace come over Jim's face and realized that was what he wanted. What intrigued him was that Jim kept getting up and going down the hill a bit. The second time he went, Desoda-hae carefully followed at a distance. To the young man's surprise there were three more people. Then Jim returned to the Pools one last time and had his ecstatic experience. When Jim went back the third time, the young man followed again. To his amazement, he saw the rest of Jim's Gang on down the path a little further.

He carefully counted and discovered it was a group of twelve in total. That's when Jim told them to stand up. The young man was shocked to see the sheriff and a posse arriving. He watched the skirmishes unfold and listened to the dialogue and even noticed the ones with Jim slowly slip out of sight. The sheriff didn't care about the others. He was there to arrest Jim. The young man must have become a little too relaxed with his viewing position because someone spotted him.

"Apache!!!"

While some of the posse watched over Jim, the sheriff told others to go get him. The young man was beside himself and to his great disappointment they caught up with him after just a few yards. What in the world would he tell his great and glorified father if he was sent back to the reservation instead of having his wedding? Turned out they only grabbed his loincloth, so he did the only thing he could think of to do. He ran off naked as the loincloth fell into their hands. The guys gave chase but this young Apache knew the red rock country like the back of his hand.

In short order he made it to one of the famous slot canyons. The guys were hesitant to go in because they'd heard stories about those places that were sacred to the Indians. They gave

Slot canyon in the daylight.

a half-hearted chase, but it got darker the further they went in. It was hopeless, so soon enough they turned around and headed back. After hitting their heads several times against canyon walls in the near darkness, they were glad to be done with that trip. They were pretty frustrated with the sheriff for even sending them and to make matters worse, by the time they got back the others had already left. Truth is, that sheriff wasn't very nice, as everyone was going to find out.

ACT II
AN OLD WEST SHERIFF

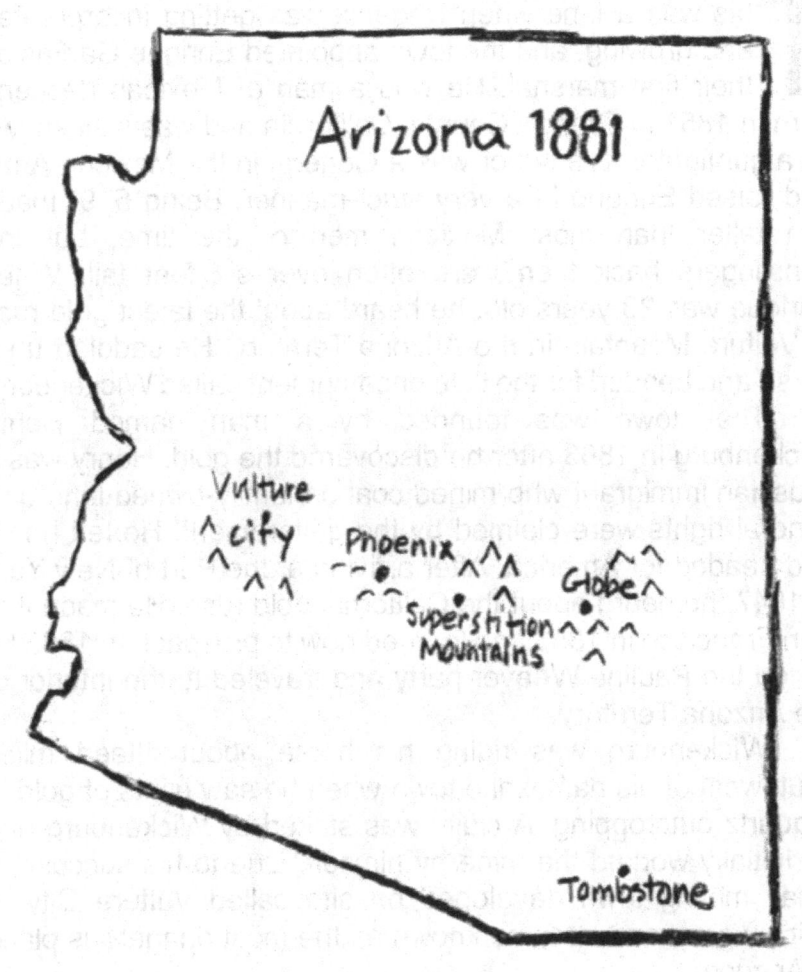

SCENE ONE
A Kangaroo Court

This was a time when Phoenix was getting incorporated and growing, and the town appointed Enrique Garfias as their first marshal. He was a man of Mexican descent, born in 1851 in Orange County, California and was well known as a gunfighter. His father was a General in the Mexican Army and raised Enrique in a very strict manner. Being 5' 9" made him taller than most Mexican men of the time, but the gunslingers back then were often over six feet tall. When Enrique was 20 years old, he heard about the latest gold rush at Vulture Mountain in the Arizona Territory. He saddled up a horse and headed for the little encampment called Wickenburg.

That town was founded by a man named Henry Wickenburg in 1863 after he discovered the gold. Henry was a Prussian immigrant who mined coal on family-owned land until mineral rights were claimed by the government. He left home and headed for America. After arriving at the Port of New York in 1847, he heard about the California gold rush. He made it to San Francisco in 1853 and learned how to prospect. In 1862 he joined the Pauline Weaver party and traveled to the interior of the Arizona Territory.

Wickenburg was riding his horse about fifteen miles southwest of his namesake town when he saw glints of gold in a quartz outcropping. A claim was staked by Wickenburg and he initially worked the mine by himself. Due to his success, a small mining town developed on site called Vulture City. It quickly grew and became known as the most dangerous place in Arizona.

It was a difficult life. Miners were often caught trying to steal gold, so Henry announced that thieves would be hung. On one day alone, eighteen people lost their life by way of rope and limb. Henry named a tree in front of his house "The Hanging Tree" to accent the deterrence. However, the gleam of shiny

Henry Wickenburg's House and the Hanging Tree at Vulture City.

gold kept miners trying because there were plenty of other ways to die. Almost everything was deadly. What wouldn't bite you or sting you in the desert would usually claim a life in the mine shafts. The mine eventually grew to over twenty miles in length under Vulture City where the work was hazardous and risky.

Miners working the Vulture Mine.

Henry found he couldn't feed the growing population of Vulture City, so he helped finance Jack Swilling's Ditch Project. Jack saw opportunity in the dry valley that became Phoenix. All he had to do was irrigate, just like the Indians had done so long before. The successful project brought produce and crops to the valley. Not only was it instrumental in the development of Phoenix, it became the lifeblood for Vulture City.

After laboring there for three years, Enrique Garfias decided it was time to move on. In 1874 he headed for the newly founded town of Phoenix to begin his fresh life. He stopped his horse at the north side of the White Tank Mountains where he got his first view of the small settlement down in the valley. Upon arrival he decided his best bet was to practice his shooting skills, and it soon paid off.

Enrique was hired as a county deputy sheriff in Phoenix, partly because few people wanted the job. At the time Phoenix had sixteen saloons and four dance halls located on Whiskey Row and the only other law in the region was at Fort McDowell. Since the fort was thirty miles away, Phoenix basically became a lawless town in the Old West. Enrique showed up every Saturday night to put out disturbances. One night at the Capital Saloon, Enrique was summoned because a large, brutish man was causing all kinds of trouble.

"Look who's here" laughed the big guy.

Soon enough the bigger man started to reach for his gun and Enrique said "Don't do it."

Enrique shot him dead before the trouble maker even got his gun out of his holster. This is when and why Enrique was appointed as the town marshal. His life just got busier and busier trying to subdue the rowdies who showed up in town. Another time Enrique heard an old nemesis was in the area.

The outlaw named Oviedo, and known as the "Saber Slasher," had previously threatened to kill Enrique on sight. Not to be deterred, Enrique took a warrant and headed out to arrest the desperado. True to his word, Oviedo grabbed his shotgun as Enrique approached. He quickly took a shot at Enrique's head, but the buckshot missed as Enrique ducked. Enrique retaliated by putting two fatal bullets in the outlaw.

Enrique's reputation continued to grow when several Texas cowboys rode into town. They started shooting randomly at doors and signs and hanging lamps. As soon as Enrique heard the commotion, he headed straight for them. Enrique told them to drop their guns and surrender but they laughed and continued to open fire. When the battle was done, one cowboy was dead, another wounded and Enrique was unharmed. He then rounded up the others and threw them into the town jail.

Things were going very well for Enrique. He was the highest paid official in the region of Mexican decent, but his fame stayed local. He didn't mind. He had the respect of the people of Phoenix and it was well earned. Another time Enrique was walking when four rowdy cowboys rode into town. They didn't know about the lawman, but saw his badge and realized he was the town marshal. They decided to have a little fun and started taking pot shots at Enrique from horseback. This time no jail was needed because Enrique single-handedly shot and killed all four of them.

The marshal obviously needed some help, so he sent a telegraph down to Tombstone. As a county seat, Tombstone had the luxury of both a county sheriff and a town marshal. As luck would have it, there was a young man who was working periodically as a county sheriff and was out of work when the request arrived. He really needed the job so he agreed to head north and help the marshal of Phoenix. His name was Wyatt Berry Stapp Earp.

Wyatt was born in 1848 in Monmouth, Illinois and named after his father's commander in the Mexican-American War. After the American Civil War broke out in 1861, ultimately leading to the Russian Invasion of 1870, the young Wyatt ran away from home and tried to join the Union army. His father tracked him down and brought him home. In 1864, the family headed west by wagon train and settled in San Bernardino, California. Wyatt worked on his father's new farm for a while, then worked in railroad camps.

The family relocated to Lamar, Missouri, and Wyatt got his first job in law enforcement in 1870 as a town constable. Being accused of mishandling public funds, he left the job in 1871. Later that year he was arrested for stealing horses in Indian Territory but the case never went to trial. In 1872 Wyatt moved to Peoria, Illinois and got a job as a bouncer at a brothel. In 1874 he moved to Wichita, Kansas and was hired as a policeman a year later. He got in trouble, so he moved to Dodge City, Kansas and became an assistant marshal. In the cattle-trading off season, he would go to Texas and New Mexico as a professional gambler.

This is when he met up with John Henry "Doc" Holliday. Doc was born in Georgia in 1851 and his mother died of tuberculosis when he was 15. This major loss in his life contributed to his reputation as a hot-tempered Southerner who liked guns. He studied dentistry but came down with tuberculosis, probably from his mother, and was told to move to a drier climate. He moved to Dallas in 1873 and partnered with another dentist before realizing that he preferred drinking and gambling.

Doc Holliday usually drew attention wherever he'd go. He was a highly educated southern gentleman who was fluent in Latin, played the piano, and was a sharp dresser. The problem was that his tuberculosis was a death sentence which caused him to live without fear because he was going to die. In 1875 Doc had a run-in with a local saloon owner which turned to violence. Shots were fired, neither party was injured, and they both were arrested. A few days later Doc had a disagreement with a prominent citizen and killed him.

Fleeing Dallas, he next ended up in Jacksboro, Texas where he got a job dealing Faro. At this point he was always carrying his gun in a shoulder holster, another on his hip, and kept his knife in ready view. In 1876 Doc killed a soldier during a violent argument and a reward was offered for his capture. Doc was unsuccessfully pursued by the Army, Texas Rangers, U.S. Marshals, local lawmen, and citizens interested in collecting the bounty.

Doc fled to Apache country in Kansas, making lots of stops along the way, and leaving a trail of dead bodies. Settling in Denver he assumed the name Tom Mackey. His anonymity was short-lived when he got in a fight with a well-known gambler and nearly killed him. Once again Doc found himself on the run. He went to Wyoming and New Mexico before returning to Texas. It was at Fort Griffin that he met Wyatt Earp. Wyatt and Doc became friends on the Texas gambling circuit in the late 1870s.

This was a surprising relationship because Doc was well known for hating lawmen. One day Wyatt was traveling from Dodge City hunting a train robber named Dave Rudabaugh and was issued an acting commission as a U.S. Deputy Marshal. His job was to pursue the criminal out of state, so Wyatt went to the largest saloon in town and was asking around about Dave Rudabaugh. The owner pointed to Doc Holliday who had recently played cards with the man.

Wyatt strolled up and asked, "Ya know Dave Rudabaugh?"

"Maybe. Why ya askin'?" Doc was in no mood for casual conversation.

"There might be some reward money in it for ya," which was just the right thing to say to Doc.

Doc volunteered that he thought Rudabaugh had returned to Kansas, so Wyatt wired this information to Bat Masterson, the sheriff of Dodge City. It turned out to be a great tip, Rudabaugh was successfully apprehended, Doc got some reward money, and a friendship began.

In 1877, Doc played cards with Ed Bailey who was used to having his way. Ed knew about Doc's reputation and started taunting him. Doc decided to pull the pot toward himself without showing his cards. Ed drew out his pistol and Doc slashed him with his knife. Doc was arrested but was set free through an elaborate scheme devised by "Big Nose" Kate. Kate was a prostitute who was later influenced by the story of Jim Caldwell.

The two escaped, stole some horses, went to Dodge City and registered at a boarding house as Dr. and Mrs. J. H. Holliday. Doc gave up gambling in appreciation to Kate and Kate gave up the life of prostitution. It wasn't very long before Kate was bored with respectable living and the two split up. One night several Texas cowboys arrived with their cattle. Leading the rough and tumble group was Ed Morrison, who was humiliated by Wyatt a few years back in Wichita.

The boys started shooting out shop windows then started harassing customers at the Long Branch Saloon. When Wyatt walked through the swinging doors he found several gun barrels pointing at him.

Morrison growled "Yer time has come, Earp!"

Next a voice came from behind Morrison, "Throw yer hands up," as Doc put his revolver to Morrison's temple.

The cowboys dropped their guns and Wyatt ushered them to the Dodge City Jail. Wyatt never forgot that Doc saved his life that night, which solidified their friendship.

In the late summer of 1879 Doc tried one more time to start his dentistry business. A few weeks later he was nearly bored to death, got out of the business, and bought a saloon. As usual, Doc got in trouble and headed back to Dodge City. Once there he discovered that Wyatt had left for a new silver strike in Tombstone, Arizona. He then searched around for Kate and found out nobody had seen her for quite a while. With no reason to stay, Doc decided to seek his fame and fortune in Tombstone. Doc made a stop in Prescott, Arizona and hauled in $40,000 in winnings, and to his delight he found none other than Kate. She, too, was in Prescott on her way to Tombstone so the two of them arrived together in early summer of 1880.

When Doc got to Tombstone, he found Wyatt and all of the Earp brothers. Morgan came from Montana, James traveled with Wyatt from Dodge City, and Virgil came from Prescott where he had been a Deputy U.S. Marshal. Virgil appointed Wyatt as the acting City Marshal because he needed help with the outlaw Clanton Gang. The arrival of Doc Holliday was hailed as a great addition to the Earp's fight with the Clantons. Soon thereafter, Kate moved to Globe, Arizona some 175 miles away to run a boarding house.

Boarding House in Globe, Arizona.

Kate would come to Tombstone from time to time and ended up having arguments with Doc. She would get drunk and become abusive, so in early 1881 Doc threw her out for good. Throughout the summer of 1881, the threats against the Earp brothers by the Clantons increased. This is when the telegraph came from Marshal Garfias in Phoenix:

MARSHAL VIRGIL EARP,

NEED HELP.
ARRESTING RING LEADER.
HOLE IN THE ROCK GANG.
HERE IN PHOENIX.

CORDIALLY,
MARSHAL ENRIQUE GARFIAS

Virgil agreed to send his brother Wyatt, but wanted to make sure it was a short term job as the Clantons were a handful. Marshal Garfias assured him it wouldn't take long. The only problem was that he didn't have time to deal with a person like Jim Caldwell.

It was a long ride for Wyatt, but he'd been around a lot of America. He knew that once he saw Superstition Mountain, he'd be on the south side of Phoenix. Farmers of the area heard stories from the Pima Indians about fearing the mountain. They took these fears to be superstitions which is how the mountain got its name. Wyatt knew about it because a U.S. War Department map had labeled it for the first time in 1870.

Superstition Mountain.

Wyatt and his posse of Arizona Territorial Rangers arrived back in Phoenix with their criminal, Jim Caldwell, and went straight to the marshal's jail. They went through the open rooms with their dusty floors in the front part of the jail and headed back to where the jail door and barred windows were. They waited for Marshal Garfias to return and most of the posse gathered inside the small rooms. As fate would have it, Pedro had followed them into town. He took a seat outside and rather blended in with the guards in the darkness.

Turns out Marshal Garfias had been receiving lots of complaints against Jim, so he had his deputies looking for reasons to put him to death. That night many people heard what was going on and went to the jail to offer testimonials. When the marshal finally arrived, he started listening to their stories, but

Just inside the door of the dusty jailhouse.

nothing was worthy of a firing squad or hanging. As one person would file out, he would whisper to the next person filing in to just make up a story. The marshal realized that the stories were conflicting, so he asked Wyatt to go outside and create a kangaroo court.

One person stood up and said, "We heard him say he could bust out of the jail."

Another said, "No, I heard him say he didn't care if we all rust out in hell."

In short order they were laughing and enjoying this chance to pick on Jim.

Someone excitedly offered, "That crazy guy once said it was fine to be poor in spirit, but I think its better to pour spirits and drink 'em!" Laughter poured out of the ever-growing crowd like a bottle of smooth whiskey.

Another said, "He even tried to change the Good Book. Jim talked about not commitin' adultery, as the Good Lord told us, but Jim claims that just lookin' at a woman with lust is as good as adultery."

"No it ain't," snarked another, and they all started howling with laughter.

"He also told us that if yur right eye causes you to sin, tear it out and throw it away. I didn't much appreciate that," said a man with a patch over his right eye.

Another said, "I heard he stole a diamond." Now that would be a serious offense but they had no proof so the strange comment faded away.

Obviously they were having too much fun to be useful, so Wyatt gave the bad news to the marshal. Enrique was getting very agitated at this point, so he went back to the prisoner himself and asked Jim, "Why is it so many people don't like ya?"

Amazingly, Jim offered no response in his own defense. Then the marshal asked, "Who do you think you are, God?"

Jim finally spoke up. "Those are your words."

Enrique said, "That's all we need!" He then turned to Wyatt and said "You heard him! He's so crazy he thinks he's God."

He then looked around the room where people were crowding in. "What's yer decision?"

Even though Enrique had lots of latitude to carry out sentencing, he wanted their approval.

"He deserves death!" they yelled together as the sound echoed down the streets of Phoenix.

SCENE TWO
Villains

That's when the fun began. This villainous group of characters pulled Jim outside the jail and started spitting on him. "Hey, he spit in that old guy's eyes, so he must think that's a great thing to do," suggested one in the crowd.

When they were done with that, another person tied a kerchief around his wet eyes. Some thought he was trying to dry Jim's eyes but that was far from the truth.

"Let's play a game," he said. "Hey Jim. Since ya' think yer God, and God knows everything, tell us who hits you."

One at a time men stepped forward and punched him in the gut. "Come on, at least take a guess," they would say.

This continued for a while and Jim never uttered a word. He probably couldn't have even if he wanted to. The guards finally stepped in and folks figured they'd seen enough, but that wasn't the case. The guards wanted in on the fun and took turns beating him while blood oozed from his nose and eyes.

Abuse at this level may have seemed overboard, but everyone knew death was worse. At this point Jim fell to the ground and the guards began kicking him. Others wanted their opportunity but the guards kept this mistreatment to themselves. One guard was particularly glad to have his opportunity for payback. It seems that one day Jim was talking to a crowd and isolated one man, which just happened to be this guard, and said "Follow me."

The man responded that he was interested, but he first had to go back and bury his father. That's when Jim said the coldest thing this man ever heard. Jim said "Let the dead bury their own dead." Just thinking about that nauseated the man who was now a guard standing over him. With one swift kick he finished the abuse heaped on Jim who was barely conscious.

Pedro moved further back in the crowd when these awful events started happening. The early morning light was beginning to unfold across the valley and it became harder for

Morning across the Phoenix valley.

Pedro to just blend in. Sure enough, Pedro noticed a woman in the crowd who just stood there staring at him.

"What's yer problem?" Pedro snarled in hopes of scaring her off.

"Ain't you one of the Hole in the Rock Gang that ran around with Jim?"

"Why?" Pedro asked evasively.

"Yer obviously Mexican and I heard he had two Mexican brothers in his group."

Pedro denied it, saying "No idea what yer talking 'bout. There's plenty of Mexicans in these parts and we all don't look the same, ya know."

When she responded that he sounded like a Mexican, he moved further back in the crowd. A strange thing happened at that moment. Just as Pedro denied knowing Jim, a coyote howled off in the distance. That meant something to the people because the Native American tribes saw the coyote as a major mythological figure. Their superstitions were passed on to the early settlers of the West leaving them cautious about coyotes.

The myth about coyotes had to do with death and its origin. The native people of the Old West told a story about death being the result of a debate between two animals:

One favored death and the other immortality. Raven wanted death, but said you could never quote him. Coyote wanted sleep, but lost the vote at the council of animals. Raven's daughter was the first death so all of a sudden Raven wanted to change his vote. From that time forward Coyote was known as a trickster because he announced that the decision was made and could not be changed.

Not to be ignored, this same woman started talking to the others in the crowd outside the jail.

"This guy's one of 'em," as she pointed to Pedro, and again he denied it. Now others were joining in,

"I think she be right. He fer sure be Mexican."

Now Pedro had to think fast on his feet. He knew that Jim didn't believe in lying but then again, he wasn't Mexican, he was American because of the Gadsden Purchase. What Jim had said in the past was "Do not swear at all, and let yer word be Yes or No; more than this comes from evil." Pedro thought for a moment then said "no."

Everyone went on edge when the coyote howled again because it seemed closer. Truth is, death was closer, at least for Jim.

Morning had finally come, but it was an eerie look. The nearby hill turned blood red, almost symbolic of what was in store. Marshal Garfias consulted with his assistant, Sheriff Earp, and the rest of the posse that stayed through the night. They no longer had execution privileges since the Russian overlords were around. As a group, they agreed that Jim was going to be turned over to Dmitri. Dmitri was the Russian assigned to oversee the Phoenix area and the only one authorized to carry out the death penalty. They checked the ropes tied around Jim's hands, then had him stand up and led him away to be handed over to the Russian authorities. The extra strong binding on Jim's hands was done to send a message that this was a dangerous man.

Blood red rocks.

Back when Benedict left The Rusty Tavern, he was feeling beyond angry and looking for revenge. Jim himself had said to "go do what yur gonna do," but the problem was Bennie had no idea what he was gonna do. Jim also said that things weren't going to end well for him and that someone was going to report him to the authorities. "Maybe that's what I'm supposed to do," he thought, but what would he report about Jim that was bad enough for an arrest?

As Bennie considered his task, he slowly began to believe that he never really belonged to the Hole in the Rock Gang. Sure, it was nice that Jim talked about treating people with dignity and respect and all that, but Bennie was getting more comfortable by the minute with getting back to his true self. What was that garbage about equality anyway, questioned Bennie. Everyone knows them Mexicans are short so they don't have to stoop so far down to work the ground, he believed. But the truth was that he himself was barely five foot tall. And nobody can trust an Injun, he said to himself. Why did I ever join that group anyway? Jim's ideas make no sense, he alleged as his thoughts waned and his feelings grew.

Bennie rode his horse back into town and was ready for anything. He felt free from all those restrictions Jim recommended living by, and after a while he found himself on Whiskey Row. This was a place Bennie hadn't been to since joining the Hole in the Rock Gang and it felt good. Bennie bellied up to the bar and ordered a whiskey. People drank their whiskey fast and furious in those days because it was cheaper than beer, wine, coffee, tea, or milk.

With the soaring consumption of whiskey in the Old West, it became synonymous with gambling. The two together proved to be deadly, so the government contracted P. T. Barnum to produce a play to try to get Americans to think before they drink. "The Drunkard" became the most popular and widely performed

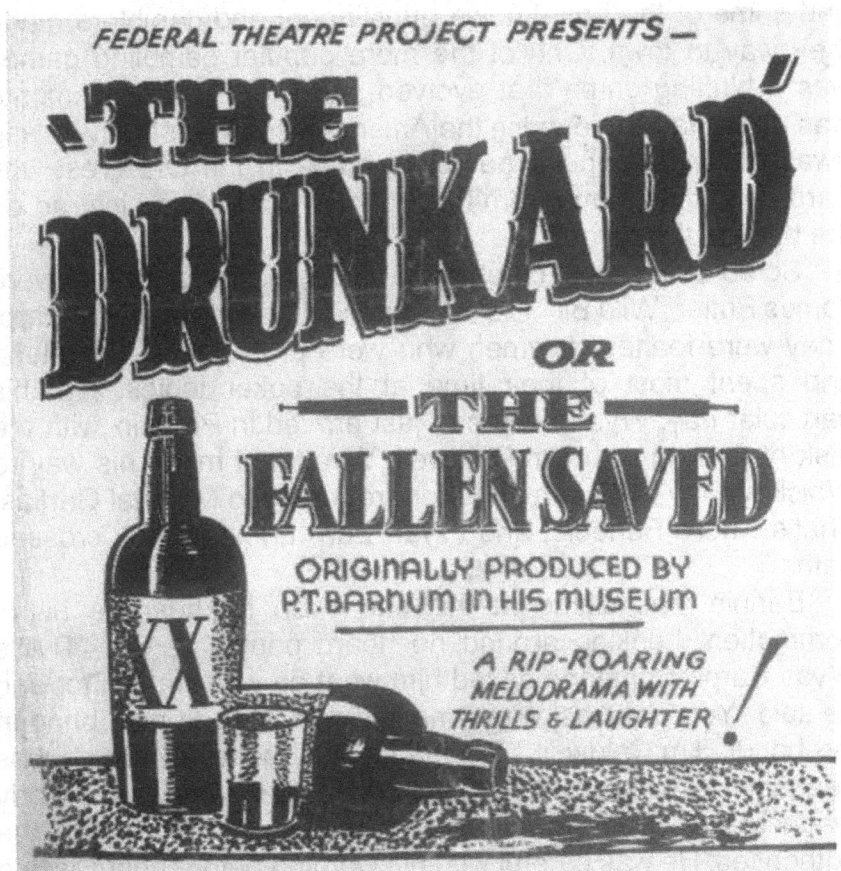

P. T. Barnum's "The Drunkard."

play in America. It offered entertainment but did little to slow the voracious appetite cowboys had for liquor in the Old West.

Gambling was also out of control. Saloons, brothels, and gambling halls appeared almost over night near Army forts, wagon trail river crossings, and mining districts. As Phoenix grew, one-story wooden buildings replaced dirt-floored tents, and some of the best-known gunslingers and gamblers made their way to town. One of the more popular gambling games was a bluffing game that evolved into poker. Mexican monte was particularly enjoyed in the American southwest, but far and away the most popular gambling game in the Old West was Faro, taking its name from the Egyptian pharaohs pictured on the back of the cards.

Some of the most celebrated names of the Old West were James Butler "Wild Bill" Hickok, Bat Masterson, and Wyatt Earp. They were fearless lawmen who were professional gamblers, and spent most of their time at the poker tables. On this particular day, Wyatt Earp had just arrived in Phoenix with the task of dealing with Jim Caldwell. Wyatt first made his way to Whiskey Row to relax a bit before reporting to Marshal Garfias. That's where Benedict and Wyatt Earp unexpectedly crossed paths.

Bennie was sitting at the bar when he heard a bit of commotion. Looking around he heard people saying "That's Wyatt Earp!" Someone asked him what he was in town for and he said "Your marshal wired me in Tombstone to help bring in the bandit Jim Caldwell." Bennie couldn't believe what he was hearing. He was kind of glad that the decision was already made to arrest Jim, so he didn't have to turn Jim in to the authorities. He was careful with his wording before approaching Wyatt.

"Did I hear ya say yer lookin' for Jim Caldwell?"

Wyatt shot a steely-eyed look at him and said, "Why do ya wanna know?"

Bennie felt a cold shiver run through his soul when he said, "I might be able to help."

Not having much patience, Wyatt said, "Ya can help or ya can't. Which is it?"

Bennie said "I was just with 'em at The Rusty Tavern."

"OK, let's corral him in," Wyatt said with a strange sense of destiny.

Bennie, being the one who always had money on his mind, said "What's in it fer me?"

"Whatcha wantin'?"

"How's $500 dollars sound to ya?"

Bennie knew some stories about these gambling lawmen and the vast sums of money they took in. That's why Wyatt had gone to Tombstone in the first place. The town was freshly founded in 1877 by Ed Schieffelin who found silver in the wilderness. The town was first known as Goose Flats, but in 1879 it was renamed to Tombstone. By 1881 it grew rapidly, outpaced only by San Francisco and St. Louis.

Tombstone also had a few theatres, but the most prominent one was The Bird Cage Theatre. Opening in 1881, it was a gambling hall, saloon, and a brothel. It got to be known as the wickedest and wildest night spot in the entire Old West, frequented by the Clanton Gang, the Earp brothers, Bat Masterson, and Doc Holliday. Upstairs was for prostitutes and their customers, the basement was for gambling, and the main floor was the saloon and theatre. The first floor also had a stage for live performances with a sunken orchestra pit.

The Jim Caldwell Trilogy

The Bird Cage is where silver became king. People didn't like carrying cash, so with silver being mined in abundance, folks were plunking down silver coins for their entertainment. Even Wyatt Earp enjoyed the change of pace from cash to silver coins. He found he could carry lots of them in his buffalo leather satchel bag.

Bird Cage Theatre in Tombstone.

When Wyatt heard Bennie asking for $500 cash, he didn't flinch. He had plenty of silver coins, so Wyatt offered him thirty pieces of silver. They immediately struck a deal and headed over to Marshal Garfias' office. His office was surprisingly decent for a new town. Enrique Garfias wasn't in, so the boys took a seat and waited.

Marshal Garfias' office.

"So where ya think Caldwell is?" asked Wyatt.

Not wanting to get cheated, Bennie said "I know their favorite spot. He'll be there."

"Where's there?"

"I'll show ya when the coins are in hand."

Soon enough, Enrique got back and was delighted to find Wyatt Earp had arrived.

"Who's this guy?" asked Enrique, pointing over to Bennie. "Take yer boots off my desk and get out of my chair!"

Bennie awkwardly stumbled away with a grin on his face.

"I don't know," responded Wyatt, "but he claims he can take me to our bandit."

Enrique was all of a sudden pleased and asked "What's holdin' ya up?"

Wyatt said, "This guy wants $500 for his capture, so I offered him 30 pieces of silver. I've got it, but just wanted to make sure you'll pay me back."

The marshal was happy to get one more problem off his back so he approved the deal.

"Also, I want a posse of Arizona Territory Rangers."

The posse was put together faster than expected and the arresting authorities were on their way.

Bennie led the trip with his silver safely in his saddlebag. They rode north out of Phoenix until they began to see the red rocks ahead.

"We're getting close now," said Bennie. At this point he started to question his decision to lead the posse to Jim, as he imagined the faces of the men he had spent a lot of time with in the past year. But it became a fleeting thought as the silver clanked against the side of his horse. Livin' proper is fine and dandy, but money pays the bills became his closing thought.

When they arrived at the trail head to the Seven Sacred Pools, they dismounted and prepared their guns for battle. Bennie said "Ya don't need no guns. I guarantee they don't have any" and sure enough they simply walked up to the Hole in the Rock Gang and arrested Jim after a fairly mild skirmish. After the Eleven ran away and the young Apache wasn't caught, Wyatt and Bennie returned to the jail in Phoenix and delivered Jim Caldwell to the justice system.

Bennie was surprised when he caught a glimpse of Pedro lingering around the outside of the jail. He wondered for moment where the others had gone, but it didn't really matter. Bennie fulfilled his destiny, as Jim said he would, so he just faded back into the crowd to watch what was going to happen. To Bennie's surprise things got ugly. He thought Jim might have to spend some time in jail, so he was shocked beyond belief when the crowds called for the death penalty.

Actually, Bennie was shaken to the core. Thoughts started racing through his head like "Jim certainly didn't deserve this kind of treatment" and "He was a good man. I'm the bad guy."

Bennie was ripped apart inside. He kind of liked getting back to his old self but he knew he was wrong. So when he heard that Jim was condemned, he had a change of heart. He went up to Wyatt as Jim was being taken away and put the thirty pieces of silver back in Wyatt's hands.

"I'm wrong for betraying my friend," bemoaned Bennie.

"How could I care less?" Wyatt offered coldly.

Actually, Bennie went numb inside and didn't care about anything at this point. First he threw the coins onto the dusty floor of the jail and watched them roll around. Several coins spun on their end and mesmerizingly lowered themselves in ever increasing circles speeding toward oblivion. Bennie got dizzy at first, but that's when he knew what he was going to do. He took some rope from his saddle and headed to the nearest tree. He didn't even pause as he threw it over a limb and hanged himself.

As for Jim Caldwell, the Americans were required to turn to the Russians to accomplish the death penalty. Nobody liked the Russians, and southwestern Americans were still in shock that they were governed by Russia. Sure, the local sheriffs and marshals did their job, but ultimately Russia was in charge. So now it's time to find out how it came to be that the Russians were the overseers of that part of America.

<u>INTERLUDE</u>

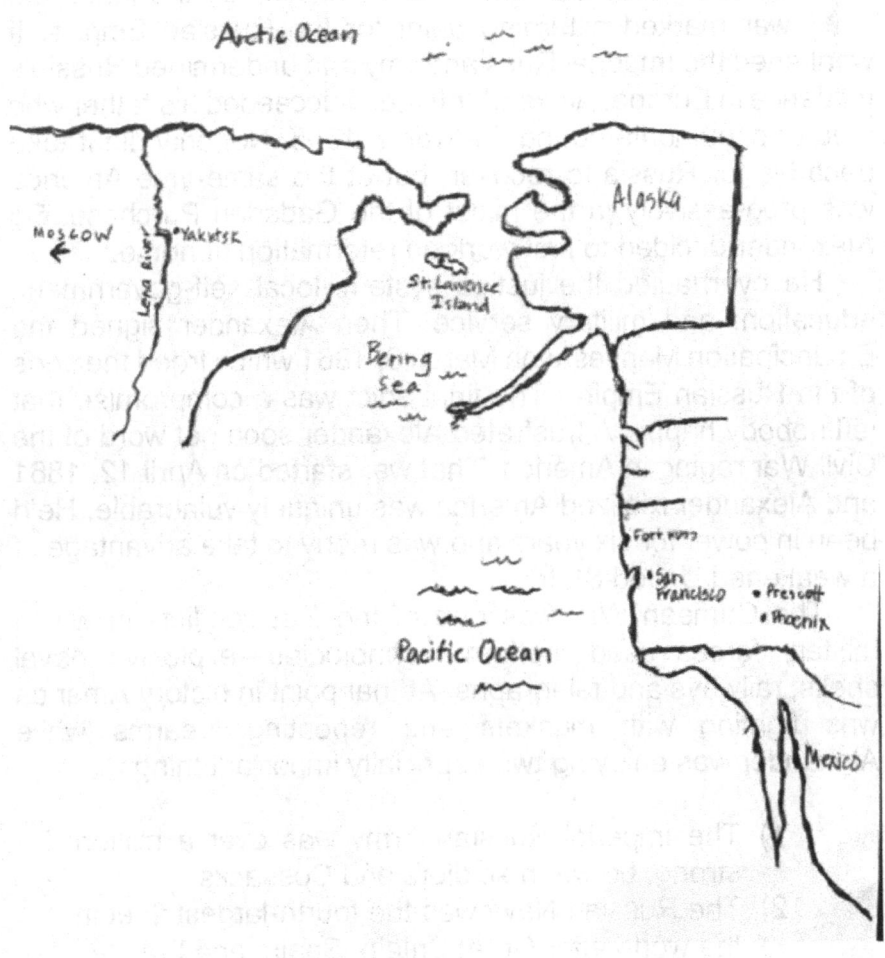

THE RUSSIAN INVASION

The stage was first set by Russia's humiliating defeat in the Crimean War that ended in 1856. To say the least, the war marked a turning point for the Russian Empire. It weakened the Imperial Russian Army and undermined Russia's influence in Europe. Alexander II then succeeded his father who died of pneumonia during the war in 1855. Not only did it take decades for Russia to recover, but at the same time America was progressively in the midst of the Gadsden Purchase. So Alexander decided to first work on reformation at home.

He overhauled the justice system, local self-government, education, and military service. Then Alexander signed the Emancipation Manifesto on March 3, 1861 which freed the serfs of the Russian Empire. The final edict was a compromise that left nobody happy. A frustrated Alexander soon got word of the Civil War raging in America. That war started on April 12, 1861 and Alexander realized America was uniquely vulnerable. He'd been in power for six years and was ready to take advantage of a weakened United States.

The Crimean War was one of the first conflicts in which military forces used modern technologies—explosive naval shells, railways and telegraphs. At that point in history America was fighting with muskets and repeating firearms while Alexander was enjoying two especially important things:

1) The Imperial Russian Army was over a million strong, between soldiers and Cossacks.
2) The Russian Navy was the fourth-largest fleet in the world after Great Britain, Spain, and France.

Emblem of the Imperial Russian Army

Emblem of the Imperial Russian Navy

The problem was that Alexander was more eager than ready. His idea was to attack the less settled part of western America, but the time just wasn't right. He needed to accomplish more reforms at home before trying to impress Europe with an invasion of the United States. The good thing was that as America was exploring and settling the West, Russia was exploring Siberia and their own Far East. Russia needed time to expand its military to the east, in preparation for an invasion, and Alaska became the calling card for drawing their attention toward the rising sun.

The 1867 Treaty of Cession became the second thing that set the stage for invasion. The U.S. purchased Alaska from the Russian Empire for $7.2 million. One of its provisions was that "uncivilized Native tribes" would be subject to laws the U.S. might adopt in regards to aboriginal tribes. Tensions were low at an international level, but they were all but out of control in the United States. To get a feel for the ethnic mix of people in the time of Jim Caldwell, here's how it looked:

1) Americans
2) Mexicans
3) Native Americans
4) Native Alaskans
5) Russians

The treaty with Russia was done under amicable circumstances because both Russia and the U.S. felt they gained from it. Or at least most people thought that way. Critics in the U.S. quickly called it "Seward's Folly" in disgust with Secretary of State William Seward who negotiated and signed the deal. On the Russian side, they immediately began to regret the decision. This is when they started to seriously put together a plan for the Russian invasion of America. The first railways were making progress ever since service was opened between St. Petersburg and Moscow in 1851, but the road system was inadequate. This scheme helped that problem as a quiet expansion of troops began in earnest from 1867 to the invasion in 1870.

The Imperial Russian Navy was impressive, but it had a limited capacity for sailors. It was going to take a joint venture of the Army and the Navy to mount an invasion of America. The advantage the Navy had was familiarity. They had voyaged to their North American colonies in Russian America (Alaska) and Fort Ross in northern California. They also had visited Pacific ports on the eastern seaboard of Siberia. This gave a wealth of information for an invasion.

They also were aware of St. Lawrence Island. The Russian explorer Vitus Bering originally arrived there on St. Lawrence's Day in 1728 and the island was subsequently named after the day of his visit. The value of this island was its size, being 90 miles wide and 22 miles from north to south. And its location, just 36 miles from the Chukchi Peninsula in the Russian Far East. The island was sparsely inhabited and was first occupied around the time of Christ. The usefulness came in its many abandoned huts. The local Yupik people were never permanent, depending on resource availability and changes in weather patterns.

Tsar Alexander decided to use his navy to take and store supplies in these huts on the island for the army to use for and during the invasion. All that needed to happen now was move as many troops as possible across Siberia. That wasn't going to be easy, but the payoff was nothing less than regaining

Abandoned Yupik hut.

Russia's influence in Europe. And it took every bit of three years to manage that feat.

The Imperial Russian Army had fourteen grades in their ranks of officers, but two people became most important in the story of Jim Caldwell. They were Lieutenant General Dmitri Ivanov and Major General Sergey Popov. Dmitri was the higher ranking official between the two, so he often took the lead. Dmitri was from Pavlovsky Posad, a suburb of Moscow that was founded in 1844. The town was an industrial center where Dmitri learned to do hard work before entering the military. A tall and stout man, Dmitri was the ideal leader for the army.

Sergey had a very different story. He was from Yakutsk and was a Cossack, which was a Russian military warrior. He was short and stocky and didn't look the part of an army trailblazer, but he was. His rising through the ranks happened because of the location of his childhood. Yakutsk was about 3,000 miles east of Moscow, directly in line with their planned journey to the Far East. He had journeyed to Moscow before, so his knowledge of that trek was priceless.

Sergey was also well known from participating in the Battle of Balaclava during the Crimean War, where he served directly under Commander Pavel Liprandi. That victory was so popular that it was memorialized just six weeks after the event in Alfred, Lord Tennyson's narrative poem "The Charge of the Light Brigade." For years after that war, Sergey loved quoting a famous line from the poem: "Theirs not to reason why, theirs but to do and die."

When the decision was made to proceed with the plans to invade the American West, Sergey was among the first to find out. He had settled in Moscow and became friends with Dmitri. His task would be to lead the troops, although Dmitri was in charge. As the army slowly advanced across Siberia in groups, these two guys began thinking about where they would like to govern in America. They were both interested in settling in the Arizona Territory as they had heard some raucus stories of the Old West.

Sergey liked snow, since his childhood was spent on permafrost. He found out that Prescott was in a beautiful, forested area in the northern mountains and let Dmitri know of his interest. Meanwhile, Dmitri wanted warmth as the Siberian weather was a bit much for him.

"I hear Phoenix good. It hot. Better zan Siberia!" exclaimed Dmitri.

"Yes. I'll go with you there," Sergey said in Russian, but Dmitri reminded him they needed to practice their English. It would make the transition to Russian governance much easier.

It was a grueling experience for the army to cross Siberia. During this advancement east, the navy quietly went about their task of supplying the abandoned Yupik huts on St. Lawrence Island for the invasion. During their free time, which wasn't a lot, the soldiers liked to read. This is when Leo Tolstoy was putting out his serialized version of *War and Peace*. That was useful because when the book was finally published in 1869, it was 1,225 pages long and unaffordable. Fortunately, Dmitri had a copy sent to him from a rich friend and it made a huge difference at just the right time.

The troops were a bit more than two years into their journey and morale was low. When Dmitri got his copy he pored through it with excitement. It was about the effect of the Napoleonic wars on Russian aristocracy, but the quote that he shared with the troops was "The strongest of all warriors are these two – Time and Patience." It was just what they needed to inspire them to finish with renewed vigor at the Chukchi Peninsula.

They had followed south of the Arctic Circle for most of the journey, and were overjoyed to finally see water at the Bering Sea. One zealous soldier exclaimed in Russian "I can see Alaska from my tent!" From here it was a matter of moving some of the troops to St. Lawrence Island by way of the Navy. The others would be shipped to Fort Ross in preparation for the

Fort Ross in northern California.

invasion. Fort Ross (the name is derived from the same root as the word "Russia") was the hub of the southernmost Russian settlements in North America from 1812 to 1841.

Fort Ross was established as an agricultural base to supply Alaska, and was the site for the first windmills and ship building in California. The Russian people also introduced glass windows, stoves, and all-wood housing into Alta (meaning upper) California. Russian presence expanded during this time from the Fort inland with farming communities. Juan Bautista Alvarado was the Mexican Governor of Alta California who decided to buttress the area against Indians, Russians, Americans, and the British as it was then the Mexican territory of California.

Alta California ceased to exist as separate from Baja California in 1836. Then the end of the Mexican-American War in 1848 ceded Alta California to the United States. Three years later California became the 31st state of the union. All of this made it so California thought nothing of Russian troops slowly arriving at their old Fort Ross in 1870. The plan for the Russian Invasion of the west coast of America was beginning to unfold.

Lieutenant General Dmitri Ivanov organized troops at Fort Ross as they arrived on ships and Major General Sergey Popov supplied soldiers with extra provisions at St. Lawrence Island. As waves of infantry finally gathered together with their naval counterparts, they headed south for San Francisco. While the city was founded in 1776, San Francisco didn't become a city until 1850 and a consolidated city-county until 1856. The city was still in its infancy, so it was totally taken by surprise just fourteen years later with the beginning of the Russian Invasion of 1870.

Dmitri and Sergey and their massive numbers of troops just walked right into the city and took over without bloodshed. It was just like what happened when Persia walked into Babylon in biblical times and conquered without violence. Indeed

Dmitri's constant reminder to his troops that time and patience were the true warriors was what ultimately paid off. The troops were elated. The dream of their beloved Tsar was being realized. Russia would regain the esteem and fear of Europe and Dmitri and Sergey were already beginning to imagine their victorious reception upon their return.

The same success on the part of the Russians extended into the Arizona Territory. While it's true that America's population at the time was over thirty one million, its vast size caused the population to be spread out. Russia was soon reigning over the Old West, partly because they weren't foolish enough to attack the heavier populated East coast where most of the Civil War played itself out. The Russian invasion only lasted eleven years, but it played an important role in the story of Jim Caldwell and the Hole in the Rock Gang.

The invasion came to an end in 1881, because back home in the motherland Tsar Alexander II was assassinated. His noble reforms weren't appreciated and a period of repression led to revolutionary terrorism. Alexander was killed in the streets of St. Petersburg from a bomb thrown by members of the "People's Will" group. His successor was his son, Alexander III. This Tsar was understandably reactionary. First, he reversed the liberal reforms of his father so he could enjoy autocratic rule. Then, his oppressive rule needed his military in full force, so he recalled his troops from America.

It was just as well. America was rapidly expanding to the west due to railroads, factories, mining, and finance. Immigration from Europe and the Eastern United States also led to speedy growth, based on farming and ranching. Even labor unions became increasingly important in the industrial cities. Prohibition and racism was added to the cultural problems, so it seemed America was ready for its own battles. That's how the invasion ended, but here's how our story continued. Dmitri settled into the newly incorporated city of Phoenix and Sergey settled into the former Territorial capital of Prescott.

ACT III

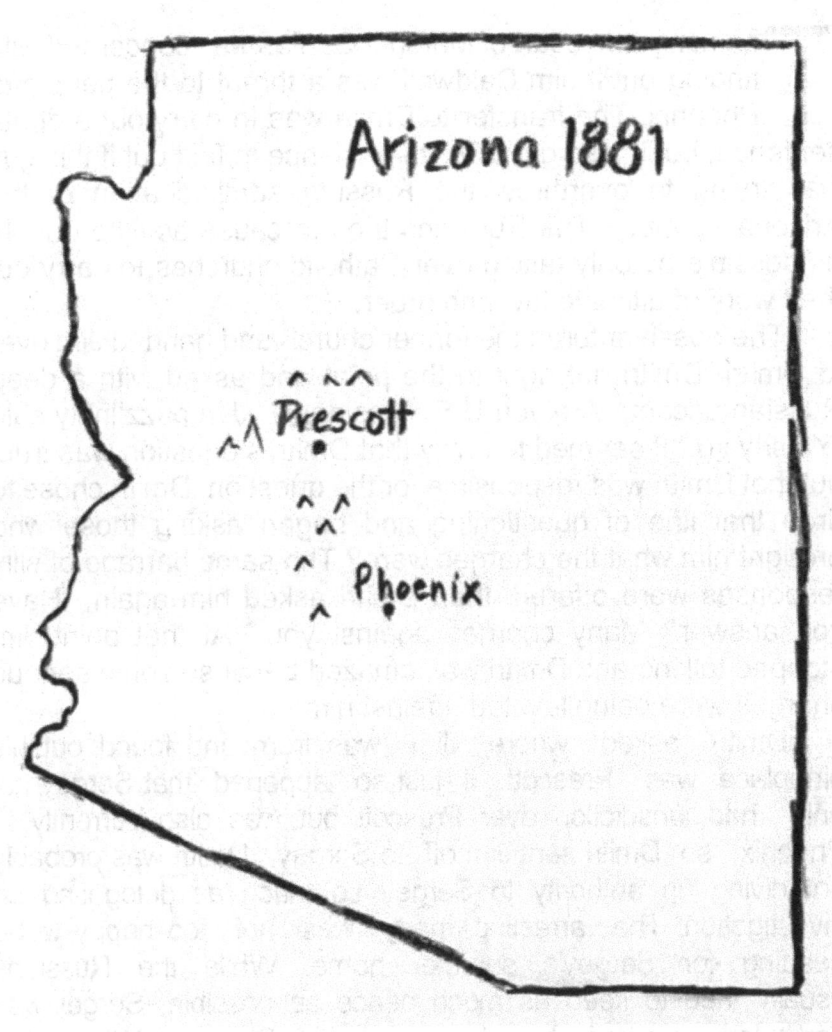

THE HANGING JUDGE

The kangaroo court of Marshal Garfias was concerned with finding out if Jim Caldwell was a threat to the people of Phoenix. The transfer to Dmitri was to carry out a death sentence, but it also gave Dmitri a chance to find out if this guy was trying to overthrow the Russian administration of the Arizona Territory. The Russians tried to cause as little trouble as possible by only taking over Catholic churches to carry out their work of ultimate law and order.

The posse entered the former church and handed Jim over to Dmitri. Dmitri got right to the point and asked with a deep Russian accent, "Are you U.S. President?" Jim puzzlingly said "Ya say so." It seemed to imply that Dmitri's question was true, but that Dmitri was responsible for the question. Dmitri chose to drop that line of questioning and began asking those who brought him what the charges were? The same barrage of silly responses were offered, then Dmitri asked him again, "Have you answer? Many charges against you." At that point Jim stopped talking and Dmitri was amazed because some serious charges were being leveled against him.

Dmitri asked where Jim was from and found out his birthplace was Prescott. It just so happened that Sergey not only had jurisdiction over Prescott but was also currently in Phoenix, so Dmitri sent Jim off to Sergey. Dmitri was probably not giving up authority to Sergey so much as delegating an investigation. The arresting party was not too happy to be heading for Sergey's summer home. While the Russians usually tried to keep as much peace as possible, Sergey was particularly disliked by the people of Phoenix. When the

Dmitri's office.

Russians first conquered the area, Sergey took the finest piece of property he could find and visited it often from Prescott.

Just walking onto the property made everyone's blood boil. It had been owned by the wealthiest man in Phoenix and Sergey didn't spare a dime in making it opulent when he took it over. As the posse brought Jim onto the gardens, they found themselves even more frustrated. This oasis in the middle of the desert had a small lake and waterfall, plenty of ducks and green trees that seemed so out of place in the hot, dry area. Complaints continued as they made their way through the gardens and into Sergey's vacation home.

Sergey was waiting with gleeful anticipation to see Jim, but it was with malicious intent. Sergey's mind went back to the time he tried to see Jim after having Jim's cousin hung from the gallows. It was with great frustration that the visit didn't come to pass. Yet another provocation came about when friends warned Jim that Sergey wanted to have him killed. Jim shockingly told them to "Go and tell that fox that I have my own timing for my death." So finally, here stood Jim in Sergey's place and he was savoring every element of the interrogation.

"What bring you my way, comrade?" taunted Sergey as he nearly foamed at the mouth.

Jim had no response.

"Kind of stupid you are?" asked Sergey as he moved up nose to nose with Jim.

Jim could smell Sergey's rotten egg breath, but offered no response.

"You have idea how serious zese allegations are against you?"

The question was met with a blank stare as Jim stood there dripping in blood.

Sergey's gardens.

"I enjoyed watching your cousin hang from end of rope. Life drain out. He no good," Sergey said in an attempt to get some sort of response. But Jim wasn't going to give Sergey that pleasure. That's when the posse that brought Jim in started vehemently accusing him of all manner of evil doings.

"This guy thinks he's better than us and makes us feel belittled" one little man offered in a rather pathetic way.

Another said "He's a traitor!" which rather riled up the people gathered in hopes of seeing a lynching.

Then someone said "Everyone knows he's in a gang. I think its name is the "Hole in the Head Gang," and everyone started laughing. At this point, Sergey was enlivened to get back to treating Jim with contempt. He had good reason because people never treated Sergey in such a manner as did Jim Caldwell.

"You probably think you're Rutherford B. Hayes," Sergey offered in an attempt to mock him as if he were the President of the United States.

In a moment of disgust, Sergey put a robe on Jim saying "I salute President of U.S."

He then sent Jim back to Dmitri. Sergey and Dmitri had a falling out over authority a while back, but this experience with Jim brought them back from enemies to friendship.

The posse brought Jim back to Dmitri by way of one of the many mining operations that were springing up all over the Arizona Territory. They found gold near Wickenburg, silver near Tucson, and copper in Jerome. The one precious metal they

One of the many mines in the Arizona Territory in the 1880s.

didn't find in the Arizona Territory by 1881 was diamonds. This continued to cause some confusion because one of the allegations against Jim was that he had stolen a diamond. The only way would be from a woman's necklace, but there was no evidence at all to support the charge.

When they arrived back to Dmitri, he decided to carefully stay out of this argument the Americans were having about wanting the death penalty for Jim. Crowds of people were also gathering so he knew he needed to do something. The locals had a festival where an old custom of releasing a prisoner was observed. Dmitri smiled when he realized he could completely put the "Jim" problem in their hands.

There just so happened to be a prisoner in jail who had committed murder during the insurrection against the Russians. His name was Jackson and he would be the perfect foil. Sure enough the crowd began to ask Dmitri to honor their custom, so he said "You want me release guy who think he God?" Dmitri knew that the local authorities were tired of Jim and that he had been handed over out of jealousy. Their dislike for Jim was more like a violent hatred for good, so Marshal Garfias and Sheriff Earp started stirring up the crowd to release Jackson instead of Jim.

Dmitri fetched both Jackson and Jim and stood them before those gathered. "Look, I also bring Jim so you know I find no case on him." Jim came out wearing a cap and coat the Russian soldiers put on him and Dmitri said to them "Here the man! What you wish me do?"

They shouted back, "Hang him!"

Dmitri asked "What he done to deserve death?"

The crowds shouted even louder saying "Hang him by the neck until he dies!"

The one man gallows erected in Phoenix.

Realizing the crowd could turn into a riot, Dmitri took some water and washed his hands in front of the angry mob, saying "I innocent of zis man blood." He also said "to me to lightbulb" which, because of the recent invention of the lightbulb, became a favorite new Russian phrase that meant "I don't care." Then he released Jackson to the people and the crowd cheered his unexpected return. Truth is, Jackson was a very bad man and all he was doing was serving time in jail. Dmitri thought it all seemed so strange that those crazy Americans wanted a bad man freed and a good man killed. But at least it was their decision. Dmitri then had Jim flogged and he handed him over to be hung. The soldiers began saluting Jim and mockingly saying "Hail to President!" They hit him, spat on him and knelt down in homage to him. They then took him out to hang him.

ACT IV
DEAD AND BURIED

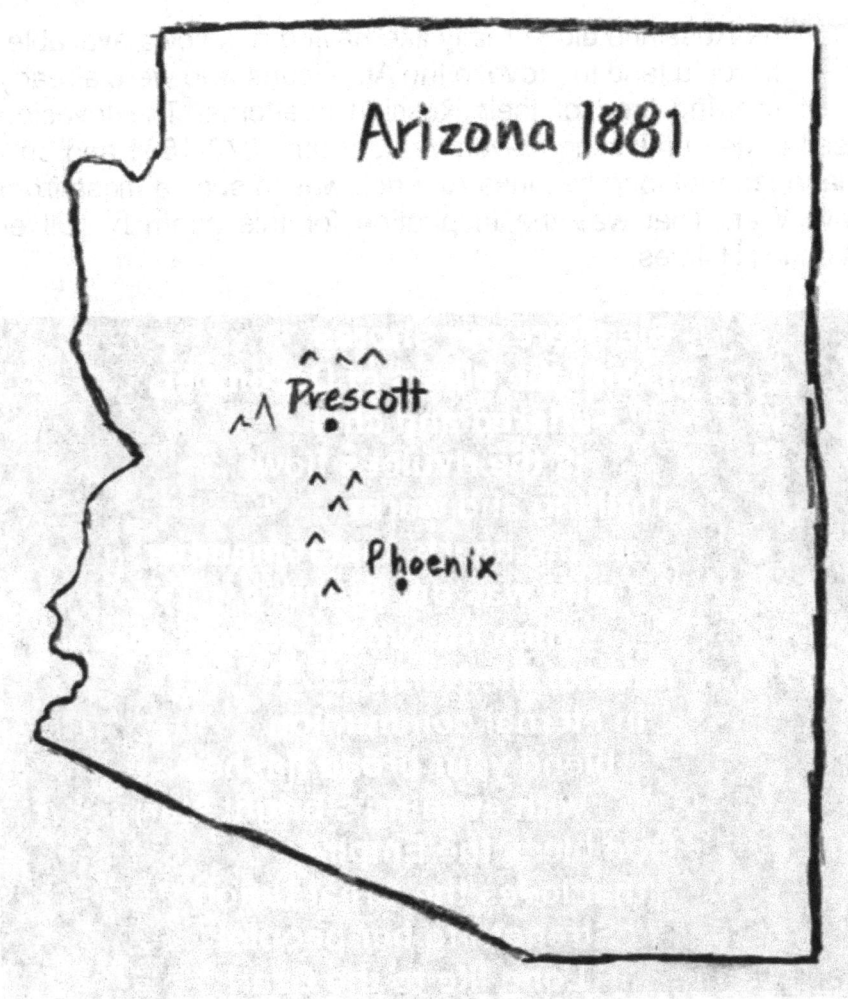

SCENE ONE
The Gallows

The Russians didn't really like having a gallows available. It would tend to provoke the Americans who were already growing tired of their Russian overlords. The invasion itself ended up lasting eleven years, from 1870-1881 and only managed that long because America was in such a mess from Civil War. That was the inspiration for this poem by Oliver Wendell Holmes:

> Bleak are our shores
>   with the blasts of December,
>   Fettered and chill
>   is the rivulet's flow.
> Thrilling and warm
>   are the hearts that remember,
>   who was our friend
>   when the world was our foe.
> Fires of the North
>   in eternal communion,
>   blend your broad flashes
>   with evening's bright star;
> God bless the Empire
>   that loves the Great Union
>   Strength to her people!
>   Long life to the Czar!

It was surprising how much respect America had for Russia just before the invasion, as witnessed by the preceding poem. Emancipation was on the mind of both countries and change was in the air. Even the great Mark Twain described a short visit with Alexander II in chapter 37 of *The Innocents Abroad*, describing him as:

> "very tall and spare,
> and a determined-looking man,
> though a very pleasant-looking one
> nevertheless.
>
> It is easy to see that
> he is kind and affectionate.
> There is something
> very noble in his expression
> when his cap is off."

So the Russian soldiers led Jim to a place just outside the town where there was a nearby mining operation. The two vertical end pieces were set in place when it was decided there would be a hanging, but the crossbeam was left off. This was usually reserved for the criminal to carry to the gallows as a final form of punishment. At this point, Carly, one of the remaining eleven, couldn't stand what was happening. He stepped forth and offered to carry the crossbeam for Jim.

"Sorry," Carly whispered to Jim. "This is all so horrible. I don't even understand what happened."

Jim tried to acknowledge but he was too beaten and bruised to be able to respond.

Many people were following the events unfolding, including a group of women and none other than Big Nose Kate. While Kate had waffled back and forth about giving up prostitution when she was with Doc Holiday, her life was completely transformed when she saw the tragic events against Jim Crawford. Later, some of Jim's followers taught her what they learned from Jim. The lifestyle of equality and justice were just what she needed to carry on with her new life. In fact, her life was so radically new because she ended up being cured of seven evil spirits.

As for the cluster of ladies gathered at the crucifixion site, they called themselves the "Daughters of Phoenix." They too were renegades of sorts. At a time when few women got an education, these women gathered each week at the local library and taught themselves to read. They were all single and had no interest in men, and over time they developed an interest in writing poetry. This event of a decent man being sentenced to death seemed like a great occasion to develop their unusual style of poetry. They found that when events moved them, it made writing even easier. In the days that followed, they each wrote about their experience. They shared their individual poems and then developed a single poem to express their feelings:

"Blessed are the barren,
and the wombs that never bore,
and the breasts that never nursed.
Say to the mountains, 'Fall on us';
And to the hills, 'Cover us.'
For if they do this when the wood is green,
what will happen when it is dry?"

Don't bother to ask for an interpretation. This collection of misfits was fun to listen to but nobody ever got their point. Perhaps that's what they wanted. It was definitely a man's world and they managed to carve out their unique identity in a rather hostile environment. Writing became their offspring and they enjoyed nursing their stories along each week.

Then the hanging party arrived at the gallows by a place known as "The Skull." The crossbeam was carefully attached to the two vertical end pieces and the noose was flung over the top. A couple of soldiers offered him a drink of whiskey as a last wish, but Jim turned it down. Then, to the disbelief of many, they hung him. The Russians were pretty excited about the cowboy boots Jim was wearing. They were a nice pair of western boots, so their love of gambling caused them to roll some dice to see who would get them.

Dmitri didn't bother to lower himself to the point of attending the hanging, so he left instructions for the soldiers. They were to leave an inscription on the crossbeam that read "This man thought he was US President." Soon thereafter, two more bandits were hung, one on his right and one on his left. It was

The place known as "The Skull."

a most cruel way to hang all three of them because they left the noose loose so as to bring about death slowly.

Some in the crowd taunted Jim as he took his waning breaths. They yelled things like "Ya think so much of yerself, show us something truly amazing and save yerself!" Even Marshal Garfias and Sheriff Earp joined in the mockery. Unbelievably, even the two bandits taunted him, but at least they had a remote hope that somehow the rope would break and they'd be rescued.

That's when Jim, with the noose still a tiny bit loose, slowly choked out seven more thoughts before he died:

1. "God, why have you forsaken me?"
2. "God, forgive them."
3. Then he looked at one of the criminals slowly losing his life and said "Today, we're going to heaven together."
4. "God, please take me now!"
5. Then he looked at Carly who was in the crowd and said "Watch over the Daughters of Phoenix."
6. "God, I'm thirsty."
7. "God, I've completed my task."

At his death, people started complaining.

"What did he mean about a task?" asked one.

"What was his concern with the Daughters of Phoenix?" asked another.

Even the marshal was frustrated, "Jim thought that rotten bandit was going to heaven? I'm not even sure about Jim!"

And the sheriff offered his two cents worth with a wry smile, "At least he felt forsaken."

Dmitri surprised everyone with a visit asking "You feel earthquake few minutes ago?"

"Yeah, but why?"

"Curtain in my office just tore in two, from top to bottom."

All of a sudden a Russian soldier offered an unexpected claim, "I think there was something real special about this man."

The Daughters of Phoenix agreed and quickly penned another one of their strange poems:

And the earth was shaken,
and the rocks were rent;
and the tombs were opened,
and many bodies of the
fallen-asleep
holy ones
were raised.

And it wasn't just the Daughters of Phoenix who took interest. Seems that women from all over heard about the troubles Jim was having. They arrived too late, but women just kept coming to the hanging site and looking on from a distance. Some came from Tucson and some from Globe, in support of their friend Big Nose Kate. Others came from Wickenburg and still others journeyed down from Prescott. Many of them had appreciated the message of equality that Jim shared and helped to provide for the Twelve when they were in their area.

While men and women lingered around, the Russians decided they didn't want the bodies left on the gallows. The coyotes would get them in a heartbeat. Dmitri ordered their necks be broken and their bodies removed. This was to make sure they were dead. After breaking the necks of the other two criminals, who were all but dead anyway, they noticed that Jim was definitely dead. They didn't break his neck, but one of the soldiers decided to be extra cruel for the onlookers and thrust a Russian spear into Jim's side, garnering the desired outrage of the women.

SCENE TWO
The Diamond Mine

When evening had come, Jasper of Prescott, a respected member of the council of the state capital, went boldly to Dmitri and asked for the body of Jim. Dmitri couldn't get it out of his mind that somehow Jim survived the hanging. He'd heard about bandits who would show up on horseback just as a gang member was being hung, shoot the rope in two, and ride off with their friend. So Dmitri summoned a soldier and told him to check to make sure Jim was dead. He returned shortly and confirmed that there was no life in Jim, so Dmitri granted the body to Jasper.

Evening in Phoenix.

Jasper headed into town to get something worthy of wrapping Jim in. He felt bad that he missed out on the events of Jim's life but had heard enough to believe he was special. He wasn't sure about the business of Jim being God, but of course the Russians were just being mean about him being the President of the United States. Jasper made his way into a small store that recently opened and told the proprietor what he was after. The owner disappeared into a back room, and to Jasper's surprise he returned with a fine Indian blanket. More

Commodities store in Phoenix.

likely the proprietor took the blanket from his wife's belongings, but they were trying to get a new goods and services store up and running, so why not?

Jasper then returned to the gallows and found that the other two bandits had already been taken down. People heard about what Jasper was doing, so a crowd remained upon his return. He asked for some help removing Jim's body to lend an air of dignity in the midst of this tragedy. A small group of men solemnly removed the noose from Jim's neck and helped Jasper wrap the body in the blanket.

"What we gonna do now?" inquired one of the helpers.

Jasper explained that he bought an old diamond mine that was abandoned soon after opening. The miners had been told they might find a few rough diamonds, but nothing of any value came about. The opening was just big enough to make for a decent tomb. As they carried the shrouded body into the abandoned mine, someone noticed that the opening almost looked like a heart. That made them feel a little better about the terrible task they were performing.

Another follower of Jim, who wasn't one of the Twelve, was trailing behind the group and brought a large quantity of spices.

"What'd ya do that fer?"

"I just wanted him to smell good."

That seemed fair, so they carefully placed Jim's body in the unique tomb and scattered the spices around the sides and on top of the blanket. What remained was the task of closing up the tomb. It was a good thing a group of men made the short trip from the gallows to the tomb because closing was a real challenge. Once outside they find a nice big boulder, some old mining tools, and fortunately it rolled with some ease to close off the tomb.

Jim's heart-shaped tomb.

The next day, Marshal Garfias brought some people with him to talk again to Dmitri. He wished Wyatt Earp had stayed, but he said his brother really needed him down in Tombstone.

"We're hearing all kinds of crazy stories about Jim," Enrique Garfias began.

"Like what?" asked Dmitri.

"Like he's gonna come out of that tomb in three days!"

Dmitri chuckled, but Enrique continued.

"Why not secure the tomb for three days? Some of his Hole in the Rock Gang might come and steal his body and tell everyone that he came back from the dead. Then we'd have a bigger problem on our hands."

Dmitri thought it was a good idea and said "Take your deputies and make it secure," but he sent some of his own soldiers to be sure it was done right. When the soldiers arrived at the tomb, they found it with the large stone blocking the entrance. They then melted some wax, spread it between the stone and mine entrance, and let it harden. That would make it obvious if the seal was broken. Next they pressed Dmitri's insignia ring into the wet wax to make the seal official. For good measure, they proceeded to put seven seals on the stone.

The next couple of days had the townspeople abuzz with stories. Almost everyone agreed that Jim was a good person and didn't deserve what the Russians had done. In fact, they couldn't even bring themselves to say he died because that would give the Russians some sort of sick credit. Others started wanting to know more about Jim, so an obvious question arose about his family of origin. All they knew was that he was from Prescott and it turned out they had more questions than answers.

Some of the less noble folks expressed interest in the business about diamonds.

"He ended up being buried in a diamond mine!" one hard looking cowboy offered.

"Yah, and didn't he steal someone's diamond?" asked another.

All of a sudden there seemed to be more interest in this strange story about a diamond than in Jim.

"That mine never produced a single diamond" offered one of the former owners of the mine. That seemed to tone down any plans to break into the tomb.

"I helped fill the tomb with spices to keep the stench down," said one of the men who helped put the spices all around Jim's shrouded body.

"So what was the diamond business all about, anyway?" asked a man who had secretly followed the ideas that Jim tried to spread.

"I don't know," said Pedro, who had recently joined the discussions, now that nobody cared about him being one of the Twelve.

"What I do know is that Jim said the last days of his life were gonna be real tough. Kinda hardened by the terrible things he went through."

"You tryin' to say there's something good that could come out of all that mess?" asked Jimbo, who people were starting to call a disciple of Jim's rather than one of the Twelve.

Even Johnny was there, just sort of mixing in with the crowd. That made the three that Jim called upon the most, to be reunited once again in Phoenix.

"Yes," said Johnny. "I think Jim knew what was gonna happen, and somehow the story of the end of his life was a diamond in the rough."

Another in the crowd spoke up. "Maybe, just maybe."

"Why do ya say that?" asked a woman in the group.

"I get a strange feelin' that Jim's burial in Phoenix is gonna prove to mean something."

"It meant something to the townsfolk who chose that name," said Darell Duppa, who just so happened to be the one who predicted that, like the mythical phoenix rising from its own ashes, a great city would emerge from the ruins of the original Indian settlement.

"God doesn't know impossible," said an unidentified person in the group. "Maybe that's the secret of the diamond."

"In what way?" asked an intrigued person.

"Maybe there's more things to happen," said Big Nose Kate in a hopeful way.

———————

And happen they did.

THE VALUE OF THE DIAMOND
A Jim Caldwell Story – Book 3

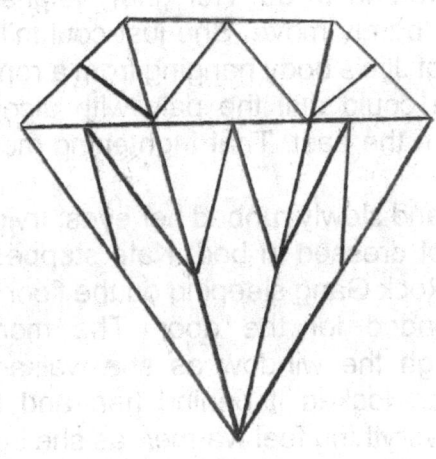

PROLOGUE
Life after Death

It was a rather chilly Sunday morning in the Phoenician desert. As the sun was peeking over the McDowell Mountains, Big Nose Kate was desperately trying to wake up. She had made a commitment to a daily journey to the gravesite of Jim Caldwell, yet a couple of days later it was the last thing she wanted to do. Her grief weighed her down so much she could barely move. She just couldn't get that image out of her head of Jim's body hanging from a rope. Kate thought that maybe she could dull the pain with alcohol, after all, it always worked in the past. That frightening memory jolted her awake.

She sat up and slowly rubbed her eyes, trying to find focus, then clumsily got dressed in bed. Kate stepped over some of the Hole in the Rock Gang sleeping on the floor of the boarding house, and headed for the door. The morning sun was streaming through the window as she walked by, then she opened the door, locked it behind her, and left. The direct sunlight made everything feel warmer, as she began her trudge to the abandoned diamond mine that served as Jim's tomb. "Why am I doing this?" Kate asked herself, but the truth was that she just wanted to be near the man she loved more than anything. It seemed like an endless journey as she dragged one leg in front of the other, while aching all over.

When she finally arrived, she noticed something strange about the stone that covered the entrance. Looking closer, Kate was surprised to see six of the seven seals broken. Dmitri, the Russian overlord for Phoenix, had ordered his soldiers to spread melted wax between the stone and mine entrance. He also told them to press his ring into the wax to make an official insignia. This was to provide proof that nobody could tamper with the dead body, because Marshal Garfias heard some wild stories about resurrecting from the dead. Out of fear, the soldiers decided to seal the tomb seven times for extra protection.

Kate could see that the first six seals were broken, so she blinked her eyes and moved in closer. The remaining seal was definitely missing the insignia, and she guessed that the soldiers were simply in a hurry, causing them to miss putting the final insignia in place. Out of curiosity, she reached her hand toward the seventh seal, and it too broke. Now a lot of folklore develops around unusual stories like these, but what people later said was that, "there was silence in heaven for about half an hour."

What happened next took Kate's breath away, and she became paralyzed with fear. While standing at the entrance, the gigantic boulder slowly rolled to the side. Her instinct was to run, but her feet wouldn't move. Right then a wonderful fragrance wafted out, and the spices that were left around Jim's body helped bring Kate's mind back to the moment. "What should I do?" she wondered, as the cool air also drifted out of the diamond mine and further helped to clear her mind.

Against her better judgment, and almost like an out-of-body experience, she slowly stepped into the cold, dark, makeshift tomb. Once inside, her eyes took a bit of time to adjust, so she rubbed them, and was stunned because she couldn't believe what she saw. It was something that would forever be talked about in the annals of time. To her absolute terror and deep confusion, she was confronted with…are you ready for this?...

nothing. As in no body. As in an empty tomb that had been meticulously sealed to prevent this sort of thing from happening. At that point she nearly fell down trying to get out of there, because one's rationality is completely lost in moments like that.

Once out of the mine, she fled in terror, wondering if the grave robbers were still nearby. Then she remembered that the tomb was still sealed, which further confused her. After fumbling to unlock the door at the boarding house, Kate breathlessly burst through the door. The boys were awake and Pedro said, "Whoa, there! What's your problem? And for heaven's sake, lock the door." For a moment she thought that the nothingness she saw in the diamond mine was a cue to say nothing…so she didn't…then she did. She mumbled some confusing gibberish which brought the rest of the gang together to see what was going on.

"Take a deep breath," said Pedro, so Kate complied because she was already feeling a bit light-headed. Johnny had just finished making a pot of coffee, so he handed her a cup of Arbuckles' Ariosa Blend.

Kate said thanks and took a few sips, then they sat and waited to hear what was going on. She rocked back and forth trying to soothe herself, and finally screamed, "Jim's body's gone!" and, as you can imagine, the reaction was varied.

Jimbo said, "Not surprised they broke in and stole his body. The marshal wanted that to happen, 'cause of all that talk 'bout Jim risin' from the dead."

Johnny mumbled, "Maybe she's back to drinking."

Then Pedro said, matter-of-factly, "Just tell us what happened."

Kate took a moment to compose herself, and with a bit of tremble in her voice, said, "When I got to the tomb this morning, the stone was still blocking the entrance."

"So how'd ya know his body was stolen?" asked Matt.

"Just let her tell her story," growled Bart.

After a moment Kate explained, "Six of the seals were broken, but the seventh seal was still in place."

"So his body wasn't stolen?" asked Carly.

"I don't know," replied Kate, with a bit of exasperation. "All I know is that I reached toward that seventh seal and then it broke."

"So you broke it?" inquired Junior.

"No!" yelled an irritated Kate. "But then the boulder rolled to the side." Now they were getting interested.

"What did you find?" asked an impatient Pedro.

"Nothing" said Kate. "The tomb was empty."

"Either the tomb was empty because the stone was moved before you got there," suggested Johnny, "or it was moving because you were tipsy." Several laughed, but the look they got from Kate quickly ended their fun.

"This ain't no laughing matter!" complained Kate.

Then Pedro said, "Okay, I'll go see for myself what's going on." He left in a bit of a huff, and went to the outskirts of town where the mine was located. While approaching, he thought to himself, "If Jim got out of that tomb, when it was still sealed and he was dead, the ole worthless diamond mine just might find it has value."

It was full daylight when he arrived, and he was beyond surprised to see the stone rolled away. He thought it was too big and heavy for Kate to have moved it, so he started feeling fear as he stooped to look in. All he saw was the Indian blanket Jim's body had been draped in, and lots of spices strewn about, still filling the air with a wonderful aroma. One would think Jim's body was stolen, but not Pedro. He decided to believe Kate about the breaking of the seventh seal, and being the first one into the formerly sealed tomb. What Pedro decided to believe was about resurrection. People had talked about it since Ezekiel's prophecy in chapter 37, which said, "You shall know that I am the LORD, when I open your graves, and bring you up from your graves, O my people. I will put my spirit within you, and you shall live." (vv. 13-14).

Pedro was beside himself with excitement. He went running back to the boarding house and yelled gleefully, "I knew it! If anyone could beat death, it was gonna be Jim." Others kind of wanted to go see, but since two had already shared the same story from separate trips that the tomb was empty, they decided to stay. That night, the Gang closed and locked their boarding house room, out of fear that they would be blamed for taking Jim's body. Was Kate right, that the body was taken, or Pedro, that Jim had resurrected from the dead? Tommie didn't particularly care, so he went out to have a drink at a bar. Several rushed to the door to lock it after Tommie left, because whatever the truth was, strange things were certainly happening.

It turned out that Tommie missed the most momentous occasion one could possibly imagine. As the Gang sat around the table and chairs in the lamp-lit room, Jim himself appeared to them. To say the least, they were in shock as they rubbed their eyes. Pedro was the first to speak, saying, "Locked doors couldn't keep him out any more than a closed tomb could keep him in." The darkness of the room caused the others to squint, because they feared they were seeing a ghost. Then Jim spoke, "Peace be with you." He told them that the good words he had shared with them on the hillside, the parables he told, and the great powers God wrought through him, were now theirs to continue. They were speechless, and then frustratingly, Jim disappeared.

Pretty soon there was a knock on the door, and they all nearly fainted. Pedro sheepishly made his way to the door and asked in a befuddled manner, "Who's there?" The answer quickly came back, "It's me, Tommie. Who'd ya think it was?" A relieved round of laughter broke out and Pedro unlocked the door and let him in. Jimbo told Tommie the story about Jim's appearance, and Tommie was the only one who laughed. "I thought I was the one who had too much to drink," retorted Tommie, and this time nobody laughed. He looked around, saw folded arms and serious looking eyes, and said "I'm sticking to my guns on this one. You don't call me Doubting Tommie for nothing!"

About a week passed and the Gang was confused, because they didn't know what to do. They stayed put all week in the locked room and things were started to get musty. They believed that Jim had been resurrected from the dead, and they really felt it was important to be of one accord, but Tommie wouldn't budge. They routinely gathered at the dinner table during that week, and talked about what Jim had said. It would be easy enough to continue sharing his stories and parables, but they weren't too sure they understood what Jim meant by God's powers now being theirs to continue. Unfortunately, they also rather taunted Tommie about his unbelief, and he was beginning to feel excluded. That's when Jim appeared again in the boarding house.

The Gang was overjoyed to see him, but Tommie was the one this time who was speechless. They all moved in closer to be near Jim, while Tommie moved back. He hit the bunkbed behind him and fell onto the bottom mattress. Everyone looked back, and Tommie appeared as white as the ghost he thought he was seeing. Jim looked at him and said, "Tommie, stand up." He knew he was in trouble, but not sure why. As he stood up, nearly knocking over a lantern, Jim said, "Do not doubt, but believe." Tommie gathered his senses and delightfully surprised everyone by saying…"I believe!" Jim then said, "Blessed are those who will never be able to see me, but choose to believe." Jim then once again disappeared, and Tommie took some time to be embarrassed.

It was a rather sleepless night for all of them, as they pondered the meaning of everything that had happened. The next morning they discussed what to call themselves, because they felt 'Hole in the Rock Gang' was about the past. Since Pedro was the go-to guy for naming, they asked him for some ideas. After scratching his head a bit, he mentioned that when Jim appeared, he called them to continue the things he had done. A huge grin then spread across Pedro's face and he said, "I guess you could say we were 'called well.' Get it? Let's call ourselves Caldwellians." Nobody liked it at first, but somehow the idea stuck, and after a while they adopted their new name.

Meanwhile, before continuing with other things that happened after Jim's resurrection, we need to first get caught up on a couple of important events from the fall of 1881. Deputy U.S. Marshal Virgil Earp moved from Prescott to Tombstone, to help deal with the outlaw Clanton Gang. Virgil quickly appointed his brother, Wyatt Earp as the acting City Marshal, who was also pleased to see his good friend Doc Holliday had arrived in town. On October 25, Ike Clanton was openly breathing threats against the Earps and Holliday. After a heated argument, the unarmed senior Clanton member said "Get ready for a showdown!" The next day the Clanton Gang met in a vacant lot to bushwhack Doc Holliday, but they were surprised when the Earps showed up with Doc. The Clanton Gang made their way toward the O.K. Corral, and as the Earps passed by, they found the troublemakers waiting at the end of an alley. Virgil tried to arrest them, but what happened next was a blur. Some of the Clanton Gang cocked their pistols, shots were fired, and several died. The Earps and Doc Holliday were tried for murder, but it was decided that they acted within the law.

Another important thing that happened in the fall of 1881, was the end of the Russian Invasion. Back in the motherland, Tsar Alexander II was assassinated. His successor was his son, Alexander III, who wanted to avoid his father's fate. The first thing he did was to reverse the liberal reforms of his father by assuming autocratic rule. This kind of oppressive rule needed the full force of his military, so he recalled his troops from southwest America. They moved out about as fast as they moved in, and the invasion that started without bloodshed, mercifully ended in a withdrawal without bloodshed.

_____

In the meantime, the boarding house they were staying at was starting to smell, and Pedro was feeling a bit antsy. "I don't like it," announced Pedro, "that we're now just a group of eleven, after Bennie hung himself."

"Let me remind you that Bennie's death made us a group of twelve," countered Big Nose Kate.

"Not really," complained Pedro. "You liked to call us a baker's dozen, but we ain't thirteen any more either."

"Right," argued Kate, "because we're now a group of twelve!"

"But the twelve," continued Pedro, with frustration in his voice, "referred to the twelve men, and now Bennie is gone."

"Men!" Kate stomped her foot on the ground and raised her voice, "At least Jim didn't discriminate against women!" Most of the men in the room looked uncomfortable, but didn't want to deal with her.

"So, what's yer point, Pedro?" asked Bart, proving that Kate was right about men, and even more correct about Jim.

"We need to honor Jim's plan of having twelve of us," explained Pedro.

Carly then chimed in with, "We've got enough problems. Don't need more, unless ya gots a solution."

"Not that hard," said Pedro, "all we have to do is add another to our group."

"Since you don't seem to want to follow Jim, when it comes to equality," offered Kate, "I guess I need to push you all on this issue, so I vote that you add me." The guys rolled their eyes and ignored her, which made her even madder. "So, at least we can all agree on one thing. You guys, and I do mean guys, find it difficult to live the life Jim taught!"

"You're right," Pedro said in a dismissive way, then suggested "let's add one of the people among the crowds who heard Jim talk and saw the great things he had done."

"You mean one of the men among the crowds," complained Kate.

Talking as if Kate wasn't even there, Johnny asked, "How about Clint?"

Almost at the same time, Bart said "I was impressed with Cooper.

Pedro then suggested, "Let's do this the way Jim did things. Let's pause in prayer and ask for guidance from God."

Kate threw her arms up in the air and said, "Nice job of practicing selective spirituality."

They agreed that they were doing a nice job, and continued to ignore her because now she was using big words that they didn't understand. Then they bowed their heads, including Kate, who was now outside their prayer circle, because they wanted Kate to understand that they were going to do things the way Jim did. Pedro simply prayed "Our father in heaven, please show us which one of the two people you have chosen."

Kate added, "Lord, he means, which one of the two men, because Pedro really isn't interested in you having your way, if it includes a woman." Now she was stepping on toes, as if she were a preacher. Come to think of it, she was the first person ever to preach the good news of the empty tomb. This comment rather abruptly ended the prayer, without so much as an "amen."

At least Matt affirmed the hypocrisy as he complained, "This was easier when Jim was around."

"I agree," said Pedro with a lot of frustration, "but this is what we have now. Anyone have an idea which person God wants us to choose?"

"No," answered Jimbo, "but I've got a coin. How about I flip it? If its heads we go with Clint, and if its tails we go with Cooper.

"And if it lands on its edge, we go with me," Kate suggested sarcastically. "And what a great idea to let God speak through gambling!"

The men agreed that God was speaking through Jimbo, not Kate. Then Pedro angrily offered out of his biblical ignorance, "God surely couldn't speak through a donkey." Several nodded in agreement, so he flipped the coin. All eyes were steadfastly watching the coin as it went into the air. It came down, hit the floor awkwardly, and rolled toward the wall. They almost knocked each other over following it, and their eyes went wide open as it started to tip against the wall.

Pedro stomped the floor in anger and the coin fell over. He happily said, "Tails. Looks like God wants Cooper to join us."

"Looks more like Pedro wants another man to join us, if you ask me," complained Kate as she turned and walked away.

Nobody was asking Kate, and since Bart was the one who suggested Cooper, he was sent out to retrieve him. The room was rather chilly that hot afternoon in the Arizona desert, so they sat and waited without talking.

Cooper was downtown working at the new post office when Bart found him, and Bart simply said "Cooper, the Lord has chosen you to become a witness with us to Jim's resurrection." This became the first sign that things were going right, because Cooper was happy to be added to the group. When Bart and Cooper returned to the boarding house, they were very excited and began sharing the stories of Jim's resurrection and his appearances.

"I guess I just have one question," mentioned Cooper. "I heard a lot of his stories and saw many of the things he did. How did Jim do all those things?"

"It was the power of God working through him," stated Pedro, as a matter-of-fact. "And when the resurrected Jim appeared to us right here in this room, he said that the stories and powers were now ours to continue."

"I guess I have another question," announced Cooper. "If you have so much power, why are you all holed up here like a bunch of scared kittens in a box?"

"Good question," stated Johnny.

Bart seemed embarrassed for a moment, and decided they needed to be empowered by their personal stories, so he shared how his life had changed. Matt gave a glowing testimony of the radical change in his lifestyle, and Kate had the most impressive story of the effect Jim had on her life. Cooper decided right then and there that he was dedicating his life to becoming what they were starting to call Caldwellians.

Rather on a high, Pedro said "Let's go to The Rusty Tavern. I sense something great is getting ready to happen," and the others could feel it, too.

As they opened the door to leave, Kate said, "Kinda feels like we're leaving the tomb. Maybe now we can start living the resurrection life."

They all agreed, but Pedro cautiously said, "Or at least we'll try."

Getting in the last word, Kate said, "Nope. This new life is something we do or don't do. No such thing as trying. That would be like being a little pregnant!"

The Jim Caldwell Trilogy

ACT I
THE ROAD TO TUCSON

Arizona 1881

SCENE ONE
The Caldwellians

It was exactly fifty days since the Jewish celebration of Passover, making this the Jewish day of Pentecost. This day commemorates the power of God coming down to Mount Sinai, giving the gift of the Torah. Nobody in the group knew that because there weren't many Jews in the Arizona Territory. After the relatively short ride to The Rusty Tavern, they were surprised to see a large crowd gathered inside and out. Our Caldwellians dismounted and headed through the multitude. As they expected, there were no seats or tables available in the Tavern, but soon Jimbo announced that a table was freeing up outside. They packed themselves around the table with the late morning sun glistening on their faces.

Suddenly there was a loud sound like a pack of coyotes, followed by what looked like sparks of fire resting on the heads of each of the Caldwellians. Pedro looked over and saw fire even resting on the head of Kate, and she returned a peaceful smile. At that point hey were filled with the Holy Spirit and began speaking in other languages, which amazed and astonished the onlookers. One man said, "That guy is speaking Apache," and another said, "I hear someone speaking Russian. I thought we were rid of them!" A large group of Chinese immigrants had come for the California Gold Rush, and a Chinese man who had settled in Phoenix announced that he heard someone speaking Chinese. All were amazed and perplexed and more than curious. Finally, a man came stumbling out of the Tavern and said "I know drunk talk when I hear it!"

Pedro then stepped forward and got everyone's attention.

He wasn't sure what to say, but he knew Jim's spirit would be with him, so he opened his mouth and spoke from the heart. "I assure ya we ain't drunk. We just arrived and couldn't even find a table, much less place an order, but listen to what I have to say." He paused for a moment, surprised to see people paying attention, then said, "Jim Caldwell, as you well know, performed deeds of power, wonders, and signs that God did through him. Then you had a fake trial, and sentenced him to be hung by the Russians."

"Rightly so," yelled a large man holding a mug of beer.

Ignoring him, Pedro continued. "But God raised him from death, and freed him from the diamond mine that served as his tomb, because death could not hold him. Jim was raised up to heaven by God, and all thirteen of us here today are witnesses." He again flashed a smile at Kate and she returned an approving look.

Someone yelled, "That's a bunch of hogwash!" and went back into the tavern. Others went back to eating and drinking, while still others came forward and asked what they should do.

Pedro said to those interested, "Change your lives, and be baptized, so that your sins may be forgiven; and you will receive the gift of the Holy Spirit."

So those who welcomed his message were baptized that day. They headed to the nearby Agua Fria River, where Pedro, Jimbo, and Johnny just naturally waded out. The rest of the original Caldwellians lined people up to get baptized, and they were overwhelmed to see more and more people coming down from the Rusty Tavern. It was an exciting and heart-warming time, as God smiled on them. Someone yelled, "Look, a rainbow around the sun!" It became a fitting end to a memorable day, as people left, filled with the Holy Spirit.

An ever-growing number of Caldwellians began devoting themselves to the teaching of Jim, as taught through the original Caldwellians. They began gathering daily for fellowship, and prayer, and learning. Many exciting things started happening over the next several weeks, and people were in awe because wonders and signs were being done by the Caldwellian leadership.

Soon they settled into the Catholic Church in downtown Phoenix, now that the Russians were gone, and the priest was happy to let them use it for their new movement of the Holy Spirit. They also did a rather strange thing, probably to show their commitment. The followers sold everything they had, then the leaders distributed the proceeds to all, as any had need. Things were going very well indeed for the Caldwellians, and their numbers continued to grow.

One day Pedro was at the Church for some prayer time, when a man who hadn't walked since birth was carried to the entrance. The man hadn't been to the church for a long time, due to the Russians, and was happy to be back in his favorite begging spot. When Pedro was done, he headed to the exit, and the lame man asked him for money. Pedro looked intently at him and said, "I got no money." The man looked away in frustration, then Pedro said, "But what I have I give you; in the name of Jim Caldwell, stand up and walk." The man felt his ankles strengthen, then Pedro took him by the hand and helped him stand up. He then ran around the street in from of the church praising God.

People came pouring into the church, because they knew the man, and were amazed when they heard what Pedro had done. They hailed Pedro as a hero, brought him back into the church, and said they wanted to hear more from him. The priest was there, and offered to let Pedro speak from the pulpit. Pedro stepped up and said, "Jim Caldwell did many great works, and he always said it was the power of God working through him. When he was resurrected from the dead, we saw him, and he told us that the powers were now ours to continue. To this we are witnesses. And the lame man now healed is a testimony of God's power, to all of us gathered here. Change yer ways, and turn to God so that your sins may be wiped out."

While Pedro was speaking, Marshal Garfias was just outside the church and had several people complaining to him. The marshal headed into the church with several of his deputies, interrupted Pedro, and declared, "People are annoyed." He then said, "You can't be claiming that Jim was resurrected from the dead." He then explained, "I didn't care for that Russian Dmitri, but he had a great idea about sealing Jim's tomb. That way we would know his body hadn't been stolen. Fact is, the seals were broken, so it's not too complicated to understand how his body disappeared. You yourself probably took it!" The crowd started yelling at the marshal, so he drew his gun and shot it into the air to squelch any questions about his authority. He then arrested Pedro, who was still at the pulpit, and put him in custody. One might think that would stop this new group, but many more became believers that day.

The next day, the clergy showed up at the jail and asked Pedro, "By what power did you heal that man?"

Then Pedro, filled with the Holy Spirit, said to them, "If you are questioning me because of a good deed done to someone who couldn't walk, and are asking how he was healed, let it be known to all of you, that he was healed in the name of Jim

Caldwell, whom you hung and whom God raised from the dead."

Having nothing to say in opposition, the clergy retreated just outside the jail for a discussion. They said, "What will we do with him? Everybody already knows what he did. Let's join the marshal in warning him not to speak about Jim." So they returned to the jail and ordered him to be silent about Jim Caldwell.

Pedro then shocked them with his response, "Whether it is right in God's sight to listen to you rather than to God, you must judge. As for me, my answer is 'No!' I will not keep from speaking about all that I have seen and heard."

After the marshal released Pedro, he went back and told all of the believers what the clergy had questioned him about. In return, they prayed for boldness to continue the signs and wonders through the name of Jim Caldwell. After the prayer, something like an earthquake happened, and they were all filled with the Holy Spirit. They found that they were of one heart and soul and agreed to speak with boldness. With great power the Caldwellians went about giving their testimony to the resurrection of Jim, and they were filled with grace. They continued to care for one another's needs through the proceeds from selling their property.

But a man named Jesse, with the consent of his wife Sadie, sold a piece of their property. Then they decided to keep back some of the proceeds before laying it at Pedro's feet. Normally, this would not be a problem, but Pedro's spiritual authority was at stake. As is common in a small community, everyone knew everyone else's business, and soon this minor problem came to Pedro's attention. Pedro knew that the community decision to give property was not required, it was simply voluntary. Being caught between his authority and their choice, he decided to spend some time in prayer.

God nudged Pedro's mind toward a story in 1 Kings 14:1-8, so Pedro opened a Bible and read the story. It troubled him deeply, because he didn't get the point. He read it several times, and soon wished that Jim was there to help him. All of a sudden he realized it was about deceit, and the evil it brings. Pedro thanked Jim in his heart, called Jesse to himself, and asked, "Why has evil filled your heart to lie to the Holy Spirit and to keep back part of the proceeds of the land?" Not only did Jesse refuse to answer, but many of the disciples were listening. Pedro then asked, "How is it that you have contrived this deed in your heart?" Again, there was no answer. Then Pedro declared with powerful authority, "You did not lie to us but to God!" Immediately Jesse got on his horse to flee, but he only got a few feet away until his horse stumbled. Jesse fell off his horse, landed on his head, broke his neck, and died. Those who witnessed this thought it might be a good idea to be honest.

About three hours later, word got around about what happened to Jesse. Crowds started gathering, as is so common when terrible events occur. Then Jesse's wife Sadie returned from a short visit with a friend. She didn't know what happened to her husband, and nobody wanted to talk about it. Pedro heard she was back, so he called for her, and said, "Tell me whether you and your husband sold your land." Sadie said with a bit of confusion, "You know we did." The crowd made a muffled sound, then Pedro said, "Why did you put the Spirit of the Lord to the test?" Now she was very uncomfortable and started to sweat. She looked around and saw everyone watching her, so she rather angrily stammered, "I don't know what you mean." Pedro clearly explained that the common life they all were in was first and foremost about responding to the nudging of the Holy Spirit. He then said, "When evil fills the heart, there is no room for the Holy Spirit." Immediately, Sadie clutched her chest, fell down at his feet and died. Yet again, there was fear about what it meant to be committed to this group of believers, between deaths and healings.

Word got around about this second death, and the original Caldwellians found themselves rather isolated. At the same time, stories were also spreading about the many signs and wonders that were happening. The leaders gathered each day at the Catholic Church in downtown Phoenix, where nobody dared to join them, but the people still held them in high regard. Actually, the number of believers kept growing, mainly due to the healings the disciples were performing. People showed up each day while the Caldwellians continued the work of Jim Caldwell. Maybe the most interesting thing of all was that people were starting to gather from towns around Phoenix; from Prescott and Tucson and Tombstone. They even saw people from Wickenburg and Vulture City, and they were all cured of various infirmities.

Just as things seemed to be going well, the clergy became jealous. They easily convinced Marshal Garfias to put the Caldwellian leadership in jail, where the most unexpected thing happened. During the night, an angel appeared and said to them, "Go back to the church and tell the people the whole message about living the Caldwellian life." As Pedro was about to mention they were locked in jail, the door swung open. Pedro, Jimbo, and Johnny looked at each other then stepped out. They looked around and since they saw no guards in sight, they shrugged their shoulders and left with smiles on their faces.

While the disciples were obeying their divine calling the

next morning, the clergy showed up at the jail. They found the jail empty, rubbed their heads, and wondered what might be going on. Then someone from town burst through the front door of the jail and said, "The men you had arrested yesterday are in your church, and they're back at it, teaching the people!"

The church's priest led the posse back to his church, went in and said to the disciples, "We gave you strict orders not to teach in the name of Jim Caldwell." Pedro answered, "Yeah, and you had us arrested, but you can see how well that worked out." The priest was fuming as Pedro said, "We must obey God rather than any human authority." When the clergy heard this, they were all enraged and wanted to kill Pedro, but a deputy showed up and talked the clergy into thinking rather than feeling.

The deputy took them to a back room of the church where the priest angrily said, "This is my church. Pedro's the problem." The deputy said, "Calm down. Even the marshal doesn't know what to do with them. But let's try this. Leave them alone, and if what they do and say is of human origin, it will fail; but if it is of God, you will not be able to overthrow them." This reasoning convinced the clergy, but on their way out, leaving the Caldwellians in, the priest yelled back with his fist raised, "Do not speak again of Jim Caldwell!" As the clergy passed through the door, Pedro looked back at his disciples and said, "This ain't over, fellas."

Now during those days, when the disciples were increasing in number, a problem came to Pedro's attention. Their idea of meeting the needs of all wasn't working, so Pedro called the whole community together and said, "We are growing fast, and that's a good thing, but needs are going unmet. We've gotta continue Jim's works and words, but I think some need to be appointed to distribute our communal possessions." There was an audible sigh of relief because quite a few had been discussing the problem, and they were more than ready to hear a solution.

Pedro continued, "Let's get seven people of good standing. People who are full of the Spirit and of wisdom, to appoint to this task. That will give the rest of us plenty of time for prayer and sharing our stories with others." This pleased the community of believers, and the first name they came up with was Jack. He was a man full of faith and the Holy Spirit. The other six who were appointed were Rose, Boone, Carter, Hank, Belle, and Cheyenne. This group of men and women were brought before the Twelve, who laid their hands on them and offered prayers for their work.

They created a system to manage the assistance to those in need, and as new people joined, they gave the group their possessions. Hank and Belle were in charge of selling the items. Cheyenne and Carter were responsible for the money. Then Rose, Boone, and Jack took care of distributing the money as people had need. Great things continued to happen around Phoenix and even many of the clergy joined the movement.

Jack became the man of the hour. He did his work making sure the community's possessions were meeting the needs of all, and in his spare time he did great wonders and signs among the people. He was a likable sort, and people enjoyed him. Well, not all of the people. Some tried to argue with Jack, about who was in the most need. It seems that even when you are about doing good things in the name of the Lord, someone will find fault, but they could not withstand the wisdom and the Spirit with which he spoke.

Not quick to back down, the trouble makers started a rumor that Jack spoke blasphemously against God. This would not be tolerated, so the clergy had him dragged before them. As Jack stood up, they expected to see an angry face, but instead they saw that his face was like that of an angel.

The priest of the Catholic Church, where the twelve had begun their movement, asked him straight out, "Have you been blaspheming God?" Jack replied with a testimony from his heart: "The God of glory appeared to our ancestor Aapo, and said 'Leave your country and your relatives and go to the land that I will show you.'"

"Yah, why don't you leave?" yelled one of the clergy.

"Let him speak," responded another.

"Aapo left his country of Guatemala," continued Jack "and settled at Calakmul. After his father died, God had him move from there to a land of promise."

"Yah, not like this God-forsaken place!" yelled someone in the growing crowd of listeners, as several laughed.

Jack continued, "Then Aapo became the father of Hugo, and Hugo became the father of Tobillo, and Tobillo became the father of the twelve patriarchs."

"We know our Bible!" complained one of the clergy, angrily.

Jack ignored him and said, "The patriarchs sold Eloy into Honduras, but God rescued him and enabled him to win favor with the King, who appointed him ruler over Honduras. Now there was a famine, and our ancestors could find no food. But when Tobillo heard there was food in Honduras, he sent our ancestors there on their first visit. On the second visit Eloy made himself known to his brothers, and Eloy's family became known to the King. Then Eloy sent and invited his father Tobillo to come to Honduras. He died there as well as our ancestors, and they were laid in a tomb."

"I don't hear any blaspheming going on here. I say let Jack go," suggested one of the clergy who had recently joined the movement.

"I want to continue," offered Jack, "because the story gets better. At this time Abund was born. For three months he was brought up in his father's house, but then he was abandoned. The King's daughter adopted him and brought him up as her own son. So Abund was instructed in all the wisdom of the Hondurans and was powerful in his words and deeds.

"When he turned forty, it came into his heart to visit his relatives. When he saw one of them being wronged, he killed the Honduran."

"Now we're talking," a cowboy in the crowd said with a smile. "Sounds like our Wild West." This time others hushed him, because they liked hearing a good story.

Again Jack continued, "The next day he came to some of them as they were quarreling and said 'Men, you are brothers; why do you wrong each other?' But one pushed Abund aside, saying, 'Who made you ruler and a judge over us? Do you want to kill me as you killed the Honduran?'" An uneasy feeling went through the crowd at this point, as murder seemed to be brewing in their attitudes. "This cast great fear into the heart of Abund and he fled. He became a resident alien in the land of San Salvador and became the father of two sons."

"You might be thinking about packing your bags yourself, there young man" said another cowboy. Then he ominously said, "We don't cotton to no blasphemers."

"Forty years later," Jack went on, seemingly unaware of the growing anger in the crowd, "an angel appeared to him in the flame of a burning bush. When Abund saw it, he was amazed.

As he approached, there came the voice of the Lord: 'I am the God of your ancestors, the God of Abund, Hugo, and Tobillo.' Then the Lord said to him, 'Take off the sandals from your feet, for the place where you stand is holy ground. I have heard the groaning of my people in Honduras and have come down to rescue them. And now I will send you to Honduras.'

"Doesn't that sound like blasphemy?" inquired a person in the crowd.

"No," said the priest. "At least not yet."

Then Jack said, "It was this Abund who led his people out of Honduras. He performed many wonders and signs in Honduras, at Lake Izabal, and in the wilderness for forty years. Our ancestors were unwilling to obey him, and wished to return to Honduras. They told Abund's brother, 'Make gods for us who will lead the way for us.' So they made a calf, offered a sacrifice to the idol, and were delighted with what they had done."

"Is this guy supporting idolatry?" quizzed a clergyman who wanted to get rid of Jack.

"Let him talk," said the priest. "I think the way he's telling this story is giving us plenty of rope to hang him."

"Our ancestors," Jack said with growing strength, "had the tent of testimony in the wilderness. Then they brought it with Geovanni to Tenochtitlan, and it was there until the time of King Montezuma. But it was the Spanish conquistadors who built God's temple, so hear me out. The Most High does not dwell in houses made with human hands. As the prophet Isaiah says,

'Heaven is my throne,
and the earth is my footstool.
What kind of house will you build for
me, says the Lord,

or what is the place of my rest?
Did not my hand make all these
things?'"

Anger was at an all-time high now in the crowd, but Jack expressed it first and directed it at them. "You stiff-necked people, uncircumcised in heart and ears, you are forever opposing the Holy Spirit, just as your ancestors used to do. Which of the prophets did your ancestors not persecute? They killed those who foretold the coming of Jim Caldwell, and now you have become his betrayers and murderers. You are the ones that received the law as ordained by angels, and yet have not kept it!"

In hindsight, Jack would have been better off keeping his temper, because the clergy certainly didn't. They became enraged, were grinding their teeth, and wanted blood. That's when Jack was filled with the Holy Spirit and gazed into heaven. There he saw the glory of God and Jim Caldwell standing next to him. "Look," Jack said, "I see the heavens opened and Jim Caldwell standing next to God!"

That was it. The clergy were beyond furious, then rushed in on Jack. They knocked him down, dragged him out of town and prepared to hang him. While they tied the noose around Jack's neck, he prayed, "Lord, receive my spirit." As they kicked the support out from under Jack's feet, he was heard saying "Lord, do not hold this sin against them." When he had said this, his body swung slowly as his last breath left him. Someone in the background looked on with a rather evil smirk of approval. That someone was Jose Maria Perez, who hated a fake story more than anything.

The next day a severe persecution began against the

movement started by Jim Caldwell, and it was Jose Maria Perez who rallied the oppression. He made a visit to Marshal Garfias and got deputized, so he could track down Jim's followers and arrest them. So Jose Maria Perez began his legal campaign of hatred and violence. He entered house after house and asked if they were followers of Jim. If they said "no" he would leave them alone, but for those who confessed their allegiance to the Caldwellians, he dragged them off to the downtown jail and the marshal gladly locked them up.

After the tragic loss of Jack, Rose stepped up to the task of sharing the stories of Jim Caldwell. She was one of the seven, along with Jack, who had been appointed to dole out the proceeds to those in need. After the persecutions began, and the followers were scattered, Rose went down to Tucson. She spoke with great eloquence about Jim and the crowds listened eagerly. She was rather short of stature, so she stood on a wooden crate, and they were astounded at the signs she did. She exorcised demons out of many who were possessed, and cured many others who were paralyzed or lame. So there was great joy in that city.

In contrast to Rose, there was a magician named Alexander Herrman. He had traveled all over the world, and now was settled into Tucson and performing his art. He was well known as the first magician to pull a live rabbit out of a hat, and the people of Tucson were amazed by him. They would often say, "This man is the power of God that is called Great." That created a tension in the town about who they thought was the greatest, so they listened carefully to what Rose was saying. It didn't take long until many realized that Rose was promoting God, and Alexander was promoting himself.

When those who believed Rose was the real thing, because she was proclaiming the kingdom of God in the name of Jim Caldwell, they were baptized. At first, Alexander was jealous. He wanted the crowds for himself, so he paid attention to what Rose had to say. He had been more attracted to Rose's spectacular accomplishments than her spiritual message, but actually, he simply found her quite enticing. His travels made it difficult to think about marriage, but now he was settled down. He didn't think he would have any chance with Rose, because he was a bit short and stout, so he did what he could do. Alexander became a believer and was baptized. Truth is, what he started dreaming about was to tour with Rose for profit, and of course, to marry her.

Now when the Twelve up in Phoenix heard that Tucson had accepted the word of God, Pedro and Johnny went down to pray for them. They soon discovered that the people were only baptized, but had not yet received the Holy Spirit. Then Pedro and Johnny laid their hands on them, and they received the Holy Spirit. This was a profound moment in the life of the believers, as they praised God, exchanged hugs, and offered holy kisses. Now when Alexander saw this great event, he offered money, saying, "Give me also this power so that anyone on whom I lay my hands may receive the Holy Spirit." But Pedro said, "May your silver perish with you, because you thought you could obtain God's gift with money! You have no part or share in this, for your heart is not right before God. Repent, and pray to the Lord that you may be forgiven."

Alexander was stunned, and said, "Pray for me that I will

not lose my silver." Pedro shook his head in frustration. He couldn't believe how lost Alexander was, especially considering he had been baptized. Pedro called Rose over and had a long chat with her about the difference between baptism by water and baptism by the Holy Spirit. He said, "Baptism by water remembers what Jim received from his cousin the Dipper, and baptism by the Holy Spirit is the leading of Jim here and now. After a good discussion, because this was new to all of them, Pedro and Johnny got on their horses and returned to Phoenix.

After they left, an angel of the Lord said to Rose, "Get up and ride your horse toward the south to the road that goes down from Phoenix to Chihuahua, Mexico." (This is a wilderness road.) So she got up and went. Now there was a court official of the President of Mexico, who was in charge of his treasury. He had come to Phoenix to worship and was returning home. When his stage coach stopped at Nogales for more passengers, he pulled out his Bible and started reading from the prophet Isaiah. Then the Spirit said to Rose, who had also stopped for a break at Nogales, "Go over to the man on the stage coach who is reading his Bible." So Rose went and heard him reading the prophet Isaiah. Rose asked, "Do you understand what you are reading?" He said "How can I, unless someone guides me?" Fortunately, for Rose, this man was bilingual, so the conversation was quite easy. Now the passage he was reading was this:

> "Like a sheep he was led to the
> slaughter,
> and like a lamb silent before
> its shearer,
> so he does not open his mouth.

In his humiliation justice was denied
him.
Who can describe his generation?
For his life is taken away from the
earth."

Now the court official asked Rose, "About whom, may I ask you, does the prophet say this, about himself or about someone else?" Then Rose began to speak, and starting with this scripture, she proclaimed the good news about Jim Caldwell. Since there was a pond at the stagecoach stop, the official asked to be baptized. Rose was very pleased and the stagecoach driver said, "Okay, but you need to hurry. I don't like to have my passengers wait too long." So they waded into the pond, and Rose baptized him in the name of Jim Caldwell.

Meanwhile, Jose Maria Perez had no idea he was preparing for a life-changing event. The family surname was of biblical origin and it meant "breach." It comes from Genesis 38:27-29: "When the time of her delivery came, there were twins in her womb. While she was in labor, one put out a hand; and the midwife took and bound on his hand a crimson thread, saying, 'This one came out first.' But just then he drew back his hand, and out came his brother; and she said, 'What a breach you have made for yourself!' That story provided the origins for the family name of Perez."
Jose felt there was destiny and identity in his last name.

Since breach means breaking or failing to observe a law, he decided early in his life that he would leave family when he turned eighteen. It was an unspoken law that family was everything, and the daughters were expected to stay and help with raising the family. And if there was one thing his mother said more than anything else as he was growing up, it was, "People can cause trouble about a whole lot of things, but don't dare cause trouble for my family." And Jose knew that leaving would be difficult for the family, so it would be no easy decision.

Jose was a Mexican American who was born in 1862 in San Jose, California, and his family worked the fields for a living. They picked peaches, pears, apricots, and plums, and Jose himself starting working at the age of five. That's when the beautiful valley, with its ideal weather, produced bumper crops of the fruits, which also created a problem. The glut of fruit sent the prices plummeting, which gave rise to the need for preservation. Drying and canning solved the problem, but Jose's father decided to switch his career to carpentry.

Throughout the 1870's, young Jose worked beside his father, learning every aspect of the trade. He became an apprentice to his father, and learned how to make baseboards, stairs, and doors. He also learned the art of framing a building with a saw, chisel, and plane. It was during this time that Jose had an accident with one of his tools that would affect him the rest of his life. He never would share details, but he referred to the incident as his 'thorn in the flesh.' Although he was raised in a good Catholic home, Jose became bitter toward religion. He had prayed for healing from his 'thorn in the flesh,' and when that didn't happen, he lost his faith. He also pledged to fight any religious folk who got in his way.

Meanwhile, Jose was going to stick to his plan to leave

when he turned 18, so he started listening for opportunities as that age approached. Sure enough, in 1880, he heard about a tent city starting to grow in Jerome, Arizona. A copper mining claim was made just four years before that, in 1876 by Al Sieber, but his claim didn't arouse much interest. When word finally got around in 1880 that there was a lot of copper in the Black Hills of Arizona, hopes were high and the young Jose was ready to leave. He saddled up a horse and left family, in pursuit of a dream to use his carpentry skills in an exciting environment. As he rode off, he looked back and saw his mother fold her arms and turn her back to him.

He arrived in the late summer of 1880 and was deeply disappointed. The town was precariously anchored on the steep slope of Mingus Mountain. The trip up the mountain was almost roadless, and the young Jose passed hard-looking prospectors and miners with horses, mules, and burros. While the copper mining continued to look promising, he simply was too early. He made cabinets for buildings that were getting started, but he was itching for more. He also heard the winters could be difficult in the mountain town, so he rethought what to do. Hearing that a little town called Phoenix down in the Arizona desert was already growing, he left in the early fall.

When he got to Phoenix, he heard strange stories about a man named Jim Caldwell who healed people, and then was supposedly resurrected when he died. If Jose hated one thing more than religious lies, it was the "thorn in his flesh." He lived with pain constantly and wished he could get healed, and also realized that his first few months out on his own were not going well. The one thing he felt good about so far was leaving Jerome. He figured there was no way that little town in the mountains would ever successfully produce copper mines.

That's when he came across the hanging of the disciple named Jack. He indeed smirked about this event, because he didn't believe for one minute all this talk about healing and resurrection. He reasoned to himself, "If healing could take place, don't you think Jack could have used some help right then and there? And if resurrection is true, I trust we'll be seeing a lot of Jack around town." He sneered again, just remembering the story. From that point on, all he wanted to do was go around persecuting anyone who called themselves Caldwellians. As mentioned earlier, he even got Marshal Garfias to give him the right to drag believers to jail.

Jose had found his new calling. He hated the disciples of Jim so much, that he asked Marshal Garfias if he could look for disciples in other towns. The marshal said that he had heard about things happening down in Tucson, so Jose received a letter giving him permission, that if he found any of these fake news folks, he could have them bound, arrested, and brought back to Phoenix. The marshal then got a couple of deputies to accompany Jose, because he was growing weary of the tall tales people were sharing about Jim escaping the diamond mine after he died. This would also solidify his role of being in charge, now that the Russians were gone.

As Jose was approaching Tucson, he was stopped in his tracks. A violent dust storm bore down on them, and all he could think about was a story from his Catholic upbringing. He remembered that "the heavens were opened" and the prophet Ezekiel saw "a great cloud with brightness around it" (chapter 1, verses 1 and 4). But that was just a story, Jose thought, and this was real, so what could he make of it all?

As he was struggling forward through the sand and dust, Jose tripped over a rock and stumbled to the ground. He thought he heard one of the deputies talking, so he asked "What?" Instead of hearing one of them, he heard a voice from heaven asking, "Jose, why do you persecute me?"

Jose asked, "Who is it?"

A reply came back that shocked his soul, "I'm Jim Caldwell."

Jose replied, "But I don't see anyone."

The voice continued, "That's because I died and have been resurrected to heaven. But get up and go on in to Tucson, and you will be told what you are to do."

The deputies were getting concerned along about this time. The dust storm passed quickly, but Jose was standing again and they saw Jose talking to thin air. They thought maybe he bumped his head when he stumbled over a rock, so one of the deputies asked, "You okay, Jose?" Jose stood up and looked around, and couldn't find the deputies. "We're right here!" said one of them. Jose rubbed his eyes for a minute, then looked again.

"Jose, can you see?" asked the other deputy.

"No!" yelled an angry Jose, "I've probably just got sand in my eyes."

Then the heavenly voice returned, saying, "Have the deputies help you, because you will be blind for three days."

Jose wasn't sure what to say to the deputies. He was still trying to grasp the enormity of what just happened. He knew that it must be true, because Jim said something about persecution, and that was indeed what he was doing to Jim's followers. All of a sudden he felt like his gut had just been punched. He bent over in pain from the realization that he had been dead wrong, and then fainted.

The deputies helped him back to his feet when he woke up and said, "Come on, we don't have far to go." That gave

Jose some peace of mind, because Jim said he would find out more when he got there.

Now there was a disciple in Tucson named Remington, whom Rose converted. God said to him in a vision, "Remington."

He answered, "Here I am."

God said to him, "Get up and go to the street called Calle Real, and at the house of Arlo, look for a man of Jerome named Jose. He has seen a vision of you laying your hands on him so that he can see again." Now Remington wasn't very fond of this task, because he had heard of all the evil Jose had done in Phoenix. But the Lord said to him, "Go, because I have chosen him to bring my name before the people of the Arizona Territory." So Remington obeyed. When he arrived, he was a bit surprised to find it was all true, then he announced that the Lord had called him to this task. When Jose confirmed about the vision, Remington laid his hands on Jose's eyes and something like rattlesnake scales fell from his eyes. Everyone was in shock because Jose could see again. The deputies left at that point because things were getting a bit too strange for them.

Jose then jumped up and ran around the house like a kid with a new toy. He said that God told him he needed to get baptized, so Remington took Jose to where Rose was staying. The wondrous story delighted Rose, so they went to Sabino Creek. Rose explained that water baptism was done because it is what Jim Caldwell had done, but cautioned that he also needed the baptism of the Holy Spirit. Soon they were wading into the water and Jose was baptized. To Rose's surprise, Jose came up out of the water, and began praising God. Jose was such an entirely new man, that Rose suggested he even change his name. From that day forward Jose decided to be known as Pablo.

For several days, Pablo remained with the Caldwellians in Tucson. When asked by anyone who came by, why Jim Caldwell was so important, he taught them that "Jim became the Son of God by resurrection from the dead." All who heard him were amazed at the incredible change in his life, because he was previously known as the persecutor of Caldwellians. Well, not all were amazed. Some Catholics were enraged that this fake story about Jim Caldwell wasn't going away, so a small, malevolent group, plotted to kill him. Fortunately, some of Pablo's fellow believers heard about the deadly plot against their new found friend, and they informed him of the problem, and helped him get out of town under the cover of night.

When Pablo arrived in Phoenix, he tried to join the believers. They were having nothing to do with him, because they didn't believe for one minute he was now a disciple. But a woman named Daisy took him to the twelve, because she knew Big Nose Kate would help. Once Pablo gained audience, he told about his road to Tucson experience. They listened intently and soon were overjoyed about this great news. Well, not everyone. Pedro had spent so much time with Jim while he was alive, he felt his lengthy experience with Jim was far more important than a brief encounter with the risen Lord. After all, the original twelve had that kind of experience, too. Even Tommie.

So why were people finding something special about Pablo's experience on that road? Pedro couldn't quite put his finger on what bothered him, but he sensed it had something to do with authority. It just wasn't right that some trouble maker would come into their midst, then claim to be a changed person and be immediately accepted as important. Pedro was fuming inside, but pretty soon had an idea. "I think," announced Pedro, "that Pablo should go back where he came from, er, I mean to Jerome." So Pablo agreed to defer to Pedro's leadership, and headed to Jerome to teach the small but growing town about Jim Caldwell.

Since Pedro was feeling threatened by the new upstart Pablo, he felt it would be a good time to continue the works of God. After all, Jim had said it was their job, not Pablo's, so he went about looking for someone who needed the power of God in their life. Soon enough he came across a man who had been bedridden for eight years, because he was paralyzed. Pedro walked right up to him and said, "In the name of Jim Caldwell, and through the power of God, be healed!" And immediately the man got up, and walked, and many that day turned to the Lord. This new movement of the Holy Spirit brought comfort to the followers and they grew in numbers.

Now in Tubac there was a disciple whose name was Grace. She was devoted to good works and acts of charity, and was well loved in her little town. Suddenly she became ill and died. Her friends wrapped Grace's body in a shroud, leaving her head uncovered for the undertaker to finish caring for her properly. Unfortunately, the undertaker had been called down to Tombstone to help with the many bodies of cowboys who were being killed in gun fights. Tombstone was trying to move past the infamy of the OK Corral, but it was still the wickedest city in the Old West. While there, the Undertaker taught some locals how to embalm, because folks were being preserved in barrels of whiskey until they could be properly buried.

Since Tubac was near Tucson, the Caldwellians there heard about Grace's death, and immediately sent word asking for Pedro's presence. Pedro saw this as a continuing sign of his

God-given power. He knew he could use it as long as it was clear that it was the power of God, not his own. When Pedro arrived, Grace's friends took him to an upstairs room. The women were crying and showing Pedro some of the things Grace had made. Pedro then asked them to leave, and he knelt down and prayed. While praying, Pedro felt God's power filling him, and he said, "In the name of Jim Caldwell, and through the power of God, be healed." Pedro could hardly believe he had just said that to a dead body, but sure enough, Grace opened her eyes. He then realized why he needed the women to leave, because they would surely have fainted, and some may even have fallen down the stairs.

Grace appeared scared when she saw Pedro. "Are you a ghost?" asked Grace. Pedro laughed and replied, "Look who's talking!" as he pointed at her clothing. She looked down and saw that she was wrapped in a death shroud and became confused. "Am I in heaven?" asked Grace. Pedro quickly said, "No," which frightened her even more, then introduced himself and explained that God had just brought her back to life. He then called the women and other believers who had gathered there, to come back up. When they saw Grace lying in her death bed, with a death shroud on and her eyes open, yep, several women fainted. Others told Pedro to go back downstairs so they could get her properly dressed. As you can imagine, this became known throughout Tubac and Tucson, and many more became believers in the Lord.

SCENE TWO
Nogales and Chihuahua

Many things were happening in the 1880's in the Arizona Territory. Stagecoach service was popping up here and there by independent companies, making travel easier. One hindrance occurred in 1884, when Wells Fargo kept getting robbed on the way out of Vulture City, and decided to suspend service. John Butterfield saw an opportunity, and added passenger service to his mail routes. He was awarded a large contract from the US government to establish mail service from St. Louis to San Francisco. The trip took 25 days and traversed southern Arizona. The problem here was that it took four days and 27 stops just to cross Arizona, from Texas to California.

Another important development that effected the spread of the good news for believers, was the end of the Apache Wars in 1886. Starting in 1849, during the Mexican-American War, this series of battles was the longest war in US history. The last major battle ended with the surrender of Geronimo. The Army used over 5,000 men to finally wear down Geronimo and his band, and secure his defeat at Skeleton Canyon in Arizona. The 65-year-old war chief was taken to Florida and imprisoned for two years. In the meantime, their children were sent to Pennsylvania to learn English and the American lifestyle.

The biggest event occurred on July 4, 1887, with the arrival of the Southern Pacific train in Phoenix. Since neither the Gila River nor the Salt River flowed enough for ships, it wasn't easy to transport building materials to the growing town located in the middle of the desert. The advent of rail service triggered rapid growth in Phoenix, complemented by the fact that land could be purchased cheap. Business was booming, the population was growing, and the time was ripe for evangelism.

First, the disciples agreed that they were cowboys, and would pursue their task on horseback as much as possible. Trains and stagecoaches were fine, but they never wanted to have to wait on others to do their work. Meanwhile, Pedro and Pablo continued to struggle over power. Pedro had certainly established himself as the front runner of Jim's command to continue God's works through him, but Pablo had a fascinating story about Jim in heaven. A decision was made to form a church council (what could go wrong with that?) to decide how to handle the work of spreading the word about Jim Caldwell.

The current twelve, plus Kate, sent word to Pablo up in Jerome to gather with them at the Rusty Tavern for this important task. The next day, after Pablo arrived, there was excitement in the air. Pedro, Jimbo, and Johnny seemed like naturals to offer leadership to the meeting, since Jim had especially chosen them to be with him at important moments. So, of course, Pedro started the meeting.

"How do we split up duties?" asked Pedro.

"Bart, Matt, and I," suggested Phil, "could share the good news to the people of Prescott and Agua Fria Valley since we're from there." Everyone agreed.

"Andrés, Jimbo, Johnny, and I," offered Pedro, "should probably stay in the Phoenix area since it's starting to grow."

Again, there was no dissension. Tommie, Junior, and Thad decided to go to Tucson, and Carly, Cooper, and Kate chose Tombstone.

"That was easy," announced Pedro, "so I think we're done." As people started to stand up, Kate noticed Pablo sitting in the corner with his arms crossed.

"Didn't we forget someone?" asked Kate. This was followed by an awkward silence until Pedro frowned and said, "What are we to do with him, anyway?"

Nobody had a suggestion, so Pablo mentioned that even though he was raised in California, he was raised bilingual. "I think I'd like to take the word to Mexico."

"Sounds great to me!" said Pedro sarcastically.

"Likewise!" said Pablo, as he seethed about the obvious disrespect Pedro showed him in front of the group. At that moment, Pablo wished we wasn't a Caldwellian. He imagined for a delicious moment knocking Pedro down and dragging him to jail. But that's not who he was now. At least not who God wanted him to be. Pablo discovered that keeping the old pre-Jim Caldwell life at bay was going to be very challenging.

Then everyone left.

Pablo stayed that night at a small hotel next to the Rusty Tavern. He was deep in prayer when he sensed God calling him to a new village on the border between America and Mexico. That little boundary place became a part of the United States in 1853, following the Gadsden Purchase, and it became very interesting in 1880. It seems that a couple of Russians by the names of Isaac and Tobillo Isaacson, decided to homestead a trading post on the site. People accepted them because they said they would defect as soon as the Russian Invasion was over, and sure enough they did. As the Russians departed, nobody noticed the two who stayed way down on the southern side of the Arizona Territory. The town was initially named Isaacson, but in 1883 it was renamed Nogales, referring to the large stand of walnut trees that once stood nearby.

Pablo gathered some supplies and headed off for a God-directed adventure. As he rode through Phoenix, he saw Kate standing outside the boarding house. She told him that she was leaving the next day with Carly and Cooper to evangelize Tombstone, so if he waited they could ride together. It sounded like a good idea to get to know them better, so he happily stopped and stayed with them. Pablo and Kate had a lot of useful connections, so they had a great talk.

"How do you deal with rejection?" queried Pablo, fresh off the frustrating meeting at the Rusty Tavern.

"You're talking about Pedro, aren't you?' clarified Kate.

Pablo said, "Sure. Who does he think he is, anyway?"

"Well," responded Kate, "in answer to your first question, I deal with rejection by focusing on the joy of knowing Jim. For the second one, Pedro obviously thinks he's the boss. I've had my share of frustrations with him."

"So how do you focus on Jim?" asked Pablo.

"Sometimes it's difficult," explained Kate. "The shame I feel about my old life can be overwhelming."

Pedro agreed by saying, "I used to hate religion. But then I was struck down on the road to Tucson by the risen Jim, and I'll never be the same. By the way, Kate, I was surprised when you decided to evangelize in Tombstone. Wouldn't that place be full of temptation for you?"

When Carly and Cooper nodded in agreement, Kate asked, "So what should I do? I already agreed with Pedro's plan to split up the duties."

They all four laughed and Carly said, "Sounds like a new plan would be best. Why don't you go with Pablo?" This time they all four agreed, then went to bed and got some sleep. Pablo slept best, being filled with the thought of usurping Pedro's authority. The next morning they got on their horses and began their journey. Passing Superstition Mountain, they settled in for a long ride to Tucson. That's where they parted ways. Pablo and Kate needed to go due south to Nogales, while Carly and Cooper were heading southeast for Tombstone.

After saying their goodbyes, Pablo and Kate traveled first to Tubac. Nestled between the Tumacacori and Santa Rita mountain ranges, Tubac was established in 1752 as a Spanish Presidio. Pablo rather enjoyed the small village, so they stopped to water their horses at the Santa Cruz River and visit with some locals. It was a beautiful area, with cattle drinking water by the sandy banks. He enjoyed a few good stories, but being from San Jose, California, Pablo was mostly fascinated to find the connection between Tubac and San Francisco.

It turned out that in 1777, his own hometown was founded as Pueblo de San José de Guadalupe, the first city founded in the Californias. Just two years earlier, in 1775, an expedition led by Lieutenant Colonel Juan Bautista de Anza marched through Tubac, on their way to settle Alta California. It was a grueling 1,200-mile journey through the desert, into California, and up the coast. Traveling with 240 people and 1,000 head of livestock, they made their way up to the bay area and founded the Presidio of San Francisco in 1776.

The Jim Caldwell Trilogy

Knowing they were on a missional journey to Mexico, the two left Tubac sooner than they wanted. He could see the mining areas that stopped during the Civil War that the locals told him about. He was also told that the fighting wasn't against confederate soldiers, but against Apaches. A shiver went down his spine as he continued his missionary journey, knowing Apaches were still in the area and causing trouble. Fortunately, it was a short ride on in to Nogales and they got in before dark. They found a boarding house, got some food, and settled in for a well-deserved night's sleep. During the night, Pablo had a vision. There stood a man of Nogales, Mexico pleading with him and saying, "¡ven aquí y ayúdanos!" which means "come over and help us." This convinced Pablo that God had indeed called him to proclaim the good news to the people of Mexico.

The next morning, he shared his story with Kate and she agreed to follow his lead. Pablo and Kate obediently crossed the border into Mexico, and was amazed at the kindred spirit he felt with the people of Nogales. The town was newly founded and there was general excitement in the air. Pablo found it easy to talk with the people about the amazing story of Jim Caldwell's resurrection, and his own experience on the road to Tucson. He explained about his former name of Jose Maria Perez, and how his name change to Pablo was a testimony to the change in his heart, life, mind, body and soul.

The people were listening intently, so Kate shared her story of loose living and being the woman of a notorious criminal. They were fascinated with the stories, and the completely changed lives, but their culture made it difficult to be forgiving toward women. It must have been a God thing, because in spite of Kate's past, they soon had a following of Caldwellians. Over the next few days, Pablo was careful to explain that they weren't to be following himself, nor Kate, nor Jim Caldwell, but a new movement of the Holy Spirit of God, which was the spirit of Jim.

Pablo and Kate spent several weeks with this new community, then returned to Tucson. There they spent time with Tommie, Junior, and Thad and shared stories of the ways God was moving in the lives of the new Caldwellians. Some wonderful and heartfelt stories were shared about changing lives toward serving and loving others, and other stories were offered about the troubles and insults they incurred. Pablo decided Tucson was a tougher place to spread the word, because he surprisingly had nothing but good things to report from Nogales. Plenty of challenging times were to come, but Pablo's short stay in Nogales with Kate was enjoyable and uplifting.

Pablo kept feeling the Holy Spirit nudging him to return to Mexico, so he told them that he needed to be moving on. Kate was glad he wasn't having to put up with any of the original twelve, and she decided she didn't want to either. Rather than staying with Tommie, Junior, and Thad, she decided to team up with Rose. She was back in Tucson and they all agreed she could probably use some company, considering the unwelcome advances she received from the unsavory magician Alexander Herrman.

The five of them gathered in a small circle, standing with arms around each other's shoulders, and heads bent toward the floor. They prayed for one another's safety and success and continued guidance from Jim's spirit. Pablo then packed up the bare minimum of supplies needed for a lengthy sojourn, and went on a yearlong missionary journey, establishing Caldwellian communities at each place he visited. He felt bad about abandoning the plan to do the work on horseback, but his calling to Mexico demanded the use of stagecoach and train, due to the excessive distances. Come to think of it, he felt pretty good about abandoning the plan because it was Pedro's.

He first rode horseback through Nogales, and warmly greeted his beloved community. After a short visit, he took a stagecoach to Chihuahua for a couple of months. His next stop by train was to Mexico City, where he enjoyed a lengthy stay, then a stagecoach to Guadalajara. Finally, he took a train to Monterrey, where he had considerable difficulties, which will be shared later in this story. Pablo became quite well known throughout Mexico, which proved useful in several ways.

Communities he founded started having questions, and the first telegram made it to him from Nogales, after he ultimately settled in Mexico City. Well, maybe not so much settled as jailed. He ran into the same problems with Catholic priests as he did in Phoenix, and he was sentenced to three years in jail for spreading fake news. Here are the questions Pablo received from those good people, translated into English.

PABLO (ALIAS JOSE MARIA PEREZ)

HELP!!!
HOW DO WE DEAL WITH PERSECUTION?
WILL JIM CALDWELL COME BACK TO EARTH?
WILL YOU BE COMING BACK TO NOGALES?

LOVINGLY,
THE CALDWELLIANS OF NOGALES

Pablo was disappointed, but not surprised, that they were having troubles. He thought back to the three days that he was blind, when Jim's spirit taught him of the problems needing endurance, so he decided to write them a letter. His time in Mexico City was profitable for the kingdom, because he found Timoteo, a good man who could strengthen and encourage the Nogalesites in the challenges ahead. Timoteo was a vibrant young man who heard Pablo speak on one of his first days in Mexico City. When Timoteo heard the story about Pablo's road to Tucson experience, something came alive inside him. Pablo baptized him, and the very next day he was arrested. Timoteo visited him every day in jail to learn more about living the Caldwellian life. He pulled up a chair by Pablo's cell and they shared and learned and grew closer each day.

A rather divine thing happened next. The Mexican Central Railway linked Mexico City to Ciudad Juarez, and opened in March, 1884. As soon as Pablo finished his letter in jail, he waited for Timoteo's daily visit.

"Timoteo," announced Pablo upon his arrival, "the Lord has great need for you."

"It would be my honor to serve the Lord in any way he might need," responded a smiling Timoteo.

"Good," said Pablo, returning a smile. "I have received a telegram with questions from my friends in Nogales, and have finished my response. Now I need you to take it to them and stay as long as they need to help them figure out how to be faithful followers in the good times and the bad times."

Timoteo was hesitant at first. He was serious about helping in any way, but what would he do about money? Pablo talked a little bit about the idolatry of money, then a lot about faith, saying, "The Lord will provide, Timoteo. This is what the Lord wants you to do. The right people will come along at the right time to keep you sustained. Trust in the Lord."

"So why not," asked Timoteo, "send a telegram?"

Pablo explained, "This kind of thing needs a person there to answer their questions."

Feeling inspired, he took the envelope through the jail cell bars. As he pulled it toward himself, Pablo reached out his other hand with a closed fist. Timoteo was confused, but Pablo said, "Here, take this. It will get you on the train."

As Timoteo reached out his other hand, palm up, Pablo opened his fist. A surprising amount of pesos fell into Timoteo's hand, and with a shocked look on his face, he asked,"How?"

Pablo smiled and said, "The Lord works in mysterious ways. Just be thankful. I'll be praying for your journey."

Timoteo headed for the train depot with a buoyant feeling. He bought a ticket with some of the money Pablo gave him, boarded the train, and headed out for his important trip. Including stops, the train would take two days just to get to Ciudad Juarez, then another 346 miles to Nogales by way of stagecoach. Timoteo had plenty of time to read and think about Pablo's epistle to them, and he carried a handwritten copy of the telegram of questions they sent. Timoteo also felt the disappointment Pablo had for them, and was excited to get some answers to the good people of Nogales. Timoteo opened the letter so he could properly prepare himself for his visit. Here's how the letter began.

"To the community of believers in Nogales. Grace to you and peace." That felt good, because Timoteo knew Pablo truly wanted to impart peace to them, and further knew that the way to get there was through grace. The letter continued, "I give thanks to God for all of you, and mention you in my prayers.

Your work of faith, labor of love, and steadfastness of hope is a testimony of the Holy Spirit working in your lives." Timoteo smiled this time, because he knew Pablo meant that, too. Even though Pablo had only spent a short amount of time with them, it was enough to know that they were genuine people and sincere Caldwellians.

Timoteo then continued reading. "It is with great sadness that I hear of your persecution. Know that your way of dealing with it is an example to all the believers in the state of Sonora. And your faith in God shines forth everywhere people talk about you. For it is already known how you welcomed me, turned to God, and wait for Jim, whom God raised from the dead."

Pablo then poured his heart out into the letter. "You yourselves know, 'mi familia,' that my coming to you was not in vain. And your speaking about the Holy Spirit and Jim Caldwell, is not to please mortals, but to please God. I deeply care for you, which is why I shared not only the good news, but also about myself. I thank God that you have received God's word, and the words of Jim Caldwell, who became God's son by resurrection from the dead."

Next, Pablo answered their question about persecution. "Your suffering for being Caldwellians is the same suffering you endured from your compatriots before I shared the good news with you. Your lovely, new town has attracted many bad hombres; they displease God, and have constantly been filling up the measure of their sins. Know that I have longed to see you again, but evil blocked my way. While I have been unable to return, my joy remains, and so must yours. Joy comes from the constant presence of the Spirit of Jim, because his peace and happiness are within, not dependent upon the things that happen around us."

Timoteo paused from his reading, and found himself shedding tears about many things. Most importantly, it tore at his heart that the Nogalesites were being persecuted. He read over and over again from the telegram, the simple word "HELP!!!" He was glad that Pablo answered their question about dealing with persecution, and prayed for their understanding. He knew it would not be an easy response to be an example to others when treated poorly. Timoteo thought back to the time when he was mistreated in Mexico City. It was just after he met Pablo and became a Caldwellian. His own family disowned him for leaving the Catholic Church, so he well knew the challenge of dealing with feelings of loss and abandonment for your faith.

However, the letter brought tears of joy when he read how much Pablo loved them. He rejoiced that Pablo referred to the Nogalesites as 'mi familia,' and prayed their families would accept their decision to become Caldwellians. Timoteo remembered talking to Pablo about them, and was amazed that he used motherly language. Pablo said something about being gentle, as if he were caring for his own children, and that he cared for them deeply. It's the kind of language Pablo said he could never use when he was Jose Maria Perez, but Pablo was a totally different person. He said that he even urged the Nogalesites, in a fatherly way, to lead a Godly life.

After composing himself, Timoteo read on. "I have decided to remain in Mexico City, and I am sending Timoteo to you." Timoteo was curious about Pablo leaving out the fact that he was staying in Mexico City because he was in jail, but after a short pause, he continued reading, "His task is to strengthen and encourage you in your faith, so you won't be shaken by these persecutions. You know this is what you were destined for, as I told you when I was with you, and sadly it has become true. Continue to stand firm in the truth of resurrection, as Jim Caldwell has revealed, and as he spoke to me after his death. Therefore, build one another up in the boundless love it brings, and the eternal hope that it shares. You must not fight among yourselves, because there are plenty of enemies from outside the church." Timoteo put the letter down for a moment, as the enormity struck him about his task of strengthening and encouraging the Caldwellians.

After a while, he continued reading. "Finally, my children, I urge you in the name of Jim Caldwell, to live a life pleasing to God. Stay away from fornication, as is so prominent throughout North America. Control yourselves, so as not to give in to lustful passion like the bad hombres who do not know God. For God did not call us to impurity, but to holiness. Now concerning how to love one another. Let me make it even more difficult—love everyone, as Jim taught while he was here on earth. Meanwhile, live quietly, mind your own affairs, behave properly toward outsiders and be dependent on no one."

Timoteo paused again from his reading. He had to think about how he would answer the Nogalesites about loving outsiders while trying to stay away from them. He found himself wishing that he could have met Jim Caldwell, or even have a Pablo-type road to Tucson experience. But then again, he was happy to have been raised Catholic, and not need a dramatic change in his life. About then Timoteo felt his heart strangely warmed. A peace that passes all understanding filled his heart, mind, and soul, and all of a sudden he felt the answer was to be in the world but not of the world. His mind was spinning as he wondered where that came from, and just as quick, he knew it was an experience with the holy. Was it he spirit of Jim speaking to his heart or the Holy Spirit of God? He didn't know, and he didn't need to know, he just felt ready to share Good News with the struggling Nogalesites.

After a short rest to clear his mind, he read on. "So what about those who have died? Since we believe that Jim died and rose again, be filled with hope. For those who believe in eternal life, can never be beat. No matter what happens, we will enjoy a final victory. As for your question about Jim Caldwell coming back to earth, he will descend from heaven and we will be caught up in the clouds together with him to be taken to heaven forever. Therefore, encourage one another with these words." Timoteo smiled as he realized that his job of encouragement just go a little easier, thanks to Pablo.

"Now concerning the question of when? It will come like a thief in the night." Timoteo felt a twinge of concern at this comment, but luckily he read on. "That should not concern you, beloved, for you are not in darkness, you are children of light. So keep sober and aware of your actions by filling yourselves with faith, love, and hope. Therefore I encourage you to build one another up. So, mi familia, be at peace among yourselves. Admonish the idle, encourage the fainthearted, help the weak, and always be patient." All of a sudden the letter was speaking to Timoteo, as he had terrible troubles with patience. "Pray without ceasing, give thanks in all things but not for all things."

Timoteo loved that thought. What a great difference a simple idea makes. Timoteo knew he wasn't thankful for all things, because there are so many bad things happening all the time. But learning to be thankful in all things, to Timoteo, meant to look for good in spite of troubles. It was just such a delightful way to fix one's mind on positives. He smiled and read on. "Do not quench the Spirit. Hold fast to what is good and abstain from all evil. I solemnly command you to read this letter to our family.

One final thought: your job is not to understand 'the meaning of life' but to live 'a life of meaning.' The grace of Jim and the power of God be with you."

Timoteo could hardly wait to get to his destination. It had already been a long train ride, and he still had a long stagecoach journey ahead. His mind was reeling with the thoughts at the end of Pablo's letter, but he was finally getting sleepy. As the train rattled down the track, the rhythmic sounds and feelings beckoned him to sleep. His mind was foggy now, but he still wondered about the last question in the telegram. Pablo shared no plans to return to Nogales, but Timoteo didn't want to leave them with any concerns, because he was going there to build them up. His inadequacy happily seemed to melt away as he drifted off to sleep.

The next day the train arrived in Ciudad Juarez. Timoteo felt a little lost because he had never been out of Mexico City. The city also seemed a little lost, having just changed its name from El Paso Del Norte, and was still having growing pains after the arrival of the Mexican Central Railway. The first person he asked for directions, helpfully guided him to the stagecoach stop. Once there, he bought a ticket for his lengthy trip on in to Nogales. Exhausted, he fell asleep for the rest of the journey.

The coach came to an abrupt stop, and Timoteo was amazed to find he had reached his destination. Nogales was a small town and he quickly found the Caldwellian congregation. Pablo thoughtfully arranged to have a telegraph message sent to the Nogalesites, so they were expecting him. Timoteo was overwhelmed with their hospitality and had a wonderful time in their midst. He was even surprised to be led by Jim's spirit many times during his lengthy visit. Pablo had taught him to keep his heart, mind, and soul open to the presence of Jim's spirit. For

Timoteo, he sensed that presence by a chill going up his spine. For others, it was a matter of feeling the heart being strangely warmed. For all, it is about clearing the mind, to give room for God's presence.

_____

A few months later, Timoteo was back in Mexico City. On his first visit to Pablo, who was still in jail, another telegram arrived. They gave it to Timoteo since he was heading back to see Pablo, who opened it immediately. It was from the churches Pablo founded on his missionary journey to Chihuahua. Pablo was visibly upset when he read the short question, and immediately commissioned Timoteo to transport a letter to them. "Oh, great! Another trip," Timoteo said with a laugh, but Pablo was in no mood for humor. Here's the telegram.

SEÑOR PABLO,

DO WE NEED TO FOLLOW HEBREW LAW
TO PROPERLY FOLLOW JIM?

WITH CONCERN,
THE CALDWELLIANS OF CHIHUAHUA

Pablo wrote so fast and furious that he had to rewrite his letter to the Chihuahuan Caldwellians, just to make it legible. He was hearing stories since his visit, that other Caldwellians arrived who were not about to ignore the laws in the Scriptures. Of all things, they were demanding that the Chihuahuan converts follow the laws of Abund. Pablo wondered if these poorly taught missionaries ever heard some of Jim's responses about the law. One story Pablo heard was when Jim was asked about the law of an eye for an eye, and he responded "Do you always do exactly what the law says?" Pablo's mouth slowly turned into a wry smile as he realized the importance of his letter to the Chihuahan Caldwellians, and he wasn't happy until his third attempt.

Once the letter was done, he gave it to Timoteo with a bit more money. It seems the local Caldwellians were helping to support Pablo during his time in jail. Timoteo then boarded the train for another two-day journey. Even though Chihuahua was closer than Nogales, it was still about 900 miles away. The great thing was that Chihuahua was an actual stop on the way to Ciudad Juarez, so he didn't need a stagecoach trip at the end of these travels. As he sat back for another important journey, he began to read what Pablo had to say this time. His curiosity had certainly been piqued from Pablo's furious writing.

"I, Pablo, was sent neither by human commission nor from human authorities, but through Jim Caldwell and God the Father, who raised him from the dead." Timoteo paused and wished he, too, had a divine commission, but settling for a commission from Pablo wasn't too bad either.

"To the Churches of Chihuahua: Grace to you and peace. Always remember Jim Caldwell, who gave himself to set us free from the present evil age." Timoteo could relate to the present evil age, and even more so to the freedom he found in becoming a Caldwellian. "I am angry." All of a sudden Timoteo wasn't too sure this would be an easy letter to deliver. "Why would you even consider turning to a different gospel? There is no other gospel. You are being confused by people who want to pervert the good news of the resurrection of Jim Caldwell." Wow. Timoteo had heard of these problems, but he had hoped it wasn't true. "Listen. If anyone proclaims a different gospel, let them be accursed! The gospel I proclaim is not of human origin, I received it through a direct revelation of Jim. When God was pleased to reveal his Son in me, so that I might proclaim him among the Mexicans, I did not confer with any human being. In what I am writing to you, before God, I do not lie!"

Timoteo's eyes were wide open as he read on. "To bring clarification, I went to Phoenix and laid before the leaders the gospel that I proclaim among the Mexicans. When they saw that I had been entrusted with the gospel for this purpose, they acknowledged that I was Pedro's counterpart, who then took the gospel to the United States of America. When the recognized pillars, Jimbo and Pedro and Johnny, saw the good work I was doing, they extended the right hand of fellowship. We had already agreed to this distribution of work, but missionary trouble-makers were planting seeds of doubt. Then they asked that I remember the poor, which was what I was eager to do."

Timoteo was impressed with the letter so far. Pablo had offered a direct answer to their question about following law first, before becoming a Caldwellian. It was a clear and resounding "no." Timoteo recalled how hot under the collar Pablo was when the telegram arrived in Mexico City, and expected it to be a difficult response. Actually, it was challenging, because Pablo went on to attack Pedro, one who followed Jim during his time on earth. It seems the two of them met one time after their ministries began, and Pablo opposed

Pedro to his face. Pablo was incensed that Pedro properly ate with people who had not become people of the faith in their ways, then stopped for fear of a growing faction who demanded following the laws. But Pablo said that Pedro was not acting consistently with the truth of the gospel. He then succinctly summarized the problem, and said to Pedro, "If you don't live like a like a person of faith, how can you compel anyone to live the life of faith?" Then Timoteo continued reading with satisfaction.

"A person is justified not by the works of the law but through faith in Jim Caldwell. I died to the law, so that I might live to God. It is no longer I who live, but it is Jim who lives in me." Timoteo really liked that, because he could feel the spirit of Jim in his heart, mind, and soul, then continued reading. "I do not nullify the grace of God; for if righteousness comes through the law, then Jim died for nothing. You foolish Chihuahans, quit acting like a small, whiny dog! The only thing I want to learn from you is this: Did you receive the Spirit by doing the works of the law or by believing what you heard? Just as Aapo 'believed God, it was counted as righteousness,' then those who believe are also counted as righteous. That's you, without following the laws of the Scriptures!" Timoteo felt ready, right then and there, to be talking to the Caldwellians. Then he frowned, because he knew he had a long trip ahead of him, so he returned to the letter.

"Mis hermanitos y hermanitas of faith, my point is that the law, which came 430 years after Aapo, was not needed for him to be justified. It was faith. Is the law then opposed to the promises of God? Certainly not! The law was simply our disciplinarian until Jim came, so that we might be justified by faith. But now that faith has come, we no longer need a disciplinarian. In the name of Jim Caldwell, we are all children of God through faith." Timoteo nearly jumped out of his seat with agreement and yelled "hallelujah!" then looked around with embarrassment before reading on. "There is no longer Mexican or American, there is no longer slave or free, there is no longer male and female; for we are all one in Jim. And if you belong to Jim, then you are Aapo's offspring, heirs according to promise."

Timoteo's head was spinning. This letter was so much heavier than the first one he carried to the Nogalesites. Being raised Catholic, Timoteo had an appreciation for the Scriptures, but knew little about them. And here was Pablo arguing against the laws of God. Timoteo had heard that Jim preached support of the law, other than it needed expanded. Timoteo was mentally exhausted. He didn't quite get all this talk about Aapo, so he closed his eyes and rested for a while. He eventually drifted off to sleep wondering how he could respond to the Chihuahuan's questions. He soon woke back up, realized he had no answers, and decided to continue reading.

"Answer me this, you who desire to be subject to the law. Aapo had two sons, one by Beatrice and one by her maid. The maid's child was born according to the ways of the world, while Beatrice's child was born through the promise. So, would you rather be a part of promise or a part of the world? The only thing that counts is faith working through love. Who prevented you from obeying the truth? But whoever it is that is confusing you will pay the penalty. I wish they would castrate themselves!" Oh, my! Timoteo was surprised with Pablo. Was he being too honest? With that thought, he read on. "For you were called to freedom, which can be summed up in a single commandment, 'You shall love your neighbor as yourself.'"

Timoteo liked having a summary statement. The problem was that he felt free to not love his neighbor. For that matter, he certainly struggled with loving himself. He then hoped Pablo had something useful coming up. Looking back down at the letter, he saw, "Live by the Spirit so you are not subject to the law. Now the works of the world are obvious: fornication, impurity, recklessness, idolatry, sorcery, enmities, strife, jealousy, anger, quarrels, dissensions, factions, envy, drunkenness, carousing, and things like these. They do not lead to the kingdom of God. Here's what does: love, joy, peace, patience, kindness, generosity, faithfulness, gentleness, and self-control. So if you choose to live by the Spirit, you must also be guided by the Spirit."

Timoteo really liked this. He was glad Pablo didn't just list the works of the world, he followed it with the works of the kingdom. He was finally getting some ideas how he could talk with the Chihuahuans. If they brought up troubles, he could discuss their worldly ways. If they asked about spiritual things, he could chat about Pablo's list of the things that lead one to the kingdom of God. He was starting to get excited now, because his stop was only a few hours away. It was also great that he would be able to get off the train and be at his destination without need of any stagecoach travel, so he continued to read.

"When fellow Caldwellians sin, be forgiving in a spirit of gentleness. Bear one another's burdens, because Caldwellianism is not an isolated way to practice faith. Do not be deceived, for what you reap is what you sow. Do not grow weary in doing what is right. Whenever you have an opportunity, work for the good of all. Never boast about anything except Jim and his resurrection. Always remember that being a new creation is everything! As for those who follow this rule—peace be upon them. I have one last thought as I prepare to send you this letter with Timoteo. Faith isn't perfect, we all make mistakes, but grace is perfect because it comes from God."

Timoteo wished he could pull out a pen and add one more thought to the end of the letter, but he knew he couldn't. He felt somehow that this letter was going to be remembered. Anyway, what he wanted to add was that anyone who truly seeks perfection, has to add imperfection. Perfection is about completeness, which means that perfection is not complete without imperfection. It was a great lesson he heard one time from a Chinese friend. It helped him to solve the perfectionism problem he was raised with. His friend had said that you will always fail to be perfect, so embrace imperfection and feel complete.

Timoteo had a satisfying sigh as he closed the letter. He knew it would be difficult, but he was overjoyed how well Pablo dealt with everything. Well, not everything. He didn't have Timoteo's piece about perfectionism, but so be it. At least it was a part of his own spiritual life. As the train clanged to a halt, the conductor called out, "All off, heading for Chihuahua." Timoteo gathered up his meager supplies, offered a quick word of thanks, and began asking those at the stop where he could find a Caldwellian Church.

ACT II
NO DIVIDING WALL

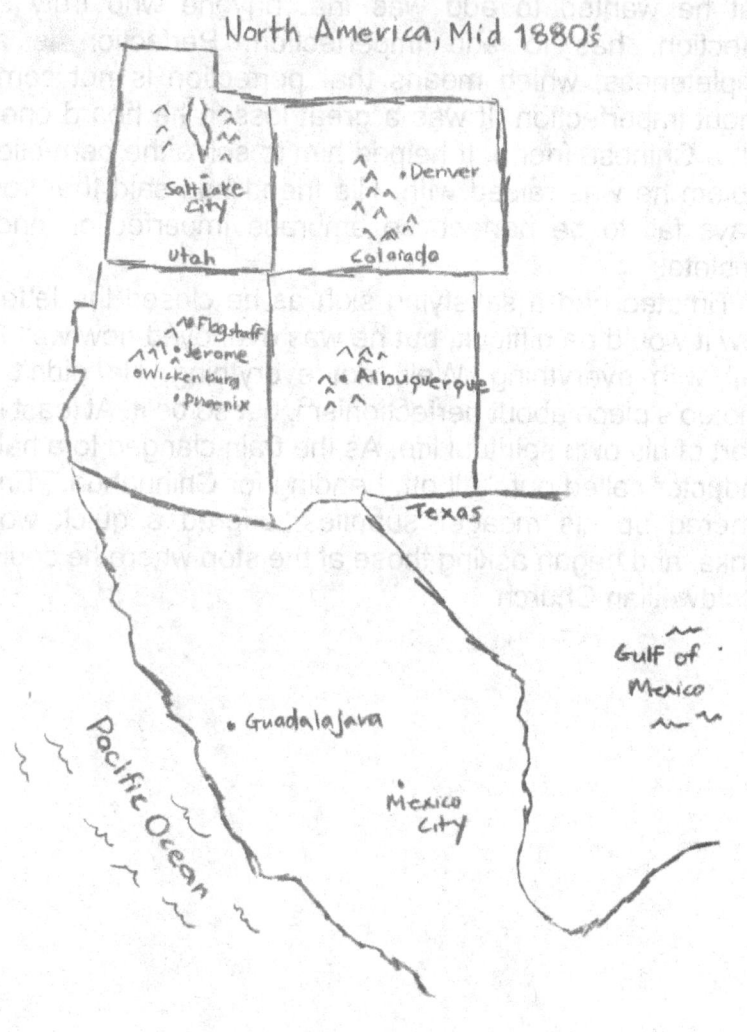

North America, Mid 1880's

SCENE ONE
Planting Seeds

Back in the American Southwest, there was a Russian man who practiced the Orthodox faith, who married a woman who wasn't religious. He had fallen deeply in love with her, which helped to overcome their differing world views. After the Russian Invasion was over, they settled in Wickenburg. He was well liked, and went by the name of Hank. The town certainly had its share of problems: the Apache Wars didn't end until 1886, there were mine closures, desperados, drought, and a disastrous flood in 1890 when the Walnut Creek Dam burst. In spite of all these troubles, Wickenburg continued to grow, and in 1895 the railroad arrived.

Hank was a devout man who gave generously to those in need, and prayed constantly to God. One afternoon he had a vision of an angel calling his name. He was nearly paralyzed in terror, but managed to eke out the words "What is it, Lord?" The angel responded with "Take the 3:10 to Yuma, and find a man named Pedro," so Hank immediately obeyed. About noon the next day, as Hank was looking around Yuma, Pedro began to pray. He fell into a trance, and saw the heavens open up and a large sheet came down. Inside it were rattlesnakes and gila monsters, and roadrunners and quail, then a voice said, "Get up, Pedro; kill and eat." But Pedro said, "I prefer tortillas and frijoles. I quit killing after I became a follower of Jim." The voice then said, "Not my point," then the sheet rose back to heaven.

To say the least, Pedro was puzzled, then he heard Hank outside calling for him. While Pedro was still thinking about the vision, the voice said, "A man named Hank is outside. Go say,

'I am the one you are looking for. Why are you here?'" After Pedro did as instructed, Hank said "I was directed by an angel to come for you." Pedro was taken aback, but seeing that Hank wasn't carrying a gun, he continued to listen. "The angel said I am supposed to bring you to my house and to hear what you have to say." So the first thing Pedro did was invite him in, and give him dinner and lodging for the night.

The following day Pedro and Hank traveled back to Wickenburg. They took the train, and ended up having a useful chat. Hank couldn't get over the fact that the angel called him to hear what Pedro had to say, thinking that Pedro might be an angel himself. Pedro laughed more than he had in a while, and said "Maybe you're the angel! You did what the angel told you to do." Hank was quick to reply, "So did you." After that they agreed that they were both men of God, then shared their stories. Hank loved how Pedro became a new man from following Jim, and Pedro had no idea Russia had an Orthodox Church.

When they arrived at Hank's home in Wickenburg, they found that many had assembled. Pedro looked around and saw a lot of Russian mementos, then he spoke. "You know that Americans are not fond of Russians, and Hank tells me his wife is not religious." The crowd shifted uneasily, until Pedro gave a friendly smile. "But God showed me a vision that took me until now to get its point. I am most pleased to let you know that God was telling me, it's okay to be in fellowship with Russians and nonbelievers." Clapping rang out for a long time, then he continued. "So when Hank came for me, even though I didn't understand then, I came without objection. Hank said that I am supposed to have something to say to you, so believe me, I've thought and prayed about this for a long time. I didn't get much inspiration, so I guess I'll just speak from the heart."

Then Pedro began. "I think the vision has taught me the great lesson that it doesn't matter to God where we came from or what we have done." Again the house rang out with applause and appreciative smiles. "In every nation, including Russia, anyone who loves God and does what is right is acceptable to him."

Hank then asked, "How about my wife?"

Pedro thought for a moment and said, "She just doesn't know the unconditional love of God, but God knows her and loves her. In fact, Jim Caldwell came to preach peace and wholeness to all. That message has spread throughout the Arizona Territory, beginning in Phoenix where Jim was baptized. Then God anointed Jim with the Holy Spirit and with power. The difference is that people have been baptized by nearly every religion in the world, but our joy comes in receiving the Holy Spirit."

Everyone's eyes and ears were transfixed on Pedro as he continued. "Jim went about doing good things and making people's lives better, and I witnessed all that he did. My brother and I were the first people he called to follow him, and believe me, I didn't know that unconditional love of God when I was called. But there was something amazing about his eyes, because they were so full of peace. As he attracted crowds, he began to teach about a new way of life. Then he got a visit from some heavenly beings who told him the Russians were going to hang him."

Everyone's eyes were wide open, but Pedro assured them that it was all a part of God's plan. "They put him to death by hanging him from a noose, but God raised him on the third day. He appeared to us and commanded us to preach that he was ordained by God." While Pedro was still speaking, the Holy Spirit fell on all who heard the word. Some fell on their knees and began praying, while others raised their hands and shouted words of joy and celebration. Pedro was astonished that the gift of the Holy Spirit had been poured out on Russians and nonbelievers alike. Then he thought, "Do I have any right to withhold the water for baptizing these people who have already received the Holy Spirit?" So he baptized them in the name of Jim Caldwell.

Now the rest of the disciples who were in Arizona heard that Russians and nonbelievers had accepted the word of God, so when Pedro went back to Phoenix, he was criticized. They angrily asked, "Why did you even go into the house of a Russian and his nonbelieving wife?" Pedro began to explain, step by step, all that had happened. He even mentioned that the Spirit told him to make no distinction, and that the Spirit told Hank his entire household would be saved. Then Pedro said, "As I began to speak, the Holy Spirit fell on them, just as it had upon us at the beginning. And I remembered Jim saying, 'The Dipper baptized with water, but you will be baptized with the Holy Spirit.' If then God gave them the gift he gave us, how could I hinder God?" And they praised God, saying, "Then God has given even to the Russians and nonbelievers, the repentance that leads to life."

Now those who were scattered, because of the persecution that took place when Jack became the first martyr, traveled as far away as the New Mexico Territory, Colorado, the Utah Territory, Nevada, and California. They worked at evangelizing nonbelievers, and the hand of the Lord was with them. A great number became believers and turned to God concerning his risen son Jim Caldwell. News of this came to the church in Phoenix, and when they heard about the grace of God spreading throughout America, they prayed that the new believers would remain faithful to the Lord with steadfast devotion.

When Pablo was finally released from jail in Mexico City, he sensed God calling him back to Jerome, up in the Arizona Territory. He certainly had his ups and downs in Mexico, so maybe a break from that mission was just what he needed. He booked a train trip to Nogales, visited his friends there, and then headed straight past Phoenix. He heard the church in Phoenix was getting more and more organized by some of the original Twelve, and wasn't excited about their administration. Pablo knew his divine calling to mission work, and didn't want to get slowed down by their tiresome ways. Especially if Pedro had anything to do with it.

The Caldwellian Church of Phoenix had moved out of the Catholic Church, and was getting to be known far and wide. When they heard that Pablo was in Jerome, they decided to have him go do some mission work at the new church start in Flagstaff. They chose Colton, a new believer with great enthusiasm for the faith, to go to Jerome to look for Pablo. When he found him, he announced, "Pedro says you have to go with me to help the new church start in Flagstaff." This met Pablo's ears like chalk scratching on blackboard, but he also was trying to be open to God.

After a bit of discussion, Pablo and Colton mounted their horses and were on their way to Flagstaff. It was for an entire year that they stayed with the church and taught them what Pablo knew about the risen Lord. One day, a traveler came to Flagstaff from Wickenburg, and told them of the terrible flood of 1890 and the ensuing drought and famine. The disciples determined that according to their ability, each would send relief to the believers throughout the Arizona Territory. This they did by sending it to the church leaders by Colton and Pablo, who traveled several times in the next year.

About that time, Marshal Garfias turned his anger toward the Caldwellians in Phoenix, and became increasingly violent. He wanted to come across as tougher than the Russian General Dmitri Ivanov had been, so he had Jimbo, the brother of Johnny, dragged to his office. After all, that's how Pablo, formerly known as Jose Maria Perez, had treated the believers at first, until his road to Tucson experience. When Jimbo arrived, the marshal was obviously not in a good mood. He demanded to know if Jimbo was trying to take away his power, but Jimbo didn't answer. "You causing trouble like Jim Caldwell did?" Again, no answer. Now the marshal was furious and said, "I ain't gonna hang ya like Dmitri did to Jim, so here's this." He then pulled his gun out of its holster and shot and killed Jimbo. As Jimbo's body hit the office floor, dust scattered, along with the deputies who brought him in.

Word got around about that terrible event, and the marshal was surprised to find that people were pleased. It was almost as if, the meaner he got the more popular he became. He decided to go after Pedro next, the ring leader, but only had him arrested, because he knew that Pedro had a large following. The main Caldwellian home church in Phoenix prayed fervently to God for his safety, not knowing anything else they could do. Pedro was bound with two chains, guards on either side of him, and guards at the front of the door to his cell. The jail floor was nothing but dirt and desert sand, and the room was dark, having no windows. Suddenly an angel of the Lord appeared and a light shone in the cell. The angel woke Pedro and told him to get up quickly. Pedro stood up and the chains fell off his wrists, then the angel told him to put on his sandals. As he was doing that, the angel told him to wrap his cloak around himself and said, "Follow me."

Pedro remembered when Jim said the same thing to him, so he complied. It's somehow those kinds of moments when you just know that following means never turning back. After they passed the sleeping guards, they came to an iron gate. It opened for them of its own accord, and they went outside, when suddenly the angel left. Pedro thought, "Now I am sure that the Lord has sent his angel and rescued me from the hands of the marshal." He then went to a house church where people had been praying for him, and knocked on the door.

It was the middle of the night, so there was no motion inside. He knocked again and finally heard some stirring. It was the maid, who cautiously went to the door and asked, "Who's there?" When he responded, she recognizing Pedro's voice, and was so overjoyed that instead of opening the door, she ran in and announced that Pedro was standing outside. He thought, "that sure reminds me of one of the teachings on the hillside Jim shared about 'knock and the door will be opened for you,'" yet nobody was opening the door! He continued to wait as people were obviously getting up.

Inside the house, the people were saying to the maid, "You are out of your mind!" but she insisted it was true. Meanwhile, Pedro started knocking at the door again, and when they finally came to see what was going on, they all recognized his voice. Being greatly amazed when they let him in, he motioned with his hand to be quiet. After all he had just escaped jail, so they quietly brought him in. Pedro then told them how the Lord brought him out of the jail, and they were deeply encouraged that God was still doing great things. Pedro then encouraged them to fully share his story with all the believers, saying "my story of faith in the face of obstacles is your story, too. Just not with the same people. There are those who will hate you because of your faith, but the outcome is still the same." After a quick nap, he left before daybreak.

Now when Marshal Garfias got up that morning, he was sipping his coffee and feeling great that Pedro was successfully behind bars. He was sitting back in his favorite chair with his feet comfortably resting on the edge of the desk. The serenity of that moment was soon interrupted when a jailer frantically knocked at his door, and gave him the bad news that Pedro had escaped. The marshal nearly fell out of his chair, spilled his coffee all over himself, and was beyond furious.

He jumped up and ran to the jail, and to his disbelieving eyes he found the gate open. When he looked in, he saw the two chains laying on the floor, and he felt sick to his stomach. He angrily asked the guards, "Who let Pedro out?" The guards claimed innocence, but it was obvious that Pedro couldn't have gotten out on his own. The marshal asked "Who has the key for the chains?" and again the guards said they didn't have it, and they didn't know where it was. He quickly touched his pocket to make sure he didn't have it either, and to his shock and embarrassment, there they were. Now the marshall was far too proud to admit it, so he stared at them in the kind of way no one wants to get stared at. The two guards who were supposed to be on either side of Pedro, and the guards who were at the front door, knew they were in trouble. One guard suggested it was an act of God, so the marshal said "Maybe this is, too!" Garfias then drew his gun and shot and killed all four guards, right then and there. He didn't need any witnesses, in caseone of them noticed the key in his pocket. When Pedro got word of this, he made his way to Wickenburg and stayed there.

This story surprisingly made the marshal even more famous than he had been before. He thought the town's people would be angry, but they heard stories about how Pedro escaped with divine help. It turned out that they were impressed that he dared to arrest Pedro in the first place. Being of Mexican descent, he never expected acceptance in Phoenix in the first place, but his fame just kept growing. Tales of his heroics as a gunfighter when he first arrived were not only remembered but embellished. The marshal was so enamored with his growing fame, that he announced he would give a speech. When that day came, he was overjoyed to see a great crowd, probably the biggest gathering of people anyone had ever seen. To help with his short stature, and growing ego, he stood on a crate draped with a blanket to hide it.

As he was talking, the people were chanting, "The voice of a god! The voice of a god! The voice of a god!" This inflated Enrique's ego to biblical proportions, and he lapped up the praise as if it were earned. It was almost like Enrique tasted the forbidden fruit as Adam did, which says "of the tree of the knowledge of good and evil you shall not eat, for in the day that you eat of it you shall die" (Genesis 2:17). Well, Enrique was certainly chewing a nice juicy piece of ego fruit, when right in the middle of his speech, an angel of the Lord struck him down. Marshal Enrique Garfias clutched his chest, started choking, then fell off the crate and died. Meanwhile, the word of God continued to advance and gain believers.

Now in the church in Flagstaff, there were many prophets and teachers. While they were worshiping the Lord and fasting, the Holy Spirit said, "Set apart for me Colton and Pablo for the work to which I have called them. To witness equality, have Kate and Rose come up from Tucson and join them." As soon as they arrived, the Caldwellian congregation laid their hands on the four of them and sent them off. The adventure became Pablo's missionary journey to North America. So, being sent out by the Holy Spirit, they first went to proclaim the word of God among the Havasupai Tribe of the Grand Canyon. Colton was a bit surprised at this choice, so Pablo admitted that he always wanted to see the Grand Canyon. The fact that the Havasupai Reservation had just been founded in 1880, made it even more intriguing, so the four of them headed northwest around the San Francisco Peaks and across the Coconino Plateau.

As they got closer, they took the short expedition north to see the Grand Canyon, and camped that night near the rim. Pablo was so excited that he barely got any sleep, was up well before dawn, walked carefully toward the edge, and sat down to await the view. It turned out to be better than anything he could have ever expected. As the sun slowly rose, his jaw gradually dropped. The mist dispersed with elegance, and the darkness was displaced with an almost eerie light. Pablo rose to his feet in awe, as the canyon walls first appeared, with their varying colors of orange and brown and green and yellow. Then the endless depths and distances of the valleys and peaks revealed their sublime majesty. The other three joined him, and Colton noticed tears in Pablo's eyes. He patted him on the shoulder and said, "Sure glad ya chose this place to visit."

After Rose and Kate agreed, Pablo composed himself and said "I heard about John Wesley Powell's Colorado River expedition here in 1869, and have wanted to see this place ever since. My joy is complete, because that incredible story is now a part of my memory." Colton smiled, and they all agreed that they gained a whole new appreciation of why the Indians of the area, who had been there for over 1,000 years, called it sacred ground.

Packing up their meager supplies, they headed west in search of the most remote community in the U.S. They had to leave their horses at the top of the Havasu Canyon, to take the long, and steep path eight miles below the rim of the Grand Canyon. Finally, they arrived at Supai Village. It was not common to have outsiders, so Pablo asked to see the Shaman. The Shaman expressed interest in hearing what Pablo had to say, but the chief got word of this and opposed the meeting.

Suddenly, Pablo was filled with the Holy Spirit, looked intently at the chief and said, "You son of the devil, you enemy of all righteousness, full of all deceit and villainy, will you not stop making crooked the straight paths of the Lord?" The chief was more surprised than anything, because Pablo was on the chief's territory. Then Pablo continued, "And now listen—the hand of the Lord is against you, and you will be blind for a while, unable to see the sun." Immediately mist and darkness came over him and he went about groping for someone to lead him by the hand.

The Shaman arrived just in time to see and hear all of this, and he was astonished, so he motioned for Pablo and Colton to come with him. The women wanted to go, but the Shaman said no. The three of them walked to the famous Havasu Falls, and the Shaman had a big smile of joy on his face as they arrived. He said to Pablo, "This is our paradise. The beautiful blue-green waters even gave us our name. We proudly call ourselves the Havasupai Tribe, which means 'People of the Blue-Green Water.' You two are very fortunate to be allowed to come here. It is sacred to us."

"Is that why you wouldn't let the women folk come?" asked Pablo. The Shaman did not answer, but soon enough they sat down in their idyllic setting. First they smoked a peace pipe, then the Shaman talked extensively about the ancient spirituality of the indigenous peoples. He shared about the soul and afterlife, the spirits and gods, and the sacred hoop of life. He explained that their ways were about honoring the connections of life, to the point of asking a twig for forgiveness when they needed to break it off to build a fire.

Pablo felt properly honored to be hearing these stories. He then followed by sharing the good news of Jim Caldwell and his resurrection, and how he himself was blind for three days while the risen Lord taught him. At that moment, Pablo was filled with the Holy Spirit, and asked the Shaman if he wanted to be baptized. They agreed that their spirituality seemed to fit together, so the Shaman agreed to baptized. The three of them waded out into the warm, soothing water and Pablo baptized him in the name of Jim Caldwell. As the Shaman rose from the water, he said he felt like he died and was reborn, much like the

Shamanism that has been practiced for over 100,000 years.

They spent several days at this wonderful site, talking at length about their experiences. Finally, they shared prayers in celebration of this wondrous place, and mutual learnings, then returned to the village. The chief had has sight back and wasn't too happy to see Pablo and Colton. The Shaman calmed him down and told him about their experience by the Falls. Pablo and Colton then gathered Rose and Kate and bid their farewell. Once they got back to their horses at the top of the canyon, Colton asked, "Where now?" Pablo responded, "I hear interesting things about Salt Lake City" so they headed off for a lengthy journey north.

It proved to be a difficult and frustrating trip, trying to get around the Grand Canyon. Pablo knew the only way over the Colorado River was after they would be close to Nevada. He expected plenty of improvements, since Nevada became the 36th state in 1864, and they were more than delighted to find a bridge across the Black Canyon. After a while they rode into a small settlement with a structure that was built in 1855 by Mormon missionaries. Pablo wanted to stop and chat with the Mormons, but he felt the Holy Spirit calling him to go on up to Salt Lake City and see it for himself.

As the four pressed forward, they shared stories they heard about the City. They agreed that it was settled by the Latter-day Saints, and knew that Brigham Young was their leader. They further agreed that those pioneers were seeking religious freedom, but beyond that they knew nothing. That's when they decided to not talk further about things they didn't know. The time proved fruitful, as they got to know each other much better during their 400-mile journey to Salt Lake City.

Pablo said he would never forget the site when they first

saw the City. He was beyond surprised to find out it had grown to a population of over 200,000, but that view of the City sitting against the majestic backdrop of the Wasatch Mountains was already worth the trip. They entered the city, and asked around for a guide of sorts to tell them about the metropolis. A nicely dressed young man shared six things he saw as important:

1. In 1846, the ill-fated Donner Party trekked across the valley through Emigration Canyon.
2. By 1857, there was a public outcry against the Church practice of polygamy.
3. Gold and silver was discovered in the Wasatch Mountains.
4. In 1869, the first transcontinental railroad was completed at Promontory Summit.
5. Bitter conflicts broke out between the LDS-controlled local government and Federal authorities.
6. To achieve statehood, the LDS Church agreed to ban polygamy.

Pablo said to him, "We would like to worship with an LDS church," so the young man directed them to a local chapel for a service. On the Sabbath day they went into the chapel and sat down. They were pleased to find a pleasant welcome and friendly worshipers. The service began with hymns and prayers, then the bishop looked at Pablo and Colton and said, "Brothers, if you have any word of exhortation, you are most welcome to give it now." So Pablo stood up and with a gesture began to speak.

"The God of our ancestors made the Mayans great during

their stay in the land of the Hondurans, then led them out. For forty years he put up with them in the wilderness." Most of the congregants laughed because they knew a patient God. "He then gave them their land as an inheritance, and later gave them judges until the time of the prophet Samuel. Then they asked for a king, and God gave them Saul, who reigned for forty years. Then he made Montezuma their king, and at long last God gave us Jim Caldwell. Before his coming, Jim's cousin was offering a baptism of repentance, asking, 'Who do you suppose that I am? I am not the savior, like the one who is coming after me.'

"You descendants of Aapo's family, and others who fear God, to us the message of this salvation has been sent. Because the residents of Phoenix and their leaders did not recognize him, they condemned him. Even though they found no cause for a sentence of death, they killed him. They took him down from the noose, and laid him in a former diamond mine for a tomb. But God raised him from the dead, and for many days he appeared to his followers, and they are now his witnesses. And we bring you now that good news. Let it be known to you, my brothers and sisters that through this man forgiveness of sins is proclaimed to you. In the name of Jim Caldwell, everyone who believes is set free from all those sins."

As Pablo and Colton were going out, the people urged them to speak about these things again the next Sabbath. When that day came around, thousands gathered to hear the word of the Lord. But when the bishop saw the crowds, he was filled with jealousy and contradicted what was spoken by Pablo. He began to talk of John Smith and the Book of Mormon, but Pablo tried to speak over him, saying, "It was necessary that the word of God should be spoken first to you. Since you reject it and judge yourself to be unworthy of eternal life, we are now turning to the nonbelievers."

When the unbelievers from the city heard this, they were glad and praised the word of the Lord, putting them on the road to eternal life. Thus the word of the Lord spread throughout the region. But the LDS members incited the devout women of high standing and the leading men of the city, and stirred up persecution against Pablo, Colton, Rose, and Kate, and drove them out of their region. So they shook the dust off their feet in protest against them, and departed. Kate was quite incensed, but Rose managed to calm her down. Soon Colton asked Pablo the now common question, "Where to now?" He responded, "I believe we are being called to go to Denver."

As they headed out for a grueling trip, Colton asked if there was any chance they could sell their horses and take the Transcontinental Railroad. Right then they found themselves within eyesight of the train depot. Colton declared it a sign, and Pablo agreed that it would be okay, because they all were developing back and shoulder troubles. It was easy selling their horses, and then they had plenty of money to take the train and buy horses again later, so they did it.

Getting on the train was a useful experience. It truly gained them insight into spreading God's word to a wider audience. Colton struck up a conversation with another traveler, who explained that "the railroad was originally a goal of President Abraham Lincoln. The route began in Omaha, Nebraska where the Union Pacific Railroad built westward, while the Central

Pacific Railroad Company would start in Sacramento and build eastward. Each company received $48,000 in government bonds for every mile of track built. The Native Americans often attacked the workers, as they felt threatened by the progress of the white man and his 'iron horse' across their native lands." Colton was mesmerized by the story, so the man continued.

"Chinese laborers were hired and were toiling under brutal conditions to bring the line east. Irish immigrants and Civil War veterans were hired and started bringing the line west. The Central Pacific workers built huge wooden trestles to traverse canyons and they blasted tunnels through granite mountains. By1869, the two companies were working only miles from each other. They agreed to meet on Promontory Summit, just north of the Great Salt Lake, and on May 10 a Golden Spike was driven.

"I was there for the ceremony, and it was a great celebration for linking the Central Pacific and Union Pacific. A telegraph cable immediately went out to President Grant with the news that the transcontinental railroad had been completed." Colton asked how he knew so much, and he replied that he was the one who carried the message for the telegraph. After hearing a good story, Colton drifted off to sleep, happy that they weren't doing this part of the missionary journey on horseback. Pablo had also been listening, but he kept nodding off, while Kate and Rose were fast asleep.

As Denver slowly came into view, Colton got a bit homesick. It was one thing to be all the way up in Salt Lake City, but Denver was another 500 miles from his home. About that time the train whistle blew, and Colton felt lonely and tired and sorry for himself. As he shook off the sadness, the train came rolling to a stop and the four of them got off. It was a chilly day in the mile-high city, so they first looked for a boarding house to put them up for a while. They easily found a place and settled in with their few belongings, then headed out for a short stroll of the city. Soon Kate announced that her brother lived in nearby Redstone, Colorado and she wanted to go visit him.

"We're not going," Pablo flatly announced.

"Well, I think I am," countered Kate.

Colton was confused and asked, "Aren't we following the lead of the Spirit?"

"Yes," offered Kate,"and the Spirit is leading me to see my kin. What you don't know about me is that I was born in the Kingdom of Hungary as Maria Katalin Magdolna Horony. I miss my family, and I sense my destiny in that direction."

Rose had tears in her eyes and said, "We need to let her go," and at that, Big Nose Kate departed. She immensely enjoyed the visit with her brother, then started dating an Irish blacksmith from Aspen, Colorado. They got married on March 2, 1890, and after working mining camps in the area, they moved to Bisbee, Arizona where she ran a bakery. She left her life of missionary work, but continued to live the Caldwellian lifestyle. Her experiences with Jim Caldwell changed her, like coal into a diamond.

As the remaining three continued their walk, they were amazed at how fast America was growing. They realized that their isolated experiences in the Arizona Territory weren't a good barometer of life outside the desert. Denver had only been founded since 1858, but by 1890, it had grown to be the 26th largest city in America, and the fifth-largest city west of the Mississippi River. Manufacturing soared over this same period of time to $40 million, however this attracted other problems like crime and poverty. What was familiar was the rampant gambling, prostitution, and alcohol, which was in its early stages of fighting for prohibition.

This is what gave Pablo his initial inspiration. He heard people on the streets talking about the new Charity Organization Society, which coordinated services and fund raising for many agencies. He also found out that Myron Reed, pastor of the First Congregational Church, was questioning the Society's efforts to distinguish the "worthy" from the "unworthy" poor. Pablo returned that night with the decision to share the good news about Jim Caldwell to the people of Myron Reed's congregation.

The next morning Pablo, Colton, and Rose were filled with the Holy Spirit as they found the church, and the pastor was in. They sat in his office, and their zeal was so contagious, Pastor Reed invited Pablo to speak at his church on Sunday. Rose was also a great speaker, but the church wasn't open to women preaching. The pastor explained that they were interested in fighting injustice, but it became obvious he couldn't see it right under his nose. As they left the church, Rose asked, "Do you know what yer gonna say?" Pablo replied, "Of course not but I'm sure the spirit of Jim will guide me." Rose smiled at that thought as they returned to their boarding house.

Sunday morning couldn't come quick enough, because their missionary journey so far wasn't all smooth sailing. The Havasupai chief seemed to be a deterrent, but Pablo and Colton ended up having a great experience with the Shaman. The Mormon people were very open to Pablo's message, until the bishop opposed him. They wondered what the Congregational Church would have in store for them, so they spent the next few days in prayer and fasting. This renewed their energy, so they could fulfil God's purpose in their lives.

At long last, they were making their way back to the church. It was a pleasant building, dominated by the charisma of the pastor. As they walked in, members proudly told them that Pastor Reed was not just their minister, he was also a lawyer and a political activist. Making their way toward the front, Pastor Reed hobbled toward them, so some parishioners explained that he was shot in the leg while serving in the Union Army. Colton looked at Pablo in a way that seemed to show deference, so Pablo quickly whispered, "Don't forget, we've got the spirit of Jim."

Rose was invited to join them up front, then Pastor Reed opened the service with hymns. To show his efforts toward equality, he offered to have Rose lead the time prayers. Colton felt out of place facing the congregation, but Rose led the congregation with beautiful prayers. At long last, the pastor turned the service over to Pablo. Colton was still nervous, but Pablo spoke eloquently and with conviction about Jim Caldwell. They were surprised when church folk became believers, so they remained for a long time afterwards and Pablo and Rose both spoke boldly for the Lord. As the time grew from one to two to three hours, Pablo began doing signs and wonders of healing and imparting hope. Things were going great for the missioners, but not for long.

Word got around the city over the next several days about the stories of Jim Caldwell, and the residents became divided. Some believed the stories while others thought Pablo, Rose, and Colton to be charlatans. As is so often common, the troublemakers won out, and began breathing threats against them. Pastor Reed hurried to their boarding house, and with apologies, suggested they leave town. All of a sudden they sensed their work was done, so Pablo, Colton, and Rose packed their things and headed for the train station. As usual, Colton asked, "Where to next?"

Truth is, Pablo wanted to go to Albuquerque, but the ticket person started explaining all kinds of problems with the railroads not wanting to work together. The man droned on about the Denver and Rio Grande Western Railroad and their agreement problems with the Atchison, Topeka and Santa Fe Railroad. Pablo really wasn't interested in a history lesson, so he finally interrupted and said, "I'll take three tickets to Santa Fe." He was frustrated that they couldn't get him all the way to Albuquerque, but he knew it would all work out. After they disembarked at Sant Fe, they bought three horses with the extra money they still had, and then completed their trip to Albuquerque.

The first thing Pablo announced was that he was kind of done with speaking in churches, so they spent some time riding around Albuquerque. The Spirit of Jim was certainly not confined within the walls of a church, so they hoped for some new good fortune with street preaching. Pablo was just soaking up the culture, because the town was a distant outpost of the Spanish empire, and its residents were mostly people who looked like himself. It was also the site of Native American pueblos when Europeans first arrived in 1540, and was officially founded in 1706 by Don Francisco Cuervo y Valdés. It soon became an important trading center on the Chihuahua Trail from Mexico.

That's when Pablo saw his first opportunity to do his

missionary work in Albuquerque. He stopped, and motioned to Colton and Rose to dismount. They walked up to a man sitting by the street, and soon discovered he had been crippled from birth. Pablo started sharing his story with the man, when he sensed the man had faith to be healed. Speaking in a loud voice, Pablo said, "Stand upright on your feet." Crowds had already gathered when the man sprang up and began to walk. They all knew the man who had been healed, so they shouted, "¡Los dioses han llegado a nosotras en forma humana!" which means "The gods have come down to us in human form!"

To their surprise, the crowds rushed away. It turned out that there was a local shaman just outside town who listened to the story that excited the crowd. It didn't take him long to suggest they offer sacrifices to Pablo and Colton for their great gift. The people headed off in different directions to find the best gifts they could gather. Returning to Pablo and Colton, they brought turquoise and silver jewelry, and a very rare Yawanawá necklace made in Brazil, and some onyx figurines from Mexico.

Pablo was touched, but knew that the praise was going the wrong direction. He finally said, "Friends, why are you doing this? We are mortals just like you, and we bring you good news, that you should turn from these worthless things to the living God, who made the heaven and the earth and the sea and all that is in them. In past generations he allowed all the nations to follow their own ways; yet he has not left himself without a witness in doing good—giving you rains from heaven and fruitful seasons, and filling you with food and your hearts with joy."

But the crowds did not listen. In fact, they were downright incensed. They felt Pablo was unappreciative of their gifts, and one person questioned, "Did he just call our gifts worthless?" The crowd was quickly turning angry, as another said, "You are not a god, we now agree with you, for gods would not turn down such precious gifts" At that point things turned very ugly for the visitors, and Pablo and Colton were severely beaten. They were dragged out of town and left for dead, but they decided to leave Rose alone. She got some water, tended to their wounds, and after several hours, they woke up. They were bloodied and in severe pain, as Rose asked, "Pablo, Colton. You alive?" Pablo weakly responded, "I think so," and Colton nodded his head yes.

They laid there for a while, taking inventory of their injuries, and were glad to find they had no broken bones. When Rose finally managed to drag them to their feet and lean them against their horses, Pablo curled a smile that their horses were also loyal. The horses had stayed nearby, and were more ready for the remaining trip than their riders. Rose first tried to push Pablo up on his horse. He was facing his horse in a standing position as Rose firmly placed her hand on his buttocks. She said, "If this isn't ministry, I don't know what is!" but nobody had the energy to laugh. With one big shove, Pablo sprawled over the saddle. He slowly turned over, with lots of help from Rose, and many moans and groans. Likewise, Rose helped him move one leg over the saddle and he carefully sat up.

"Next!" exclaimed a joyful Rose, but Colton had no joy. She said, "Oh, come on. At least I learned some things from getting Pablo on his horse." Working together, Colton got on his colt and readied himself, then Rose mounted her steed. Even though they were bloodied and had torn clothes, Colton managed to ask, "Where to now?" Pablo said, "I think we've done enough here." They both laughed through the pain and all three headed back to the church in Flagstaff.

It was more than a 300 mile journey ahead of them, and

the first several miles were just grueling. As time passed by, so did some of their pain. They slowly learned how to sit in the saddle in less difficult ways, but they still wanted to stop. Pablo suggested it would be too hard to get on and off again, so they rode until dusk. It was cool in the mountains, so when the sun set, they picked a campsite, got off their horses, and Rose prepared a fire. It reminded Pablo of their first night by the Grand Canyon, and he wondered how Kate was doing. Missing her robust attitude and amazing testimony, he drifted off to sleep.

Each day was a challenge, but at least they knew they were always getting closer. Wounds were slowly healing and so was their spirit, and it really helped having Rose with them. She did a great job of keeping them positive. Crossing the Puerco River was a celebration of its own, as they knew it meant they were back in the Arizona Territory. They followed the Purerco River and passed some magnificent scenery. They saw fallen trees that looked like colorful stone, and Colton hoped that someday the area would be preserved.

The next day they passed through a small, unincorporated town. They were standing on a corner in Winslow, Arizona and thought the small General Store was such a fine sight to see. They went in and got some cheese, hardtack, coffee, and dried fruit, and praised God for the opportunity to get some supplies. That lasted them all the way home, but when they arrived, the Caldwellians were appalled at their appearance. They helped them dismount, assisted them into the church, and told them to get some rest.

The next morning, the church gathered together to hear all that happened on their missionary journey. First they celebrated having come full circle in their travels through the

American West, then explained Kate's absence. Most of the Caldwellians were wide-eyed at their accounts of troubles in Salt Lake City, Denver, and Albuquerque, and decided then and there that mission work was not for them. Pablo was feeling a bit defensive, so he shared the good experiences they had on their journeys and was a bit surprised when the stories finished so fast. Pablo ended by saying, "Well, at least a door has been opened for faith in Jim Caldwell. Sometimes you just plant the seeds of faith and let others reap the harvest." And they stayed in Flagstaff with the Caldwellian church members for some time.

SCENE TWO
Mexico City and Guadalajara

While in Flagstaff, Pablo got a telegram from Mexico City. His experiences, both in Mexico and North America, helped him answer the concerns expressed by the Caldwellian Church.

HOLA PABLO,

REMIND US OF THE KEY POINTS OF THE FAITH.
REMIND US HOW TO LIVE THAT FAITH.

APPRECIATIVELY,
THE CALDWELLIANS OF MEXICO CITY

Remembering the troubles he had in that city, he lightly chuckled as he addressed them as "saints." Knowing the seriousness of his task, he proceeded with "Grace to you and peace from God our Father and the Lord Jim Caldwell." Now that this was his third response to a telegram, he decided to again refer to Jim as Lord, like he did when writing to the Nogalesites. He knew 'Lord' was the term used to refer to the deified Russian emperor, and that was precisely his point. Not only was it a political and religious statement, it followed the revolutionary thinking of Jim Caldwell. Jim was greater than any human idol, because the resurrection was what set him apart.

Well, not just resurrection. Jim had innumerable redeeming qualities, and just thinking about them again brought joy to Pablo's heart. He still struggled to understand why, of all people, Jim chose him to "know" about the resurrection. For whatever reason though, he was certainly dedicating the rest of his life to sharing that profound good news.

Pablo then scribbled some initial ideas for an opening prayer in his letter to them. He had heard that prayer was extremely important to the historical Jim, so he started with a beatitude. Pablo felt particularly good as he exhorted the Capitalinos to be "holy and blameless before him in love." The next words he jotted down were redemption and forgiveness, then he made sure to use the word mystery, since it seemed so relevant to his own experience. Then he thought that he certainly needed to include the word hope. He learned a lot about hope as he sat in jail for three years feeling hopeless. He put his pen down and thought and prayed about his responses as he sat in his room in the modest church home.

After a while, he wrote that he was remembering them in his prayers, and specifically prayed that they would receive a spirit of wisdom. He knew the problems the Capitalinos faced with living in a city near such a magnificent place as Teotihuacan. It is just thirty miles northeast of Mexico City and consisted of the Pyramid of the Sun and the Pyramid of the Moon, connected by the Avenue of the Dead. The problem was that the locals made miniature souvenirs of the pyramids for visitors from all over the world, which made the business one of near idolatry. It was almost a carnival atmosphere, which seemed exceedingly strange and frustrating to Pablo because the ancient Aztecs considered it a sacred place. It reminded him of the time he stood at the Grand Canyon, which made him hope even more that tourism wouldn't some day ruin it's majesty. This all seemed too depressing, so Pablo decided to go outside and get some fresh air.

It was a crisp and cool day in the mountains of northern Arizona. The birds were chirping and squirrels were running around the yard, and Pablo couldn't quite put his finger on the joy he felt. It crossed his mind that there seemed to be a spiritual connection between everything. That was just what his spirit needed to continue with this important letter, so he sat outside on the front porch. He penned his hope that this wisdom would enlighten their hearts, so that they might know God's will for them. He noted that God put his power to work when he raised Jim from the dead, and suggested that Jim would take a seat of honor in heaven.

Pablo wanted to finish this opening prayer saying something new, or at least since his letter to the Nogalesites. After thinking for a moment, he smiled because it came to him that his inspiration while being in the out-of-doors was starting to materialize. The interconnectedness of life slowly became visualized in a strange way. Pablo saw Jim's head on top of a church. It wasn't a disembodied image, but a connected one. Jim may no longer be with them physically, so why not have them think of the church as his body? This concept would now let Jim be the head over all things for the Caldwellian churches.

He then stopped for a moment to remind himself about the first concern in the telegram. He glanced at it and remembered that they wanted to know the key points of the faith. Pablo decided to begin by talking about life without God, then compare it to life with God. He was pleased with how he was going to begin the body of his letter, but first he needed another break to really get in touch with Jim's spirit. Pablo walked down to a local café to get some coffee, and immediately thought about The Rusty Tavern back in Phoenix. He sat outside and sipped his drink, and soaked up some sun, then it hit him. Thoughts of his old life just flooded back, and even he was surprised about the dramatic change it was to the new life in Jim.

As he hurried back to his room's porch to continue his letter, he wondered where Timoteo might be. He proved to be a great ambassador for Jim, and did a wonderful job carrying Pablo's letters to the Nogalesites and Chihuahuans. But now he was on his own, evangelizing in the name of Jim Caldwell, so Pablo wasn't sure what he would do to get this letter to the people of Mexico City. When he got back to his room, he again prepared to put pen to paper. So, life without God, eh? Pablo started writing furiously about how sin causes one to live as if they were dead. He warned that a Godless life fills the soul with the desires of the flesh, leaving us as children of wrath, like everyone else.

Pablo paused again, realizing that just thinking about his old life was turning his soul dark. He felt his chest tighten as he thought about dragging Caldwellians to Marshal Garfias, so he proceeded with thoughts about God being rich in mercy. Tears started to fall as he penned "by grace you have been saved." His mind wandered back for a moment to his road to Tucson experience and a smile crept across his face. Knowing how undeserving he was, Pablo continued with "For by grace you have been saved through faith, and this is not your own doing; it is the gift of God—not the result of works, so that no one may boast." He then wrote about being created anew in Jim Caldwell, and that it should be our new way of life.

The old life, Pablo explained, was the life without the spirit of Jim. It was a lonely life, not knowing promise nor God. But now in Jim Caldwell, we are brought together. We have peace, because there is no need for hostility, not even towards those who wrong us. There is no dividing wall, because one humanity can be created in the name of Jim. He continued writing with, "So then we are no longer strangers and sojourners, but members of the household of God. And we are joined together spiritually, into the Caldwellian Church that is open to all. When I say all, I mean all. That is, it does not matter where we came from, or what we look like, or what we have done. God loves us and is interested in who we are now and where we are going. When the community comes together in such a loving way, we become a dwelling place for God."

Pablo stopped again, and was pleased. He felt inspired about what he had written, and prayed about what else God wanted him to tell the Capitalinos. Immediately he sensed the spirit of Jim leading him to talk about the mystery of God's plan. It was time to tell them that all people were chosen by God, and that the Caldwellian Church was to make God's wisdom known. What better way to show inclusion than to tell his own story, so he shared quickly about his unique revelation from the risen Lord. Pablo was excited to share that this great mystery had never before been revealed, but now it was theirs to know: anyone can share in the promise of Jim Caldwell, through the good news of his resurrection.

Pablo concluded this part of his letter with prayers for the Caldwellian Capitalinos. He wanted them to be strengthened in their inner being, because he knew that spreading the news of God's love through Jim would be a challenge. He then wrote something about how he sincerely prayed for them to have spiritual power, and that they needed to have Jim's spirit dwelling in their heart. The reason was because he knew that having Jim's spirit within would ground them in love. Then he prayed that they might be able to comprehend the breadth and length and height and depth of God's work. He liked that. It seemed to express the fullness of their task. Finally, he desired that they would be able to know the love of Jim which passes all understanding.

Satisfied, Pablo looked back again at the telegram. A smile crept across his face, because he was glad they wanted to know how to put their faith into practice. Theory, he thought to himself, was virtually worthless if you don't do anything about it. He begged them to live a worthwhile and meaningful life, because the meaning of life is to live a life of meaning. The way to do that is to be humble and gentle and patient. Pablo was on a roll now, and the words just flowed. "There is one body and one Spirit, just as you were called to the one hope of your calling, one Lord, one faith, one baptism."

He then explained that we were given grace according to the measure of Jim's gift. Again the inspiration just flowed with, "The gifts he gave were that some would be vaqueros, some caballeros, some evangelisticos, some padres, and some maestras." He encouraged them to find their gifts, so they would mature to the measure and stature of the fullness of Jim. Pablo then exhorted them to speak the truth in love, for the purpose of building the community in love. He further insisted that they put away their former life, and be renewed in their mind. That way they would be clothed with the new life.

Pablo couldn't help but think something needed to be written about the things that destroy Caldwellian community, so he encouraged them to put away falsehood. Especially because Caldwellians were accused of spreading fake news, he demanded that they exorcise gossip from their lives. He knew that would be an endless challenge, so he told them to treat it like an evil addiction. He knew first hand about the damage gossip could do. The whole reason he spent three years in prison in Mexico City was because the 'policia' listened to the gossip that said resurrection was fake news. All of a sudden he felt hot all over with anger, and decided to address that issue.

He explained that it was okay to be angry, but not to sin, because anger is just a feeling, while sin is what we do with it. He then decided to give them something to think about: "all sin is wrong doing, but not all wrong doing is sin." He hoped they would dwell on that long enough to understand it. Further, he was emphatic that they must put away all hatred that dwells in the heart. Instead, they needed to be the first to be forgiving, because God showed the way by forgiving us through the death of his son Jim. Finally, he encouraged them to be imitators of God, to live in love, because Jim first loved us and gave himself up for us.

Something kept bothering Pablo about the old life everyone has, before they turn to the new life of Jim. He suggested that fornication and impurity should not even be mentioned, then implored them to act in the ways of Jim. He warned them that obscene, silly, and vulgar talk was entirely out of place in the community, then plainly said that no one should be deceptive. To really make his point, he wrote that they should not even associate with those who do, then he realized one of Jim's first followers was Big Nose Kate who had been a prostitute. And Matt had run a house of prostitution. "Oh well," he thought. "I guess that's part of why this whole thing is called a mystery." Then he decided that you can't judge a book by what's on the outside.

He also realized that the Capitalinos needed practical advice, and it needed to be simple and straightforward. So he wrote that the old life was darkness, but the new life is light, so take no part in darkness, but shine light on it. He explained that the days are evil, so it is of utmost importance to understand God's will. Don't get drunk on spirits, but be filled with the Spirit. He wrote that they should, "Sing psalms and hymns, making melody to the Lord in your hearts." Then he wrote that they should give thanks to God at all times and for everything in the name of our Lord Jim Caldwell.

Pablo paused again to refresh and spend some time in prayer. He felt certain that he was being properly inspired, but wasn't sure where to go next with his letter. After a quick nap, he decided to share some of those thoughts he had when he started, about the church being Jim's body. The words began to flow, so he wrote "Submit to one another out of reverence for Jim." He hoped the readers wouldn't misunderstand, because his point was about equality. He continued about having Jim as the head of the church in community as well as in the family, and this is put to use in love. If the spirit of Jim loves the church, then the spirit of Jim loves the family, and we are all one: Jim, church, and family. Pablo then scribbled another note about making it all very practical through respect.

About that time, a young family went walking by. The baby in the stroller was doing fine, but the child walking next to the stroller was very loud and angry. Pablo couldn't believe that neither parent did anything while the child was screaming and throwing a fit. Pablo thanked God for this useful interruption, and began writing about family. "Children, obey your parents." That didn't seem too confusing, so he bolstered this statement with scripture: "Honor your father and mother." Figuring that many readers wouldn't know scripture, he explained that Exodus 20:12 contained a promise. For those who obey this commandment, they should be able to live long in the land where they dwell. He then warned parents to not provoke their children to anger. Having no children, Pablo felt that was enough to say about that.

He was ready to close out his letter, but something kept nudging him to give the Capitalinos an image of protection. All he could think about was the cowboy clothes he heard that Jim wore. Before he knew it, he was writing about being strong in the Lord and in the strength of his power. He penned that they should put on the whole cowboy outfit of Jim, so they could stand against evil. This inspired Pablo to remind them that their struggle was against the rulers and authorities and cosmic powers of this present darkness. Now Pablo felt he needed to be bold, so he turned his image of Jim's cowboy outfit into the Mexican cowboy clothes of the vaqueros.

To fight spiritual evil, he pleaded with them to stand firm in the whole outfit of God's protection. He wrote that they should "put on the sombrero of salvation, so it covers your head like the waters of baptism. Wrap yourself in the bolero of righteousness, and wear it as a reminder of the good works you are called to do. Toss the serape of faith over your shoulders, and let the fringe at the bottom drip troubles away. Climb into the chaps of truth, so you are bolstered with God's way. Slide your feet into the botas of peace, so that you can walk this life like Jim Crawford did. Finally, strap on the spurs of God's word, and use them as the machete of the Spirit."

Pablo felt great about that piece of inspiration. He followed it with a request for himself, that he would be given a boldness when he spoke of the mystery of the gospel. He then let them know he would be sending Diego, who could tell them everything about his situation. He explained that Diego was a dear brother he met among the Caldwellians of Flagstaff, and that he was a faithful minister in the name of Jim Caldwell. Diego's main purpose was to encourage their hearts in the exciting and challenging task of living as a Caldwellian.

He then closed his letter with a benediction. Pablo wished them peace and love and faith, from God the Father and the Lord Jim Caldwell. Something frustrating entered his mind at that moment, and for some reason he couldn't bring himself to offer blessings to those who didn't have an undying love for Jim. He felt it wasn't right, but a little impish grin came across his face when he thought of a subtle way to hold back blessings. He picked up his pen and wrote his last sentence: "Grace be with all who have an undying love for our Lord Jim Crawford."

He then put his letter in an envelope and sealed it. He gathered the church members together to lay their hands on Diego's head for a blessing, and said, "Dear God our Father and Jim our Lord, we pray safety for Diego's journey. He has many miles to travel on several kinds of passage. Give him rest and nourishment all the way to Mexico City. We are thankful for his boldness to accept such a great challenge, and pray he may arrive with health in his mind, body, and soul. Be with him as he turns this letter over to our dear brothers and sisters in that great capital city." Diego then mounted his horse and rode off for an initial stop in Phoenix. A member of the church said, "If that letter makes it all the way to Mexico City, it could only be by the grace of God."

Pablo was pleased how the Caldwellian church was growing all over North America. He got word from Phoenix that church structure was settling in and the word about Jim was still growing with great speed. He also rejoiced that his work with the people in Mexico was having wonderful success. He thought about Pedro's work with the people in the United States, and quickly moved on to a more enjoyable topic. He stopped for a moment, and wondered why he was so willing to not think about Pedro, and it bothered him deeply. Then again this was a struggle about authority, and Pablo realized he was still frustrated about how Pedro treated him as inferior. Pedro insisted that his direct experience with Jim during his earthly ministry was far superior to Pablo's direct experience with Jim from heaven.

The fury that built up inside him came quickly and was unholy, and he even began questioning his calling to spread the news about Jim. Pablo wondered why he couldn't let this issue go about Pedro disrespecting him, and he felt remorse for a moment, then a light bulb went on. Even though he was imperfect in so many ways, God still used him to write letters to help others. It was one of those moments that changes things. Or could have. He quickly got back to thinking about Pedro's faults. With some false bravado, Pablo hoped that some day Pedro would realize that the church was about living like Jim did when he was on earth. He started focusing on how wrong Pedro was, and that his problem was that he needed to be led today by the Spirit of Jim from heaven. Both parts are essential to the Caldwellian life. He decided the sad thing was that Pedro was actually envious of him for having his transforming experience, but because they never talked honestly with each other, the problem never got resolved.

Toward the end of Pablo's stay in Flagstaff, he got another telegram. He enjoyed hearing from churches in Mexico that wanted his help, because it inflated his ego. This helped deter his anger about the unhealed 'thorn' in his flesh, which now just might be more about Pedro. It was good to know the churches that he founded, and the ones that were already there, were surviving. Times were certainly difficult in the United States and Mexico, but life was changing rapidly. Pablo just prayed that the spirit of Jim would continue to find open souls, so they could be led in a holy way. He opened the letter and found it was from the good people at the church of Guadalajara. Pablo fondly recalled the people there, and loved the city that he considered to be the quintessential representation of Mexico. Here's what was on the telegram:

ESTIMADO PABLO,

YOU ARE IN JAIL? WE'RE CONCERNED!
WE ARE ALSO CONCERNED THAT SOME
  AMERICAN MISSIONARIES ARE PREACHING A
  DIFFERENT GOSPEL THAN YOURS.
AND WE ARE HAVING TROUBLE WITH OUR
  LEADERSHIP.

ATENTAMENTE,
THE CALDWELLIAN CHURCH OF GUADALAJARA

As Pablo read over the concerns, he welled up with anger inside. He wondered "Why would missionaries change the message? How dare they!" And when he read about problems with the leadership, his soul burned hot. As he sat in his room, he had plenty of time to settle down. He needed a clear head before he replied, so he rested, then prayed, and then started writing, even though he was disappointed that he let his old self slip out.

"To all the saints in Guadalajara, and the overseers and helpers; grace to you and peace, in the name of Jim Caldwell."

That felt pretty good. He again loved the implication that the overseers and helpers were not part of the saints. After all, they were part of the problem. He continued by sharing his thankfulness for the Guadalajran believers, and that he prayed for them all the time. He wrote about his confidence that everything would be okay, either in this life or the next. Pablo was strangely moved as he wrote, "For God as my witness; how I long for all of you with the compassion of Jim." He genuinely meant it, even though his heart was filled with anger about the situation. He then talked about his hope for their growth in knowledge and insight.

As for his being in jail, he explained that he was released after three years in Mexico City, and is now in the United States. He then wrote, "I want you to know that what has happened to me has actually helped to spread the gospel. It has become known to everyone here that my imprisonment was for our Lord Jim Caldwell. Not only that, but the new believers are daring to speak with greater boldness and without fear." He went on to say that some were making fun of the story of Jim, but others were proclaiming Jim out of love. He then asked, "What does it matter? Just this, that Jim is proclaimed in every way, whether out of false motives or true; and in that I rejoice."

Pablo urged them to believe that he would always be delivered from a prison, because his salvation would deliver him to the next life, even if he didn't get out of jail in this life. Then he wrote, "It is my eager expectation and hope that I will not be put to shame in any way, so I need to speak the truth. Jim will be exalted now as always, whether by life or by death." He tried to explain that, at least for himself, living was about Jim, and dying was even better, but he realized this could be taken wrong. That's when he added that it was more necessary for them to live for the sake of glorifying and sharing about Jim. After all, Pablo wasn't ready to die either. He had demons of his own he was still fighting, and hoped that doing good for the rest of his life would keep him on the straight and narrow.

He decided he needed to shift his focus to the wonderful people of Guadalajara. Pablo stopped again and waited for some inspiration, which came with surprising ease and speed. He proceeded to tell them to live a life worthy of the gospel. He exhorted them to stand firm in the guidance of the spirit of Jim, and to strive together with one mind for the faith of the gospel, so they can keep from being intimidated by their opponents. He told them to know, without doubt, that if they accomplish difficult tasks, they can celebrate that it was God working with them. Then he told them a great secret: "For he has graciously granted you the privilege not only of believing in Jim, but of suffering for him as well—since you are having the same struggle that you heard I had."

Pablo felt a need to offer more encouragement, since suffering isn't very appealing, so he wrote, "If there is any consolation from love, any sharing in the Spirit, any compassion and sympathy, make my joy complete: be of the same mind, having the same love, being in full accord and of one mind." He felt this was so important, he offered the following advice on how to keep it from happening. He told them to not be selfish or conceited, but regard others as better than yourselves. He begged them to put the needs of others as a primary concern, because that would give them the same mind as Jim Caldwell.

All of this inspiration was doing something to Pablo. He didn't fully understand it, but he decided to write it down. The words strangely fell from his pen and he wrote the words in a creative fashion, unlike he'd ever done. To him it felt like poetry, but when he was done writing, he realized it was about the story of Jim's life:

Let the same mind be in you
that was in Jim Caldwell,
who was a child of God,
just like you and me,
but he took the form of a cowboy,
being born a human.
And being in human form,
he humbled himself
and became obedient to the point of death—
even death by a rope.

Therefore God also highly exalted him
when he arrived in heaven,
and gave him the name
that is above every name,
so that at the name of Jim
every knee should bend,

in heaven and on earth,
and every tongue should confess
that Jim Caldwell is Lord,
to the glory of God the Father.

Pablo reread what he wrote, and thought that someday it might become a song. But however it might be used in the future, he prayed that it would show the way of humility and obedience. He hoped they would catch the significance of humiliation being replaced with exaltation. Pablo then complemented them for their obedience, not only when he was present with them but also when he was absent. He also suggested that the more they worked together for good, the more they could fend off the outside troublemakers.

Again he stopped, and this time he thought about God's children complaining in the wilderness, so he wrote, "Do all things without murmuring and arguing, so that you may be blameless and innocent, children of God without blemish in the midst of a crooked and perverse generation, in which you shine like stars in the world." He wasn't sure that even he believed that, but it should provide impetus for their proper behavior. He further suggested that sacrifice was something they should rejoice in, for it was the way of Jim.

He stopped for a moment, looked back at the telegram, and got angry reading about missionaries preaching a different gospel. Actually, he was so angry that he expressed it in his letter, writing that they should beware of the low life dogs who are evil missionaries. Pablo knew he had to cool down, so he waited for a while and prayed about it. Soon he was back to writing, only this time it was in a positive light. He explained that nothing was more important than knowing the spirit of Jim, and that comes through faith. Pablo had to be careful here, because Pedro and The Twelve actually knew the earthly Jim. He had to make sure the Capitalinos understood his road to Tucson experience was so powerful, that their faith in the risen Lord would also be as good as Pedro's historical experience.

Pablo thought that maybe he needed to correct himself. He wrote that he was certainly not perfect, but he was on the road to being complete, and that is only because Jim Caldwell brought him into the family of believers. Then the words just flowed. He wrote, "this one thing I do: forgetting what lies behind and straining forward to what lies ahead, I press on toward the goal for the prize of the upward call of God in the name of Jim Caldwell. Let those of us then who are mature be of the same mind; and if you think differently about anything, this too God will reveal to you. Only let us hold fast to the gospel message given from God, through Jim, to me, and shared properly with you."

He got frustrated again about the improper message the missionaries were sharing with them. In fact, he got so mad that he wadded up the letter and threw it into the trash can. He took a break to cool down, which was frustratingly often. Getting new writing paper, he again put pen to paper, but the anger just wouldn't go away. "For many live as enemies of Jim; I have often told you of them, and now I tell you even with tears. Their end is destruction; their god is the belly; and their glory is in their shame; their minds are set on earthly things." Pablo reminded them that they are citizens of God's Kingdom here on earth, which will lead them to becoming citizens of God's Kingdom in heaven. He finished his thought by telling them that they were his beloved church, and that they were his joy and crown. He felt very two-faced about all of this, but knew that it wasn't easy to practice what you preach.

That being done, he looked back at the telegram, and saw that they were also having troubles within their leadership. "Will the maddening problems never stop?" he wondered. Pablo decided to name two women he knew, and urged them to stop causing trouble. He then asked a special friend in the church to help the two women. He felt divine revelation seeping into his heart, which he desperately needed, then wrote, "Rejoice in the Lord always; again I will say, Rejoice." Pablo then wrote that they should spend much time in prayer, thanking God for the precious gift of life. He explained that the peace of God surpasses all understanding, but it would guide their hearts and minds in the name of Jim.

Pablo knew he had to close out his letter on a positive note. After all, being a messenger of good news does not mean ignoring the bad news, it just means that the good news is what we Caldwellians choose to do. He wrote that "whatever is honorable, whatever is just, whatever is pure, whatever is pleasing, whatever is commendable, if there is any excellence and if there is anything worthy of praise, think about these things." Pablo wished he could do that, then got back to his favorite topic, celebrating their concern for him. Again he felt Jim's spirit nudging him in his writing, so he penned "I know what it is to have little, and I know what it is to have plenty. In any and all circumstances I have learned the secret of being well-fed and of going hungry, of having plenty and of being in need. I can do all things though Jim who strengthens me."

Pablo sat back and thought about that last piece, and agreed with it. His mind went back to the time he persecuted the Caldwellians and he felt a twinge of shame. Then he realized that without his background, he would be in no need of his road to Tucson experience. Yes, coming to know the spirit of Jim was what faith was all about, and anyone could have that experience. Pablo was content for now, which was needed because he was going to talk to them about money. He knew that was a delicate issue, so he had to proceed carefully to keep from being misunderstood.

He reminded the Guadalajarans that they were the only Caldwellian church that helped in the early days. And he was especially grateful that when he was beginning his Mexican work in Nogales, they even sent help for his needs more than once. Then he acknowledged the current gifts they sent, and called them "a fragrant offering, a sacrifice acceptable and pleasing to God." He said that God would satisfy their needs too, and give the glory to God. He finished by telling them to greet every saint in the name of Jim Caldwell, and bid them the grace of Jim to be with their spirit, then closed with "amen."

Another departure was arranged by the Caldwellian community of Flagstaff. They were called upon to equip Timoteo and Eduardo who had been chosen for this journey to Guadalajara. They needed horses to get to Nogales, then a train to Guadalajara. It wasn't as far as Diego had to go to deliver Pablo's letter to the people of Mexico City, but it was still a monumental trip. Pablo called everyone together and they formed a circle. He put Timoteo and Eduardo in the middle of the circle, then had everyone move in close and put their hands on either their head or their shoulders. Pablo put his hands on each of the heads, then prayed over the men and the letter, and sent them off with requests for divine protection.

ACT III
FAMILIARITY BREEDS CONTEMPT

Mexico, Mid 1890's

SCENE ONE
Teotihuacan

Pablo and Colton and Rose were appalled to hear that, even in the U.S., there were missionaries and evangelists who were demanding that the Caldwellians follow the law that was given to Abund. Pablo stood wide-eyed as he listened to heretical stories claiming that without the Law you cannot be saved. Pablo quickly called a meeting with the church in Flagstaff, and they decided to send Pablo, Colton and Rose to Phoenix to discuss this insidious problem with the mother church. They were informed that the church was getting organized, and now even had elders. Pablo rolled his eyes and said, "Sure wish the church was more about serving others than helping themselves!"

When they got to Phoenix, they were warmly welcomed. They settled into the new church the Caldwellians were working from and shared many stories about their travels through Mexico and America, with all of its ups and downs. They delighted in recalling the memories of people coming to Jim's abundant life by way of faith, and the four letters he had written in response to telegrams from churches. To Pablo's surprise, one of the elders stood up and said, "It is necessary to keep the law of Abund. Without them, there is no salvation!" It was all Pablo could do to restrain himself as his face grew hot with anger again. He felt like grabbing someone's riding crop and giving the man a good horse-whipping.

Instead, the mother church decided to call together its leadership to discuss the matter. The next day, the small group of decision makers gathered around a table. As usual, they left one chair empty to symbolize Jim Caldwell's presence. Pablo watched with curiosity, because he was very surprised to see that Johnny, one of the original twelve, had taken over the position of leader. Pablo was not one to keep quiet, but this development kept him on the sidelines. At least for a while.

Soon enough, Pedro spoke up. (You remember Pedro, Pablo's nemesis?) He stood up and reminded them about the Holy Spirit falling on unbelievers during his visit with Hank in Wickenburg. He said, "In the early days, God made a choice among you, that I should be the one through whom the unbelievers would hear the message of the good news and become believers. And God, who knows the human heart, testified to them by giving them the Holy Spirit, just as he did to us; and in cleansing their hearts by faith he has made no distinction between them and us." Then Pedro yelled, "Now therefore why are you putting God to the test? We believe that we will be saved through the grace of the Lord Jim, just as they will. Enough with this talk of needing the law!"

The church was silenced by Pedro's speech, so Pablo, Colton, and Rose began sharing their stories with the leaders, after explaining about Kate's departure. For one fleeting moment, there was a sense that Pedro and Pablo were working together. The leaders of the mother church were amazed that Pablo and Colton got to the famous Havasu Falls, and were overjoyed to hear the Shaman agreed to be baptized. They were astounded that Pablo, Colton, and Rose traveled by horseback all the way to Salt Lake City, and they were stunned to hear that Pablo spoke at an LDS Church. After hearing that the sermon was well received, they were not surprised to hear that angry mobs later that week ran them out of town. The elders were pleased to hear that they chose to take a train, and could barely believe Pablo decided to head next to Denver. Pablo had to remind them it was the leadership of the spirit of Jim.

The apostles and elders continued to listen, as Pablo shared his story about Pastor Ross inviting him to preach at his First Congregational Church. Pablo told about doing signs and wonders in their midst, how the townspeople became divided, and how Pastor Ross encouraged them to leave while they could. Colton then talked about their experience in Albuquerque, and how Pablo healed a man crippled from birth. The elders applauded, until Colton told them the crowd thought Pablo was a god. Rose said that when they brought gifts to Pablo, he turned them down, but the crowd was offended. "What happened?" inquired Johnny, to which Colton said, "We were nearly beaten to death." All of a sudden, several elders decided missionary work wasn't for them.

Rose shared about their excruciating journey back to Flagstaff and the letters Pablo wrote in response to telegrams form churches he started. Pablo continued with stories about his journey to Mexico, and after he finished talking, Johnny said, "Listen to me. Pedro has told us how God first looked favorably on the unbelievers." Pablo was visibly upset, because he was thinking that it seemed like a waste of time that he ever bothered to share his stories. Then Johnny continued, "This agrees with the words of the prophets, as it is written,

'After this I will return,
    and I will rebuild the dwelling of Montezuma,
      which has fallen;
    from its ruins I will rebuild it,
      and I will set it up,

so that all other peoples may seek the Lord—
even all the unbelievers over whom my name has
been called.

Thus says the Lord, who has been making these
things known from long ago.'

In light of these reports, I have reached the decision that we should not trouble those unbelievers who are turning to God, but we should write to them to abstain from idols and from fornication."

Pablo thought this was all a bit unnecessary, because he himself had direct guidance from the spirit of Jim, but then he calmed down and decided to cooperate with this newfangled church administration. The elders decided to send Pablo, Rose, and Colton back to Flagstaff with a letter. Pablo was a bit surprised, but glad to hear they were moving in the right direction. Here's what the letter said, as signed by Johnny.

"Greetings to the converted brothers and sisters of Flagstaff. Since we have heard that certain persons who have gone out from us, though with no instructions from us, have said things to disturb you and have unsettled your minds, we have unanimously decided to send back to you Colton and Pablo, and Rose, who have risked their lives for the sake of our Lord Jim Caldwell. For it has seemed good to the Holy Spirit and to us to impose on you no further burden than these essentials: that you abstain from idols, and from fornication. If you keep yourselves from these, you will do well. Farewell."

So they mounted their horses and headed off to Flagstaff. Pablo enjoyed passing familiar sights, like the Rusty Tavern and the road to Jerome, even though things were changing around them quickly. When they got to Flagstaff, they gathered the faithful together and gave them the letter. When they read it, they were happy, so Rose, Pablo and Colton remained in Flagstaff to teach and preach the word about Jim. After some days Pablo said to Colton, "I want to return to Mexico to see how the churches I started are doing." Colton was open to the possibility, but demanded a new friend of his come along. Pablo wasn't used to demands, so the friendly discussion quickly became an argument. In fact, it became so intense that they parted company. Colton headed north with his new friend to the places that had been visited in the United States, and Pablo ended up selecting an exciting new recruit from the Caldwellian Church in Flagstaff named Jasper. Together they headed south to Mexico, along with Rose.

The three of them took the train to Guadalajara, the capitol of the Mexican state of Jalisco, because it was more than 1,300 miles away. They caught the train at Nogales, Arizona, and Pablo was disappointed with himself for not crossing the border and visiting the Caldwellians in Nogales, Mexico. When they finally arrived in Guadalajara, they were mesmerized by the size and beauty of the city. Acting like tourists, they visited the city center, which was dotted with colonial plazas and landmarks. They were in awe of the neoclassical Teatro Degollado, then took a seat in the central plaza. Soon a mariachi band stopped at their table and a waitress took their order. Seeing how tequila was born there, they ordered a margarita. Jasper felt strange about ordering alcohol, but Pablo settled him down by saying,

"When in Guadalajara, do as the Guadalajarans do." Rose stunned them by ordering a Vino Mezcal de Tequila de Jose Cuervo. Noticing their faces, she said, "Hey guys, remember, I'm not Kate."

After spending several days in the city, they wanted a calmer atmosphere, so they headed to the outskirts of town. Since it was the Sabbath, they were delighted to find a peaceful spot by the Rio Grande de Santiago River, where there was also a small group of women gathering stones for their craft. They sat down by the women, and Pablo began sharing his gospel message. They were very hesitant, as they were suspicious of men, not to mention "Americanos".

One of the women was named Guadalupe. She was from Aguascalientes, a worshiper of God, and a maker of fine jewelry. As she listened, the others continued to ignore him, because they also didn't understand a woman traveling with them. As Pablo spoke, the Lord opened her heart. It was nothing specific that he said, but the overall message of freedom and equality spoke deeply to her. Guadalupe immediately requested baptism, and the other women stood up and walked away. Rose asked for the honor of doing the baptism, so the two of them waded into the river and Rose dipped her in. Although Rose never met Jim's cousin the Dipper, she remembered his work and praised God for this sacred moment.

Guadalupe was so moved by the experience, she invited them to come to her home and baptize her family. They were overjoyed, and soon enough they arrived at her home and baptized all of them. It was getting late in the day, so Guadalupe said, "If you have judged me to be faithful to the Lord, stay here with us. It would be like entertaining angels." Pablo agreed for them to stay, showing his complete acceptance of her as a Caldwellian. Later, Jasper asked Pablo what Guadalupe meant about angels and he said, "Hospitality was very important to the people of the Scriptures, and it is very important to the Mexican people. Always remember that Caldwellianism is about inclusion and acceptance. It is an angelic way to live"

One day, back in central Guadalajara, Pablo and Jasper ventured into the relatively new Mercado San Juan De Dios. It was a grandiose market packed with people selling beautifully embossed leather goods, jewelry, spices, fruit, and delightful fragrances. They heard there was a corner of the market that specialized in religious, spiritual, and occultist objects, so their curiosity tilted them in that direction. That's where they met Juanita Maria. Pablo asked her last name, and she stared at him and said, "None of your business." To help dull the embarrassment, he said, "That sure is a long last name." Being ignored, Pablo looked around and saw magic soaps and potions, incense and candles, and statues of folk saints like Santa Muerte (the saint of death).

Jasper said he was beginning to get nervous, but Pablo ignored him and said to Juanita, "I hear you can perform cleansing rituals." The young woman said, "That would cost you 30 pesos," and Pablo agreed to the price. Jasper again voiced concern, but Pablo rather scolded him for his lack of faith and asked Rose to take care of him. Juanita Maria then invited Pablo into a cramped space behind her stall, to which Jasper grabbed him at the last second and said, "I have a bad feeling about this." She motioned for Jasper to stay outside, to which he happily complied, and as the two of them disappeared behind a thin curtain, Rose reminded Jasper to have faith.

To be honest, Pablo wasn't sure what he was getting himself into, but at least he felt safe. Juanita Maria then told Pablo to raise his arms, and she brushed his legs, torso, arms, and head with a handful of rosemary plants. He asked what it was for, and she responded in a dull voice, "It's a cleansing ritual. Be quiet." The bells on her bracelet lightly jingled while she uttered a prayer in a strange voice. The calming blend of sounds and soft touches were wonderfully accented afterward, as she sprayed a pleasant perfume on him.

After this, Pablo looked Juanita in the eyes and asked, "Who owns this stall?" He was concerned, because he had heard that the owners of the stalls in the marketplace often charged exorbitant rates. She just looked down at the ground and didn't answer, so he went out to the front of the stall and yelled, "In the name of Jim Caldwell, I order the owners of this stall to stop taking advantage of this woman." Jasper was appalled and Rose tried to comfort him. Needless to say, there was quite a stir in that part of the mercado. Jaunita froze in fear, people came running over to see what was going on, and the owners of Juanita's stall rushed over and seized Pablo and Jasper.

As the locals yelled at the out-of-towners, some started throwing fruit from a nearby stand. One of the owners got even angrier when he was accidentally hit in the head with a mango. With a bit of blood flowing from his brow, he started screaming at the crowds, "Stop it! Get out of the way so we can teach these gringos a lesson, but leave the gringa alone!" Then they knocked Pedro and Jasper to the ground, and dragged them by their feet to the authorities of the marketplace. Pedro and Jasper grabbed at tables along the way, knocking over a few stands and tripping up several people.

When they arrived at the authority's office, they were quite a sight. Standing up, Jasper had to pull an embroidered blouse off his face and Pablo picked several necklaces off his clothes. The owners said, "These men are disturbing our mercado." Everyone in the crowd laughed at the understatement. Needless to say, things weren't going quite as well as Pablo had hoped, and he didn't feel as though he had been cleansed as well as Juanita's ritual claimed. The police were summoned and quickly showed up, and asked, "Who started this?" Everyone pointed at Pablo and Jasper, so both of them were arrested, and Rose trailed behind.

They were unceremoniously thrown into jail, and the police ordered the jailer to put them in the innermost cell and to fasten their feet in the stocks. After midnight, Pablo and Jasper were praying and singing hymns, and their fellow prisoners were listening. Suddenly, a violent earthquake shook the very foundations of the prison, and their jail door creaked open and their chains fell off. When the jailer woke up and saw the open cell, he feared he would face a firing squad. But Pablo shouted, "Don't be worried. We are here." The jailer rushed in, and fell down trembling before Pablo and Jasper and pleaded, "Please sirs. I don't want to die! I have a family! Please take me wherever you go, for you surely have more power than the police."

Pablo was concerned with this confusion of power, so he said, "This is not my power, it is the power of God and the Lord Jim Caldwell." The jailer then asked, "What must I do to become a follower?" Pablo said, "Just believe in the Lord Jim Caldwell, and get baptized." At that, the jailer invited them to his house, mostly because he wanted this kind of power to keep himself and his family safe. As they walked out into the night, they were pleased to see Rose sitting nearby. When they all arrived at his home, everyone listened to Pablo share the gospel, then the jailer shared what happened at the jail. One by one, they decided they wanted baptized, and Pablo and Jasper baptized them all. The jailer's wife even presented their newborn, and he, too, was baptized.

Pablo and Jasper were greatly encouraged by all of this, but thought that leaving town might be in their best interest. The jailer expressed concern for his safety, so they all bowed their heads and Rose prayed for their newfound faith and that God would protect them. Jasper then suggested they get involved with a local Caldwellian community. After a short discussion, Pablo, Rose, and Jasper decided next to travel northeast to León, where there was a Catholic church. On three Sabbath days in a row, Pablo talked with people on their way out of church. He explained from scripture that it was necessary for Jim to suffer and to rise from the dead, and then said, "It is Jim Caldwell whom I am proclaiming to you." Some of them were persuaded and joined the trio, but their fellow Catholics became jealous. With the help of some ruffians in the marketplace, a few Catholics formed a mob and set the city in an uproar. When the city officials heard of this, they asked Pablo, Rose and Jasper to leave, which they did, with grace, if not a little annoyance. On the way out, Pablo looked back and said, "We've been kicked out of better places than this!"

Venturing on further to the northeast, they came to San Luis Potosí. This time, the folks coming out of the local Catholic Church were more receptive of the message that Pablo shared.

In fact, they welcomed it eagerly, and examined the scriptures for themselves to see if the scriptures might indeed be about Jim Caldwell. Slowly, several of them became believers. But when some of the Catholics of León learned that the word of God had been proclaimed by Pablo in San Luis Potosí as well, they came there too, to stir up and incite the crowds. Then the new believers immediately sent Pablo and Jasper to the coastal city of Tampico.

Upon arriving there, Pablo was deeply distressed to see the city was full of idols from their heritage. He argued in the zocalo every day with those who happened to be there. Also some revolutionaries of the young Pancho Villa movement debated with him. They had little patience with Pablo and his message, because they were interested in making money to help force out Mexican President Porfirio Diaz. After the southern United States outlawed international slave trade in 1807, early revolutionaries illegally smuggled African slaves across the border at Brownsville, Texas. They debated with Pablo, calling him a "babbler," while another proclaimed, "And no Mexican will believe in a man with an American name like Jim Caldwell."

That's when the revolutionaries decided to go just outside the city to debate at the Las Flores Pyramid. They proudly passed by the neoclassical Palacio Municipal and the Tampico Cathedral in the Plaza de Armas, then on to the Plaza de Libertad. Pablo, Rose, and Jasper were properly impressed, then they arrived at Las Flores. One of the debaters said, "The earliest settlements here are very old," and another shared that "Amerigo Vespucci himself visited here." That's when someone in the back came forward with a doll and announced, "This represents the Aztec Quetzalcoatl deity. He is the god of life, light and wisdom, lord of the day and the winds. May we know what this new teaching is that you are presenting?"

Then Pablo stood in front of the pyramid and said, "Tampicans, I truly think you are very religious. As I went through your city and looked carefully at the objects of your worship, I was particularly intrigued with one thing. I saw an altar here at the pyramid with an inscription that said, 'A un dios desconocido' (which means, 'To an unknown god'). What therefore you worship as unknown, I know as the God who made everything. The God I worship does not live in shrines, and we should not think that the deity lives in pyramids made by human hands. Nor in statues of gold, or silver, or stone. There was a time that God saw our human ignorance, now he commands all people everywhere to repent. God has fixed a day on which he will have the world judged in righteousness by the actions of Jim Caldwell, and of this he has given assurance to all by raising him from the dead." When they heard of the resurrection of the dead, some scoffed; but others said, "We will hear you again about this." At that point, Pablo, Rose, and Jasper left, but some joined them and became believers.

After that, they journeyed north and west to Monterrey. There they found a man named Carlos who was Catholic, who had recently come from El Salvador with his wife Elena. It turned out that Carlos was of the same trade as Pablo, so they were invited to stay at their house. They were cabinet makers, and worked together during the week, then every Sabbath Pablo would talk outside the Catholic Church. He was trying to convince people that Jim Caldwell was resurrected from the dead. When they opposed and reviled him, in protest he shook the dust from his clothes, and decided to go witness to the unbelievers. While that proved fruitless, Pablo was overjoyed to find that the official of the Catholic Church became a believer in the resurrection of Jim.

One night Pablo stepped out onto the balcony of Carlos' home. It was a crystal clear evening, and the city streets were still abuzz with people shopping. That's when the Lord said to Pablo, "Do not be afraid, but speak and do not be silent; for I am with you, and no one will lay a hand on you to harm you, for there are many in this city who are my people." He stepped back into the house and told Jasper and Rose about the vision, and they found a sense of peace after many trying experiences in Mexico. They ended up staying in Monterrey for a year and six months, teaching about Jim Caldwell.

Things changed at the end of that time, when a new governor became in charge of the city. The Catholics made a united attack on Pablo and brought him before the tribunal. They said, "This man is persuading people to worship God in ways that are contrary to our beliefs." The governor asked for details, and one man said, "He talks of baptism in the name of Jim Caldwell." Just as Pablo was about to speak, the governor said, "If it were a matter of crime or serious villainy, I would be justified in accepting your complaint. But since it is a matter of questions about your own ways of thinking, see to it yourselves. I do not wish to be a judge of these matters."

After many good, bad, and ugly experiences in Monterrey, Pablo said farewell to the believers. He, Rose, and Jasper boarded a train bound for Mexico City, accompanied by Carlos and Elena. When the five of them arrived, Pablo immediately went to a Catholic church and had a discussion with the Catholics. Things went well, so Pablo decided to stay, in hopes that he wouldn't be jailed again.

The Jim Caldwell Trilogy

Now there came to Mexico City a Catholic named Francisco, who was an eloquent man, well-versed in the scriptures. He had been instructed in the way of Jim Caldwell, and spoke with burning enthusiasm and taught the things concerning Jim, though he knew only the baptism of the Dipper. He began to speak boldly in local churches, but when Carlos and Elena heard him, they took him aside and explained the ways of Jim more accurately. Francisco expressed surprise that a woman would be instructing him, so Carlos said, "If there is one thing that Jim Caldwell taught more than anything else, it was to treat all of God's people with dignity, equality, and respect."

Soon Pablo found some disciples in the City who joined the Caldwellian Church he visited on his missionary journey there. He asked them, "Did you receive the Holy Spirit when you became believers?" They replied, "No, we have not even heard of a Holy Spirit." Pablo shook his head, then asked, "Into what then were you baptized?" They answered, "Into the Dipper's baptism." Pablo said, "The Dipper baptized with the baptism of repentance, telling the people to believe in the one who was to come after him, that is, in Jim Caldwell." On hearing this, they were baptized in the Spirit in this way: Pablo laid his hands on them, the Holy Spirit came upon them, and they spoke in tongues and prophesied. Altogether there were about twelve of them.

Pablo then entered the Catholic Church and for three months he talked with them, and argued about the kingdom of God. When some refused to believe and spoke evil of the ways of Jim Caldwell before the congregation, Pablo left them and argued daily in the lecture halls. This continued for two years, so that all the residents of Mexico City, both believers and nonbelievers, heard the story about Jim. Pablo shared that Jim simply taught to deny yourself and follow him. God did extraordinary things through Pablo, when some Catholic exorcists came along. They tried to use the name of Jim Caldwell during exorcisms, saying, "I order you by the Jim whom Pablo proclaims." But the evil spirit said, "Jim I know, and Pablo I know; but who are you?"

To say the least, this didn't go over very well with the exorcists. The evil spirits frightened the exorcists, who ran away wounded and disgraced. When this became known to all residents of Mexico City, everyone was awestruck, and the name of Jim Caldwell was praised. Also many of those who became believers confessed and disclosed their practices. A number of those who practiced magic collected their books and burned them publicly. Pablo said, "Banning books doesn't work. Let the people find what is true and what is false through their own experience." This impressed the Capitalinos so much that the word of the Lord grew mightily and prevailed.

Now after these experiences, Pablo resolved in the Spirit to get back to Phoenix. He said, "After I have gone there, I must also see San Francisco." About that time no little disturbance broke out about the ways of Jim Caldwell. A man named Antonio, a silversmith who made silver shrines of Teotihuacan's (which means "the place where the gods were created") Pyramid of the Sun, brought no little business to the artisans. These he gathered together, with the workers of the same trade, and said, "Men, you know that we get our wealth from this business. You also see and hear that not only in Mexico City but in almost the whole of Mexico, this Pablo has persuaded and drawn away a considerable number of people by saying that gods made with hands are not gods. And there is danger not only that this trade of ours may come into disrepute but also that the Pyramid of the Sun will be scorned, and it will be deprived of its majesty that brought people from all over the world to worship it."

When they heard this, they were enraged and shouted, "Great is Teotihuacan's Pyramid of the Sun!" The city was filled with the confusion, and people rushed to the Pyramid. Pablo wished to go into the crowd, but Rose, Jasper, Carlos, and Elena would not let him. Even some local officials, who were friendly to Pablo, urged him not to venture into the nearby open-air theatre. Meanwhile, some were shouting one thing, some another; because the assembly was in confusion, and most of them didn't even know why they were there. The one thing they had heard was that Pablo was somehow causing trouble about their main source of income.

Soon the crowds made their way to the open-air theater, and for about two hours all of them shouted in unison, "Great is Teotihuacan's Pyramid of the Sun!" But when the town clerk had quieted the crowd, he said, "Citizens of Mexico City, who is there that does not know that the city of the Capitalinos is the gate keeper of Teotihuacan and that the Pyramids fell from heaven? Since these things cannot be denied, you ought to be quiet and do nothing rash. Neither Pablo nor his friends are pyramid robbers nor blasphemers of our gods. If Antonio and the artisans with him have a complaint against anyone, the courts are open; let them bring charges there against one another. If there is anything further you want to know, it must be settled in the regular assembly. We no longer sacrifice animals or humans at Teotihuacan, and we are not going to start now. Do you not realize you are in danger of being charged with rioting today? There is no cause that you can give to justify this commotion."

Someone in the crowd yelled, "But that man might cause us to lose our business!"

The town clerk replied, "The law doesn't operate on what might happen. You would need to have proof, so go away." When he had said this, he dismissed the assembly.

SCENE TWO
Monterrey

During Pablo's lengthy stay in Mexico City, and just two weeks before his awkward time at the nearby pyramids of Teotihuacan, a telegram arrived from the Monterreyans. He had written to the Caldwellian Church of Monterry once before about immoral church members, but they seemed to have lost that letter. Here are the questions they had this time:

> DISTINGUIDO PABLO,
>
> TELL US MORE ABOUT COMMUNITY.
> ANY ADVICE ABOUT MARRIAGE?
> COULD YOU TALK A BIT ABOUT FOOD?
> WHAT ARE SPIRITUAL GIFTS?
> PLEASE WRAP UP YOUR TEACHINGS IN A SINGLE
>   SENTENCE.
>
> SALUDOS,
> THE CALDWELLIAN CHURCH OF MONTERREY

Pablo sat back in his chair in the room he was staying, and folded his arms. He had to clear his mind about his departure from Monterrey before he could answer the telegram. There were some difficult people in that church, and it crossed his mind that "mission work wouldn't be so bad, if it weren't for the people." After chuckling to himself, he also thought that wishing something from the past was different, was little more than "wishcraft," so he sat back up and grabbed pen and paper.

"My dear Monterreyans," Pablo began, "you are called to be saints." He then thought about how easy it is to forget that calling, and admonished himself about his attitude. He then continued, "God has freely given you grace, and now I pray God's peace upon you, so that you might all know and experience the way the world is called to be, and all relationships within it." He then offered thanksgiving for them, as now had become customary for his responses to telegrams, and encouraged them that they were not lacking in any spiritual gifts. Even though they were asking for more information about spiritual gifts, it was too important of a topic, so he acknowledged the issue and decided to build toward it.

He wrote that they should first of all expect God's strengthening Spirit, and to know that God is faithful. That gets people ready by focusing on God rather than themselves. He even gave them some new hope that God was on their side, and that they were called into fellowship with one another, thereby becoming the body of Jim here on earth. That sounded a bit strange, but if they could just learn the great secret that their actions make Jim's life real again here and now.

The writing was flowing well, but Pablo realized he needed to heed his own advice. Hopefully, it was God's advice he was sensing, by the nudging of the Spirit of Jim. So he looked back at what he wrote and appreciated the thought of expecting God's strength. He absolutely knew that God was faithful, and acknowledged that he had trouble focusing on God rather than himself. There was a lot to like about the old Jose Maria Perez, but he was now Pablo. Getting his mind back into the task, he continued.

Pablo appealed to them to stay away from divisiveness, and to be united "in the same mind and the same purpose." He then shared the sad news he had received that there were some quarrels among them. He wanted to go quarrel with them right then, but shook his head over the fact that he would be directly opposing his own teaching. He further delineated the problem was that some claimed to be followers of Pablo, some of Francisco, some of Pedro (that made Pablo shiver just a bit), and some of Jim Caldwell. Pablo then got mad: "Has Jim been divided? Was Francisco hung by a noose for you? Or were you baptized in the name of Pedro?"

All of a sudden Pablo got furious. Not so much at them, but at himself. He thought that this Caldwellian thing was much easier to write about and think about, than do. Yet his divine task was to live out the new life, so he could write about it with genuineness. That was a challenge. His old life, before the road to Tucson, was quite polished, which gave him permission to give this new life some time. But then again, he didn't have time. These people needed help now. He could barely believe how his attitude kept seesawing back and forth, so he stopped. He prayed, "Lord, teach me patience. Give me humility. Thanks for putting up with me so far, and help me to practice what I'm trying to teach. Oh, and by the way. If you want somebody else to take over this opportunity, just let me know. I promise I won't go back to the way I was before." A sly grin crossed his face, because he knew that wouldn't happen.

This letter writing thing was exhausting, so Pablo decided he needed a break. He went down to the local zocalo and ordered a nice *pan dulce* from a street vendor. He sat down on a bench in a busy area and started into the slightly sweet treat. The first bite took him back to his childhood, when his mother made the bread every day. He savored the snack and the memories, then felt the urge to get back to his task at hand. His church in Monterrey needed him. As good as the food was, his need to be needed was more important.

As soon as he got back to his rented room, he tried to get back to his train of thought. "Now understand this. Baptism is important, but not the one who baptized you!" He looked upward and asked, "How's that for humility?" He almost heard a groan before looking back down. Then he wrote what he considered to be his main point. "My job is to proclaim the good news of Jim, and Jim resurrected." After pausing for a bit, Pablo continued: "For the message about hanging by the neck is foolishness to those who are headed for destruction, but to us who are headed for wholeness, here and in the hereafter, it is the power of God." For effect, he added a verse from Isaiah, then had a question. "Where is the one who is wise? Where is the debater? Has not God made foolish the wisdom of the world?"

He seemed to smile a lot when writing. Maybe these letters were even better than talking in person. It also crossed his mind that these writings could even be useful past his time on earth. Shrugging his shoulders, he continued, "For unbelievers demand signs and philosophers desire wisdom, but we proclaim Jim Caldwell hung with a rope, a stumbling block to the unbelievers and foolishness to the philosophers. But to the saints who are called, Jim is the power and wisdom of God, because God's foolishness is greater than human wisdom."

Pablo thought that was pretty good, then exhorted them to believe that none of them have any reason to crow, except to celebrate the risen Lord. He was on a roll again, so wrote, "God chose what is foolish in the world to shame the wise; God chose what is weak in the world to shame the strong; God chose what is low and despised in the world, so that no one might boast in the presence of God." Wow. Pablo loved this inspiration business. For good measure, he offered a quote from Jeremiah, then continued: "For I decided to know nothing among you except Jim Caldwell, and him hung." He then mentioned that his own weakness in preaching became the avenue for God's power.

He further wrote about God's wisdom, and said, "None of the earthly powers understood it; for if they had, they would not have hung the Lord of Glory." Feeling a strong need to undergird this thought, he again quoted a verse from Isaiah, then wrote, "These things God has revealed to us through the Spirit; for the Spirit searches everything, even the depths of God." Then he wrote that, "We have received not the spirit of the world, but the Spirit that is from God, so that we may understand the gifts bestowed on us by God." Again he was alluding to spiritual gifts, but he felt he still needed to write more before that topic. Then Pablo wrote another verse from Isaiah, and ended with, "But we have the mind of Jim."

All of a sudden Pablo felt anguished. He meant it about having the mind of Jim, but the reality was that it was almost impossible to get everyone united in that task. Pablo then got frustrated and wrote, "I could not speak to you as mature people, but rather as people of the flesh, as infants in Caldwellianism. I fed you with milk, not solid food, for you were not ready for solid food." He then complained that they were immature due to their jealousy and quarreling. And their division about who should get their admiration was explained with this: "I planted, Francisco watered, but God caused the growth." He then encouraged them with: "Do you not know that you are

God's temple and that God's Spirit dwells in you? For God's temple is holy, and you are that temple, and you belong to Jim, and Jim belongs to God."

He threw his pen against the wall in anger. He was writing things that were true, but would anyone listen to him? After a moment, he picked his pen back up and explained, "I sent Timoteo, who is my beloved and faithful child in the Lord, to remind you of my ways in Jim Caldwell, as I teach them everywhere in every church. But some of you, thinking that I am not coming to you, have become arrogant. If you think I'm not up to the challenge of confronting you face-to-face, you are wrong! But I will come to you soon, if the Lord wills, and I will find out not the talk of these arrogant people but their power. Let's see how they do when they aren't talking behind my back! For the kingdom of God depends not on talk but on power. What would you prefer? Am I to come to you with a stick, or with love in a spirit of gentleness?" Pablo realized that he far preferred the stick, so he needed to clear his mind before answering more of the telegram. He took some deep breaths and his mind drifted back to the serenity of Havasu Falls in the Grand Canyon.

He sat back for a while, then decided to call it a night. It was good to have time to respond to this telegram, because it wasn't going to need to travel nearly as far as his first four. As he laid back in his modest bed, he was grateful that it wasn't a jail cell. Then he decided to spend some time in prayer. He was quite tired, and drifted off to sleep in the middle of his prayer. The next morning he got ready, had a nice breakfast, and got back to work. He started to look for the telegram when he remembered they had a question about community. He was surprised to find words on it smudged from holding it so tight.

Anger welled up inside Pablo one more time. He had heard that his church, the Caldwellian Church of Monterrey, had someone who was practicing sexual immorality. He quickly put pen to paper and wrote, "For though absent in body, I am present in spirit; and as if present I have already pronounced judgment in the name of Jim Caldwell on the man who has done such a thing." Then he remembered hearing that some were boasting. Getting straight to the point, he said, "Your boasting is not a good thing. Do you not know that a little yeast leavens the whole batch of dough? Clean out the old yeast so that you may be a new batch. Let us not celebrate with the old yeast, the yeast of malice and evil, but with the new *pan dulce* of sincerity and truth."

Pablo then reminded them that his first letter, one they seemed to have conveniently lost, was about not associating with sexually immoral persons. Somehow they misconstrued that admonition to be about those outside the church, so now he's specifying that it is about those inside the church. He went on to include anyone among them "who is greedy, or an idolater, reviler, drunkard, or robber." He even told the church not to celebrate communion with them, then added, "For what have I to do with judging those outside? Is it not those who are inside that you are to judge? God will judge those outside." He knew he had to take it to the extreme because subtleties didn't seem to get through to them, and then he attached a verse from Deuteronomy.

He hoped they were beginning to understand that community comes from like-mindedness, which comes from cleansing the heart, mind, and soul. That's when he was reminded that some church members were suing each other in the Mexican court system. "Can it be," he questioned, "that there is no one among you wise enough to decide between one church member and another?" He decided he needed to get really tough at this point, so he wrote, "Do you not know that wrongdoers will not inherit the kingdom of God? But that's not you! You were washed, you were made holy, and you were made right in the name of the Lord Jim Caldwell and in the Spirit of our God."

Then Pablo wrote, "All things are allowed, but not all things should be done." He added, "And God raised Jim and will also raise us. Do you not know that your body is a temple of the Holy Spirit within you, which you have from God, and that you are not your own? For you were bought with a price; therefore glorify God in your body." Pablo put his pen down and wondered if they would understand his point. They wanted to know about community, so he prayed they would come to the knowledge that the church was the body of Jim Caldwell, alive and working through them. When they join him through membership, they establish the beautiful and illusive thing called community.

Pablo again took a break to ponder their next question. Even though it was a straight forward question for advice about marriage, they had also previously asked a variety of questions about the topic, so he reminded them of that fact first. "Now let's get back to the things you wrote about. Are you ready? It is well for a man not to touch his spouse." He grinned and thought, "That won't go over well." He then wrote about the importance of sexual morality, and how spouses should treat one another equally. And that they should devote themselves to prayer, so they can honor and respect one another's gifts. Next he offered some of his own opinions about unmarried individuals, and wanted them to be free from anxieties so they could have "unhindered devotion to the Lord."

He looked at his telegram and wasn't too interested in talking about food. He knew where their question was coming from. They wondered if it would be okay to eat food offered to the ancient Mexican gods, so he responded, "No idol in the world really exists," and "there is no God but one." Then he wrote that, "Food will not bring us close to God," but ended with, "if food is a cause of their falling, I will never eat meant, so that I may not cause one of them to fall." Pablo added that "I have become all things to all people, that I might by all means save some. I do it all for the sake of the gospel, so that I may share in its blessings." He finished his thoughts by sharing some warnings gleaned from Abund and the exodus.

Finally, Pablo could get on to their question about spiritual gifts. They asked a silly question about head coverings for women, and he thought that would be a great way to begin a talk about spirituality. He explained that it simply went back to an old way of thinking that a bald woman was somehow inferior to other women, not to mention their terrible attitude toward women in general. He suggested that "if you're spiritually immature, you might want to have all women wear head coverings. That way you won't know the difference, because you won't know who's bald. A far better way would be to grow up and not worry about head coverings."

He then moved on to their concern about the Lord's Supper. This being so deeply important, he told them what he knew from the risen Lord, and from Pedro (ugh!) who was at the Rusty Tavern where the Lord's Supper was instituted. He wrote that Jim Caldwell, "on the night when he was betrayed took a loaf of bread, and when he had given thanks, he broke it and said, 'This is my body that is for you. Do this in remembrance of me.'" Pablo got choked up for a moment, then wrote, "In the same way he took the cup also, after supper, saying 'This cup is the new covenant in my blood. Do this, as often as you drink it, in remembrance of me.'"

He then continued with, "Now there are varieties of gifts, but the same Spirit; and there are varieties of services, but the same Lord; and there are varieties of activities, but it is the same God who activates all of them in everyone. To one is given wisdom, and to another knowledge, to another faith, to another gifts of healing, to another the working of miracles, to another prophecy, to another the discernment of spirits, and to another various kinds of speaking talents. All of these are activated by the Holy Spirit, who allots to each one individually as the Spirit chooses."

He explained that believers become one body through baptism, and that the body does not consist of one member but of many. He glorified in the fact that the body of Jim, now the church, in its unity through baptism, expressed diversity in its members. Pablo prayed that they would capture the importance of this message: "If one member suffers, all suffer together; if one member is honored, all rejoice together." He further explained that, "Now you are the body of Jim and individually members of it. And God has appointed in the church first apostles, second prophets, third teachers; then deeds of power, then gifts of healing, forms of assistance, forms of leadership, various kinds of speaking. But strive for the greater gifts. And I will show you a still more excellent way." At that point a mighty wind blew into Pablo's writing area, and all he wanted to do was get this more excellent way right. As Pablo began to write, he sensed it was a poem straight from the heart of God.

If I speak like Poncho Villa,
    even in an angelic voice,
        but do not have love,
  I am nothing more than a bad mariachi band
      with clanging maracas.

And if I say I can look into the future,
    through crystal balls
        or the past through a seance,
           or even change the present,
        enough to move a pyramid,
  but do not have love,

        I am nothing.

If I give all my worldly possessions away,
    then brag that about it,
        that is not love, and

        I gain nothing.

Love waits,
    love is caring,
        love is not
      jealous
  or boastful
      or arrogant
        or uncivil.

It does not insist on its own way,
  it is not irritable or resentful.

Love does not celebrate wrong,
　　but rejoices when truth wins.

It bears all things,
　　believes all things,
　　　　hopes all things,
　　　　　　and lasts and lasts.

　　　　Love is eternal.

But as for crystal balls,
　　they will get cloudy and break,

　　　　　as for seances,
　　　　　　they will cease;

　　　as for the present,
　　　　it too will come to an end.

Right now we know only in part,
　　and even that is limited.

But in heaven we will be complete,
　　and the partial will come to an end.

When I was growing up,
　　I spoke like an infant,
　　　　then I acted like a child,
　　　　　　and finally I reasoned like a teenager.
　　But when I became an adult,
　　　　I took on more grown-up ways of thinking.

For now we see a riddle,
dimly,
but then we will see,
face to face.
Now I know only in part,
then I will know
fully,
even as I have been
fully known.

And now:
faith,
hope,
love.
These three have great potential within us.
But the greatest will always be

Love.

    Strangely, Pablo felt exhausted. He thought he would be exhilarated, so he put down his pen and took a walk. He wished he could be in Monterrey, rather than just writing to his church. A smile broke across his face as he remembered the Sierra Madres as a towering backdrop to the city. That perked him up, so he quickly returned, as it was getting dark outside, and he realized he needed to say more about spiritual gifts. He remembered how several parishioners were enamored with the gift of tongues, so he wrote, "Those who speak in a tongue build up themselves, but those who prophesy build up the church."

Pablo started breathing harder, and realized he was now quite upset. He figured that those who spoke in tongues would feel his insult, so he decided to couch his message in the idea of an even better way. He thought for awhile, then quite simply encouraged them all to build up the church with praying, singing, and blessing all of God's creation. The point would be to have outsiders experience God's love in their midst, so that they might declare, "God is really among you."

That geared his mind toward worship, so he wrote, "God is a God not of disorder but of peace." He worried that people in the future would somehow hear the loud voices of men complaining about women, but he hoped they would even more loudly hear his voice about equality. It wasn't a popular message, but he had been clear from the beginning, and it was intensified when Elena assumed a powerful teaching position in Mexico City. Pablo just wished the men of Monterrey could be more accepting of women having equal positions in the Caldwellian church. Overcoming millennia of patriarchal attitudes was going to be a challenge for them, so when it comes to worship, Pablo demanded decency, equality, and orderliness. He hoped they would understand that it was also God who demanded that we love all.

One last look back at the telegram brought him to a thought-provoking task. He remembered the old saying that a sermon should be able to wrap up in a single sentence, and that's what they wanted him to do with all of his teachings. That was surprisingly easy, so he wrote,

"All of this is to say to you, with nothing but love, to always stand firm, don't be wishy washy, and always do your best because your work isn't for nothing."

He sat back and looked at his summary, and felt content, until he realized he had a lot more to say. Instead of continuing, he decided to set the letter to the side for a few days and let it all germinate. He truly felt inspired by most of what he had to say, but it is always good to give things some time. Rushing seems to miss things. He decided to take the short trip to Teotihuacan and sit among the ruins and the tourists. The Aztec legends about this place say that it is where gods were created. He chuckled in agreement as a souvenir vendor tried to sell him a miniature pyramid trinket. That was all he needed to get back to writing.

Upon returning to his room, he quickly grabbed his letter and pen and started writing about the resurrection. "Jim," Pablo wrote, "was buried in a diamond mine, that revealed its secret when he was raised on the third day. Then he appeared to Pedro, Kate, the twelve, Jim's brother, and the apostles. Last of all, as to one untimely born, he appeared also to me." He went on with, "since death came through a human being, the resurrection of the dead has also come through a human being; for as all die, so all will be made alive in Jim."

Again he felt some special inspiration, so started writing: "Listen, I will tell you the greatest mystery of all time! We will not all die, but we will all be changed, from death to life." As had become Pablo's style, he strengthened his comment with a scripture verse, this time from the prophet Hosea. Then he shared the bigger secret that we don't have to wait until we die to experience the change from death to eternal life, because the Caldwellian lifestyle is about dying to the old life here and now and rising to the new life in Jim.

Somehow that steered him to give guidance on collecting a love gift for the church in Phoenix. He kind of felt like a souvenir vendor, but the purpose was to build the kingdom, not personal profit. He also mentioned that he hoped to visit them, and "perhaps I will stay with you or even spend the winter." Then told them he wanted to stay in Mexico City until Pentecost, "for a wide door for effective work has opened to me, and there are many adversaries."

Pablo shared that if Timoteo comes, they should take care of him, "for he is doing the work of the Lord just as I am." Then he talked a bit about Francisco, who questioned if a visit to Monterrey was a part of God's will for him, but Pablo assured them that he would come when he had an opportunity. His heart was strangely warmed, then he wrote, "Keep alert, stand firm in your faith, be courageous, be strong. Let all that you do be done in love." He prayed that this encouraging admonition would help them in the challenge of the divine practice of equality.

He urged them to serve the saints who ministered among them, and "everyone who works and toils among them." He sent warm greetings to them from Carlos and Elena's house church, who told them to greet one another with signs of holy friendship and affection. Not wanting to end too sappy, he wrote "Let anyone be accursed who has no love for the Lord." Then concluded with "The grace of our Lord Jim Caldwell be with you. My love be with all of you in the name of Jim, who taught us how to live and die with dignity."

Pablo folded the letter, prayed over it, and put it in an envelope. The trip to Monterrey was just over 550 miles away, and happily, the train went straight there. Still, it was a lot to ask of anyone to deliver his letter, but he felt a need to remain in Mexico City. He then found Francisco and made his request. Francisco had heard of the lengthy trips others made for Pablo, so he was more than happy to make the relatively easy journey.

They said their goodbyes, and Francisco departed.

_____

It was a nice sunny day in Mexico City, and things were going well at each of the several Caldwellian Churches that were now up and running in the City. Then another telegram arrived. He opened it up and immediately felt sick, because it was again from the Monterreyans. His sickness wasn't so much physical, as emotional, and spiritual. "What's wrong with these Monterreyans?" he wondered. "Why do they struggle so? Why can't they be more like my friends here in Mexico City?" He was beyond frustrated that he was needing to write a third letter to them. He always suspected they disliked the first letter, and just threw it away. His second letter ended up being longer than any he had written before, and now this telegram. He wanted to strangle them. Well, not literally, but not too bad of an idea either. They were always looking for an easy way to do things.

He looked over the telegram and understood the struggles behind the questions. One particular individual was a real pain in Pablo's backside during his last visit, yet he knew he was going to have to continue showing them an even better way. "How," he thought, "do I share that fine balance of building up the right while tear down the wrong." There was plenty to think about as he looked over the telegram, and plenty to be frustrated about. He was beyond exasperated that they didn't want to be in mission to others. "Why do they only think about themselves? Don't they understand that selfishness is the exact opposite of the Caldwellian lifestyle?" To get his mind straightened out, he talked at length with Jasper and Rose.

When he was ready to write, a strange thing happened to Pablo. He discovered how difficult it is to keep ego at bay. He well knew that he was impatient, but when he read that the Monterreyans were questioning his character, he took it personally. "Not honorable? How dare they?" He had just complained to himself about their selfishness, while at the very next second he was thinking of himself. "This Caldwellian lifestyle just might take a lifetime to master!" He wished Jim Caldwell had never made "deny yourself" such an important part of following him. Anyway, here's how the telegram actually read.

MUY SENOR MIO,

WHAT IS MINISTRY?
DO WE HAVE TO GIVE MONEY TO PHOENIX?
WE'RE NOT SURE YOU'RE HONORABLE.

SALUDOS CORDIALES,
THE CALDWELLIAN CHURCH OF MONTERREY

Pablo wasn't feeling too generous, but he went ahead and started with "Grace to you and peace." He knew if he began his letter with his true feelings, the letter would never get read. Then he went into different ways of expressing a need to console one another, because their mutual sufferings were for the gospel. He then defended himself for not returning to Monterrey, writing, "But I call on God as witness against me: it was to spare you that I did not come again to Monterrey." He figured they would never believe that, so he went on to say, "I made up my mind not to make you another painful visit." At least that was honest, but then he defended himself by referring to the problem causer. "But if anyone has caused pain, he has caused it not to me, but to some extent—not to exaggerate it—to all of you." He went on to recommend the congregation forgive the trouble maker, offer him consolation, and simply love him.

Getting all of that out of the way, Pablo turned to the congregation's first question about ministry. He wrote that it is "God who has made us competent to be ministers of a new covenant." He then talked about the ministry that Abund brought in with the Law, and compared it to the ministry that Jim Caldwell brought in with the Spirit. He wrote down that, "Since it is by God's mercy that we are engaged in this ministry, we do not lose heart." He reminded them that the job of ministry is not to proclaim ourselves, but to proclaim Jim Caldwell, and ourselves as servants of Jim. That actually helped to settle him down from the anger he felt.

That must have helped, because Pablo felt the movement of the Spirit within and wrote, "But we have this treasure in clay jars, so that it may be made clear that this extraordinary power belongs to God and does not come from us." He hoped they would understand that ministry is not about them. The treasure is God within, while we are the breakable earthen pottery. He could relate so much to this image of brokenness, and after his road to Tucson experience, he understood that it truly is not about the clay jar, it's about the treasure within. If he focused on the clay jar, he would still be angry about the unhealed 'thorn' in his flesh. Pablo then quoted a Psalm, and said, "Because we know that the one who raised Jim will raise us also, and will bring us with you into his presence." Then he encouraged them to not lose heart, because "this slight momentary affliction is preparing us for an eternal weight of glory."

Pablo loved that. He wondered, "Did I really just write that?" He reveled for awhile in the thought of eternal glory, and then shook his head as he thought the weight for him would be due to giving glory to God rather than himself. He mumbled that, "The old life sure is hard to turn away from." Then he felt a need to teach. He exhorted them to, "Walk by faith, not by sight." It was a fundamental truth, so he amplified it with, "So if anyone is in Jim, there is a new creation: everything old has passed away; see, everything has become new!" It seemed self-serving to him at first because he wanted them to reconcile with him, but he knew it would be an example of the way to practice ministry. Pablo put it this way: "All this is from God, who reconciled us to himself through Jim Caldwell, and has given us the ministry of reconciliation."

To do ministry is a community event, so he further encouraged them to work with him, and offered a quote from the prophet Isaiah. In case they didn't get it, he wrote, "See, now is the acceptable time; see, now is the day of salvation!" If they could only understand that forgiving him when they were angry with him, was a great sign of the power of reconciliation. He concluded this line of thinking by writing, "I have spoken frankly to you Monterreyans; my heart is wide open to you. There is no restriction in my affection for you, but I fear there is restriction in your affection for me. You remind me of the Rio Santa Catarina that runs through your splendid city. While it is beautiful, it only runs one way. Don't act as immature Caldwellians, but let us open wide our hearts and prove that we are doing ministry."

Feeling exhausted, Pablo took another break before looking back at the telegram. He strolled down to the zocalo and did some people watching. It wasn't long until a poor beggar went up to a street vendor and asked for some free food. Pablo reached into his pocket to perform a charitable act, when he saw the vendor give the man the food. This was so inspiring that he thanked God and ran back to his room. He grabbed pen and paper and quickly glanced at the telegram which read, "Do we have to give money to Phoenix?"

Pablo chuckled and decided to teach them a lesson, to motivate them toward being true believers. He hoped it would ultimately stir them up to compete in generosity. He told them about the wonderful response in Nogales and Guadalajara, even during some difficult times they were having. He said, "They voluntarily gave according to their means, and even beyond their means." He let them know that those two congregations in particular begged for "the privilege of sharing in this ministry to the saints." He then wrote, "Now as you excel in everything—in faith, in speech, in knowledge, in utmost eagerness, and in your love for me—so I want you to excel also in this generous undertaking."

Pablo felt a need for a scripture verse again, to support his teaching on generosity. He finally settled on a verse from Exodus about the wilderness wanderings. He then tantalized them with this: "I am sending the brother who is famous among all the churches for his proclaiming the good news; and not only that, but he has also been appointed by the churches to travel with me while I am administering this generous undertaking for the glory of the Lord himself and to show our goodwill." Pablo decided to sum up his response to the question about the need to help others. He wrote that the point is this: "the one who sows sparingly will also reap sparingly, and the one who sows bountifully will also reap bountifully." He then added a final zinger with, "for God loves a cheerful giver."

That seemed to be enough about generosity, so Pablo looked back at the final comment on the telegram. They don't think I'm honorable? He warned that he had a divine power to destroy arguments, and that he was "ready to punish every disobedience." He reminded them that some of the parishioners said, "His letters are weighty and strong, but his bodily presence is weak, and his speech contemptible." That really angered Pablo, especially when they shared that they were impressed by other missionaries. He took a deep breath and chose to just say that they do not show good sense. His final admonition was, "Let the one who boasts, boast in the Lord. For it is not those who commend themselves that are approved, but those whom the Lord commends."

Pablo then suggested that since they thought he was foolish, why did they put up with him? He then accused his competitors of proclaiming another Jim, another spirit, and another gospel. Then he stated that "I may be untrained in speech, but not in knowledge." And he flatly told the Monterreyans that his competitors were not his equal, and called them false prophets and deceitful workers. He taunted them for calling himself a fool, because if they were so wise, why did they let the other missionaries take advantage of them? Then he got real with, "I am talking like a madman—I am a better one: with far greater labors, far more imprisonments, with countless floggings, and often near death. The God and Father of the Jim Caldwell knows that I do not lie."

He then said that if he had anything to boast about, it was that he "was caught up to the third heaven—whether in the body or out of the body I do not know; God knows." He went on to write, "I heard things that are not to be told, that no mortal is permitted to repeat." He thought for a moment that he himself is a mortal, so maybe he could repeat some of it. But, of course not, so he continued, "Therefore, to keep me from being too elated, a thorn was given me long ago in the flesh, a messenger of Satan to torment me, to keep me from being too elated." That thorn turned out in part to be his pride, and his anger about not getting it healed. Pablo didn't want the thorn, but God said to him, "My grace is sufficient for you, for power is made perfect in weakness."

This made sense in Pablo's world. If he could only deal with his thorn of pride, he could turn himself over to depend on the grace of God. He looked back at what he just wrote, that "power is made perfect in weakness," then he grinned from ear to ear. For the first time he truly understood that when he lets go of his pride, it doesn't make him weak. It makes way for God to be powerful. The same goes for his lack of healing. It wasn't supposed to happen. He continued writing, "Therefore I am content with weaknesses, insults, hardships, persecutions, and calamities for the sake of Jim Caldwell; for whenever I am weak, then I am strong."

Pablo wondered what else he could say. After thinking for a bit, he decided they needed another visit, so he wrote, "Here I am, ready to come to you this third time." He cringed for a moment while thinking about the painful challenge of doing ministry there. It was the last thing he wanted to do, but it was something God was calling him to do. So he tried to soften them a bit with, "If I love you more, am I to be loved less? Everything I do is for the sake of building you up. I fear that when I come again, my God may humble me before you, and that I may have to mourn over many who previously sinned and have not repented of the impurity, sexual immorality, and recklessness that they have practiced." He looked at what he just wrote and thought that it sure was difficult to focus on building them up.

He continued with, "This is the third time I am coming to you." Too repetitive? No, he decided, because it shows that this is on them not him. He reminded them that any "charge must be sustained by the evidence of two or three witnesses." He then mentioned, "I will not be lenient," and exhorted them to examine themselves to see if they are living in the faith. He explained that "we cannot do anything against the truth, but only for the truth." He then said, "So I write these things while I am away from you, so that when I come, I may not have to be severe in using the authority that the Lord has given me for building up and not for tearing down." He frowned for a moment, realizing most of this letter was tearing down, but so be it.

Pablo closed out the letter, saying, "Finally, brothers and sisters, farewell. Put things in order, listen to my appeal, agree with one another, live in peace; and the God of love and peace will be with you." He smiled as he agreed with that final statement, then gave them a threefold blessing. "The grace of Jim Caldwell, the love of God, and the communion of the Holy Spirit be with all of you." He once again summoned Francisco to deliver his letter to Monterrey, and Francisco was more than happy to oblige.

ACT IV
THE PRISON LIFE

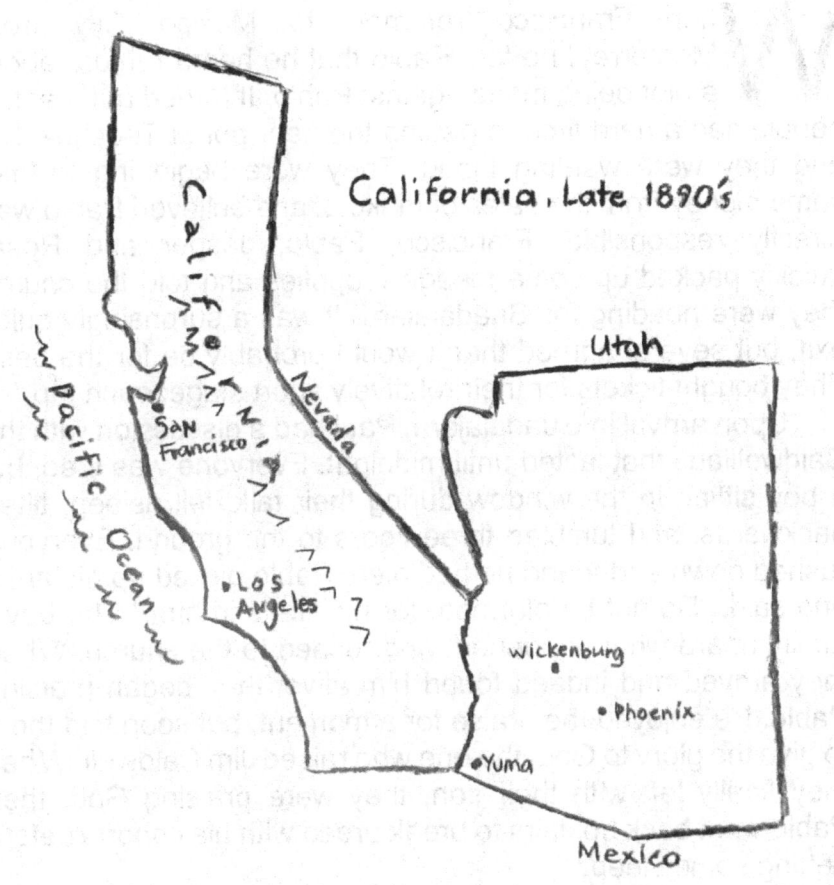

California, Late 1890's

SCENE ONE
It's a Long Way Home

When Francisco returned to Mexico City from Monterrey, he told Pablo that he heard rumors about a plot being made against Pablo. It turned out that the people had a hard time forgetting the near riot at Teotihuacan, and they were wanting blood. They were beginning to lose some money from the sales of trinkets, and believed Pablo was directly responsible. Francisco, Pablo, Jasper and Rose, quickly packed up some meager supplies and told the church they were heading for Guadalajara. It was a surprisingly quick exit, but several agreed that it would probably be for the best. They bought tickets for their relatively short stagecoach trip.

Upon arrival in Guadalajara, Paul had a discussion with the Caldwellians that lasted until midnight. Everyone was tired, but a boy sitting in the window during their talk, fell asleep, tilted backwards, and tumbled three floors to the ground. Everyone rushed down and found he had died. Pablo picked up his arms and said, "Do not be alarmed, for his life is in him." The boy's family heard what happened, and rushed to the church. When they arrived and indeed found him alive, they began praising Pablo. He enjoyed the praise for a moment, but soon told them to give the glory to God, the one who raised Jim Caldwell. When they finally left with their son, they were praising God, then Pablo went back upstairs to break bread with his cohorts before getting some sleep.

A few days later, Pablo got a telegram from the Caldwellians back in Mexico City. They hated that he left so unexpectedly, so they asked him to sum up his teachings. He sent word back to them that the value of the diamond is about having faith in the risen Lord. Then he wrote, "And now, as a captive to the Spirit, I am on my way to Phoenix, not knowing what will happen to me there, except that the Holy Spirit testifies to me in every city that imprisonment and persecutions are waiting for me." He told them that they would never see his face again, but they should keep watch over themselves and the whole flock. He then wrote, "And now I commend you to God and to the message of his grace, a message that is able to build you up." He also reminded them that Jim himself said, "It is more blessed to give than to receive," so always be in mission and balance it with evangelism.

Pablo and Francisco collected an offering from Guadalajara for the mother church in Phoenix, then traveled on to León. Pablo was delighted to find a church had been established by the few converts he had there, and decided not to request an offering, because they were a fledgling group and it would be too easy to lose focus. Next they went to San Luis Potosí and were overjoyed to find a large, successful Caldwellian congregation. He requested and received a nice offering, then didn't bother to stop in Tampico. He had no luck establishing a Caldwellian community in that city of idols.

He instead went on to Monterrey. He said he would return, and finally the city was within sight. He stopped and prayed, "Lord, I don't want to go," and his prayer was met with a resounding silence. He kind of felt sick inside going back to this place that treated him so poorly. As expected, they greeted him with a lack of enthusiasm because, as far as they were concerned, he mainly wanted the collection they had taken for the mother church in Phoenix. Right on cue, Pablo asked if they had done as requested, and they begrudgingly handed over the small amount. Pablo kept a straight face when he saw the offering, but wanted to throw it back, because it strangely felt like blood money. Instead, he accepted it, and without further comment, the foursome made their departure. Still within in hearing distance, someone yelled, "You shouldn't have a woman in your group." Pablo was glad to be done with that challenging group, and they chose not to respond.

They left Monterrey by train to travel to Chihuahua. When they arrived, Pablo was quite surprised that they were happy to see him. He had been quite harsh about the disingenuous missionaries, but they had moved on from that concern. They had settled into a nice rhythm of evangelism and mission, and were growing. Pablo explained that he was heading for the mother church in Phoenix, and was asking churches in each of the cities he visited to collect an offering. They not only did that, but asked him to stay until Sunday to preach. He was honored, the service went well, the offering was exceptional, and Pablo shared a concern that he was starting to have too much money for comfort. They talked about it for a while, and chose a bodyguard to accompany them to Phoenix. His name was Chuy, and he was a big, muscular man, just right for the job.

All five crossed the border at El Paso, and Pablo was happy to be back in the United States. They were surprised to see Caldwellians there, and accepted their hospitality by staying the night. The next day they left for Tucson, where they stayed at the house of Philip the evangelist. He had four unmarried daughters who had the gift of prophecy. One day during their stay, a prophet came and took Pablo's belt. He bound Pablo's feet and hands with it, and said, "Thus says the Holy Spirit, 'This is the way the marshal in Phoenix will bind Pablo and hand him over to the courts.'" Immediately, his cohorts suggested not going to Phoenix, but Pablo was, how shall we say it, bound and determined? Since he couldn't be persuaded, they finally said, "The Lord's will be done." Secretly, Pablo was glad to have Chuy along, in case things got ugly.

As they prepared to leave, a man from Nogales arrived. He was so glad he caught them, because they had only heard a rumor that Pablo was in Tucson. It turned out that the Caldwellian Church of Nogales decided to quickly gather an offering and send it up to Tucson. Pablo was so touched, he sat down and quickly penned a letter of thanks to the first friends he had made in Mexico. Bidding him a safe journey back to Nogales, the host said goodbye to Pablo's group, and they were on their way.

When they arrived in Phoenix, the brothers and sisters in the Lord welcomed them warmly. They were more than happy to put them up, and were interested in hearing some stories about Pablo's Mexican journey, but he was exhausted. Pablo gave his apologies and they all headed off for room for the night. The next day everyone went to the mother church to visit the leaders, and all the elders were present. After greeting them, Pablo related the things God had done among the Mexican people through his ministry. They were mesmerized as he related the many years worth of stories.

As they celebrated this good news, someone asked about the collection for them from the churches in Mexico. Pablo smiled and turned to his bodyguard Chuy, who didn't seem to be present. In a panic, they checked everywhere, until someone mentioned they saw a man with a large satchel riding east out of town. Francisco wanted to chase him, but the locals said he was probably heading for the Superstition Mountains. Their interests quickly waned, because far more money had been lost in the Superstitions than ever got found. In fact, the Legend of the Lost Dutchman still brings shivers to listeners, about people meeting foul play and even death in those mysterious mountains.

Word got around quickly about Pablo losing the money. It was badly needed by the mother church in Phoenix, because a recent drought had the people living in hard times. Some of the Caldwellians were so enraged that they seized Pablo and dragged him into the streets. It seems to be a bad plan to come between people and their money. The Caldwellians were threatening to kill Pablo, when Pedro made an appearance. He was no longer in charge, but seemed to be enjoying the troubles Pedro was having. One would think that two pillars of the Caldwellian movement could overcome their differences, but all Pedro could think about was that Pablo was getting his comeuppance. After all, he had dragged Caldwellians to jail, so maybe this was his due reward.

Meanwhile, the new marshal, after Marshal Garfias' untimely death, heard the uproar. Immediately he brought some deputies with him and they stopped the yelling. They arrested Pablo and ordered him to be bound around his feet and hands with his own belt, just as the prophet in Tucson had said. The marshal then inquired what the problem was, and some in the crowd shouted one thing, and some another. The mob started getting unruly again, so the marshal fired a shot in the air to get their attention. The same shouting ensued, and as he could not learn the facts because of the uproar, the marshal ordered Pablo to be brought into the barracks. The violence of the mob was so great that he had to be carried by the deputies. The crowd that followed kept shouting, 'Away with him!'" Seems money was quite important to more than just the Caldwellians.

Just as Pablo was about to be brought into the barracks, he asked if he could address the crowd. He noticed there was a great variety of people: Catholics, Methodists, nonbelievers, townsfolk, and some Caldwellians. The marshal turned down his request, but Pablo suggested the crowd would calm down. The marshal said, "Okay, we'll give it a try, as long as it works." Pablo went to the steps, bound, and accompanied by deputies. He nodded his head to the people for silence, and there was a great hush, so the marshal motioned for him to proceed.

He said, "I am a Mexican American."

Immediately someone in the crowd yelled, "Go back where you came from!"

Pablo went on to explain that he was "born in San Jose, California, and moved to Jerome before coming here to Phoenix. My Catholic upbringing was at the Basilica of St. Joseph where I learned much about the Scriptures. I was injured as a youth, which I call the 'thorn in my flesh,' and prayed for healing, which still has not come."

"And no divine help is coming your way today, either!" yelled an angry man.

"I persecuted the new movement of Caldwellians," continued Pablo, "for being the bearers of fake news. They claimed to do healings and said strange things about life and death. They even offered baptism as a way to die to the old life and take on the new life they were offering. I was given permission from Marshal Garfias to persecute Caldwellians in Tucson, and I went there to bring them back to Phoenix for punishment. While I was on my way and approaching Tucson, about noon a great light from heaven suddenly shone about me."

Someone yelled, "Yeah, it's called the sun!"

Most didn't laugh because they wanted to hear the story, so Pablo continued. "I fell to the ground and heard a voice saying to me, 'Pablo, Pablo, why are you persecuting me?' I answered, 'Who are you, Lord?' Then he said to me, 'I am Jim Caldwell of Prescott whom you are persecuting.' Now those who were with me saw the light but did not hear the voice of the one who was speaking to me." The crowd was quiet now and listening. "I asked, 'What am I to do, Lord?' The Lord said to me, 'Get up and go to Tucson; there you will be told everything that has been assigned to you to do.' Since I could not see because of the brightness of that light, those who were with me led me to Tucson.

"A certain Jesse, who was a devout man according to the law and well-spoken of by all the Catholics living there, came to me; and standing beside me, he said, 'Brother Pablo, regain your sight!' In that very hour I regained my sight and saw him. Then he said, 'The God of our ancestors has chosen you to know his will, to see the Righteous One and to hear his own voice; for you will be his witness to all the world of what you have seen and heard. And now why do you delay? Get up, be baptized, and have your sins washed away, calling on his name.'"

"What's this got to do with losing our money?" asked a member of the Caldwellians.

Pablo just continued, "After I had returned to Phoenix and while I was praying in the church, I fell into a trance and saw Jim saying to me, 'Hurry and get out of Phoenix quickly, because they will not accept your testimony about me.' And I said, 'Lord, they themselves know that in every church I imprisoned and beat those who believed in you. And while the blood of your first witness Jack was shed, I myself was standing by, approving and keeping the coats of those who killed him.' Then he said to me, 'Go for I will send you far away to Utah, Colorado, New Mexico, and all over Mexico itself.'"

Up to this point, most of the people in the crowd listened to him, but then they shouted, "Away with this guy. He's just trying to save his own skin!"

The deputies brought him into the barracks and had him flogged, to find out why there was such an outcry against him. Discovering that this was a religious problem about money, they took him to the Catholics and had him stand before them. Pablo said, "Brothers, up to this day I have lived my life with a clear conscience before God." The Catholic priest in charge ordered those standing near him to strike him on the mouth. At this, Pablo said to him, "God will strike you, you dying saguaro cactus!"

Those standing nearby said, "Do you dare to insult God's priest?"

Pablo focused them, saying, "I am on trial for stealing money that I did not steal!"

Then a great clamor arose and some stood up and said, "We find nothing wrong with this man. Besides, the problem is with his fellow Caldwellians."

When the troubles became violent, the deputies took Pablo by force and brought him back to the barracks. That night the Lord stood near him and said, "Keep up your courage! For just as you have testified for me in Phoenix, so you must bear witness also in San Francisco."

In the morning, the Catholics and many others joined in a conspiracy and bound themselves by an oath, "neither to eat nor drink until they had killed Pablo." They went to the marshal and said, "We have strictly bound ourselves by an oath to eat nothing until we have killed Pablo. Now then, you must bring him to our bishop on the pretext that you want to make a more thorough examination of his case. And we are ready to do away with him before he arrives."

Now a Caldwellian heard about the ambush; so he went to the barracks and told Pablo. After that, he went to the marshal and also told him about the ambush. He said, "Do not be persuaded by them, for more than forty of their men are lying in ambush for him." The marshal summoned two of his deputies and said, "Get ready to leave by nine o'clock tonight for Wickenburg with forty men." He also told them to have a horse for Pablo to ride and take him safely to the governor. Then he wrote a letter to be handed to the governor that said:

"Greetings, Governor Irwin,

This man was seized by the Catholics and others and was about to be killed by them, but then I came with some deputies and rescued him. Since I wanted to know the charge for which they accused him, I had him brought to their bishop. I found that he was accused concerning questions of money for church purposes, but was charged with nothing deserving death or imprisonment. When I was informed that there would be a plot against the man, I sent him to you at once."

With appreciation for your help,
Marshal Wilcox

So Pablo was taken to the governor under the cover of night. When they came to Wickenburg and delivered the letter to the governor, they presented Pablo also before him. On reading the letter, he said, "I will give you a hearing when your accusers arrive. Then he ordered that he be kept under guard. Five days later the Catholic bishop arrived, along with a representative of the Caldwellians. When Pablo had been summoned, an attorney for the Catholics began to speak. "Governor, we appreciate all you have done to help our Arizona Territory, but to detain you no further, I beg you to hear us briefly. We have, in fact, found this man a pestilent fellow, an agitator among all the Catholics throughout America and Mexico, and a ringleader of the sect of Caldwellians. By examining him yourself you will be able to learn from him concerning everything of which we accuse him."

The governor said, "And what about the representative of the Caldwellians? Come and share what you accuse this man of doing." Nothing happened at first, so the governor was obviously getting frustrated, then before he could complain the crowd separated. Both Pablo and the governor were squinting to try to see who was coming forward. As he approached, Pablo's jaw dropped. Of all the people it could be, it turned out to be none other than Pedro. Pablo's blood coursed red hot through his body, and all he wanted to do was break his chains and wrapt them around Pedro's neck. The two men stared at one another for a long time, while the crowd experienced an awkward silence.

The governor finally said, "I don't have all day, speak now or I'll have you jailed, too."

"Your honor," Pedro said in a rather halting voice, "all I can say is that the man standing next to you was charged by the Caldwellians to collect an offering from the churches in Mexico, to help us in Phoenix. He accomplished this task, which we greatly appreciated, but when he arrived, he didn't turn over the money."

Then the governor motioned for Pablo to speak, and he said, "I cheerfully make my defense, first to the Catholics. They did not find me disputing with anyone in their church, nor stirring up a crowd. Neither can they prove to you the charge that they now bring against me. As far as the second charge, according to the Caldwellians, I stole the money collected for the Caldwellian church of Phoenix. It is true that the money made it across the border with my bodyguard Chuy, but it is not true that I stole it. We have reason to believe Chuy returned with the money to Mexico."

"Who do you mean," questioned the governor, "when you say we?" At that point, Francisco, Jasper, and Rose were in the crowd and raised their hands, so the governor motioned for Pablo to continue.

"I do my best always to have a clear conscience toward God and all people." But the governor, who was rather well informed about the Caldwellians, decided to adjourn the hearing by saying, "I will decide your case in the next few days," then ordered Pablo to be kept in custody.

Several days later, Governor Irwin brought his Catholic wife to hear Pablo speak concerning faith in Jim Caldwell. And as he discussed justice, self-control, and the coming judgment, the governor became frightened and said, "You need to leave. I will send for you again later." At the same time the governor hoped that the money collected by Pablo would show up and prove Pablo's innocence. For that reason, the governor sent for him on numerous occasions and conversed with him. After two years had passed, Governor Irwin resigned his position and President Benjamin Harrison appointed Oakes Murphy as the successor.

Three days after Governor Murphy arrived in the territory, he went from Wickenburg to Phoenix where the bishop gave him a report against Pablo. Then the bishop requested, as a favor to himself, to have Pablo transferred to Phoenix. The governor replied that Pablo would remain in Wickenburg, but they could travel back there with him, and "if there is anything wrong about the man, let him be accused." When they returned, the governor took his seat and ordered Pablo to be brought out.

Several Catholics made the trip to Wickenburg, and brought serious charges of theft against him, which they could not prove. Pablo simply denied all charges, but the new governor wanted to do the Catholics a favor. He asked Pablo, "Do you wish to go to Phoenix and be tried there by me on these charges?" Pablo said, "I have done no wrong to the Catholics, as you very well know, so I request to see President Harrison." The new governor replied, "You want to appeal to the President?" then with a laugh he said, "To the President you will go."

President Harrison enjoyed promoting the Transcontinental Railroad, by taking occasional trips across the country to San Francisco. Governor Murphy decided to send Pablo to San Francisco in hopes of gaining audience with the President at some point. It was at the train station that the three faithful companions from his Mexico trip said their goodbyes. Francisco was going back to Mexico, while Jasper planned to return to Flagstaff. Rose decided to reclaim her ministry in Tucson, but all four had tears in their eyes as the train embarked for Los Angeles.

Pablo was accompanied by a deputy, who thoughtfully told Pablo that if he hadn't appealed to the President, he probably would have been set free, but at least he was deemed to not be a risk. As the train lumbered down the newly laid tracks, Pablo had a nice view looking south. As he stared out at the majestic South Mountain, he couldn't help but remember the risen Lord saying, "You will be my witness in Phoenix, and the Arizona Territory, and to the ends of the earth." He thought that San Francisco must surely be what Jim Caldwell meant by the end of the earth. Pablo started falling asleep as he noticed the Gila Bend Mountains on his right. It helped that it was hot out in the desert, making him want to sleep, as the train continued clacking down the track in a rhythmic pattern. Even the deputy was comfortable that Pablo was no danger, so he too fell asleep. This lonely stretch of train track slowly brought them to across the punishing desert to Yuma, where they stopped at the depot.

Founded in 1873, Yuma quickly became known as a stopover place for immigrants heading for the California gold fields. A rough collection of outcasts quickly caused the crime rate to surge, and in 1875 the town built the Yuma Territorial Prison. As Pablo and the deputy got off to stretch for a bit, the deputy pointed at the prison and said, "Pablo, you sure you want to live out the rest of your life in a place like that?" Pablo was sure about his innocence, so he brushed off the comment. Meanwhile, the engineer got word that a bad dust storm was raging across the desert between Yuma and Los Angeles.

Pablo said to the engineer, "I can see that the trip will be dangerous and with heavy loss, to the train and also our lives."

But the engineer paid no attention to Pablo saying, "We made it here from Phoenix and we'll make it to Los Angeles."

"All aboard!" the conductor barked a few minutes later.

A moderate south wind began to blow, but the engineer still

believed they could achieve their purpose. As they made their way northwest of Yuma, the winds slowly became more violent and the engineer asked for assistance from the conductor.

"A dust storm is kicking up," announced the engineer, "and I can barely see. Are we getting close to Lake Cahuilla?"

"Sorry sir," replied the conductor. "I lost sense of where we were quite a while ago."

The winds were so strong that the desert sand felt like sandpaper scraping across the face. The engineer reluctantly slowed down, then a powerful thud was heard and the train slowed to a stop.

"What happened?" screamed someone on board, while others fell out of their seats.

"We're gonna' die out in this desert!" yelled another.

As many passengers were getting up to see what was going on, the conductor walked hurriedly through the cars and cautioned everyone to stay in place. He said, "You might not find your way back on board due to the dust storm, so sit down!" By the time he got up to the locomotive, the engineer had struggled to the front and found the problem. As the winds howled, they had a hard time hearing one another, but soon enough the engineer said, "We ran into a herd of cattle standing on the tracks."

They were stranded there for several anxious days. The nights were even worse as the coyotes gathered to devour an evening's dinner of freshly killed beef. Each day people helped as they could to remove the dead carcasses from the tracks, and even Pablo did his fair share of work. The people had been without food for a long time when Pablo said to the engineer, "You should have listened to me, but I urge you now to keep up your courage, for there will be no loss of life among us."

"How do you figure?" he asked.

Pablo responded, "Last night an angel stood by me and said, 'Do not be afraid, Pablo. You must stand before the President, and God has granted safety to all those who are traveling with you.' So keep up your courage, for I have faith in God that it will be exactly as I have been told." The engineer shook his head back and forth and went back to work.

Just before daybreak, Pablo spoke to his fellow passengers, urging all of them to take some food, saying "It's been a long time that we have been without food, having eaten nothing. I urge you to take some food from the dining car. It will help you survive." After he had said this, he took bread; and giving thanks to God in the presence of all, he broke it and began to eat. Then all of them were encouraged and took food for themselves.

Once they were finally ready to travel again, the conductor told everyone to take their seats. The train lurched forward and crossed the bloody tracks, and they were at last on their way. When the Southern Pacific train pulled into the Los Angeles station, the passengers were greeted with unusual kindness. Since it had begun to rain and was cold, the station workers kindled a fire and welcomed everyone. Pablo had gathered a bundle of brushwood and was putting it on the fire, when a Mojave rattler bit him. When the people saw what happened, they were perplexed at his calmness. They were expecting him to swell up or drop dead, but after they had waited a long time and saw that nothing unusual happened to him, they changed their minds. And the deputy even felt stronger about the goodness and innocence of Pablo.

The final leg of the journey went smooth, and the train chugged into the San Francisco depot. Pablo was then told that he would be allowed to live by himself, with the deputy who was guarding him. Three days later he called together the local leaders of the Catholics and said, "Though I was arrested in Phoenix and handed over to the authorities here in San Francisco, they wanted to release me because there was no reason for the death penalty in my case." But when the Catholics objected, because they complained that Pablo stole money and spread fake news about the resurrection of Jim Caldwell, he was compelled to appeal to the President. The authorities replied, "We have received no letters from Phoenix about you, and no one here has said anything evil about you. But we would like to hear from you what you think, for with regard to the Caldwellians we know that everywhere it is spoken against."

After they had a set day to meet with him, they came to him at his lodging in great numbers. From morning to evening, Pablo explained the matter to them, testifying to the kingdom of God and trying to convince them about Jim Caldwell. Some were convinced by what he said, while others refused to believe. He lived there two whole years, supported by offerings from local Caldwellians. He welcomed all who came to him, proclaiming the kingdom of God and teaching about the Jim Caldwell with all boldness and without hindrance. By the way, President Harrison never made it to San Francisco.

SCENE TWO
San Francisco

Pablo's house arrest was in a meager home in view of the Emporium, which not only housed a department store but the Supreme Court. The deputy who was in charge of Pablo since Phoenix, remained loyal to his task and even became a believer. One day, Pablo got a telegram from a local Caldwellian congregation. They had questions, and having heard that Pablo and Pedro were at odds, they didn't bother to mention it was Pedro who was their founder. Here are their questions:

DEAR PABLO,

HOW DO GRACE AND SALVATION GO
   TOGETHER?
HOW DO FAITH AND RIGHTEOUSNESS GO
   TOGETHER?
PLEASE TALK ABOUT JUSTIFICATION.
HOW CAN JEWS BE SAVED?
WHAT IS THE NEW LIFE IN JIM?

AFFECTIONATELY,
THE CALDWELLIAN CHURCH OF SAN FRANCISCO

Pablo didn't have to think very long before starting his response. He'd been thinking about these issues for a long time now, and he was feeling pretty good about the clarity he had come to since beginning his ministry. So, here's how he wrote his opening salutation.

"Pablo, a servant of Jim Caldwell, called to be an apostle, set apart for the gospel of God, which he promised beforehand through his prophets in the Holy Scriptures, the gospel concerning Jim Caldwell, who was descended from an Aztec King according to the flesh, and was declared to be the Son of God by resurrection from the dead." Pablo stopped for a moment, and hoped those last few words would sink in.

He had heard way too much about Jim Caldwell being God on earth. Jim was not. He was born a human and died a human. It was the power of the resurrection that made him the Son of God. Getting that off his chest, he continued with his salutation. "It was Jim Caldwell, through whom we have received grace and apostleship to bring about the obedience of faith among all the unbelievers for the sake of his name, including yourselves who are called to belong to Jim Caldwell.

"To all God's beloved in San Francisco, who are called to be saints:

"Grace to you and peace from God our Father and Jim Caldwell."

Pablo was delighted with his salutation, and he was now ready to hit them hot and heavy, like a tortilla fresh from the fire, with his thoughts about God. "For I am not ashamed of the gospel; it is the power of God for salvation to everyone who has faith, to the Jew first and also to the unbelievers. For in it the righteousness of God is revealed through faith for faith; as it is written, 'The one who is righteous will live by faith.'" Again Pablo smiled. He was tired of hearing people speak poorly of the Jews. Don't people understand that everything started with God choosing the Jews out of all the races on earth? How could anyone in their right mind speak against them? They are automatically included. It is the rest of us who seek inclusion.

Pablo paused and thought that this house arrest business was doing just fine for him. He then looked at the telegram and was more than ready to tackle these great questions. First was, "How do grace and salvation go together?" His Road to Tucson experience powerfully told him that God doesn't impart salvation by way of what we do, but what God does. Pablo used the Jews as an example: "Now we know that whatever the law says, it speaks to those who are under the law, so that every mouth may be silenced, and the whole world may be held accountable to God. For 'no human being will be justified in his sight' by deeds prescribed by the law, for through the law comes the knowledge of sin." He then thought that was a bit too heavy. He wasn't going to change it, but maybe answering the next question would help to make it easier to understand.

"How do faith and righteousness go together?" Pablo wanted the people from the Caldwellian Church of San Francisco to know that righteousness comes through faith, so here is what he said: "But now, apart from law, the righteousness of God has been disclosed, and is attested by the law and the prophets, the righteousness of God through faith in Jim Caldwell for all who believe. For there is no distinction, since all have sinned and fall short of the glory of God." Pablo still feared he was being too heavy with his explanations, so he stopped and prayed that God would give him a practical answer about human faith and divine righteousness. Pablo muttered a thanks to the Lord when he got what he was looking for in the person of Aapo.

He wrote, "If Aapo was justified by works, he has something to boast about, but not before God. For what does the scripture say? 'Aapo believed God, and it was reckoned to him as righteousness.'" How could Aapo be good before the law was even given? Pablo hoped and prayed that people would catch this all important point, then continued with, "Therefore his faith 'was reckoned to him as righteousness.' Now the words, 'it was reckoned to him,' were written not for his sake alone, but for ours also. It will be reckoned to us who believe in him who raised Jim Caldwell from the dead, who was handed over to death for our sins and was raised for our justification." That played well into the next item on the telegram, "Talk about justification."

This was important. Pablo wanted his readers to catch the fact that through the death and resurrection of Jim Caldwell, they are justified. All they need to do is take that blind leap of faith, just as he did. So he wrote, "Since we are justified by faith," Pablo desperately hoped they would get it that the action was completed, "we have peace with God." In other words, we are made right with God, so have confidence. Does that make everything good? He continued, "And not only that, but we also boast in our sufferings, knowing that suffering produces endurance, and endurance produces character, and character produces hope, and hope does not disappoint us, because God's love has been poured into our hearts through the Holy Spirit that has been given to us."

Pablo knew justification was a huge concept, so he wrote, "But God proves his love for us in that while we still were sinners Jim died for us." He then suggested that Adam was a type of Jim: "Death exercised dominion from Adam to Abund, even over those whose sins were not like the transgression of Adam, who is a type of the one who was to come." He explained that the free gift "is not like the trespass. For if the many died through the one man's trespass, much more surely have the grace of God and the free gift in the grace of the one man, Jim Caldwell, abounded for the many."

Pablo wasn't happy with the smoothness of his argument, so he said, "Therefore just as one man's trespass led to condemnation for all, so one man's act of righteousness leads to justification and life for all." He stopped and prayed that the readers would understand this point. In his mind, it was abundantly obvious that the one man's trespass was Adam that leads to condemnation. And if Jim was anything like Adam, then Jim's act of righteousness likewise leads to justification. They are polar opposites. He then wondered which path people would prefer to take if they only understood.

He wanted to make his point crystal clear, so he continued, "But law came in, with the result that sin multiplied." He desperately hoped people would not stop reading, because his point was next. "But where sin increased, grace abounded all the more." A bad thought crossed his mind, so he wrote, "Should we continue in sin in order that grace may abound? By no means! How can we who died to sin go on living in it? Do you not know that all of us who have been baptized into Jim were baptized into his death? We have been buried with him by baptism into death, so that, just as Jim was raised from the dead by the glory of the Father, so we too might walk in newness of life."

He thought for a moment that his argument might sound like grace could cancel moral obligations, so he wrote, "What then? Should we sin because we are not under law but under grace? By no means!" Pablo felt a twinge of anger at the very thought that freedom from law could give permission to sin. He explained that it takes obedience from the heart. To put it plainly, he wrote, "Because it is sin that leads to death, then the free gift of God is eternal life in Jim." He had one more concern that justification by faith might seem to equate the law with sin. Here's how he dealt with that: "What then should we say? That the law is sin? By no means! Yet if it had not been for the law, I would not have known sin, and the very commandment that promised life proved to be death to me. So the law is holy, and the commandment is holy and just and good."

That was a lot to think about concerning justification, so Pablo wrote a quick summary thought: "Did what is good, then, bring death to me? By no means! It was sin, working death in me through what is good, in order that sin might be shown to be sin, and through the commandment might become sinful beyond measure." Okay, Pablo was done with that. He was exhausted. He thought that it was surely divine inspiration, because he barely understood what he was writing. He called his deputy friend in and read it to him to see what he thought

"Pretty heavy stuff, I'd say," the deputy responded. "But at least it will give people plenty of food for thought!"

Pablo agreed, and then was ready to move on to a positive note. "There is therefore now no condemnation for those who are in Jim Caldwell. For the law of the spirit of life in Jim has set you free from the law of sin and death." He also wanted them to know that the Holy Spirit was the spirit of Jim, so he said, "Anyone who does not have the Spirit of Jim does not belong to him. But if Jim is in you, though the body is dead because of sin, the Spirit is life because of righteousness."

He also shared that the world, and everything in it, awaits redemption. "I consider that the sufferings of this present time are not worth comparing with the glory about to be revealed to us. For the world waits with eager longing for the revealing of the children of God. We know that the whole creation has been groaning in labor pains until now; and not only the creation, but we ourselves, who have the first fruits of the Spirit, groan inwardly while we wait for adoption, the redemption of our bodies." He then encouraged them to be hopeful and to let the Spirit guide prayer, "with sighs too deep for words." Pablo felt that Spirit, and tried to put it into some sort of poetry.

> We know that all things
> work together for good,
> for those who love God,
> who are called
> according to his purpose."

Pablo really liked the way he had answered their request to talk about justification. He closed it out with some assurances, like, "Oh, what can I say? If God is for us, who is against us? It is God who justifies. Who is to condemn? It is Jim Caldwell, who died, yes, who was raised, who with God, who indeed intercedes for us. Who will separate us from the love of Jim? Will hardship, or distress, or persecution, or famine, or nakedness, or peril, or sword? No, in all these things we are more than conquerors through him who loved us." Again he smiled as the words just flowed, "There is nothing that will ever change my mind. Whether in this life or the next. Not heavenly beings, marshals, things that haunt our past, present circumstances, nor whatever tomorrow brings. From the San Francisco peaks to the depths of Death Valley, nor anything else in all creation, will be able to separate us from the love of God in Jim Caldwell."

He was so excited about what he just wrote, that he called

for his deputy again. Since he was now a believer, he wanted to run that last bit by him. The deputy sat at his feet with attentive ears. As Pablo read that last paragraph back to him, the deputy raised his hands in celebration and said, "You are a testimony of the truth you just wrote. Neither the threat of death nor the taking of freedom can stop you. Not the Catholic bishops, nor the governor of Arizona, nor the President of the United States, because the love of God dwells inside you by the power of the Spirit of Jim Caldwell."

Pablo sensed a peace that passes all understanding, from the testimony of the deputy, but just now he was feeling a bit tired. The problem was that he was on a roll, so Pablo looked at the next question. How can Jews be saved? He started to write, "I am speaking the truth in Jim—I am not lying; my conscience confirms it by the Holy Spirit—I have great sorrow and unceasing anguish in my heart." He really was too tired to continue the letter, so he just put down his pen and paper and went to sleep.

The next morning he was refreshed and ready to tackle the last question. He wrote that not all Jews were saved in the first place. After all, God's choosing of a group of people was out of God's mercy and compassion. Pablo felt some frustration for the Jews, so next he wrote, "Nothing said they were required to participate in their election as God's people." He thought for a moment that people shouldn't even try to figure this all out, because we can understand God about as well as an ant can comprehend a human.

Pablo was feeling a need to cite scripture, to get himself on solid ground. He then noted the prophet Isaiah who said, "Though the number of the children of Israel were like the sand of the sea, only a remnant of them will be saved." He then wrote that unbelieving Jews have rejected the gospel, because they did not strive for it on the basis of faith. He again quoted a text from Isaiah with, "See, I am laying in Zion a stone that will make people stumble, a rock that will make them fall, and whoever believes in him will not be put to shame."

He explained that the problem was that they sought to establish their own righteousness by way of law. What they didn't get was that the law leads to Jim. The law was meant to bring life, but now wholeness comes from believing that God raised Jim from the dead. Pablo then thought, it's all okay. Disbelief creates opportunity for non-Jews to receive the gospel. Then he wrote: "I ask then, has God rejected his people? By no means! God has not rejected his people." Pablo frowned for a moment when he realized that it wasn't about God rejecting the Jews, it was intolerant human beings looking for opportunities to discard people who aren't like them.

He noted a story from the book of Kings, then wrote, "At the present time there is a remnant, chosen by grace. But if it is by grace, it is no longer on the basis of works, otherwise grace would no longer be grace." He explained that even if Israel failed to obtain God's grace, the "elect obtained it, but the rest were hardened." He further noted that it didn't mean the hardened were lost forever because they would become envious of non-Jews and be incited to receive salvation. His point was to always hold out hope that all people would sooner or later fall into the arms of God's grace.

Pablo was again feeling pretty good about the letter. Next he noted that not all Jewish people are Jews, because a person can be Jewish by race but not by religion. He then made the analogy of an olive tree, where Jews and non-Jews are branches. Some Jews become broken off from the tree while some non-Jews become grafted in. Then he cautioned the non-Jews about boasting, "Do not boast over the branches. If you do boast, remember that it is not you that support the root, but the root that supports you." He further cautioned the non-Jews, that, "if God did not spare the natural branches, perhaps he will not spare you." Pablo wanted to give some hope, so he finally mentioned that all believers in Jim Caldwell will be saved, whether they are Jews or non-Jews.

Pablo sat back in his chair and felt proud of what he had just sketched out, until he wryly smiled for remembering that he, too, should be careful about boasting. He then climbed into his bed and fell hard asleep. As soon as he woke up, he turned back to the telegram and read the final question: "What is the new life in Jim?" A holy smile broke across his faith because this is what he really wanted to talk about all along. Here's how he started: "I beg of you therefore, brothers and sisters, by the mercies of God, to present your bodies as a living sacrifice, holy and acceptable to God, which is your spiritual worship. Do not be conformed to this world, but be transformed by the renewing of your minds, so that you may discern the will of God—what is good and acceptable and perfect."

He then wanted to talk about the new life in Jim with respect to community, so he wrote, "Let love be genuine; hate what is evil, hold fast to what is good; love one another with mutual affection; outdo one another in showing honor. Do not lack in zeal, be ardent in spirit, serve the Lord. Rejoice in hope, be patient in suffering, persevere in prayer. Contribute to the needs of the saints; extend hospitality to strangers." Knowing the challenge of being a Caldwellian, he wrote, "Bless those who persecute you; bless and do not curse them. Rejoice with those who rejoice, weep with those who weep. Live in harmony with one another; do not be haughty, but associate with the lowly; do not claim to be wiser than you are. Do not repay anyone evil for evil, but take thought for what is noble in the sight of all."

This last bit of writing about the practical application of his heavy thinking struck a frustrating chord in his heart. He believed every word he wrote, but he couldn't shake the thought of Pedro out of his mind. Their struggle over authority served no purpose in the Caldwellian kingdom, but all he could think was that Pedro started it. If Pedro hadn't been so haughty about being an original follower of Jim's, the problems would never have begun. Then a new blinding light hit him in the form of a question. In some ways it was more transformational than the one on the road to Tucson.

Why couldn't he acknowledge the power of his own transformation by the risen Lord? Did that moment back then make no difference? He reeled in pain, because it was the first time he was ever able to admit his ego problem. He felt truly struck down. All of a sudden the words of Jim Caldwell made sense to him for the very first time: "Follow me." In others words, it wasn't about himself. He needed to put away his ego if he were to truly follow the leading's of the Holy Spirit. He stopped for a long bit of prayer, and finally realized he had to forgive Pedro, even though Pedro wasn't asking for forgiveness. Somehow the pain just drained from him, and after a little more time he was ready to get back to writing.

Pablo was truly excited for the Caldwellian community in San Francisco. Having deep affection for people he never even met, he continued, "If it is possible, so far as it depends on you, live peaceably with all. Beloved, never avenge yourselves, but leave room for the justice of God; for it is written, 'Vengeance is mine, I will repay, says the Lord.' No, 'if your enemies are hungry, feed them; if they are thirsty, give them something to drink; for by doing this you will heap burning coals on their heads.' Do not be overcome by evil, but overcome evil with good." Pablo stopped for a moment and thought about the Russians hanging Jim Caldwell. All of a sudden it crossed his mind that Jim was not overcome by the Russians, but overcame them with the resurrection.

He then exhorted them to be subject to governing authorities. He actually felt good about his witness of being subject to house arrest. It was something he could easily defy by simply walking away, but he was putting his life in the hands of God by deferring to the powers that be. Then he decided to address another problem. He told them to pay taxes, saying, "Pay to all what is due them—taxes to whom taxes are due, revenue to whom revenue is due, respect to whom respect is due, honor to whom honor is due."

The words were still flowing, so Pablo added, "Owe no one anything, except to love one another; for the one who loves another has fulfilled the law." He explained that the law can be summed up with, "Love your neighbor as yourself. Love does no wrong to a neighbor; therefore, love is the fulfilling of the law." He urged them that "salvation is nearer to us now than when we became believers," and that we should "put on the spirit of Jim Caldwell." Pablo then exhorted them about the problem of judgment, asking "Why do you pass judgment on your brother or sister? Or you, why do you despise your brother or sister? For we all stand before the judgment seat of God."

That felt right, but Pablo was ready for a break. He stepped out on the front porch where he was loosely being held captive, and did a little street preaching. The city folk seemed busy and showed no interest in his thoughts. He had more to say, but decided to put it to use in his letter. He went back in and started writing. "Let us therefore no longer pass judgment on one another, but resolve instead never to put a stumbling block or hindrance in the way of another."

He explained that the "kingdom of God is not food and drink but righteousness and peace and joy in the Holy Spirit. Let us then pursue what makes for peace and for mutual upbuilding, for whatever does not proceed from faith is sin." He then asked that God would "grant you to live in harmony with one another, in accordance with Jim Caldwell, so that together you may with one voice glorify the God and Father of our Lord." The he said, "May the God of hope fill you with all joy and peace in believing, so that you may abound in hope by the power of the Holy Spirit."

Pablo was filled with satisfaction as he realized he was finished responding to the telegram, yet he sensed, as usual, that he needed to say a bit more. He appended, "I myself feel confident about you, my brothers and sisters, that you yourselves are full of goodness, filled with all knowledge, and able to instruct one another." Almost as a sense of excuse, he gave some reasons why his letter to them was written so boldly, then he shared a quote from the prophet Isaiah. He felt bad that he was under arrest, so he wrote, "I do hope to see you on my journey and to be sent on by you, once I have enjoyed your company for a little while." He finished with the comment that "by God's will I will come to you with joy and be refreshed in your company. The God of peace be with all of you. Amen."

That felt better, but first he wanted to dole out some thank yous. He told them to pray for Rose and Big Nose Kate, "who worked with me in the name of Jim Caldwell, and who risked their necks for my life, to whom not only I give thanks, but also to all the churches." He then listed twenty-nine individuals, of which one-third were women. It was important to him to celebrate women, because Jim Caldwell was ahead of his time in teaching equality. Next, he paused for a moment and remembered how Elena and Carlos quite literally put their lives on the line for his sake during the riot in Mexico City. He once again finished by saying to, "Greet one another with a holy kiss. All the Caldwellian churches greet you."

Pablo didn't seem to want to end this letter. It turned out to be the longest one and carried the depths of his thought since the road to Tucson. All of a sudden he felt a need to add an extra warning. "I urge you, brothers and sisters, to keep an eye on those who cause dissensions and offenses, in opposition to the teaching that you have learned; avoid them." That warning came from his direct experience with the challenges of starting Caldwellian churches. He then added, "For such people do not serve our Lord, but their own appetites, and by smooth talk and flattery they deceive the hearts of the simple-minded." No little bit of frustration welled up inside him, so he added even more. "For while your obedience is known to all, so that I rejoice over you, I want you to be wise in what is good, and guileless in what is evil. The grace of Jim Caldwell be with you."

He really and truly didn't want to end this letter, because he knew it might be his last. He decided it was time to sign off with a doxology. "Now to God who is able to strengthen you according to my gospel and the proclamation of Jim Caldwell, according to the revelation of the mystery that was kept secret for long ages but is now disclosed, and through the prophetic writings is made known to all, according to the command of the eternal God, to bring about the obedience of faith—to the only wise God, through Jim Caldwell, to whom be the glory forever! Amen."

Pablo then folded the letter and spent some time praying over it. Something told him he would never get to visit that wonderful church in San Francisco, and his heart broke a little. He also heard some stories while in prison, as one does, about Pedro. It came to his attention that Pedro was the one who founded the Caldwellian Church of San Francisco. He knew it was wrong, but he smiled just a little bit about the fact that the people were asking their questions of him rather than of Pedro. He also heard that Pedro was about to be arrested in San Francisco and was probably going to be sentenced to this very same jail of sorts. His last prayer was, "Please Lord, don't let Pedro be my roommate."

EPILOGUE
Angel Island

As so often are the intriguing ways of God, Pedro got in trouble in San Francisco. To Pablo's utter despair, Pedro was sentenced to house arrest and, sure enough, became his roommate. To say they got along would be as likely as a golden eagle getting along with a rattlesnake. They argued loudly day and night until neighbors requested something be done about it. The authorities decided to send Pablo to Angel Island, the largest island in California's San Francisco Bay. In 1850, President Millard Fillmore declared the island a military reserve and during the Civil War, the island was fortified.

Pablo arrived and settled into his jail cell, and very soon he got word that Rose had left Tucson and was one her way to visit him. Well, not just him. The mother church in Phoenix commissioned her to visit both Pablo and Pedro. When she arrived, she discovered that Pablo had been moved to Angel Island, so she first settled into a room being supplied by the Caldwellian Church of San Francisco. The next day she found the house where Pedro was at, and was surprised to find Pablo's deputy staying there to keep official watch over Pedro.

Rose asked the deputy, "Why didn't you return to Phoenix after Pablo was moved to Angel Island? After all, you couldn't offer your services there."

The deputy said, "I have become a Caldwellian, and I have joined the Caldwellian Church of San Francisco. It has become my mission now to provide watch over Pedro."

Pedro said, "I thought you were here to see me!" They all three smiled and Rose gave Pedro and hug.They sat down and had a long and wonderful visit, but Rose was anxious to get on to see Pablo. They had traveled so much together through America and Mexico, and now she was concerned about his safety at Angel Island. She said her goodbyes, then went there next. The boat trip to the island was quite hazardous, with choppy waters and plenty of sharks. It took a while to gain entrance as a visitor, but before long she got through the red tape and saw him. He was brought to a small, rather chilly room, and they could only sit at a desk across from one another. It didn't matter. They both were overjoyed and praised God. After another great visit, Rose left for her room at the church, promising to return each day.

———————————

That night Pablo received a mesage from Jim. It was to give comfort to fellow believers that Jim Caldwell was already with his people through the power of the Holy Spirit. The experience woke him up, so he wrote it down. Here's the first of seven messages that Jim Caldwell wanted to share through Pablo, and this one was to the church in Mexico City. It wasn't just for that church either. It simply represented situations in many of the churches.

The first message—to Mexico City, Mexico

"I know your works, your toil and your patient endurance. I know that you cannot tolerate evildoers; you have tested those who claim to be apostles but are not, and have found them to be false. I also know that you are enduring patiently and bearing up for the sake of my name, and that you have not grown weary. But I have this against you that you have abandoned the love you had at first. Remember then from what you have fallen; repent, and do the works you did at first. If not, I will come to you and remove your lamp from its place, unless you repent. Yet this is to your credit: you hate the works of the false missionaries, which I also hate. Let anyone who has an ear listen to what the Spirit is saying to the churches. To everyone who conquers, I will give permission to eat from the tree of life that is in the paradise of God." Then Pablo decided to summarize, because he really did like getting in the last word:

Your virtue is patient endurance.
Your vice is abandoning previous works of love.
My advice is to repent or lose the Holy Spirit.

———

Pablo was a bit cautious after this somewhat troubling message, so he sat back to relax in his makeshift cell. He was about to fall asleep when he received a vision, or maybe it was a dream, he couldn't tell. Whatever happened, he looked up and saw a door to heaven standing open. At first he thought he had died, but then he heard a voice saying, "Come up here, and I will show you what must take place after this." Still not sure if the voice was talking about himself or what, he soon sensed he was there in the spirit. As Pablo looked around, he saw things that he was simply incapable of describing. Finally, he saw a rainbow and thought at least that was familiar.

The next day Rose showed up for her visit, and Pablo was

happy to have someone to talk to. First thing he did was hand the letter to Rose and asked her to get it to their friends in Mexico City in whatever way she could. Next he told her about the dream.

"You went to heaven last night?" exclaimed a wide-eyed Rose.

Pablo said, "I have no idea, but I think I was there in the spirit."

Being very hesitant at first, Rose finally asked, "What was it like?"

"That's the frustrating thing," replied Pablo. "I can't even begin to describe it."

The guard then showed up and told Rose her visiting time was up. She neatly folded the letter and told Pedro she would be back tomorrow.

Pablo barely got to sleep when the next message came to his mind. He woke up and wrote it down.

The second message—to Durango, Mexico

"I know your affliction and your poverty, even though you are rich. I know the slander on the part of those who say that they are followers and are not, but are a synagogue of Satan. Do not fear what you are about to suffer. Beware, the devil is about to throw some of you into prison so that you may be tested, and for ten days you will have affliction. Be faithful until death, and I will give you the crown of life. Let anyone who has an ear listen to what the Spirit is saying to the churches. Whoever conquers will not be harmed by the second death." Pablo didn't know this church and he felt bad for them due to the challenging letter. Nonetheless, he wrote the following:

> Your virtue is being faithful unto death.
> Your vice is the fear of suffering.
> My advice is to conquer the second death (going to Hell) through faith.

This time he decided to stay awake, and sure enough a strange vision developed. Rather than seeing anything, he heard music. Now Pablo enjoyed music, because in the midst of having his eyes rendered useless on the road to Tucson, he learned to listen carefully. In all, he heard five hymns. The first song celebrated the triune holiness of God. The second hymn gave honor to God as the creator, ending with "for you created all things, and by your will they existed and were created." The third piece of music reminded Pablo about the teachings he received from Jim Caldwell, because it talked about the opening of seals. Every Caldwellian knew the story about Kate at the diamond mine, and how six seals were broken when she arrived. As she reached toward the seventh seal, it too broke and the stone rolled away. The empty tomb proved not to have given up the body of Jim to grave robbers, because the risen Lord appeared many times to many people.

Rose could hardly wait to get in to see Pablo, and they discussed the meanings to no avail. Pablo seemed irritated, so he just handed her the next letter.

"Jim spoke to you again?" she asked.

"At least his letters," complained Pablo, "are easier to understand than these vision things."

The guard opened the door and told Rose it was time to go.

That night Pablo began to wonder what was going on. It was easily the middle of the night, and nothing had yet happened. Just as Pablo was drifting off, he was woken up for the nightly message.

The third message—to Cheyenne, Wyoming

"I know where you are living, where Satan's throne is. Yet you are holding fast to my name, and you did not deny your faith in me even in the days of martyrdom. But I have a few things against you: you have some there who hold to the teachings of gambling and practice fornication. So you also have some who hold to the teaching of the one who was martyred. Repent then. If not, I will come to you soon and make war against them with the sword of my mouth. Let anyone who has an ear listen to what the Spirit is saying to the churches. To everyone who conquers I will give some of the hidden manna, and I will give a white stone, and on the white stone is written a new name that no one knows except the one who receives it."

This time Pablo decided to argue with Jim. "Are you sure you want to start with, 'I know where you are living'? Doesn't that sound a bit threatening?" Pablo got no answer, but he felt strangely humiliated. Sort of felt like he needed to stay in his own lane. Pablo soon realized his ego was messing with him, so he at least got to write his opinions to the church:

Your virtue is that you did not deny Jim.
Your vice is spiritual compromise.
My advice is to repent or fall apart.

When he was done writing the letter, he started to remember the rest of the music vision he had the night before. When Rose arrived that morning, he excitedly shared that, "the fourth bit of singing entailed thousands upon thousands singing with full voice about Jim Caldwell. I think the hymn they were singing was, 'O for a Thousand Tongues to Sing.'"

Rose asked, "What are you talking about?"

"Sorry," he said, "It's the rest of that music vision I started to tell you about."

"Okay, but slow down," suggested Rose.

Pablo realized that the fourth hymn was about seven honors being bestowed upon Jim, of "power and wealth and wisdom and might and honor and glory and blessing."

The guard started to approach, and Rose said, "This is ridiculous. I make a treacherous water crossing every day to get here, so I want more time." The guard acknowledged the situation and walked away.

Rose then looked at Pablo and said, "Hmm, sounds like strange honors. He had God's power here on earth. He didn't care about wealth. He was the wisest man I ever knew, although I only heard him teach one time. Jim sure had might, just not in earthly terms. Honor was certainly given to him by his followers. Now what were the other two?" Pablo said, "glory and blessing." Rose kind of frowned and said, "Jim never wanted glory and he was certainly a blessing."

Pablo annoyingly said, "Thanks, Rose, not real helpful, but here's the fifth song. It was being sung by "every creature in heaven and on earth and under the earth and in the sea, and all that is in them." Pablo was a bit surprised when it said, "To the one seated on the throne and to the Lamb." That made it clear that Jim was equal to God. He knew that Jim had been presented as a human, so he was glad that in his letter to the Caldwellians of San Francisco he said that Jim "was declared to be Son of God with power according to the spirit of holiness by resurrection from the dead." That made Pablo smile because the song celebrated the fulfillment of that truth. Then Rose made her required departure after taking the third letter

That night Pablo tried to barter with Jim. "I'd like to get a good night's sleep, so is there any chance you could tell me the next message now?" It wasn't as if Jim was complying so much as the timing was right, but the message came and Pablo wrote it down.

The fourth message—to Wichita, Kansas

"I know your works—your love, faith, service, and patient endurance. I know that your last works are greater than the first.

But I have this against you: you tolerate that Jezebel, who calls herself a prophet and is teaching and beguiling my servants to practice fornication. I gave her time to repent, but she refuses to repent of her fornication. Beware, I am throwing her on a bed, and those who commit adultery with her I am throwing into great distress, unless they repent of her doings; and I will strike her children dead. And all the churches will know that I am the one who searches minds and hearts, and I will give to each of you as your works deserve. But to the rest of you in Wichita, who do not hold this teaching, who have not learned what some call 'the deep things of Satan,' to you I say, I do not lay on you any other burden; only hold fast to what you have. To the one who conquers I will also give the morning star. Let anyone who has an ear listen to what the Spirit is saying to the churches." Then Pablo offered his summary thoughts:

Your virtue is growing in faith.
Your vice is moral compromise.
My advice is to hold fast to your faith.

_____

When Rose arrived, she asked, "Did you have another vision?"

He told her that a very lengthy account was shared, that when it was done, he was able to understand it was about the struggle of the church in the midst of conflict and persecution. Pablo knew a thing or two about conflict and persecution, and Rose knew it, too. He told her that the even bigger story was about the judgments of God upon the enemies of the church.

Pablo said, "The vision started symbolically with the seven seals on Jim's tomb being opened by Jim himself. The first seal opened, and a white steed came forth meaning conquest. The second seal opened and a red stallion emerged representing war. The third seal opened and a black horse appeared signifying famine. Then the fourth seal opened, and a pale green mare was there, and its rider's name was death."

"What did it mean?" Rose asked rather anxiously.

"That's what I asked Jim", then Pablo said, "and Jim told me that the white horse rider has a bow, signifying that the enemies of God will have some victories."

"I don't like that one," Rose said cautiously.

Then Pablo continued, "The red horse rider has a sword, signifying that war and bloodshed comes when people oppose God's rule."

"Not any better," said Rose, "but understandable."

Pablo continued, "The black horse rider is carrying scales, signifying the injustice of famine that follows war.

"Still making sense," said Rose.

Then Pablo said, "The pale green horse rider signifies hell and death, which naturally follow."

"Naturally," said Rose, "but what should we do?"

Pablo told her, "That's what I asked Jim, and he replied, "Love one another. God loves people enough to give them free will. Freely choose good."

Of course, the guard showed up at that point and sent Rose on her way. She took the fourth letter, and as she walked through the door she said, "Can't wait to hear about the opening of the last three seals."

That night Pablo suggested to Jim, "Why not mix it up a little and give me the vision before the letter?" As expected, he was ignored. Being very tired, he quickly drifted off to sleep. For a while. Then the message came, waking him up, and he wrote it down.

The fifth message—to Oklahoma City, Oklahoma

"I know your works; you have a name of being alive, but you are dead. Wake up, and strengthen what remains and is on the point of death, for I have not found your works perfect in the sight of my God. Remember then what you received and heard; obey it, and repent. If you do not wake up, I will come like a thief, and you will not know at what hour I will come to you. Yet you have still a few persons who have not soiled their clothes; they will walk with me, dressed in white, for they are worthy. If you conquer, you will be clothed like them in white robes, and I will not blot your name out of the book of life; I will confess your name before my Father and before his angels. Let anyone who has an ear listen to what the Spirit is saying to the churches." Then Pablo wrote the following:

Your virtue is that you have lively works.
  That makes me, Pablo, very happy.
Your vice is that you are spiritually dead.
  That makes me, Pablo again, very sad.
My advice is to wake up your faith.

"Okay," said Rose, "continue."

Pablo barely realized he'd been moved to the visitation room, so he took a moment to clear his head.

"Wow," said Pablo, "I don't know if I was in heaven again last night or not. At least the vision took place in heaven. The fifth seal was opened by Jim, and the martyrs were pleading for vindication, and were told to 'rest a little longer.'"

"Seems tiresome," announced Rose.

Pablo smiled and agreed, then said, "Jim opened the sixth seal, granting a view of God's punishments of the wicked."

"Wouldn't it be better," asked Rose, "to simply be good people?"

Pablo responded, "I think that's the point of the vision."

"What about the seventh seal?" asked Rose.

Pablo said, "It didn't happen next. First there was an interlude of two visions of assurance that God's people are secure from the plagues and judgments."

"That sounds better," Rose said with a smile.

Pablo continued, "Then Jim Caldwell opened the seventh seal, and as the legend goes, 'there was silence in heaven for about half an hour.'"

"That sounds good," commented Rose, but Pablo said "It turned out this calm was like the eye of the hurricane. Pablo wasn't sure he was ready for more of the vision, but it came right then and there.

"You look sick, Pablo," said Rose with a very concerned voice.

He said, "Quiet. Here's more." His eyes rolled upward and he said, "There's a sequence of six trumpets, followed by another interlude and then the seventh trumpet." Pablo thought that ended it, but loud voices in heaven said,

"The nations raged,
   but your wrath has come,
   and the time for judging the dead,
for rewarding your servants, the prophets
   and saints and all who fear your name,
   both small and great,
and for destroying those who destroy the earth."

The guard heard all of this and didn't like it. He grabbed Rose's arm and said "It's time to go." Pablo had broken into a sweat, but Rose asked the guard if she could at least get the letter she was supposed to have from Pablo. It was visible in a pocket, so the guard grabbed it, gave it to her, and they left. At the front door, Rose asked if Pablo could get some medical help, but all he said was, "This island brings on all kinds of illnesses."

Pablo didn't seem to be doing much better that night, but he was startled awake by the next message. Not having much energy, Pablo went ahead and dutifully wrote it down.

The sixth message—to San Antonio, Texas

"I know your works. Look, I have set before you an open door, which no one is able to shut. I know that you have but little power, and yet you have kept my word and have not denied my name. I will make those of the synagogue of Satan who say that they are Jews and are not, but are lying—I will make them come and bow down before your feet, and they will learn that I have loved you. Because you have kept my word of patient endurance, I will keep you from the hour of trial that is coming on the whole world to test the inhabitants of the earth. Hold fast to what you have, so that no one may seize your crown. If you conquer, I will make you a pillar in the temple of my God; you will never go out of it. I will write on you the name of my God, and the name of the city of my God, the New Jerusalem that comes down from my God out of heaven, and my own new name. Let anyone who has an ear listen to what the Spirit is saying to the churches." Then Pablo added:

Your virtue is that you kept God's word.
Your vice is that you lack evangelism.
My advice is to keep the faith.

——

Desperately wanting to get back to sleep. The next vision came. It was a parable about evil, followed by yet another interlude, this one being three visions of reassurance. Then there was a sequence of the seven bowls of wrath. Pablo interrupted and asked Jim Caldwell if this was really necessary, to which Jim replied that God rules, so the readers of these visions are not to get discouraged or lose faith. The vision continued about the last days of the evil city. Pablo asked which evil city Jim was talking about, and he said, "Remember the messages to the seven churches?" Pablo said, "Yes." Jim said, "They represented all churches, and the evil city represents evil in every city."

The next day he was looking forward to his visit from Rose, but it never came. He stopped a guard and asked if there was a problem with visitations, and the guard told him that the wind was fierce outside. Boats weren't able to make the dangerous passage across the frigid, shark-infested water.

It was a long day for Pablo. He still wasn't feeling very well, and he couldn't seem to get any medical attention. In his frustration, he thought about trying to escape. Nighttime mercifully came, along with another message, which he carefully wrote down.

The seventh message—to Oaxaca, Mexico

"I know your works; you are neither cold nor hot. I wish that you were either cold or hot. So, because you are lukewarm, and neither cold nor hot, I am about to spit you out of my mouth. For you say, 'I am rich, I have prospered, and I need nothing.' You do not realize that you are wretched, pitiable, poor, blind, and naked. Therefore I counsel you to buy from me gold refined by fire so that you may be rich; and white robes to clothe you and to keep the shame of your nakedness from being seen; and salve to anoint your eyes so that you may see. I reprove and discipline those whom I love. Be earnest, therefore, and repent. Listen! I am standing at the door, I will come to you and eat with you, and you with me. To the one who conquers I will give a place with my throne, just as I myself conquered and sat down with my Father on his throne. Let anyone who has an ear listen to what the Spirit is saying to the churches." Then Pablo offered his final summary:

Your virtue is that you are not against God.
Your vice is that you are not for God.
My advice is to take a stand (in fear and trembling).

———

Rose made it back the next day and got both of the last two letters. Pablo was still looking a bit peaked, but he had a lot of vision to tell her about. The vision shifted to God's redemption, through seven visions, to give ideas of a bigger picture than we could fully imagine.

"Great," said Rose, "so tell me about them."

The first vision," Pablo shared, "was the return of Jim whose name is called 'The Word of God.'

Rose had a lot of questions about that one. She realized this would take longer than usual, so she called the guard over and offered him some money for extra time. He gladly took the money and said, "Take all the time you need." Rose then looked back to Pablo and asked, "So does that mean Jim is the Bible?"

Pablo said, "Great question! And no, not particularly. We are all the Word of God when we act accordingly."

"And that's our task," said a smiling Rose.

"The second vision was the last battle," expounded Pablo.

Rose thought that sounded ominous, but Pablo explained that it was really more about God's victory.

"The third vision," shared Pablo, "was the binding of Satan, signifying that the reign of evil is not permanent."

"I love that!" offered Rose.

Pablo continued by saying, "The fourth vision was about the millennium, which is only for the martyrs. The point being that this earth would finally get to enjoy the Garden of Eden as intended."

"This stuff gets better all the time!" exclaimed Rose.

Pablo said, "The fifth vision was about the ultimate destruction of evil."

"Wow!" shouted Rose, at which time the guard told her to keep it quiet.

The two of them sat for a minute, the Pablo said, "The sixth vision was about the last judgment, depicted by two books. One represented human responsibility, so that people are judged by what they have done. The other is the book of life, in which people are saved not by what they have done but by what God has done."

Rose thought out loud, "Seems fair."

Pablo then told Rose about the seventh vision. "It was about the New Jerusalem, where redemption is not about making "all new things" but "all things new.""

He then leaned across the table a little closer to Rose and said, "I asked Jim if we can make heaven on earth by living your kingdom here and now? And you know what he said?"

Rose could barely wait for an answer. "Jim didn't say anything," Pablo said, "but he appeared to me, and smiled and winked."

At that point Jim whispered something to Rose, and she got up and left.

That night Angel Island seemed to fulfil its name, because Pablo shockingly escaped. Nobody had ever escaped the island before, because it was far too treacherous of a crossing to swim, particularly at night. Not a lot of effort was put into finding Pablo because he wasn't deemed a threat. His body also never washed ashore and likewise, he was never found. Soon enough, people in the area forgot about Pablo, but intriguingly, word got around that his letters started arriving little by little to the seven churches. Each time, they were delivered by a man and a woman on horseback, who disappeared as quickly as they arrived.

WATCH FOR THE START OF

A King Montezuma Trilogy

The Forming of the Empire: A King Montezuma Story— Book 1

This book is a reimagining of the <u>Law section of the Hebrew Scriptures</u>, to the time of the judges. It is set in the Formative and Classic Period of Mesoamerica, beginning in the jungles of Guatemala and ending in Mexico. Coming in the spring of 2024.

The Secret of the Empire: A King Montezuma Story— Book 2

This book deals with the development of biblical kings and prophecies. The Aztec Empire ended on August 13, 1521 when Herman Cortes and the Spanish Conquistadors overthrew King Montezuma. The book reimagines the <u>Prophets section of the Hebrew Scriptures</u> by setting them in the Postclassic Period of Mesoamerica. Coming in the fall of 2024.

The Value of the Empire: A King Montezuma Story— Book 3

The Jim Caldwell Trilogy

This book tells the stories left behind after the fall of the Aztec Empire. It reimagines the legends, wisdom, art, and poetry of the <u>Writings section of the Hebrew Scriptures</u>. It is set in Tenochtitlan, which is now Mexico City. It also paves the way for The Jim Caldwell Trilogy. Coming in the spring of 2025.

ACKNOWLEDGMENTS

The *New Revised Standard Version* (NRSV) of *The Holy Bible* is used when scriptures are referenced.

Thanks goes to Dave Raines for volunteering to be my beta reader. His friendship for over forty years has been immensely appreciated, as I wandered through the wilderness of ministry. I truly believe the promised land is ahead. He also acted as my grammarian

Thanks goes to my amazing wife, the Rev. Dr. Yvonne C. Oropeza, for being my development editor. Her love, support, and talent have made an immense impact on this book.

BOOKS BY THIS AUTHOR

NONFICTION

A Serious In-Depth Bible Study Trilogy

A Natural History of Scripture: How the Bible Evolved—Book 1.

A deconstruction of biblical formation as seen through the lens of evolutionary biology.

Wrestling with Scripture: How to Interpret the Bible—Book 2.

How to interpret the Bible's original Greek and Hebrew by using word study tools.

Practicing Scripture: How to Live the Bible—Book 3.

How to put the ideas from the Bible into every day practice.

How to Lead a Celebration of Life

The Jim Caldwell Trilogy

An indispensable guide for laity and clergy to conduct a funeral with meaning and integrity.

Don't Look a Camel in the Mouth: Pilgrimages through the Land of Jesus and Paul

The author shares five pilgrimages through the Holy Land, Turkey, Greece, Italy, and the Mediterranean.

Don't Look a Camel in the Mouth: A Spiritual Journal Companion Book

This book follows *Don't Look a Camel in the Mouth: Pilgrimages through the Land of Jesus and Paul* with meditation questions for spiritual growth.

Parish the Thought: An Eye-Opening Look Behind the Pulpit

The author and his wife share stories of their 37 years in the ministry.

Austria, Germany, and the Oberammergau Passion Play

The author shares his experiences leading a group to this famous play, and the surrounding area.

The Jim Caldwell Trilogy

Your Year of Spiritual Growth: A Biblical Journey

This book creates spirituality through daily scripture readings, devotional questions, and debriefing with others.

FICTION

A Jim Caldwell Trilogy

The Forming of the Diamond: A Jim Caldwell Story: Book 1.

This is a retelling of the life of Jesus, drawn from the four gospels, looking through the lens of the American Old West. It focuses on The Sermon on the Mount, and shares some of the parables and healings

The Secret of the Diamond: A Jim Caldwell Story: Book 2.

This is a creative retelling of the last days of Jesus, set in Phoenix in 1881. It is the middle book of the Jim Caldwell trilogy. It deals with the Passion Narrative, from Gethsemane to the grave, which I call the diamond of the Gospel.

The Value of the Diamond: A Jim Caldwell Story: Book 3.

The Jim Caldwell Trilogy

This book deals with the resurrection, and tells the story of the early church from the Book of Acts and the Letters of Paul, ending with the Book of Revelation.

The Secret of the Diamond: A Lenten Devotional.

A Companion piece for *The Secret of the Diamond: A Jim Caldwell Story: Book 2.*

The Jim Caldwell Trilogy

This is a single book that includes all three books of the Jim Caldwell series.

If you enjoy my books, please review them on Amazon, Goodreads, Barnes & Noble, or any of your favorite places.